MK.
8-9-07

LADY GOLD

LADY GOLD

Angela Amato and

Joe Sharkey

St. Martin's Press New York

A THOMAS DUNNE BOOK.
An imprint of St. Martin's Press.

LADYGOLD. Copyright © 1998 by Angela Amato and Joe Sharkey. All rights reserved. Printed in the United States of America. No part of this book may be used or reproduced in any manner whatsoever without written permission except in the case of brief quotations embodied in critical articles or reviews. For information, address St. Martin's Press, 175 Fifth Avenue, New York, N.Y. 10010.

Design by Barbara M. Bachman

Library of Congress Cataloging-in-Publication Data
Amato, Angela.
    LadyGold / Angela Amato and Joe Sharkey.—1st. ed.
      p.   cm.
    "A Thomas Dunne book."
    ISBN 0-312-18541-3
    I. Sharkey, Joe. II. Title. III. Title: LadyGold.
PS3551.M18L3   1998
813'.54—DC21   98-14528
                                            CIP

First Edition: August 1998

10 9 8 7 6 5 4 3 2 1

For my hero,

my mother Nancy

—A.A.

For my parents,

Joseph and Marcella Sharkey

—J.S.

ACKNOWLEDGMENTS

Writing this book was cathartic for me. I relied heavily on my loving family and friends for support. They all encouraged me in their own unique ways. Thanks Mom and Dad for keeping my heart toasty warm; Sis, Billy, and Suzie, for your consistent love; Señor, your courage still remains with me; Billy V., for the countless laughs and endless advice; Austin C., I haven't forgotten your guidance; Ellen T., Howard S., Steve R., for believing; BuddyGirl and Sgt. C., for your unwavering friendship.

To my partner, Joe Sharkey, I am thankful you came into my world. Without you in the mix, none of this would be.

Much appreciation to our literary agent, David Vigliano, for his tireless efforts on our behalf. And we are deeply indebted to our editor, Ruth Cavin, for having faith in *LadyGold* and us! And of course, I am thankful I had the privilege to work with so many of New York's dedicated police officers, prosecutors, and defense attorneys; you are truly New York's *Gold*.

Most important, to my forever love, Samuel, for giving me the greatest gift of my lifetime, E.N.

—*Angela Amato*

LADY GOLD

CHAPTER 1

I *should have* let the answering machine pick up. Unhappily I didn't, so I heard the cigarette voice of Sergeant Duffy, who had been the Saturday-night desk officer at the Manhattan Borough Office since he'd accidentally shot himself in the groin while directing traffic outside Yankee Stadium in 1988. He said they wanted me to come in, overtime—an all-night shift.

In the living room, Kevin slurped his egg-drop soup and glowered. Like me, Kevin was a New York City police detective, and we'd both been on the job long enough to have regular weekday schedules, Monday through Friday. On Saturday nights, we liked to stay home, order Chinese, watch television. Kevin did not like changes in his routine, especially on Saturday nights.

But I was bored enough that working a shift seemed interesting, so I told Duffy, "I guess I can do it if you're really stuck. What time?"

"Immediately, if not sooner, Detective. Somebody called in sick."

"What kind of job?"

"Undercover, they tell me. Temporary assignment. Your name came up."

"An assignment so special that somebody called in sick?"

"You got that right."

"So where do I report?"

He made a noise that sounded like a lawn mower trying to start. Then I heard him flipping through some papers. "That would be . . . 257 West Twenty-seventh Street. That would be room 538—five-three-eight. Tell her what she won, Duffy! Yes, indeedy, Detective Geraldine A. Conte, you have won an all-expense-paid shift with an Organized Crime Task Force unit. To collect your prize, you must see one Lieutenant Campo, first name unknown. C-A-M-P-O. That's 257 West Twenty-seventh, New York, New York."

"Okay, Sarge," I said.

. . .

A**ctually, I liked** the prospect of a tour in an organized-crime unit. In my five years as a detective, I'd worked a lot of undercover, but never OCTF. OCTF was selective and haughty, like a hot-shot fraternity. The feds and the state were coming down on the New York Mafia families like sledgehammers, in independent and highly competitive operations. Everybody knew that OCTF was obsessed with Sally Seashore, the Glitz Godfather. Sally Seashore was public enemy number one, the most brazen of the current bosses, real name Salvatore Messina. He ran the Giavanni family and, besides murder, had so far gotten away with armed robbery, hijacking, loansharking, gambling, extortion, labor fraud, arson, assault, and conspiracy to commit all of the above. And that was just the felonies. Only a month earlier, Messina had swaggered out of federal court in his alligator loafers, acquitted of racketeering, and held a press conference. The tabloids were still swooning.

Sally had schemed and bashed his way to the top of the Giavanni heap during the 1980s, when he acquired a subscription to *The Wall Street Journal* as a fashion accessory and began dressing like a star mutual-fund manager. Unlike old-line Mafia bosses, who tended to become fresh corpses if their pictures turned up in the newspaper, Sally unfurled brilliantly white capped teeth and flashed his diamond cufflinks whenever the photographers spotted him at a trendy East Side cafe or at the marina on the Hudson below the World Trade Center where he docked his fifty-foot boat, *My FantaSea*. "Hiya, boys," he would say, like in the movies, as the paparazzi scuttled forward and genuflected to make their shots.

A criminal who gets that much attention drives cops crazy. So I figured that spending a tour with OCTF would at least be an interesting break from the depressing grind of work I'd been assigned to for the past year, the Special Victims Unit, women and children abused in ways a normal person couldn't even dream of. An infant in a dryer, cotton cycle. A little girl with a hatchet in her crotch. A wife nailed sideways to a headboard. Some days, I'd get home feeling like someone had put a spigot into my heart and drained it.

As I was about to hang up, Duffy said, "Wait, Detective. One more thing. You got to dress up nice. Supposedly this is crucial. 'Dress up nice,' it says. You got to go to some nightclub, apparently. You know, wine and dine courtesy the taxpayers of the city of New York. Tough work at time-and-a-half."

"Dress up," I said, knowing better than to ask what that was supposed to mean. To male cops, it meant they put on sportscoats and ties. Naturally, it wouldn't occur to them that a female cop would need more specific information about where they were sending her on an undercover assignment. The Waldorf? The bowling alley at Port Authority Bus Terminal?

I went into the living room and laid my arms on the top of the couch like it was a backyard fence and watched Kevin dab mustard from a little packet onto his egg roll. My dinner was barely touched.

"I have to go in, honey."

"What in the hell for?" he said, clearly peeved.

"They want me in on OT."

"When?"

"Now."

"Jesus," he said. On Saturday nights, Kevin wouldn't leave the couch if it was on fire. Annoyed at the sudden disruption in the routine, he dropped the egg roll into his soup container and pushed it away, spilling puddles of glop on the coffee table.

"For Christ's sake, Gerry. It's Saturday night. I keep telling you, you shouldn't answer the phone. You never learn. So now the whole night is shot in the ass."

"Sorry," I called over my shoulder, hurrying into the bedroom.

Kevin and I had been engaged for a ridiculous period of time: five years, reasonably happily for about the first half of that time and now merely coexisting. We lived in his old bachelor place, a one-bedroom third-floor walkup on Bleecker Street over a Chinese restaurant called Cheng's Happy Good Luck Garden.

Having Chinese food delivered from three flights down was one of those amenities that compensates for the endless inconveniences of life in New York, which is the only city I know of where adults with well-paying jobs actually choose to live like college students, the only place in America where you routinely associate with grown-ups who have never had a driver's license.

Lately, the apartment walls seemed to have moved closer together. I was thirty years old, vaguely unhappy, but too busy to do much about it. I was a third-grade detective, one of the youngest women ever to get a gold shield in the NYPD. I was also in my third year of law school, meaning I had classes most nights after work. My father, who had always treated me more like a son than a daughter, who showed me how to wire a lamp and throw a punch, wasn't much impressed when I became a detective. My enrolling in law school, though, was the proudest moment of his life.

Like most cops, Kevin loathed lawyers and thought it was ridiculous that I wanted to be one. Kevin was thirty-eight and set in stone for the rest of his life, complacently content as the years fell away toward the only things in life in which he had invincible faith, my presence and his retirement pension. Other than the calendar and the color of his hair, which had gone attractively gray at the temples in the past few years, little ever changed for Kevin. We had no pets, no plans beyond the next summer, and a vague, unexpressed understanding that we would someday get married.

He was a good and honest cop and a faithful supporter—until the night when I raced home four years earlier to tell him I'd been promoted to detective:

"What do I tell my friends? Now you're the same as me," he said.

"Honey, you'll always be the better detective," I'd assured him. But it was never the same after that. I continued loving him out of habit, the way I continued going to work.

The routine was our constitution. Usually we worked late on Fridays. Sundays, we were in bed before the ten o'clock news, meaning that Saturday nights were really our only free times together, and we had a ritual. Around five, he'd go out for the early Sunday edition of the *Daily News* and plant himself on the couch to work the "Jumble" puzzle, which he did with the intensity of a man cracking an enemy code. Around six, I'd phone Cheng's, and the delivery man would show up about a half hour later. The order was always the same. For me, beef with broccoli in garlic sauce. Kung Po Chicken Ding for him. Three fat egg rolls.

My job was to answer the door. He seemed to think it was his to make sure the delivery boy didn't slip into a higher tax bracket.

"The guy's here with the food, honey. Do you have two dollars for the tip? All I have is a twenty."

"Unbelievable," he grouched, with exaggerated effort digging his wallet out of his back pocket. "I would have gone down for it, for God's sake."

"So sue me," I told him in my most nasal New York voice. "For two bucks, I'm Ivana Trump."

The same delivery man always came, carrying the brown bag like a birthday cake. Chinese delivery having as strict a protocol as Japanese tea-serving, names were never exchanged.

"Beef with broccoli? And Kung Po?" I said, checking the order.

"Chicken Ding."

"Soup?"

"Egg-drop soup."

"Not Campbell's?"

Jokes never worked. "Egg-drop soup!"

"Honey, I'm only kidding. Egg-drop soup is right."

"Egg-drop soup!"

I paid him and shut the door.

"Two bucks," Kevin said, eyeing the food. "Ivana Trump."

"I gave him three bucks," I said, pleased at my rebellion.

"That's one buck for each flight of stairs!"

"Kevin, you're wearing out the needle playing that song. Give me a freaking break."

Actually, the routine had changed slightly over the years. In the old days, we'd go to bed at one o'clock on Saturday night and have sex. Our "appointment," Kevin always called it, with an annoying stage leer. But that had dropped from the agenda, without comment. Now, I'd slip into the bedroom around eleven to study torts or criminal procedure. Kevin stayed up late in the living room playing his old LPs, volume low, draining long-neck beers. When he had his load on, he got out his favorite album, *The Greatest Hits of the Ink Spots.*

. . .

He *sauntered into* the bathroom when I was in the shower. "Talk to me," he demanded above the splash of the water.

"I don't have a lot of time, Kevin."

He sat on the toilet lid, separated from me by the shower curtain, like in a confessional. Years ago, he might have yanked the curtain open, taken his clothes off, got under the spray.

"It's Saturday night. This is pure bullshit," he said.

"Don't start, Kevin."

He ignored me. "Instead of spending our one night together, you want to go play cops and robbers? You used to tell me you wanted to have a kid someday. What kind of a kid grows up with his mother running out on a Saturday night?"

Here we go, I thought. "The kid discussion? Again? Can we give it a rest right now?"

"You never want to talk."

The kid discussion only came up in fights. It was, I think, our way of avoiding discussing marriage. "Listen, I want to have a kid at some point," I told him wearily. "After law school, after I'm situated for a year or two. Maybe I can take a year off."

"A year," he snorted. "A year to raise a kid, and then back to the job?" He thought things might be better between us if I just stayed home with a child in our 850-square-foot apartment, whose main virtue was that it was rent-controlled at six hundred dollars a month.

"Kevin, last week I had to carry a six-year-old girl out of an apartment where her father had branded her on the behind. *With a branding iron,* Kevin. They had me hold up the kid for the tech guy to take a video."

"Like I haven't seen a lot of bad shit?"

"That isn't my point, Kevin! This is not the same world our mothers brought us into. I don't know how I could stand the risks a child faces every day."

"Well," he said, standing up. "Not that it matters much now. When's the last time we had an appointment, anyway?"

I turned off the water and reached out to grab a towel. I wasn't about to come out naked.

"I'm not getting into this now," I said, stepping out of the tub with the towel around me.

He heard the anger in my voice and backed off. "Okay, Gerry. I don't mean to give you a hard time. I'm just not happy about spending a Saturday night by myself." He looked me up and down, and tugged playfully at my towel, but I pulled away. I'd gained twenty pounds since we started living together, but he never criticized me. In fact, he'd said more than once, "I like you beefed up."

"Have it your way, Lady Gold," he said, retreating. "Lady Gold"— that was the nickname he gave he when I told him I had made detective. He knew I hated it.

The television belched a laugh track. In our tiny bedroom, where you couldn't do an about-face without hitting the mattress, I fidgeted at the closet. *Dress up nice?* It had been years since I felt a clothes panic. I riffled through the hangers and finally settled on something that my mother had bought me after I'd put on the weight. It was a two-piece silk Liz Claiborne outfit that I'd worn to my tenth high-school reunion two years before, a black skirt and yellow sheath top with puffed sleeves and wide cuffs dotted with seed-pearl buttons. The sheath hid my hips.

A blow-dryer tamed my hair, which I tied back with a gold ribbon from the box of Godiva chocolates Kevin had given me last Christmas. Eyeliner, mascara, lipstick, a little blush, and blue eyeshadow from a Bloomingdale's free sample that I'd got when I bought my mother her favorite moisturizer.

I pulled on the dress and walked out. Kevin watched with morose interest from the couch. It had been years since he'd seen me in heels and makeup.

"You look like you're going to a dance," he said evenly.

"I look okay, honey?"

He nodded. "You look real good."

I kissed him good-bye with a flush of affection that surprised both of us.

. . .

I *took a* cab to the address, an old ten-story building that was once a school administration headquarters. It was in the gloomy garment district, one of the only sections of Manhattan where you didn't see people on the street at night. The NYPD had commandeered a couple of floors, but the building was otherwise vacant. The front entrance was open. A linoleum-paneled elevator lurched up to the fifth floor as if it were on its last trip.

The OCTF office looked like a typical squad room, with dingy pea-green walls that hadn't been painted since the Kennedy administration, but it was busy for a Saturday night. About two dozen male officers, many of them in good suits, stood or sat around.

There wasn't another woman in sight. At the front entrance was one of the few sartorial delinquents, a detective in a short-sleeved shirt with a tie three inches too short lying on his paunch like something he'd spilled at lunch. He pecked with terrible intensity at a manual typewriter and would not look up.

"Excuse me," I said, more loudly than necessary, after he ignored me for more time than was appropriate.

Without a glance, he stood and waddled a few feet over to a file cabinet, mooning me with two yards of shiny trouser as he slid a file in the bottom drawer.

I rapped the top of the cabinet with my knuckles. "Hull-LO-O!" I sang, moving in close to deliberately invade his personal space. Women who become cops quickly learn the importance of body language, the common physical aggressiveness you need simply to get someone to take you seriously.

"Yeah?"

I squared my shoulders and planted both feet apart. You never smile. "I'm Detective Conte, from the Special Victims Squad."

"And?"

"And I was told to see a Lieutenant Campo." I smiled innocently. "Is he here, Officer?"

"Detective," he said hastily, finally meeting my eye. He pointed toward a tall, trim man across the room, late middle age, with wavy black hair. The lieutenant, a head taller than the three officers beside him, wore a starched white shirt with a crimson tie. In his right hand was an unlit panatela. The lieutenant interrupted his conversation when I approached. A cop with manners, I thought.

"Detective Conte," he said, shaking my hand with a firm, but not crushing grip. "Louis Campo. Listen, thanks a million for helping us out tonight. I'm really sorry about the short notice."

"No problem at all, Lieutenant."

Campo studied me. "Somebody told me you're engaged to Brian Murphy. Brian and I go way back, to Homicide. How is he?"

"It's Kevin Murphy, sir."

His face went red. "Oh! Right. Jesus. I'm lousy with names. Tell him I said hello, would you?"

He nodded at a table with a coffeemaker on it. "Some coffee, Detective?"

"Gerry," I said. "Yes, please."

He handed it over with a paper napkin, which struck me as the height of elegance in a squad room.

"They didn't tell you what this was all about, I guess."

"No, sir."

"That figures. Well, let me give you a broad outline before we get going. As you know, all anybody wants to hear about these days is, when are we going to get that bum, Messina?"

Ah, I thought. Already, we are discussing "Sally Seashore."

I knew that there were now more than a dozen separate federal, state, and NYPD operations working on Messina, some of them deliberately overlapping, others stumbling over one another like circus clowns. Yet so far, every time his picture turned up in the paper, his face was laughing.

And so I was going to fill in on one those operations in this relatively small OCTF squad. Campo explained to me that the unit was being run out of a state Special Prosecutor's Office. They had custody of a single, potentially crucial informant—a twenty-eight-year-old made member of the Giavanni family. Messina had run this mob operation since his predecessor, Jack Ponte, conveniently died of some bullets outside a restaurant.

"In and of himself," Campo explained as we sipped the coffee, "the guy we have isn't that important. He's just a punk, really. Why we're putting so much effort into him is simple. See, he could be the missing link. His *uncle* is a Giavanni underboss. You heard of Anthony 'Blackjack' Rossi?"

The name meant nothing to me.

He went on. "We're building our investigation around this nephew. You'll meet him tonight."

"What's his name?" I asked.

"Rossi, same as the uncle."

"His first name?"

Campo waved his cigar. "Hey," he called over to a detective. "What's the *first* name of the confidential informant. The CI?"

"Jeez, I'm drawing a blank, Lou. Wait. Uh, Eugenio, Eugene, Gene, Gino. Take your pick."

"Gino," Campo decided.

The other detective said, "He don't like you to call him that. He's particular."

"What do you call him, then?" I asked.

"*Eugene*," the detective replied, wiggling his fingers airily. "He's freaking delicate about it."

The lieutenant said, "*If* everything breaks the way we hope, then the nephew leads us, over the course of time, directly to the uncle. Hopefully by then we will have enough of a case to squeeze the uncle by the garbonzos, excuse my French. Maybe it's the crack in the hierarchy that brings it all down."

From what I'd gathered so far, it all sounded pretty tentative, but I figured he was boiling things down since I was only going to be on the job for one night. I didn't want to appear out of line and press for detail. I figured they already had an elaborate plan.

Only later did I realize that all they had at this point, besides the informant himself, was an elaborate budget.

"We've had the nephew in custody for about three weeks," Campo said. "Secretly. The uncle has no idea the nephew turned."

"Are they close?"

He shrugged. "From what the CI says, they used to be almost like father and son. Evidently, the uncle raised this guy. Then a couple of years ago, he sends the nephew down to Florida to run some of the family businesses—strip joints, pool halls, restaurants. The kid reported to the uncle and sent up the percentages. Now, as far as the uncle knows, the nephew came back to town because he's in some kind of jam down in Florida. Tonight, the nephew and the uncle are supposed to be getting together with friends at this nightclub. Which is where you're headed."

He laid out the scenario for me. It sounded awfully complicated for a one-night gig. There would be two other detectives along, plus backup. We were going to a flashy nightclub called Harlow's. I recognized the name; it had opened in an old warehouse on Hudson Street not far from where I lived. It was one of those places that suddenly get wildly popular with the Upper East Side crowd and the Hollywood types with their lofts in SoHo. Limousines and Jaguars double-parked every night out front and they never got tickets, which to me meant only that somebody had fixed things up with the precinct.

"You'll meet the CI and his control officer there. One of our guys, a veteran undercover detective named Rey Vargas," the lieutenant said.

"Isn't that place a little downtown for the mob?"

"Not these days," he said. "The next generation of wiseguys is coming into its own. To these guys, those joints on Mulberry Street like Umberto's Clam House are just old-age homes."

"How'd you get the nephew to cooperate?" I said.

"Simple." Campo was casual. "Eugene got himself arrested down in Florida. Luckily, somebody in the Boca PD ran the name and spotted the family connection. They called us. Bingo! Our boy was persuaded that his one alternative to working with us was five-to-fifteen in the can. It took him less than a New York minute to decide to flip. With the mob, don't believe any of that *omerta*, silence-unto-death crap, Conte. Especially the younger crew, these guys fold like a cheap suitcase."

He leaned forward confidingly. "When the detective normally scheduled to work tonight called in sick, I specifically asked them to see if they could call you in."

"Why me?"

"You have a good reputation for working with people, mainly. It's a new unit, we're just getting our act together. We needed somebody smart who could hit the ground running. That's you, from what I hear."

Being female was more than an incidental requirement, too, if I was going to be this guy's date.

"Who am I replacing?"

"Colleen Lewis. From Midtown South. You probably know her."

"Yeah," I said, and left it at that. Colleen, who was about Campo's age, had come up hard through the ranks in the days when a female cop trying to get ahead was regarded as little more than a school crossing-guard with attitude. The older she got, the more she behaved like a grouchy VFW post commander.

So she had called in sick to avoid moll duty. At least it wasn't the full-court hooker stint. Before I got my shield, hooker detail was one of the jobs I regularly pulled. The "John hour," as the NYPD called it. Dressed for the part, female cops were sent out to mingle on the streets with prostitutes, waving to johns and arresting those who offered money. As a city-employed "ho" working the John hour did major weirdness to the head. I'd get assigned a location where high-priced hookers hung out, say Fifty-ninth Street near the Plaza Hotel, where the girls could charge $100 for a half-and-half. I dressed like a businesswoman and when I finished my shift, I felt good about myself. Well, sort of. . . . But the next time I might get sent to one of those grim last stops on the hooker circuit, like the West Side crosstown streets near the tunnels, where I'd have to appear tarted up in a leather miniskirt, and the going rate for a blow job in the back of a car was ten bucks. I'd go home feeling like death eating a cracker, with my self-esteem shot for days. Kevin said I took it all too personally, but it wasn't him strutting his Catholic-school ass down the block.

In comparison, how bad could this one night be? "So what do I do?" I asked Campo.

"You'll go to this club with another detective," he said. "You know, look like you're on a date. Then the CI comes in later, and you end up with him. Like some kind of girlfriend. Hopefully, he introduces you to his uncle later on. He talks, you listen. All part of the process—"

"Lieutenant, please pardon me for inquiring, but what does 'girlfriend' mean?" I asked warily.

"Don't worry about it," he said, smiling. "It's very low-key. The CI knows the deal, he knows to look for you. You'll have some caviar, go dancing, you'll drink some wine. Look at it like a night on the old armski, courtesy of the taxpayers."

"Will I be wired?"

"We'll put a booster in your bag. The CI will have a Nagra taped under his twelve-hundred-dollar suit."

A Nagra was a body transmitter, state-of-the-art high tech. I was happy to hear they at least had decent electronic equipment. Cheap wiretap equipment was the main reason Sally Messina had beat the last federal indictment. The audio quality was so bad that the jury couldn't decide whether they were listening to the godfather Messina order one of his goons to "whack" somebody or, as Messina insisted, "smack" him, which covered the considerable distance between a felony and a violation. The feds were still trying to live that down.

"So you're going to try to collar the uncle tonight?"

He laughed patiently. "We should be so lucky. No, this is a long-term deal. We're just starting out tonight. We'll put the CI through the hoops, see how good he jumps. Anything you and he pick up on tape is a present—but remember, the uncle didn't get where he is by shooting off his mouth. You just play it by ear."

That was certainly standard department procedure, playing it by ear. People always think there's a sophisticated plan, but mostly what cops think about is scheduling, transportation, equipment and food. Strategy tends to be improvised.

"I'll be able to recognize the CI?"

"Yes, believe me. Typical wiseguy look. But Rey Vargas might not be so obvious. I guarantee you won't make Vargas for a cop. The guy spent his first ten years on the force extremely deep undercover, infiltrating Puerto Rican terrorist networks. Never went to the Academy. He never even owned a uniform."

That intrigued me. At the police academy, I'd heard about such cops—guys designated to go so far undercover that the department didn't want to risk the inevitable conditioning that occurred during basic training, where the first thing a recruit picked up was how to talk like a cop. It would only take one casual line of cop-speak—like "I'll meet you at Two-nine and Broadway"—to blow the cover. There were only a handful like Rey Vargas picked each year out of about two thousand new cops.

Campo said, "Okay, then. We want you there a good hour before Rey Vargas and the CI are supposed to walk in, which is at ten. They expect the uncle to show sometime around twelve, but he won't stay long, so it'll be a crapshoot if you get anything at all."

It was starting to look like a very long night ahead. I didn't relish the prospect of spending it cozying up to a mob informant who was betraying the uncle who supposedly raised him. Where I grew up, the name for this was "rat." Or, in Italian, *zuglar*, a filthy, stinking rodent. As a girl, I'd hear my grandmother use it when she whacked at a rat with a broom in the cellar off Mulberry Street where my grandparents made their wine.

Campo was pointing across the room to where several detectives stood near a window. "That's your partner, Danny Flanagan. That guy over there with the red hair?"

Flanagan's hair was startlingly orange. He appeared to be at least forty-five and looked like Elmer Fudd come to life. He had on a camel-hair sports jacket with black pants. Under the jacket he was wearing a blue-and-yellow Hawaiian shirt. Not that I was any movie star, but right away I could see we might have a problem with the doorman at some high-attitude downtown nightclub where they act like their letting you in is your biggest honor since someone took your virginity.

Campo told me quietly, "One other thing, Conte. You don't want to mention Flanagan's toupee. He's sensitive. He paid a bundle for it."

"He *did?*"

"Actually he has four of them, one for each week in the month, each one just a little shaggier than the other, so it looks like it's growing. Nobody mentions it, see, as a courtesy. Once you get past the wig, you'll see that Danny is a great detective, a terrific human being. Anytime somebody has a relative pass away, Danny's the guy they see for the Mass card."

He waved Danny over, introduced us, and led us into a small, neat office. On one wall was a bulletin board with a sign fanned on computer print-out paper across the top: LEADERSHIP OF GIAVANNI ORGANIZED CRIME FAMILY. Below that, somebody had carefully arranged about twenty-five photographs in a huge pyramid, on a background of construction paper. It looked like an eighth-grade class project. At the pinnacle of the pyramid, like the eyeball on a dollar bill, perched the face of "Sally Seashore" Messina, looking like it had been buffed with Turtle Wax. Just below were two portraits labeled "underboss" and "*consigliere*" and in widening rows below that came that the rest of the capos, each photo labeled with a man's given name and his nickname. Unlike those of Messina and his two top lieutenants, which appeared to be news photographs, some of the pictures of the lesser members of the hierarchy were police mug shots. Pasted diagonally across some of the photos were little tan paper sashes labeled FUGITIVE or IN PRISON and, in one case, DECEASED with the date, which was recent.

My eye wandered to the middle row, to the face of an old Italian man with black glasses, a man who closely resembled my own father. All those Italian names on that board made me feel oddly ashamed. All together, the Mafia had maybe two thousand made members among the hundreds of thousands of hardworking, law-abiding Italians in New York City. But you could quickly become uncomfortably aware of all those vowels at the ends of the names, when yours ended with one too.

While we were waiting for the technician, Campo held up an eight-by-ten glossy of a young man and said, "That's our CI." The photograph showed a face that would have looked out of place among the cutthroats and plug-uglies assembled on the board. He was actually quite handsome, with close-cropped black hair and big dark eyes. Except for the annoying sneer, it could have been a graduation portrait on somebody's mantel.

The door opened noisily. A very skinny man came in carrying a beat-up cardboard box. "This is Hal, with your wire," Campo said. It was a good thing Hal worked in the tech room. On patrol, he was the kind of guy other cops loved to make miserable. Like, they'd ask his partner, "Can I check your umbrella?"

Hal got busy taping a matchbox-sized transmitter to the waistband of my skirt, with a wire running under the back of the sheath to an earpiece. I undid my hair to cover it. The earpiece was for messages from the van. Two other cops would be in an unmarked van outside to record whatever conversation was intercepted.

The booster was a device about the size of a small cigar box. Hal tucked it into a cheap-looking bag, a knockoff Coach, and put it over my shoulder.

"Will this thing work?" I said while he fussed with the strap.

Hal bristled. "It *better* goddamn work. It costs five grand. You just think of one word, Detective: proximity, proximity, proximity! And don't dig inside that bag and manhandle the equipment. That bag is not for lipstick and Tic Tacs! Everything will work unless you do something to screw it up."

Nicely done, I was thinking as Hal deftly embraced what should be the NYPD motto: Divest yourself of all responsibility for potential screw-ups as quickly as possible.

The two cops who would stay in the van were waiting for us by the elevator. Campo had one more thing to say. "I forgot to mention, Detective—Rey Vargas, he's Puerto Rican. But his cover now is that he's a Cuban drug runner, okay?"

Let me get this straight, I thought. I've got a six-dollar pocketbook under my arm, heading to a flashy nightclub with a man in a red wig to meet a mob rat and a Puerto Rican detective passing himself off as a Cuban drug dealer to a bunch of Italian hoods.

Danny was a gentleman. He held the door when we went out even when it slammed into his leg repeatedly.

. . .

The van was a beat-up Ford that looked like it belonged to a scrap-metal dealer. Danny drove. The other two climbed in back and stuffed their sound equipment like fishing tackle behind the seat. The passenger seat had been removed; in its place was this milk crate somebody had nailed to the floor. The back window was covered with a plastic shower curtain, held in place with masking tape.

"Nice wheels," I told Danny.

"Drives beautiful," he said.

Gripping the milk crate, I noticed that Danny had pinned a red carnation on his lapel.

Danny drove fast. We were there in ten minutes. As usual, the block was packed with cars, but Danny drove right up front, under the marquee. It must have looked like a delivery, until Danny hopped out, opened my door and helped me down. There was already a line of well-dressed people snaking halfway down the block, waiting to get inside.

One of the cops in back climbed behind the wheel and backed the van down the block. He parked it in front of a hydrant with the engine running noisily.

Danny stood on the sidewalk blinking like a time-machine refugee looking for the Glenn Miller band. Around us people were rocking and giggling. The club's front door was blocked by a jukebox with legs. The bouncer's job was to guard that crushed-velvet rope against the press of the obscure, and drop it to admit those he deemed worthy. My ego started doing somersaults.

Right away, I saw that I was not dressed like the rest of the women. Four-inch heels clicked impatiently on the sidewalk.

"We may not get in," I told Danny, feeling foolish.

"We got to!"

Gently, I said, "Danny, not for nothing. Maybe we just don't look right together. Just let me go up by myself and give it a shot."

"Don't leave me out here," he protested. "I'll never get in alone." At least he wasn't laboring under any major delusions.

I told him I'd be right back, and pushed my way up to the scowling bouncer.

"Listen," I said, watching his gaze flicker away to a pair of long bare legs folding out of a white limo at the curb. "Listen! I'm here with my brother who's visiting me from Idaho. He got off a Greyhound at Port Authority this afternoon. I want to show the guy New York. It would really mean a lot to me to show him your place. I'd make it up to you when we leave."

I gave his big bicep a little squeeze and flashed a John hour look, heavy on the eyelashes. You don't have to spell out BJ with guys like this. "We're not going to stay that long, just for a drink. It's my brother's birthday."

Then I slipped him a twenty for insurance.

"You coming back later without your brother?" he asked.

"You going to be around at closing time?"

"I don't leave the door till then."

"Okay," I said suggestively.

"What's your name?"

"Gerry."

"Gerry," he repeated, like he was planning to write it down sometime.

I shot a glance down the line and waved to Danny, who bounded up like somebody called out of a game-show audience. He nearly died when they told him the cover was twenty-five dollars each. You would have thought it was his own money he was pulling out of his pocket.

Unhooking the rope, the bouncer advised me darkly, "Say he's a Euro."

You didn't walk into Harlow's. You were propelled in, like a steel ball shot up the chute of a giant pinball machine, which the place resembled, with flashing lights and people in constant chaotic motion. Two bars were set diagonally at the rear corner. On the walls, huge video screens pulsed with kaleidoscopic bursts of visual energy.

It was filling up fast. Money flashed in snatches of strobe light. A bearded man in a tux and a black eyepatch walked by with a bald girl who had a tattoo on her cheek and a hairless cat under her arm. The cat's eyes were hard as marbles.

Gorgeous models walked around selling black orchids out of boxes strapped to their midriffs. One approached Danny after we settled onto bar stools.

"Flower for your lady?" she asked sweetly.

"Nope," Danny grunted, the way you would brush off a panhandler.

I bought one myself and pinned it on my cuff. If Danny could have his carnation, I could have an orchid. I felt better immediately.

Down the bar, the bartender was leaned over talking to a guy in a baggy Armani suit. He nodded over to a drag queen dressed in a strapless gown and the guy walked over, undoubtedly to buy blow or Ecstasy.

The bartender approached us. "You want something to drink?" Danny said.

"White wine," I told him.

Danny said, "And give me a Rob Roy, straight up."

The bartender looked at him blankly.

"A Rob Roy," Danny shouted.

The bartender leaned over. "I'm sorry, man. What *is* that?"

Danny was amazed. "One part dry vermouth, one part sweet vermouth, three parts scotch. Shake with ice and strain it into a Manhattan glass. With a twist."

The bartender repeated this dubiously, as if he was thinking, Man, if you puke, it's not my fault.

Danny sipped his Rob Roy with a dour face and tried to make conversation, but you could tell it had been like a decade or so since he was out with any woman but his wife. He fidgeted and watched new people coming in like a fire-code inspector.

In a while he said, "Listen, you sit tight for a minute. I'll be right back. Watch the door for our friends."

He came back in less than a minute, very agitated.

"Jesus, Mary, and Joseph!"

"What's the matter, Danny?"

"The bathroom, is what. They got one of them universal-sex johns. Men and women using the same bathroom! At the same time! Holy Mother of God, what kind of a place is this?"

I couldn't hold back a laugh. "Are you sure you were in the right one? You sure they don't maybe just have those little cowboy and cowgirl cutouts on the doors, and you just couldn't tell which was which?"

"Believe me. It's all together, the same place. What the hell am I going to do?"

He looked like he was in pain, which made me anxious. His having to pee became *my* problem.

So I set off to investigate. The bathroom was shiny industrial chic; the back wall consisted of a long dark mirror with a waterfall cascading down over it. It was undoubtedly the urinal, since men were standing facing it. Women came and went from the stalls without a glance.

As I turned to leave, I caught myself in a mirror. Everything about me looked so wrong: Twenty pounds overweight. Skirt just below the knees. Nails too short. Hair frumpy. The blue eyeshadow. The reflection belonged to someone who worked in a day-care center.

I trudged back. Under all this pinball-machine lighting, Danny didn't look so odd anymore.

"You were right," I said. "But just sail in and use a stall before it gets too crowded."

He brightened, this alternative not having occurred to him, and wobbled away.

From the bar we could just barely see the sidewalk through a window beside the door. A flashier crowd was starting to assemble. I was glad we got there early, because it was a sure thing we wouldn't have gotten in now. A little after ten o'clock, a white stretch limo pulled up, and a tall man with dark hair got out. I thought a woman would follow, but another man slid out and stood flashing his cuffs for a moment. They were ushered right in.

Danny raised his glass in the new arrivals direction. "Here comes our boys."

At first, it wasn't clear to me which of the two was the cop and which was the informant. Neither of them was what you would describe as drop-dead handsome, but they both carried a lot of beef, solidly arranged. A couple of leggy women drifted toward them as if they were rolling downhill. The men paused, adjusting attitude as they took in the scene, and made their entrance.

Leading the way was the taller one, who I took to be the informant at first because he looked nothing like a cop. He was resplendent, a dark-featured man in a flashy navy-blue pinstripe suit with a long-collared silk shirt that seemed to say "Weekend in Havana, 1959."

Then I noticed that the one behind him was sweeping his eyes back and forth regally as he worked through the front crowd. That was a move you saw only on Mulberry Street.

Eugene Rossi appeared to be even younger than twenty-eight. He had on a double-breasted cream silk suit. He was about five foot eleven, with broad shoulders on an upper torso that tapered down to a narrow waist.

He flashed teeth like chiclets. Even though it was March and still chilly out, his face and neck were golden tan. On his feet were taupe reptile-skin loafers. Wiseguy deluxe.

The CI stopped and waited, with feet spread and hands folded, like a Vegas lounge singer about to begin "My Way." Something Rey said prompted a theatrical laugh, which he tossed over his shoulder.

Eugene broadcast fifty thousand watts of attitude. Rey, on the other hand, was a solid-state receiver. You could almost see him adjusting the signal.

Danny scooped his wet bills off the bar. Since he was acting like the taxpayer's money was his own, I made sure he left a decent tip. We pushed through the crowd to the two men. Danny caught Rey's eye and got a slight nod back. Rey gave Eugene a small nudge. "This is the girl I was telling you about." Eugene looked down at me like I was about to ask for his autograph.

Just then, one of the black-orchid girls inserted herself between them. She was very downtown, very blonde, and lithe in her skintight black leotard. She presented a large orchid to Eugene, who held it up in the light, as if looking for flaws, and then dropped it back into her box. Staring right at me, he took out his wallet full of flash money from NYPD, thumbed a hundred-dollar bill, and slid it slowly down her top until his hand reached her breast. He didn't stop smirking at me the whole time.

When she left, he said, loudly, "No offense, sweetheart, but I'd never be with someone who looks like you."

He started to walk away. I was furious. "Hey, buddy," I said sharply. "You are supposed to stay close to me."

He pulled out a crisp new twenty and held it straight up, like I was supposed to reach for it. "Go and buy yourself a drink, honey," he said.

"No, no, no," I replied, like I was talking to a child. "Listen, Gino. You don't get it. You have *got* to stay close to me. Am I making myself clear?"

"Eugene," he said, a bit more amiably as he caught my arresting-officer expression, which I knew he had seen before.

Rey stepped around to introduce himself in a way that took a little more wind out of Eugene's sails.

"You and Danny up for this game?" he asked pleasantly.

"So they tell me," I replied, tapping my bag.

Rey edged us out of the crowd toward the bar where we could talk more freely. "The guest of honor won't be here for an hour or so," he explained. "Eugene knows what he has to do, but right now we have to go over to meet a couple of his cousins."

"There they are, at the table in the corner," Eugene said, peering across the room.

Danny and I agreed to have dinner first and then join them before the uncle arrived. Rey said he would tell Eugene's people that Danny and I were friends of his from "the health club."

"The health club?" I said dubiously.

"Tell them we work in the business office," Danny suggested.

Rey glanced at my skirt. "Right," he said evenly. "The name of the club is Heavenly Bodies. On Twenty-first Street in Chelsea, just in case."

"Check," Danny said, utterly serious.

Eugene chucked Danny on the arm as they stroke off. "Nice shirt, dude," he said.

The friends were a group of Mulberry Street players and their girl-friends, staked out at what must have been their regular Saturday-night table. Except for one dignified old lady in a neat black suit, the women appeared to be in their twenties and early thirties. Miniskirts, diamonds, gold bracelets.

"They're having a grand time," Danny said morosely.

He and I took a table a little distance away as they all got up from their crowded table of twelve to welcome Eugene uproariously and meet Rey. Except for the getups, they looked like my relatives at a wedding.

After about a half hour, Rey wandered over. My earpiece had started buzzing with complaints from the cops in the van that they weren't picking up anything, which of course was because Eugene had the microphone wired on him while I had the booster.

I took the opportunity to ask Rey, "What's with this guy? He planning to work tonight or screw around over there? We aren't getting anything."

"Just hang loose," Rey said, touching my shoulder.

"Those guys in the van are driving me nuts," I complained.

"Just relax. Eugene ordered some DP sent over to you. Enjoy."

"What's that?"

"Dom Perignon."

"Gee, great. This is what you guys do?"

"This is all preliminary," Rey said, leaving.

I'd only had a few bites of dinner at home and now I was really hungry. We looked over the menu, but Danny worried that everything was way too expensive. I ordered a chicken Caesar salad, $24.95. Danny ordered the cheapest thing on the menu, bruschetti, $11.95. Before the food came, the waiter brought the champagne and set up a silver ice bucket.

Danny croaked, "What's that?"

"DP, what else?" I said knowingly.

Danny didn't want to accept it. He leaned over close to me so the waiter uncorking the bottle couldn't hear, and asked anxiously. "How much does that stuff cost?"

The wine list lay in front of me. "Looks like a hundred and thirty-five, Danny."

"We can't have that!"

"Don't worry, Danny. Good-time Charlie over there is buying, courtesy of 'We the People.' "

Eugene saw me look over and responded by raising his glass. The waiter poured our champagne, which Danny drained in one big gulp. Then he filched most of the chicken from my salad. The guys in the van groused in my ear again. Finally, Rey brought us over to their table and introduced us as friends.

When Eugene got up to dance with a gorgeous young woman, Rey leaned over. "Eugene made a call and they said the uncle is probably on his way. Something came up, though, and he's running late."

"He is coming?" I asked, keeping my voice low.

"My guess?"

"Yeah."

"Nah."

"What, is this guy jerking us around?" I demanded.

He shook his head. "These things can take a lot of time. You just roll with it."

Eugene kept dancing and never got close to me. After a while, I saw him come out of the rest room patting his chest. I didn't learn till later that he'd taken off the wire and stuffed it in his pocket. By now the music was so loud we wouldn't have picked up a conversation anyway.

"You're silent! We can't get nothing!" the voice in my ear shrieked. "Get out here so we can check the bag! Something's wrong. You're screwing the booster up! You got to stick right next to the guy! We got to get something on this goddamn tape!"

I couldn't leave. I knew I'd never get back in. You'd have thought they were expecting to hear the Watergate tapes. I tried to ignore the cops in the van.

At the other end of the table, meanwhile, Danny had joined the old lady in an animated conversation. He flashed me a wink. He had settled in like a guest at a dinner party. He was telling her jokes, and she was in stitches laughing. Dweeb that I had made him for, Danny was probably the only one of us who would actually walk out of this place with a piece or two of useful information.

Eugene approached a girl at a nearby table and whispered something to her. She rose. With his hand on her lower back, he guided her onto the dance floor.

As Eugene danced, he glanced over his shoulder occasionally to look for a reaction. I tried to ignore him, but my gaze kept drifting his way. The song was Barry White's, "I'm Qualified to Satisfy You." Eugene was close to his partner. Her eyes were closed. He moved the lower half of his body the way I'd never seen any white man do before. Despite myself, I couldn't take my eyes off him, even though I guessed that he knew it.

After a while, it was obvious the uncle wouldn't show. I felt like putting the cuffs on Eugene right then and there, perp-walk him out with a raincoat over his head.

Frowning, Rey said to me, "That guy is one piece of work. You know what he ordered for dinner?"

"The most expensive thing on the menu," I said.

"Bingo. The chateau-freaking-briand for two. Didn't eat a bite, didn't even look at it, for Christ's sake. A forty-five-dollar steak."

When the song ended, Rey walked out on the floor and Eugene barked something into Rey's ear, I couldn't hear what.

Rey came back and put his hand on my shoulder. "We're leaving. Party's over."

He paid the check for the table with a platinum American Express card. I went over to Danny. "Ready to go?" He gave the old lady a peck on the cheek. In a minute, we were out of there.

. . .

In the streetlight outside, Rey's face was flushed. Eugene rocked gently on his heels with his hands folded neatly at his waist. There were still people lined up waiting to be let in.

"What's going on?" I said, hoping I was finished with this sorry operation.

"Change in plans," Rey said. "The big guy isn't coming, Eugene says. He evidently might be able to see us instead at some after-hours joint out on Long Island, just over the Nassau county line."

"Eugene's talked with him?"

He shrugged. "He says so."

"And you're going to Long Island? *Tonight?*"

"We're all going. You too."

"You have got to be kidding."

It was nearly two o'clock in the morning. The champagne made my head hurt. I wanted to go home to bed.

Rey nudged Eugene into the backseat of the limo and called back, "We'll wait for you at the corner."

Without much enthusiasm, Danny and I moped to the van. The two cops in the back were ecstatic when we informed them we were going to be racking up OT. They radioed Campo to get approval, getting him out of bed. His orders were to follow the limo. Since Danny was in no shape to drive, one of the cops got up front. I held on to the milk crate and off we went.

The limo was waiting for us at Fifth Avenue and 10th Street. When he saw the van come up behind, the limo driver, also a cop, pulled out fast. We bounced across town. In the side mirror, I saw an unmarked radio car fall in behind us. A motorcade.

We picked up speed in the plaza off the Bowery and headed onto the Manhattan Bridge, scattering cabs out of our way.

Over my shoulder I asked Danny if he thought this was a wild-goose chase.

He said, "All's I know is what the old lady told me, which is that Tony Rossi spends Saturday night in Atlantic City, and him and Eugene have been on the outs for a while. But she says nobody tells her nothing anymore since her husband got blown up last year in the explosion at that meatpacking plant in Red Hook."

CHAPTER 2

The way we went roaring out to Long Island, you'd have thought we had the Sultan of Brunei under escort. The radio traffic kept referring to our destination as "the location," which turned out to be just a late-night dance club beside a four-lane highway on the South Shore, with a Las Vegas–scale sign on the roof hurling the word *Vertigo* at your face in blazing red-and-gold letters. The place was as big as one of those warehouse club megastores and was packed wall-to-wall with Long Island office workers hot-wiring weekend self-images in Hathaway suits, with big-haired girls in sequined jackets and leggings, limbs jangling gold chains on the crashing backbeat of music that braced you like a high wind. It was obvious this wasn't the kind of place to find a middle-aged Mafia underboss—a guy whose idea of dance music was more likely a jukebox with Dean Martin singing "Non Dimenticar" in a Mulberry Street trattoria with white linen on the tables, and waiters who bowed.

We claimed two adjacent cocktail tables the size of Motel 6 nightstands. After the waitress took our drink orders, Eugene looked significantly at Rey and tilted his head toward the men's room. They left together, which men seldom do. It made me think of boys at a high-school dance ducking out to the parking lot. Then, as now, I had only a vague idea of what they were doing.

Rey returned in a few minutes looking merry. I tried to talk business. "Rey, he's not meeting any *capo* from the Giavanni family in a place like this, uncle or not. I think this guy might be yanking our chain."

Rey cleared his throat loudly. "Don't worry about it. The PD tells us to expose the guy in public. That's all we're doing."

"It's costing an awful lot of money." I said. Eugene, bright-eyed as a chimpanzee, loped back to the table.

"Enjoy yourself! Just have a good time!" Rey told me heartily. He was watching faces that flashed in the lights sweeping the dance floor. It was a night crime scene. Eugene rose, wandered off, his taut figure dissolving in the glare.

"Excuse me," I told Rey as I got up.

"Where are *you* going?"

"I'll be back." There was no point in pretending to get any work done. In the bathroom, I yanked out my earpiece and stuffed it in the bag with the useless booster. My watch said 3:20. My headache hammered. My stomach felt queasy. I had no idea when this night would end. All I could do was ride it out. When I got back to the table, Rey was gone. I toyed with my plastic glass of wine.

The crowd was starting to thin out, which only intensified the music, a techno-fusion that could have been the Muzak on the elevators to hell. My veins throbbed with animosity.

In a while, Rey returned to the table. He rested his hand on the back of my chair just touching my hair and apologized. "I'm sorry about tonight," he said. "Try to understand, this guy's been under wraps for weeks. It's the first time he's been out, and I'm supposed to loosen him up so he can get back into his old social swing."

I didn't smile. "Well, I'm glad the taxpayers of the city of New York could show him such a good time."

"The uncle just wasn't in the cards. But I think our boy was as surprised as we were about that. You could see that for yourself. Anyway, it was a good trial run. We moved the ball down the field a yard or two."

That wasn't how I saw it, but I kept a lid on it, assuming that my tour was over. "Am I free to go home?" I said. I figured I could get a ride home in the van.

"We're all heading back," Rey said. "Ride with us in the limo instead of that crummy truck."

"I'd prefer the van."

"Suit yourself."

I didn't take the van. The sergeant drove me home in his unmarked car. It was after five by the time I got in. My first thought was to get into the shower and wash the stink of smoke off my skin and out of my hair, but I was afraid the noise would wake Kevin. I was ravenously hungry.

I saw the debris of the Chinese dinner on the coffee table in a junk-yard of little white cardboard takeout boxes with bent wire handles, one of which held a few soggy buds of broccoli sunk like swamp stumps in congealed glutinous sauce. Two waxed-paper packs of chow mein noo-dles lay beside an empty Bud bottle with a cigarette butt that had run aground in a half inch of beer. Using bottles as ashtrays was one of Kevin's more endearing table manners. This was a man who thought that putting his toast on a plate constituted putting on airs.

Gritting my teeth, I ripped open one of the chow mein noodle bags and dumped the contents into my palm. Kevin was snoring loudly when I slipped into the bedroom in my bare feet, the tossed covers exposing his muscular legs.

"Want some chow mein noodles, honey?" I said, tossing one into the heap on the bed, the way you'd feed a pigeon. Then I flung another, and several more.

His snoring sputtered and changed pitch. I waited and said, "I thought you might like a little snack. Sorry, this is all that's *left*, honey!" I beaned him right on the forehead with one of the noodles, but all that did was shift his snoring back into overdrive.

I brushed my teeth, undressed, took a long hot shower, and then got into bed. He didn't stir. As the first light of dawn showed on the win-dowshade, I was trying to push the wildly conflicting images of the night from my mind. I tossed and turned for a while, and finally his snoring stopped and I sensed that his eyes were open, but he lay there and said nothing. I turned on my side and forced myself to sleep.

· · ·

A *baby's sharp* cry melded with the wail of a siren over brick tenement walls, and I woke.

Kevin had left the television on when he went out to Mass, and then to lunch with his mother, who always served his favorite Sunday lunch: Oscar Meyer bologna on a bagel. On television, some Washington re-porter made up like a corpse was being brayed at by a very ugly fat man who used to work for Ronald Reagan. I lunged at the set to end the torture. My head throbbed; amazingly I had a hangover, which was a rare experience because I'm not much of a drinker. I remembered my first hangover, a real cling-to-the-toilet bowl howler from hell, on a high school class trip. At that moment, I thought, why would anyone ever want to deliberately do this again?

I had my coffee with the morning paper. On page 3 was a story about a mob hit.

SLAYING IN BROOKLYN
TIED TO MOB VIOLENCE

A reputed member of New York's Giavanni organized-crime family was gunned down execution-style early last night outside a restaurant and topless club that he ran in Bay Ridge, Brooklyn, police said.

The victim was identified as Alphonse "Faffy" Fortunato, of Manhattan, whom police sources described as a crew boss in the Giavanni family, which is allegedly run by Salvatore "Sally Seashore" Messina.

Fortunato, 53, was shot three times in the back of the head about 3:45 A.M. yesterday as he walked to his car after closing his business, the Strip 'n Sip Steakhouse, a restaurant on Eighty-sixth Street that employs topless dancers. Police responded after 911 calls reported the shots, but could find no witnesses to the shooting.

"If this was an underworld hit, it could signal the start of warfare between the Giavanni family and other factions," a police source speculated last night. The source could give no reason for any resumption of the mob warfare that bloodied New York streets in the 1980s.

Neighbors of the dead man on Allen Street in Lower Manhattan said he lived by himself in a two-bedroom apartment. A police source said that over the years Fortunato rose to become a trusted street soldier in a crew led by the late Jack Ponte, Messina's predecessor as Giavanni boss. In recent years, Fortunato was thought to have been bypassed for promotion and had fallen out of favor with Messina.

In the parking lot of the Strip 'n Sip lounge yesterday, a chalk outline still showed the position of the body. A man who lives nearby said, "I guess somebody had a pretty big beef with him."

The phone rang and I put down the paper.
"Gerry?"

"Who's this?"

"Rey."

"Oh. How's it going?"

"Okay. So, you got home all right?"

"No problem."

"Great. Very good."

I asked, "You see the paper?"

"No. Why?"

"Some Giavanni guy got whacked in Brooklyn."

"Oh, that. Nothing to it. Routine," he said. After a moment, he added, "I put in a good word for you, you know. The way you handled yourself last night. I already put in the word to the lieutenant."

"For what?"

"Eugene can be tough to handle. Especially for a woman. He's an asshole sometimes, but you didn't take any crap."

"What's the story with him anyway?" I said. "You really think he's going to deliver?"

"The NYPD does, and they sign the paychecks," he said. "That's what counts. We've got him in a safe house in Jersey. Keep him out of trouble. Next week we start bringing him in for debriefings. It's a bitch to commute out there, and once you're there, well, it's Jersey. . . ."

In the background, I heard a female voice that had a steak-knife edge. "Reynaldo! *Who the fuck is that?*"

"Got to go!" Rey said abruptly. "See you around." He hung up.

Not that it was any skin off my teeth anymore, but I wondered again whether the NYPD knew what it was doing with Eugene. The only other experience I'd had with mob guys was a brief encounter with an arsonist named Anthony "Tuna" Abalone, a fabulously inept informer that NYPD set up in the Plaza Hotel years ago. Tuna had somehow convinced some detectives who locked him up in Manhattan South that he could spin out spools of inside information on illegal casinos, card games, football pools, whatever they wanted, in exchange for his freedom. I was still a patrol officer, but since I knew Little Italy, they put me on the project, which they called Operation Jackpot. Tuna loved being the center of attention, but as an informant he was about as useful as the phone book. The one arrest he led us to was a numbers operation working out of the basement of a fried-chicken shop on Canal Street. We stormed the place like D day, but the only collar we made was an old Italian lady on the phone. I'll never forget how a cop drew his gun and shouted at her: "Drop the fucking pencil or I'll blow your fucking dago brains out." They made me cuff her and hustle her out to the wagon. Her hands felt like chicken bones. She trembled but said nothing. My face burned with shame.

. . .

Monday morning, I was back at my usual desk in the special victim's unit when the receptionist handed me a message to call an Inspector Lester Marcomb at police headquarters on Foley Square. I was mystified. Over the years, I'd met Marcomb on a couple of occasions. He pinned a medal on me at an awards ceremony and he was there to shake my hand when I received my promotion to detective. Later, I found out that Marcomb was the one who had put in the final recommendation for me to get the gold shield.

His secretary had said he wanted to see me on Wednesday afternoon.

When I got there, Marcomb rose up from his desk, a big smile on his face. He took off his glasses and got to the point.

"Conte, you just came off a very tough job. Your performance was first-rate. Everybody says so. Outstanding performance!" It startled me to hear him refer to my latest child murder like a ballgame.

"Thank you, Inspector," I said uneasily.

He leaned into his intercom. "Would you have Lieutenant Campo come in, Sara?"

He motioned me to a leather couch. "Well, well," Campo said, joining us.

"Of course you know Lieutenant Campo," said Marcomb.

Campo shook my hand. "How did you enjoy your little adventure last weekend?"

"It was interesting," I said.

He beamed. "Well, sorry we came up empty. But as I said, it was a dry run. All in all, we're pleased. There will be lots of other opportunities, and you never know where the threads will lead. For example, you take that supposed mob hit in Brooklyn last week. It doesn't make sense because this guy was out of the picture. We think it wasn't even a mob job. Just as a test, maybe we'll ask our new CI to see what he can find out for us, since his uncle goes way back with the dead guy. See if the CI can deliver on that one. It's one of many items on our shopping list, shall we say."

I was baffled, but he appeared to think I was following his line of reasoning. He went on. "As I'm sure you know, this is an unusual operation, unusual circumstances, what with the need to get some points on the board, with the feds pressing hard on Messina, after they screwed it up at the last trial. I think I told you that we've had the CI stashed away for a couple of weeks now. Now we're gearing up for a full-time push."

"Yes, sir. You have him in a safe house over in Jersey, I hear."

"Right, a rented house, out of the way. Round-the-clock coverage, Detective Rey Vargas and three other detectives out there full-time. Plus two sergeants, five or six uniforms, depending on scheduling considerations. The fun starts next week, when we begin formal interrogations downtown. As you know, our boy Eugenio is not the actual objective here. The objective is to get enough on the uncle so we can flip the son of a bitch. We have many avenues. The overhears will help. We'll be doing a sting at some point and pop him on a barrel of felonies. This basically is the road we're paving for our CI. We're just beginning that stage of the operation, where Gino, Eugene, runs the ball." He looked at me as if I was supposed to reply.

"That will be interesting," I said politely, "assuming the guy delivers something you can use."

"We've got plenty of time and money."

I didn't know how to reply to that. I wanted to tell him that if the NYPD was so flush, maybe they should talk to Kevin, dragging himself home every night, worried about the lack of resources he and his squad had to contend with because the criminals they were after were unglamorous Dominicans, not mafiosi. Kevin was on a major drug case, Project Bodega, involving the Dominican cartel that had snatched most of the heroin and crack trade from the Mafia on the East Side and in Inwood, where it operated out of grocery stores and Lotto shops. Dominican gangsters didn't go to the movies to learn their attitudes the way the Italian mob did. While Eugene was eating chateaubriand and drinking champagne, Kevin was risking his neck, hoping his backups hadn't been sent home by some lieutenant trying to gain a few points by cutting overtime.

Campo was looking at me earnestly. "And the point here, in case you're still wondering how this involves you, is that I need a female detective," he said. "Someone with a good head on her shoulders."

I blinked and said, "Why?"

"Very simple. Part of the job requires doing what we had you do the other night—pose basically as the CI's girlfriend. Hang out with him when he goes to meetings and socializes. Wired, of course."

I started to reply but he headed me off. "We'll work the kinks out from what happened the other night, with the uncle not showing up, don't worry. Step by step, we'll make the case on the uncle, and then move right on up to the big guy. We get the uncle by the short hairs and he starts talking, and it's off to the races."

"And you want me to do what?"

"To help handle this Eugene. Not only debrief him, but get him working for us."

"You have a plan? I mean, turning the uncle is a very big order."

He shrugged casually. "We always have strategy. And there's always a rat under a floorboard somewhere. This is the OCTF, don't forget. You'd be working with the best in the department, people like Rey Vargas."

So I was there for a job interview, and the job was evidently mine for the asking, assuming I'd ever had a choice. I considered it. Undercover work appealed to me, and I needed a change. Babysitting a guy who made my skin crawl was a drawback. But I liked Rey. Warily, I said, "For how long, did you say?"

"As long as it takes," Campo replied. "Myself, I'd figure on six months, maybe eight. But the working conditions are pretty good."

"Jersey," I said. I didn't like going to Jersey.

"My unit is based at the Jersey house, you'll like it out there. There's another unit in a safe house on Staten Island, same basic setup, except the CI is one of the Westies, that crazy Irish gang. Out in Jersey, we got the real thing."

Maybe, I thought. From one night's experience, I could see that Eugene was a slacker, not a doer. He was a con. Surely, they realized this. They had certainly factored it in.

"But how is the CI working out so far?" I said skeptically.

"He isn't working out, not yet, to tell you the truth. He's a smartass, which you know. Thinks he's a tough guy, but that's mostly when he looks in the mirror—"

"—Which is frequently—"

"—he sees a guy with no future besides the one we're offering. Anyway, now that we're almost fully geared up, we're going to start tightening the screws on our boy and make him deliver. From what Vargas tells me, the guy's starting to understand that he doesn't walk away till we say he can walk, that we have the key to his future."

"You've offered him the witness protection program?" I said.

"We take care of those who deliver," he said.

"And you want me in your unit?"

"Correct."

"You should know I'm in law school," I said. "Classes four nights a week, when I can make them. I'd be reluctant to lose that."

He shook off my concern. "We can accommodate that. The schedule will be fairly flexible, mostly steady days."

Day work was nirvana to a cop. After the past three years, managing my job while slogging to law-school classes at St. John's, I was worn out by the constant schedule-juggling. But I could see the goal line at last. Assuming a final big push, I would have my law degree within a year.

"Weekends off," Campo said, closing the deal. "Three-day weekends when we can work it out."

"Starting when?"

"You started last Saturday, as far as I'm concerned. Take the rest of the week off and we'll see you on Monday."

What the hell. "Sign me up," said.

CHAPTER 3

As the head of the OCTF unit, Lieutenant Campo worked at the safe house in Jersey and reported to Inspector Marcomb at headquarters downtown, but the man in overall charge of the operation was Noah Perlmutter-Rosen, an ambitious First Assistant District Attorney who happened to be an old childhood acquaintance from the neighborhood.

When we were kids, actually, I had known him as plain Noah Rosen, but just before he went to law school he spent the summer at a kibbutz in Israel and returned home as Noah Perlmutter-Rosen—having added the Perlmutter, he said, to honor his mother's side of the family. It didn't hurt, of course, that his mother's brother was an appellate court judge.

Even in New York City, Perlmutter-Rosen was considered quite a mouthful, so naturally people still referred to him as Noah Rosen. He was sensitive about his name. If you introduced him, you'd have to give him the whole nine yards, "*Noah Perlmutter-Rosen*," or he'd sulk.

Kevin knew that Noah and I had been in the same class at P.S. 17 and that we saw each other occasionally on a professional basis after college. Kevin also knew that Noah and I had dated for a little while in our senior year of high school, during a brief period when I considered him amusing and deeply sensitive. He loved to argue points of fact and history, not to mention law, which appealed to me in an intellectual way. Once, when we thought we might be getting serious, he assured me that his family would love me. "Italian girls who are smart, it's presumed they are Jewish," he said, and seemed perplexed when I didn't take it as a compliment.

We'd lost contact through college. After Yale Law School, Noah got a job as an assistant district attorney and his star began its rise.

Only after I became a detective, when I had to spend a lot of time in court testifying on major criminal cases, did we start to run into each other again. Only then, I think, did he regard me as being worth the occasional risk of his time.

"You've come a long way from P.S. 17," I told him as I admired his photographs while he waited for his secretary to bring in a report that he insisted, for my benefit, I thought, absolutely had to be signed before we could go to lunch.

"Oh well, you knew me when," he said with modesty that he turned off in an instant, quickly changing the subject. "Italian okay for lunch? I made a reservation."

"Sure, fine," I said agreeably. Italian. That figured.

The secretary, a stunningly beautiful young woman with the crisply confident manner of someone whose boss was going places, brought in a sheaf of papers and waited while he frowned over each page. Then he signed the last page with a fountain pen that looked like a ceramic cigar.

"Montblanc," he said when she left, softly closing the door behind.

"Anywhere you want to eat is fine," I said.

"Actually, I meant the pen. It's a Montblanc."

He handed the pen to me, and I dutifully admired it. Smiling, I laid it carefully back on his desk-pad, noticing that it had left a smudge of blue ink on my forefinger, which was something a 29-cent NYPD-issue Bic never did.

. . .

It was a cool afternoon with a sky full of sun, and we felt a little like old friends again on the short walk on crowded streets to a restaurant on Mulberry Street. The lunch crowd had mostly cleared out by now, and a solicitous waiter in a starched white jacket showed us to a Naugahyde-upholstered banquette in the front of the room, facing the sidewalk. After he brought a plate of assorted breads, drinks, and poured some ice water from a silver pitcher, I decided to get right to the point.

I said, "The truth is, Noah, I'm a little concerned about this operation. So I'd kind of like some guidance before I get in too deep."

He sipped his wine, then dabbed at his lips with the corner of a linen napkin. "What specifically are you concerned about?"

"I'll level with you. From what I've seen, this guy is very slick. I don't trust him at all."

"The CI? Why? I mean, other than the fact that he's a career criminal."

"Two things have me concerned," I said. "One, it's obvious that the success of this operation ultimately depends entirely on the performance of the CI, on Eugene delivering the goods and reeling in the uncle. Let's just say that I haven't yet been impressed by his diligence."

"Well, we're all just starting out," Noah said, unconcerned. "Getting the CI up and running efficiently will be a big part of your job, Gerry. That was one of the factors in your being chosen for the assignment."

"Which brings me to concern number two," I said pointedly. "What happens if this thing unexpectedly goes sour? I mean, I'm supposed to accompany this guy undercover from time to time, go where he hangs out, meet his friends, act like I'm one of them. From where I sit, it looks like I'm supposed to be sort of his keeper. That being the case, I want your personal assurance, Noah, that you will warn me if you see any hint that this operation is headed for trouble—"

"What kind of trouble?"

"Like they're going to pull the plug all of a sudden and everybody gets sent packing."

"Oh, that kind of trouble. Don't worry about that. There are too many big swinging dicks in the picture—from the governor's office, to city hall, the DA, the police commissioner," he assured me.

"Then you'll excuse my bluntness when I tell you that from what I've seen so far, this operation is well-financed, well-staffed, and typically half-assed. All you have is a CI who doesn't want to do time and says he'll turn in his uncle to avoid it. Yes, you have an objective. But there's no real plan yet for achieving it."

"Planning those details will be up to all of us in the coming weeks—you included," he said.

"That's understood. But I want your personal assurance that if for some reason the whole thing goes wrong—and you know as well as I do that it's a possibility—I don't want to be left out there flapping in the wind. My career is too important to me. I don't want to be the one blamed if this plan, whatever it is, turns out to be a disaster."

"It won't go sour," he insisted. "Do you know how much we have riding on this little adventure?"

"I'm beginning to get an idea. But meanwhile, at the same time, the feds are throwing everything they have into their own investigation. I take it this is some kind of a race between us and the feds. Okay, I'm a team player on our side. But what I don't clearly understand is, what's my objective?"

A patient smile crossed his face. "Indicting Sally Messina and locking him up for life. You know that as well as I do."

"Up to this point, every job I've done has had a specific, clearly defined game plan," I told him carefully. "Maybe I had to use my wits, move fast on my feet, improvise along the way, but the objective was always clear. I'm very goal-oriented. What I would like you to do is tell me exactly what the game plan is, so I don't get stuck in some half-assed operation where everybody's making it up as they go along."

He chewed on a breadstick and said, "Of course."

"So let me see if I have it right. Point A: The CI is arrested and he becomes an informer. Point B: After telling us everything he knows about the criminal activities of Sally Messina and his associates, the CI becomes the bait for us to collar the uncle. And point C: Once in custody and facing serious time in the can, the uncle has no choice but to turn informer in turn, leading to the indictment of Messina himself."

"Very good."

"And my job, along with Detective Vargas, is to get us from point A to point B."

"You got it," he said.

"And do you have any suggestions about how to do that?"

He folded his napkin decisively. "Improvise. But we start with the assurance that the CI is cooperating. He knows we have him by the balls."

I broke off the tip of a breadstick and nibbled on it. "Okay. So right now we're in the debriefing phase."

"Basically, although that could change fast with the right circumstances."

"But you agree we're off to a very slow start."

"True," he said casually. "This could take time. But the payoff is big for everybody involved."

"You know I'm not shy about taking the initiative," I went on, working down my mental list of things I wanted to have straight from the beginning. "If I see an opportunity to light a fire under this guy's ass, I'm going to take it."

"Your judgment has always been impeccable," he said. "Are you happy now?"

"I'm not complaining. But just between you and me, this is a difficult assignment for me. It's not going to be pleasant."

"They seldom are till they're over," he said, ordering coffee for the both of us. While we waited for the coffee, he gave me the old pep talk. "Gerry, you're a tough goddamn cop. As I recall, your first undercover assignment was working street-crime, going out dressed like a college girl on Times Square to lure muggers. How many times did you get clobbered doing that?"

"A few," I laughed, remembering the year I worked that miserable detail back when I was still a rookie. The waiter put the coffee cups down on the table with barely a sound.

"And on that job you made what, one hundred collars plus?"

"You've been reading my personnel file."

"Hell, it was in the newspapers. I still remember the headline in the *Daily News*: 'BEAUTY AND THE BEASTS,' it said. 'Lady Cop, Mugged 100 Times, Always Gets Her Man.' I'll bet you have it framed."

Actually, the yellowed newspaper clipping was lying almost forgotten in a pile of papers stuffed in the bottom drawer of my bureau. Some eager-beaver public relations man at police headquarters had got the story in, along with a horrible picture of me in uniform that made me look ten pounds heavier with my hair spilling out of my cap like a shipwrecked lunatic's. After that, I made it a point to keep out of the papers.

I smiled and said nothing, thinking of the rows of silver frames arranged carefully behind his desk.

To my embarrassment, Noah skipped along merrily down Memory Lane. "And what about the time you went to work as a receptionist for the East Side shrink who was running a whorehouse full of girls, all the time billing insurance companies for treating his so-called patients for depression? It took you what, twenty-four hours to nail the guy?"

"Good," I said.

"So what's the big deal now? Suddenly, you're with OCTF, hot stuff, but you're still just a cop looking to lock up the bad guys. What's so tough about keeping this guy under control?"

He paused and then said, "Oh, the Italian thing. Is there some conflict I ought to know about?"

"My being *Italian* has nothing to do with this. And there is no conflict other than that I hate what this guy stands for," said hotly.

Noah said, "Okay. Let me just play devil's advocate here for a minute. I remember that your father had a bakery in Little Italy, right?"

"He still has it."

"So let's just say that to do business down there in Little Italy, a businessman, even a guy who's clean, has to play ball, right?"

"Meaning?" I demanded, angry that he knew how to get to me.

He shrugged. "Meaning nothing more than that. Meaning he has to deal with the element that's all around him."

"Are you implying that my father is mobbed up?"

"No!" he said. "I'm playing devil's advocate, understand?"

"No, I don't understand! My father has nothing to do with this!" Nothing infuriated me as much as the assumption, which many cops still held, that a man with a vowel at the end of his name who did business in Little Italy had to be "connected."

"You don't ask these kinds of questions to Spanish, black, Chinese, Greek, Jewish officers. And God forbid you should ask the Irish," I said.

"I don't need a lecture on multiculture sensitivities, Detective," Noah replied sharply. It was amazing how easily he had managed to put me in a defensive position, like he was behind a desk and I was standing in front at attention for a dressing-down.

He got up and said, "Excuse me for a minute." Casually, he tossed his napkin on the table and headed for the men's room.

I pushed my plate aside gloomily. Noah had hit my hot button. Did he have any idea what it was like to be an Italian-American police officer and be expected to answer for the Mafia? These mob parasites made my skin crawl. Where I came from, men looked after their families; they worked hard, obeyed the law, valued education like it was made of gold. Why were the cops and the media so fascinated by the phony Mafia romance, by some street thug with an eighth-grade education like Sally Messina? On Amsterdam Avenue there was a popular restaurant named Via Veneto that had a sign out front: Italian Cuisine So Authentic You'll Be Afraid to Sit by the Window. Every time I passed by it, I wanted to throw a brick through that window.

When I was growing up, everybody my parents knew either had a job or wanted one. The Mafia made them sick with shame. To me, Mafia guys were slobs, sitting around on their fat behinds all day, gossiping with other slobs, common criminals loitering in dim rooms, nursing grudges, muttering threats. No wonder they spent their nights getting into trouble.

Noah came back looking at me with curiosity.

Why did I feel compelled to make him understand? "In answer to your question," I said, "just so there is no confusion on your part, my father is an honest, hardworking businessman. Which you should already know."

"I never implied otherwise," he said with an injured frown.

"Okay, fine. But look, you know the neighborhood, Noah. The wise-guys were always around, maybe not over on your block, where the doctors and lawyers lived, but if you owned a shop like Pop's in Little Italy, you could expect a visit from the wiseguys. When I was a kid, he used to throw them right out. His face would get all red and he'd tell me, 'They just want a piece of the pie.' What you probably don't know is that Pop's business was torched, not once but twice. After the second time, they had him worn down. He knew it was useless to resist if he wanted to keep the business. So every week, he had to pay. And the harder he worked, the more successful the business got, the more he had to pay. They looked at the damn books! Noah, they broke that man's spirit. He knew he could never get away from it."

"Why didn't he go to the cops?"

"Are you joking?" I said with amazement. "The sector cops were in there with their hands out long before the mob guys got a piece of the pie. When he was struggling to get the business going, they'd be on the take for fifty bucks a week. 'Night security,' they called it. He didn't trust the cops, and he knew the wiseguys would burn him out."

"That's tough," he said quietly.

"So that's where I'm coming from."

"I hear you."

"So what I'm saying is, probably more than anybody on this job, I want to lock these scumbags up. Eugene working for our side doesn't cut any ice with me. I have nothing but contempt for him and every-thing he represents. Besides, he won't like taking orders from me," I said. "He isn't used to women who have a mouth on them, at least one that they use for talking."

"That's for sure."

"What's for sure?"

"That you have a mouth, and that he isn't used to it. Good. Torture the son of a bitch, but remember he has to jump through the hoops."

"Now let me get one more thing absolutely straight, okay?"

"Shoot," he said.

"You have this CI nailed down tight? He's not going to go kiss and make up with the uncle and leave us in the lurch?"

"We got him cold, Gerry. He knows he's looking at jail time, and the last thing this guy wants is to go to jail."

I toyed absently with a piece of biscotti. "Okay, I can handle the CI, and with luck help get us from point A to point B. But listen, I'm fully aware of how desperate everybody is to put Sally Messina away, and how much competition there is. I know the NYPD and the state are going to have egg on their faces if the feds nail Messina first."

"They won't. We're miles ahead—"

"—That may well be, but whatever, however hairy it gets, I play strictly by the rulebook all the way. I won't cut any corners, even to lock up Sally Messina."

"Nor will I," he said, looking me in the eye.

"Okay, then."

"Okay, you have it," he said. "And if I see a heater coming at your head, I'll holler."

"That's all I ask," I told him. Before he could do it, I waved to the waiter, who glided over with the check on a little tray.

"We'll whack it up," I suggested.

He scooped it away. "No, it's on me."

On the taxpayers, I thought.

Noah labored over the arithmetic and slid a credit card onto the tray.

. . .

Outside, he said he had to go uptown. "My shrink appointment is at four o'clock," he told me, as casually as if he were saying he was going to the dentist.

I was stunned. Nobody I knew went to a psychiatrist. "Your shrink? Are you all right?"

"What do you mean? I've been going to the same shrink for eight years," he said, laughing. "Twice a week. I'm feeling great!" A cab rolled up to the curb. He waved and sped off.

CHAPTER 4

My *grandfather came* to New York from a village outside Sorrento when he was seventeen. He swept the city streets and died an honest man. As a cop, I was always proud that I patrolled the same city streets. But I never figured on Jersey, a place my grandfather would have thought as foreign as Greece. Neither, it seemed, had Eugene.

"I'm in the ass-end of the earth," Eugene was griping to Rey. I had been on the job for a little over a week and walked in on them in the kitchen. They sat beside each other at the table, their backs like twin headstones facing the door. In front of them were were two twelve-ounce glasses of a bright yellow juice.

Rey said, "You can still see the Empire State Building from here if you get on a hill."

Eugene stared glumly through beige lace curtains. "All I see is fucking trees."

"Any other complaints, bro?"

"Yeah, I'm living in a house full of cops."

"Well, I'll grant you that."

I let the screen door slam. Rey said over his shoulder, "Hey, Gerry."

As usual, Eugene ignored me. "What I expected is, is I thought they'd put me in a top-shelf joint in the city, with room service. Some place where you can actually see broads instead of trees and all this fucking grass and all these assholes in their cars singing to their radios. Man, I can't wait to get back to living some place where you can smell the street."

"Jersey's better than the can," I pointed out, knowing it would annoy him.

He glared at me, palms flat on his thighs. "I wouldn't know nothing about that."

"What, you're a virgin?"

"What kind of a shit-for-brains are you? I never been in."

"Relax, bro. She's a friend," Rey said.

Eugene drank some juice and said, "I don't need some lady cop in my face."

"Get used to it," I told him, pulling out a chair and straddling it backwards. The men repositioned themselves. They moved in synchrony, like mechanical figures in a Christmas window.

"What is that stuff you're drinking?" I asked. "It looks radioactive."

"Metrix," Eugene said. "For lean body mass."

"Ugh."

"I don't remember offering any to you. And leave it alone if you see it in the fridge."

"No problem with that one, buddy."

"We're working on a couple of six packs," Rey told me.

"I thought you didn't drink beer."

"No, abs. You see, there are six abs in the stomach—"

"Gym lingo," Eugene said with a glance that made me cross my arms. "Which you wouldn't know nothing about."

"Let it go," Rey warned.

Rey and Eugene had bonded before I came into the picture. They ate together, worked out together, and chased women together when they had the chance. They had begun to adopt each other's verbal expressions. You'd have never made them for cop and prisoner, except for the rare occasion when Rey had to let Eugene know who was boss. Eugene always backed off, but when I was around he resented losing face and that somehow became my fault.

It was a Wednesday. We were due downtown at three o'clock. Every Monday, Wednesday, and Thursday we had to bring Eugene into a conference room in the state office building downtown, where five or six OCTF officers and DAs interrogated him. The sessions usually lasted about an hour, but after the first thirty minutes, the questions tended to get either repetitive or highly speculative, as the interrogators vied with one another to look brilliant. The first day I sat in, they had already been through two of these exercises. Eugene loved an audience and played them like a Vegas emcee.

Lieutenant Campo and two baby-faced OCTF assistant prosecutors briskly shuffled their papers and made small notes at the long oval-shaped table, the way television news anchors do to avoid looking silly when the camera comes on or fades out. A female stenographer who looked like a guard at a women's prison sat sternly at a small table near the door. Noah hadn't arrived yet. When we filed in, Rey stood for a minute to size things up. Then, smirking, he took the seat at the head of the table. Eugene grabbed the spot at the far end. Noah arrived a few minutes later, deeply dismayed to find the two power seats already occupied.

Finally, he thought of a way to save face. Taking a seat beside me, he addressed the stenographer without looking at her. "Mary, would you get me a half-cup of decaf?" Mary stiffened and scowled. This was apparently not in the job description. Reluctantly, she went for the coffee. Satisfied, Noah made an elaborate production of opening his briefcase.

When the tribal rites were over, Noah told Rey to bring us up to date.

"Okay," Rey began. "Eugene, the last time we went over what you knew about some of the street rackets. Who ran what, how the money flowed. We'll get back to that. Today, we need you to give us the basic story on your Uncle Tony. Where he sleeps, who his top guys are, how he runs his businesses, who he hangs out with, what ticks him off, what gives him a hard-on. Like *This Is Your Life*."

Eugene pressed his lips together. "I have never heard of the gentleman. I have never heard of no organization called by the name of La Cosa Nostra," he said, swiping a finger across his lips as if to seal them. A blood vessel became visible in Noah's forehead. He looked like he was going to bolt from his chair, but Rey shook his head and told Eugene, "Just cut the fucking comedy, okay?"

"You guys should get out, go to the movies more," Eugene said.

"We seen plenty of movies, Eugene. This ain't the movies. This is for real," a detective from the DA's office said.

"But you been up my uncle's ass for years," Eugene replied. "What more could I tell you that you don't already got down in all them files? Okay, let me think. He likes good cigars, Havanas, but he also smokes them stinking Moustache Pete things. He likes chicks with big tits. He likes to go to Atlantic City. He don't like dogs. Hates the fuckers, actually. Don't never let him walk your dog."

Hands folded like a preacher, Campo interrupted, "Before we all begin to lose sight of why we're gathered here, Eugene, let's consider some realities. We are all—and that includes you—*all* working as a team. A team has a goal. In this case, it is to maneuver your uncle into a position where he will have no choice but to cooperate in a major investigation. We have you in custody, and you have agreed to cooperate. I want to make sure that you understand your status, as we see it. Except for your personal link with Anthony Rossi, and what you may have learned in your years of professional and personal association with him, you are basically a—"

"Piss-ant?" Rey suggested.

"Thank you, Detective," Campo said. "A piss-ant, Mr. Rossi." The smirk melted off Eugene's face. Campo continued. "Now, as has been explained to you repeatedly over the past several weeks that you have been in our . . . employ, you have really no choice but to tell us everything you know about your beloved Uncle Tony, unless you prefer the alternative, which is . . ." He turned to Rey.

"Being a butt-boy for some two-hundred-pound he-she's in Sing Sing?" Rey said.

"Well put," Campo agreed. "He is referring to incarceration in a state prison, with all the ensuing social unpleasantness."

Eugene braced his arms against the table as if trying to force it down one floor. "You saying I take the meat in the seat? *Nessuno me lo ficca in culo!*"

"Which means?"

"Nobody fucks me up the ass!"

"Sorry I asked," Campo said. "What I'm saying is that in prison you would be in a position, tough as you think you are, where certain unpleasant prospects will become a daily routine." Campo paused to take out a Lucky Strike. He was the only person I knew who still smoked Luckys. I had no idea where he found them.

"You going to smoke that thing?" Eugene demanded.

"Smoke bothers you?" Campo asked, eyebrows rising.

"It makes me gag, plus it's bad for your complexion, gives you a washed-out look."

Noah piped in, "Isn't skin care a little out of your line of work?"

"I like looking healthy."

"So you do like women?" Noah said pointlessly.

"Of course I like broads. What are you implicating?"

"What am I *implying*? Nothing! You seem awfully touchy."

Campo lit his cigarette. A languid stream of smoke drifted to the ceiling. I couldn't believe this was how they interrogated somebody. It was more like locker-room hazing at summer camp. I got impatient.

"Listen," I said, "can we get down to business?"

They looked at me like I was a substitute teacher. But Rey took over and had Eugene go through all of the basic family information about Tony Rossi: names, ages, birthplaces, and current status of parents (both dead, of natural causes); brothers (one, Eugene's father, murdered; one working on a street crew for Tony); sisters (two—the eldest married to a freelance hijacker in Queens; the younger having fled as a teenager to Salt Lake City, where she became a Mormon and renounced her family).

The résumé took nearly an hour. Once he decided to behave, Eugene was amazingly good with detail. For example, he wouldn't just say the uncle had a driver and a big car. He gave you the driver's name and description, the make of the car, the size of the engine, the color of the carpet, and the place the driver took it for a brushless wash-and-wax.

Finally, Campo talked about strategy. "Next time, and I ask you to give it a lot of thought, we start thinking about how do we get close to your uncle, without him knowing it. So far we haven't done real well on meeting him in bars."

"He's real insulated," Eugene said.

"How much money does he pull down?" I asked.

"Enough. More than a mil, is my guess, but he pisses it all away."

"How's that?"

"I told you he likes to play cards. I mean, big-time. It's nothing for him to go through twenty, thirty g's in a night of Atlantic City. He's always bitching about needing money."

"Tell me again how he makes the money, Eugene."

"Like I said before. He's a businessman, with ventures. It took him years to build a corporate structure."

"You mean Sally Messina's corporate structure, the Giavanni family empire?"

"Fuck 'empire'!" he scoffed. "You're the ones now who think it's like the movies. You people don't want to hear it, but it's true—most of these guys, they keep their money in a bureau drawer. They ain't financial geniuses, although my uncle is one of the few actual smart ones. The way it works, it don't get organized from the top. *Enforcement* comes from the top. The next levels down, the businesses run like franchises. The businesses that run without no trouble, like my uncle's, then they don't get no trouble, as long as they send a big slice of the pie uptown."

"What kind of business ventures? Legitimate ones as well as criminal ones?" I asked.

Eugene nodded. "This and that. You know most of this already. Clubs, bars . . . Lots of opportunities, most of them mixed legal and illegal—"

Noah was bored. "We could talk about bars till we fall asleep," he said in a belittling tone. "We're here to talk about Anthony Rossi. Now let me ask you, have you ever seen Anthony Rossi commit a violent crime?"

Eugene decided he was talking to fools again. "Violent? I seen him smack plenty of guys in the fucking head, if that's what you mean. I can testify personal to that because he done it to me plenty of times when I was growing up. But I don't know about it being a crime." He thought for a minute and added, "Now wait a minute, my cousin Virgiulio, once I heard him tell Uncle Tony that he stuck this guy in the eyeball with an ice pick outside some bar where the guy mouthed off at his date or some shit, which maybe makes my uncle an assessory. The guy was Jackie 'One-Eye' DeLuca, which is how he got the name, with the ice pick in his fucking eye. But Jackie wasn't a made guy at the time it happened, so maybe you wouldn't consider that a criminal conspiracy."

One of the young prosecutors was hastily writing all of this down, but Noah smacked a fist on the table so hard I was sure he hurt his hand. "Don't dick around with me!" he said hotly. "Did you ever hear Anthony Rossi order somebody to commit murder?"

"No, of course not."

"Do you know of any murders that Anthony Rossi participated in, directly or indirectly?"

"No. That ain't like him."

"Anything else?" Noah said, stuffing papers into his briefcase like an insurance salesman with another appointment.

"Hang on a couple of minutes," Rey said, holding a hand up. "Eugene, is there anybody out there, anybody maybe we don't know about, that can come in to see your uncle and shoot their mouth off about something we don't know about? You know, when you and Detective Conte need to go out together on a social occasion? You got any enemies on the street with a beef against you?"

"Not since that other thing got took care of after I went down to Florida."

"Okay," Rey said. "How about the girlfriends?"

"I know a lot of broads," Eugene replied. "Nobody has no claim on me."

"Except the state," Noah said, leaning on his briefcase and looking at the clock.

Almost as an afterthought, Campo said, "Eugene, there's something that we would like you to do. After you get back to Jersey, tomorrow, we want you to make a call. You call Uncle Tony and ask him what he hears about the hit on this guy Faffy Fortunato."

Eugene resisted. "That don't sound like nothing he would've heard of. That was someplace in Brooklyn, right? Way out of my uncle's territory."

"I know that," Campo said. "You just make a social call, talk about the relatives, talk about the weather, tell him you're looking forward to seeing him soon, then just slip in what's he hear about this Faffy."

"Okay," Eugene said suspiciously. He knew it was a test.

"Thank you all," Noah announced. "See you all next time."

. . .

Later that afternoon, in the car back to Jersey, Eugene stared at the highway landscape with the passive look you see in the window of a prison bus. I was in the backseat; Eugene always insisted on riding in front with Rey. Traffic was at a standstill. In front of us was a panel truck that had the name of a furniture store on the door, with a smaller message above the license plate: HOW'S MY DRIVING? ANY PROBLEMS, CALL 1-800-DRIVERS.

"I hate this fucking traffic," Rey muttered.

"What's the sign on that truck mean?" Eugene said curiously.

"Say if the guy cuts you off or something," I told him, "you can call his boss and they yell at him."

He turned to look at me. "The union would shut them down."

I laughed. "What, are you nuts? *Union?* Jimmy Hoffa is buried in the end zone in Giants Stadium, buddy. Where you been?"

Eugene looked puzzled. "So he has to ride around with a sign that says, 'Drop a dime on me if you don't like something, and by the way, here's the phone number for you to call'?"

"Toll-free."

"Fucking rats!"

Maybe the irony of this dawned on him, because he shut up for the rest of the ride.

CHAPTER 5

It *took me* a while to figure out why they had set up the safe house in Jersey. Keeping a low, out-of-town profile with an informant who still had to be seen occasionally in public was part of it. Eventually I learned the main reason: One of the OCTF inspectors downtown had a brother who was a big-shot economist with the United Nations. He had been sent to Saudi Arabia for a year with his wife and small daughter. When the NYPD nabbed Eugene and was looking for a place to stash him, the inspector's brother's split-level house in a quiet suburb was available at the right time, a mere twelve miles west of the George Washington Bridge.

For a city kid like Eugene, they might as well have stuck him in Ohio. To Eugene, the suburbs where most Americans, including most New York cops, actually lived were a landscape as alien as the moon. That attitude was, in fact, the first thing I realized that he and I had in common besides a vowel at the end of our names.

The inspector's relatives had left all of their furniture and most of their personal belongings, which made the place seem very weird for a police location. Besides paying the rent and not breaking anything, there were really only two requirements. One, evidently the thing the owners were most concerned about, was to keep up the lawn, the backyard in-ground pool, and the shrubs, which seemed to me to be a full-time job. Luckily, Danny Flanagan volunteered to be responsible for that part, and he did his job with what struck me as idiotic enthusiasm. The other requirement was that we had to mind their cat, a beautiful but nervous bluepoint male Himalayan that took a liking to me and nobody else. This meant that I got to feed it, brush its long hair, change its box, and generally keep it breathing until its owners came home.

Nobody could remember the name the people had for the cat, so I called it Barney, after *Barney Miller*, the only television cop show I liked. When the cat wasn't sleeping, it followed me around, but it bolted like a squirrel and hid behind the living room couch whenever it heard something. The cat was especially leery of Eugene, who walked as if he wore concrete shoes. Once Eugene saw that the cat despised him, he deliberately scared it every chance he got, which only made the cat hate him more.

"For some reason this cat just freaks when it sees you," I told Eugene.

"So what? Dogs like me."

"Well, cats sense things about people that dogs don't."

"Nobody gives a shit about the opinion of a cat," he said, bounding down the stairs.

. . .

After **I got** used to the place, I began dropping into Eugene's room for a chat, at first only because it was a good way to keep the guy talking. Like reporters, detectives seldom get their best information by firing questions at somebody and writing the answers down in a notebook. A lot of the job involves schmoozing. You banter, you press here, lay off there. You shoot the breeze, ask dumb questions, cut some slack and tug it back when necessary. In time, with luck, the story jells.

Eugene slept till nearly noon most days, and usually stayed to himself until it was time to drive him into town. He spent most of his time in his room, taking care of the elaborate grooming required to get him out the door.

The room they put him in obviously belonged to the little girl, because the curtains over the twin windows looking out onto the backyard had frilly lavender valances. There was a private bathroom just off to the side, a four-poster bed with a lace canopy, and in the bathroom a vanity table that had a pleated tartan skirt. I wondered what the little girl would have thought to know that a Mafia informer was staying in her room, but I guess a kid with parents who suddenly haul her off to Saudi Arabia comes to expect some variety in life.

Late one afternoon, I knocked on the frame of Eugene's open door. He was lounging in the chair, dressed as if for a polo match in Siena, with sharply creased tan cotton slacks and a white silk shirt, and shiny brown loafers that looked like they never touched a floor.

I pulled out the desk chair and sat down. "What's the matter, Eugene, homesick?" I said. He was staring out the window, watching a neighbor next door mow his lawn, which was as neat and green as the outfield at Yankee Stadium.

"Nothing's the matter," Eugene said. "Except *that*. He does that every three days. Is that all people do out here, cut their fucking grass?"

"Well, people out here also seem to drive to the store a lot," I said, feeling a touch of sympathy for his plight. "You'd better get used to it. After this little gig ends, you have to think about where you're going to live. It won't be New York City."

"Well, I won't mow any goddamn lawns, no matter where I go. It's undignified."

"Then you better find a way to get rich in your new life. But don't forget, it has to be legal."

Outside, the lawnmower sputtered and shut off. From a stand of trees at the edge of the property, crows shrieked, their cries louder than any car alarm in the city. A hissing lawn sprinkler slapped water across a field of grass.

Eugene looked appalled. "I can't take much more of them noises. Now it sounds like snakes. How can anybody live like this?"

"They have to water the grass. It's spring."

"Let the grass get its own fucking water like everything else. As far as I'm concerned, civilization began when the Romans covered up Rome with cement and put the grass and flowers in marble boxes."

"You ever been to Rome?" It was one of the places on earth that I most wanted to see.

He nodded. "Very beautiful," he said, looking at me. When he saw I was interested, he spent fifteen minutes telling me about Rome, where he had gone on a job for his uncle and ended up staying two months. He finished with a story about an old nun who supposedly genuflected herself to death in St. Peter's Square when the Pope appeared to give the blessing from his balcony.

Despite all the disdain I felt for him and what he represented, I began judging Eugene less harshly, if only because he sometimes made me laugh. Other things about him then caught my attention, like the fact that he kept his room neat, with his bed always made. By comparison, at the far end of the hall from Eugene's room, the male officers, two of whom always had to be on duty all night, used the master bedroom as a flophouse. Even the cleaning lady finally announced that she would not enter the room, where dirty clothes dangled from every available perch. As the weeks went by, the debris—stained cardboard coffee cups, sticky soda cans, old newspapers, tattered girly magazines, crusty ashtrays, crinkled candy wrappers, bent pizza boxes—piled up like a landfill.

At first, I wondered what the neighbors must have thought of our setup, even though we were under orders to be discreet and to park the cars well out of sight at the end of the long driveway. But then Danny Flanagan told me he had made it a point to "explain that this was only a temporary thing" to the only neighbor we regularly saw. This was an angular woman whose main activity during the day appeared to be standing in her front yard and screaming at her eight-year-old son, "*Jaaaaaaayyy-SON!*"—a cry that pierced the neighborhood with the ferocity of a firehouse siren. Danny said he was out fertilizing the rhododendrons one afternoon when he peered through the hedge and noticed the woman unloading bags of mulch from her Ford Explorer. He said he went over to offer help, which she declined.

"You're just renting the place while that family is away?" the woman had asked warily, once she was certain he wasn't going to murder her, which is evidently a huge concern in the suburbs with the approach of a stranger.

"Yeah," Danny assured her. "We're just renting the house for a couple of months until our own place is ready. We're having a place built out in the country."

The woman was glad to hear this. "It seems like you have an awful lot of people coming in and out of there," she told Danny.

"Well, it's sort of a group home."

She was horrified.

"Don't worry, it's a group home for New York City cops going through painful divorces and trying to get their lives together," Danny lied elaborately. "So you don't have to worry about burglars."

"They all do seem big and healthy-looking," the woman said.

"Oh, outwardly they're fine," Danny explained. He tapped his chest. "But inside, emotional tragedy. Getting them into the country is the department's new idea about making them whole again. It's kind of a twelve-step program. Most of them are already up to number eight."

"But what about the girl I see over there?" the woman asked.

"Oh, that's the police psychologist. She's what you call the facilitator."

To make sure there were no doubts, Danny took out his detective's shield and showed it to her. "You can tell your husband. Otherwise, this is secret, okay? Can I depend on you for that?"

Her eyes widened. "Oh, absolutely."

"Thank you. And you'll let me know if there's ever anything I can do for you?"

"Yes, thank you," the woman replied. "By the way, you're doing a very nice job with the garden. Far better than the regular people." She said she never knew their names.

. . .

Actually, Danny's fantasies aside, facilitator was a fairly accurate term to describe the part of my time that I spent there. As the only female assigned full-time in an environment of six male cops and one male informant, I was the one who did most of the grocery shopping, and, most days, even made lunch. Occasionally, I'd be a sport and make dinner before going home. Otherwise, meals were haphazard, take-out mostly.

At home, Kevin and I were bumping into each other at home less frequently than ever, since he began working odd hours on the Dominican drug-gang operation while I was on the new job. More and more, we communicated by phone-machine message and Post-Its stuck on the refrigerator. Even when we shared the same bed, one of us was asleep.

Kevin now was often gone till two or three in the morning. I was always up early. Most mornings, I'd get up before six, quietly slip out for a run around the neighborhood, and just as quietly come back to get dressed while he slept. I'd grab a cup of coffee and a bagel at a little cafe on Hudson Street, and by eight I'd be on the corner waiting for Rey to pick me up for the ride to Jersey.

I never talked about my morning run, which seldom exceeded a half mile. Rey and Eugene, on the other hand, talked constantly about physical workouts. In fact, Rey told Lieutenant Campo that a lot of the mob guys in Eugene's generation now hung out at gyms, not at dingy social clubs or restaurants like their elders did. So Campo authorized him to sign up for two full memberships, at $600 apiece, in a health club in Chelsea. After that, our commute into the city was daily, always with two hours free on the schedule for them to go to the club.

Meanwhile Rey also managed to get the department to spring for a personal cell phone. Since he was always on it, I became the designated driver on the daily trips back and forth across the river. It annoyed me that most of the calls were to or, more often, from, his girlfriend Monique, a woman who seemed to exist in a perpetual crisis.

"What's today's problem?" I asked him one afternoon when he snapped the phone shut after an urgent conversation.

"Her toilet overflowed," he said heavily. Eugene was quiet in the front passenger seat.

"And?" I asked without much interest.

Rey chuckled reluctantly. "Well, she was crying. She told me that when the damn thing overflowed she turned on all the faucets in the apartment trying to drain it. I told her that wouldn't work, to just take the lid off and push the plunger down. She was crying about getting her feet wet, but I talked her into doing it, at least. Now I have to call a plumber."

"Why not just have her call 911?"

Rey poked furiously at the little buttons on his flip-phone. Finally, he found a plumber in Queens and persuaded him to go to Monique's apartment.

. . .

Late one afternoon, we were driving a Cadillac El Dorado. Eugene called it "the Cadoo." The department had leased it to provide cover, since it would have looked odd if Eugene's old street friends spotted him in the typical stripped-down Dodge that undercover cops usually got. It was late afternoon, in traffic stalled at the light on Forty-third Street by Tenth Avenue, near the westbound approach to the Lincoln Tunnel. Eugene always insisted on having the air conditioner going, so all the windows were up.

A few car lengths ahead, a squeegee man worked his way down the length of cars, stopping at each one to swipe a dirty rag at the windshield for "tips."

The gnarly character with greasy dreadlocks and a grin that showed two broken teeth bore down on us with a beggar's inevitability. I was in no mood. When the grimy face appeared beside me, I took out my shield and pressed it against the side window.

The face contorted in an exaggerated laugh and he reached toward the windshield with the squeegee.

Eugene leaned across me calmly and said, "My man, she said no." Eugene's eyes and his voice were both piercing.

The squeegee man took one hard look at Eugene and his hands shot up like someone had put a gun to his temple. "Sorry, Mr. Mafia Man!"

he cried, backing away so fast that he collided with a van that had squeezed beside us.

Without a glance at the thwarted squeegee man groping for the sidewalk with his bucket of rags, Eugene reached over my lap and tapped the button that shut the window.

I was amazed. "How'd you do that?"

"Do what?" The traffic began inching through the light and merging at the tunnel lanes. "The guy knew I meant business," he said evenly.

"But how did he *know?*"

"Know what?"

"You know—the 'Mr. Mafia'?"

"Just because somebody's a scumbag don't mean he's stupid. This guy's survival depends on scoping people out. He has to have some street smarts, working that shit. Put your badge away before you lose it."

I snapped on the radio and found some music. In the back, Rey murmured into his cell phone, telling Monique to stop crying, the plumber was on the way.

CHAPTER 6

Weeks *became months* with the inexorability of a school year. Back and forth across the river we went. A couple of days a week, Eugene would meet friends in Little Italy, or sometimes at some apartment or coffee shop on the Upper West Side. Names and dates accumulated in files, a skein of disconnected anecdotes and free-floating assertions that I feared would never make sense. There were also many dinners with his friends at restaurants. I'd often accompany him, posing as his date, always wired with a recorder. Eugene and I went out on the town like this once or twice a week, usually with Rey tagging along as a friend. I was expected to smile and say little. The strongest impression I was getting around those smoke-free tables was the conspicuous absence of discussion about any kind of work, criminal or otherwise.

Why did I hate it when I began enjoying myself? Why did I feel guilty when I looked forward to shopping for his clothes, which the NYPD paid for? I even found a couple of good dresses on sale, paying for those myself. I got myself an expensive new haircut at a salon that was decorated to look like a flaming room full of aluminum foil.

Why did I have to resist the urge to *like* spending time with Eugene? He flaunted pleasure in life and he liked to share his joys. Kevin would have only cold contempt for Eugene. Why did I feel the need to hold on against the nudging tide of his simple exhilaration?

Day by day, I typed my standard DD-5 reports on my college portable, and left them on Campo's desk, stacks of procedural trivia—who we saw, what they said, who they knew. Beyond sheer volume of names and events, I had learned little that could be used in any criminal investigation, and certainly nothing that pointed upward from Eugene's level. We still hadn't met the uncle. Eugene always had an excuse, but my impression was that Uncle Tony simply had better things to do than see his nephew, the one who was supposed to be tending to business in Florida.

Finally, I had to force Eugene to follow Campo's repeated orders to ask Tony what he knew about the mob hit in Brooklyn, which was still unsolved nearly two months later. The phone in Eugene's room had a handset designed to look like Mickey Mouse's ears. The base was Mickey's body. He picked up the ears and tapped in the number as I stood next to him and watched. I wasn't able to use the phone downstairs to listen in because Danny was calling his wife on that one.

"Yeah, it's Eugenio. Is he there?"

A few minutes passed. Eugene's face brightened. "Hey, Uncle Tony! It's Eugene. . . . Yeah, good, good. You? Good. . . ."

Gradually, he brought the subject around to the Brooklyn hit. It was the first time I'd actually heard him talk to his uncle on the phone about anything to do with the mob.

"Listen, one of the guys was asking me and I didn't have no idea. This guy in Bay Ridge named Faffy? You know who I mean? . . . Yeah. Shit, yeah! . . . Yeah? I should of figured that . . . Not like the old days. . . . Nah, I didn't either. . . . Yeah, well, I'll call you next week. I hope we can get together soon, okay?"

He hung up and told me, "Okay, boss? My uncle don't know anything about this *goomba* got hit in Brooklyn except he says the guy probably got hit because he was just a punk. He don't know nothing except what he read in the paper. Okay?"

"Wouldn't he have heard something if it was a mob hit?"

"Nobody hears nothing these days, is what my uncle says. You heard me say it wasn't like the old days."

I had brought a law book with me and tried to read for a few minutes, but I couldn't concentrate. With the same set of facts, Eugene always saw a different world than I did. His was fluid; mine as rigid as a jigsaw puzzle. He splashed into his days as if they were the surf. I approached mine like quicksand.

For a professional thief, Eugene was generous, even if it was NYPD money. Once he gave Danny a pair of his Versace pants and even insisted on taking him to a tailor on Bank Street for the alterations. Another time, I watched him hand a ten-dollar bill to a street skell.

He was pacing on the plum-colored rug. "Why don't you put on the ball game?" I said. There was a twenty-one-inch television in the room. I'd never seen it on.

"What do you think I am? Some old fart sits around all day watching guys in kneesocks play ball on a television? If I ain't betting or booking, I don't pay no attention. Anyway, haven't you got better things to do than watch me?"

Why was I there? I could have studied in a lot more peace down the hall.

Eugene sat at the little girl's vanity table, bent over, working at his fingernails with a buffer.

"Eugene, what are you doing?" I asked.

He cast a studiously bored glance in my direction. "Grooming my nails."

"You're *what?*" I wondered what my father would say about a man who does such a thing, not to mention doing it in front of a woman.

"Hey!" he said. "I haven't been able to get out to get a decent manicure since they moved me to this fucking hole."

"Eugene, you're not putting on nail polish, are you? In my whole life, I have never seen a man do that. This is totally inappropriate behavior for a man!"

His look said he couldn't have cared less. "What kind of men do you go with? They must of all been animals."

He kept those dark eyes on me. I didn't want to give him the satisfaction of meeting his stare, but I didn't want to leave.

"You can be one fucking pain-in-the-ass broad, do you know that?"

"Please don't use that kind of language to me. Effing this and effing that. You don't have to talk like that, Eugene. It brings you down. You don't hear me using language like that."

"You *are* a fucking broad!" he said, aiming a stiff finger at me. "And you could use some fixing up yourself. Starting with the gym."

"I suggest you knock it off."

"Hey, this is my room. You came into my room. And no broad talks to me like that. Do you know who I am?"

I decided to let him have it. "Yeah, I know who you are. You're Eugene Rossi, in custody on criminal charges. You're twenty-eight years old, with a seventh-grade education, as I recall from reading your file. You're trying to save your own skin by working as a CI for the cops to rat out your beloved uncle."

He was quiet for a moment and then got up to put the nail polish away in the bathroom.

When he came out, he seemed subdued. "So what's in the book that has you so interested?"

I held up my textbook. It had a green cover.

"What's the name of it?" he asked.

"Torts."

"What's a tort?"

"That's a word in the law that means an injury under civil proceedings, as opposed to criminal proceedings. If someone makes a contract, that means he makes a promise to do something and has a duty to keep that promise. If he doesn't, he's breached the contract and wronged an innocent person. The court provides a remedy. In civil court, he'd pay with his money; in criminal court, with his time."

"Oh yeah? My way of doing this eliminates the courtroom shit. Somebody makes a contract to me, and God forbid he pulls a breach on me, I got the fucking remedy." He whacked his palm with his big fist. "*Batta-bing, batta-bang, batta-boom.* Next fucking case, bailiff."

"That's your idea of justice?"

"It worked in Sicily for years," he said. Not till then did I notice he was standing close to me, with his hand near mine on the arm of the chair. "Don't make a promise to me you can't keep. I'll be forced to remedy you," he said.

I laughed, feeling a little nervous.

He moved away and asked, "This contract I signed, right. Is that civil or criminal?"

"I can't say, Eugene. What exactly did you sign, anyway?"

"A fucking contract, Perry Mason."

"Can I see it?"

"Why?"

"Maybe I could just take a look at it for you."

"For what?"

"To see what you agreed to. Maybe there's something in there that you overlooked down in the fine print."

Actually, I felt a little ashamed at not knowing more about the hold they had over him, since I had been so busy disliking the guy. I didn't really have a good sense of what they had on him in Florida, beyond an outstanding arrest warrant from New York. What was his deal with the witness protection program? How much stake money would he get to start a new life? At the rate he was going, he didn't qualify for a bus ticket to Chicago. All of that should be spelled out in a contract.

Eugene walked over to the bed, lifted the quilted comforter and groped beneath the mattress. The contract consisted of five photocopied legal-sized pages on the letterhead of the Organized Crime Task Force District Attorney's Office.

I scanned it fast. On the bottom, Noah's signature appeared just above the place where Eugene had written his own name in a childlike scrawl. But something seemed wrong. I read it again, paragraph by paragraph. When I was through, I felt sick.

"Eugene, did you *read* this?"

"Of course. What are you asking me that for?"

"Hey, Eugene . . ." My voice trailed off. Here was a man who never graduated from elementary school. These days, I thought, it was possible a kid could get through the seventh grade as a functional illiterate. Eugene was glib and easy, he adapted to company like a cruise-line jewel thief, and five minutes after meeting him, any perceptive person knew he was smart. But he was like an actor. Put him on Rector Street in a Brooks Brothers suit with a cell phone stuck to his cheek, he could be a currency trader. Suddenly it hit me. He hadn't read the contract because he couldn't.

The agreement was as one-sided as a college-town apartment lease. It stipulated that Eugene would cooperate—fully and, most significantly, *perpetually*. He would inform, he would affirm, he would go undercover wherever they sent him. Whenever required, he would come to court and testify. In exchange, the district attorney promised only to "look favorably" on the possibility of dropping "any and all criminal charges" against him. Oddly, those charges were nowhere specified. And the word "favorably" did not strike me as a legally precise term.

Making sure he understood that I was alarmed, I asked, "What did they tell you about this agreement? It doesn't give you anything, Eugene. You couldn't have read this very carefully before you signed it."

He frowned like someone being informed he'd been chiseled at a used-car lot. "It says I tell them what they want to hear, and I go on my way," he insisted. "It keeps me out of jail and it keeps them off my back. They give me a new personality, with ID, with a suitcase full of money to live good. Then in a while it all blows over. Life is back to normal." A jumpy smile played on his face.

Did he really think it was that simple? "Do you know you can't bullshit your way out of this? That you can never go back home?" I demanded.

He snorted.

"That you have got to testify whenever they ask you to, against these people you know, people that you have known all your life? That everybody will know you are an informer? *And you have no guarantees in return.* My God, Eugene, don't you ever look ahead more than a day at a time? This is awful!"

As a cop, I worked for the DA, not the informant. But it was awful what they had done. I was furious at Noah and Campo, at all of them, for putting this guy in jeopardy, with no real guarantees that he would be any use in prosecuting Messina. They had confiscated his life. And they had the audacity to put it in writing and have him sign it.

"Am I fucked?" he said, seeing how upset I was.

"You answer that for yourself," I told him crossly. "This contract says you're going to do basically whatever they tell you to do, for however long they want you to. Anytime they ask you for intelligence information, you have to deliver, even if it means risking your neck. No limitations. In exchange, the charges against you may or may not be dropped."

"They said they would absolutely drop the charges."

"It doesn't even say *what the charges are*, Eugene. It doesn't specify the charges. Eugene, what *are* the charges? What was that warrant for?" I'd merely assumed it was for one of the usual mob raps—armed robbery, assault, extortion . . .

"You telling me you don't know?" he asked.

"No, I don't."

"Gambling and other stuff."

"Gambling?"

He nodded. "The deal is, I cooperate, then I can go away and live under new identification for a while. Then I can come back home."

He simply didn't get it. "No!" I shouted. "They are going to want you to eventually testify against these people, Eugene. Public testimony! People that you know! And those people—your uncle, for example— they'll know what you did to them!"

I shook my head to clear it. Slowly I repeated, " 'Gambling and other stuff'? What other stuff?"

"Racketeering," he said. "Major prison time."

I was bewildered at his ignorance. "And they told you they were going to lock you up if you didn't sign?"

"They meant it."

"Why didn't you get a lawyer?"

"The only guy I know with lawyers is my uncle. And I didn't want him to know. He warned me about getting jammed up in Florida. Plus, I always handled my own business deals. I never needed no blood-sucking lawyer before. They said they'd take care of me. I figured I could handle it."

"You figured you'd be able to con them," I said. "That's it, isn't it? You thought you could sign the paper and then tread water until they got tired of you, and then go on as usual. But Eugene, you've basically sold your soul here, do you know that? And for what? They don't even guarantee you the witness protection program."

"They promised those things," he said.

"Did they *force* you to sign this? I mean, you couldn't have read it and not had any questions about what it said. What did they tell you? Signing this was a very bad move, buddy."

"I signed a lot of things. It don't mean shit."

"It only means the rest of your life."

I pointed to the first paragraph. "Read this out loud to me."

He squirmed.

"Read it, Eugene!"

"Don't jerk me around!" he said. He stormed off and sat so hard on the bed that the canopy sagged like a boat sail.

"Eugene, why won't you read this for me?"

"Why don't you get the fuck out of my face, cunt! *Rompipalle!*"

"Eugene?"

"That means ball-buster," he spat, and added for impact: "Twat!"

He stood by the window. It was quiet except for the birds. He wouldn't meet my eye. "So I can't read so good, lady. Now are you happy?"

There wasn't anything I could do except offer some comfort. "Stop talking to me like that. I want to help."

"Yeah, right. Another cop that wants to help. Any more help from you guys and I'll be sucking wind in the gas chamber."

"Eugene? It's okay."

When I put my arm around his shoulder, he shook it off.

We sat quietly for a few minutes, till someone called up and said it was time to go.

"You're the lawyer," Eugene said to me before we left. "How do I get out of this?"

"I don't think this is something you can manage to get out of, buddy. This is serious business."

He had worked his courage back. "You watch."

"Eugene, you have to do whatever they ask. They got you locked in on this."

"Screw them. I'll do the time. *Batta-bing, batta-bang, batta-boom.*" He said this a little too loudly.

"No, you don't understand. Doing time is not the issue, even if you were willing, which I do not for a second believe you are. You have to understand that they will tell people that know you that you are an informant, and that you will be exposed as one. They have all of the cards here."

"Shit," he said with a dismissive laugh.

"There's no going back, Eugene."

"Fuck them," he declared breezily.

CHAPTER 7

My *college roommate* was a Texas girl who used an expression that came out of Dallas: "He's all hat and no cattle." That was Eugene. In a way, it was endearing to realize that, as criminals went, he was mostly talk. It was clear he knew how to fight and had probably knocked a few heads on the street, but over time it also dawned on me that Eugene seldom mentioned guns and showed no interest whatsoever in the one I carried in my shoulder holster.

So they had told him they had him on "racketeering," a charge that throws a pretty wide net, and which, as far as I'm concerned, could include half of the developers, investment bankers, and real-estate agents in New York City. When they had collared him in Florida on an outstanding New York warrant, all they really had was taking books—illegal betting. Campo acknowledged it when I pressed him in the hallway that afternoon.

"You got him on *gambling?*" I said.

Campo pushed a thin smile across his teeth. "Promoting gambling in the third degree."

"Not loan-sharking?" Loan-sharking was a little worse.

"Nope."

"You got him taking bets? For 'Give me Dallas fifty times'?"

"That's about right," said Campo, his smile washing away.

"And that's the whole nut on the guy?"

"Basically. You got questions about the deal here, take it up with the DA, Conte. Okay?"

I decided to do just that. After the meeting, I got Noah on the phone. He knew I was steamed.

"You're overreacting, Gerry," he said.

"We need to talk about this, Noah."

"When?"

"As soon as you can. I mean it."

I heard him flipping pages on his desk calender. Noah used the desk calendar as if he were some kind of a cardiac surgeon booked through infinity, rather than some DA on a case going nowhere.

"Tomorrow?" I persisted. "We have to be in the city by three, but I'll come earlier."

The flipping stopped. "Sure. I suppose I can get away for a couple of minutes. Two o'clock?"

. . .

Why should it have mattered to me that Eugene had been basically entrapped, or at least badly misled? After all, he thought he was getting over on everyone else; Eugene had no claim on my loyalty. Why was I prepared to offer even a small installment on it without any collateral?

A few days before, brooding over the fact that Eugene could not read or write, I had contacted a friend at the Board of Education who gave me some sixth-grade reading books and worksheets. I had dumped them on Eugene's bed when I got out to Jersey and told him, "School starts today."

To my surprise, he didn't give me any lip. Before we began I asked him why he'd dropped out of seventh grade.

His face registered no emotion. "I come home from school one day and my father's bleeding to death in the bathtub. So he's history."

"What about your mother?"

"She died in the operating room when I was born."

"That's how you came to live with Uncle Tony?"

"On and off," he said. "He moved me around a lot. Sometimes I'd stay in his house, sometimes an apartment over the club in Little Italy. Sometimes I'd sleep in the back room at his social club."

"And your education?"

"I learned what I needed to know."

"How did you end up in Florida?"

"I took an airplane."

"Get serious."

"I had to get out of town till things blew over."

"What things?"

"Some eggplant from a Giavanni crew was looking to settle a score with me."

"Somebody had a contract on you?"

"So they say."

"What kind of score?"

He studied the muscle in his forearm. "I don't know. Some problem with some bimbo, I think." When he was done flexing his arm, he continued, "His girlfriend, some *sticchiu*. A buddy of his says he seen us in the backseat of a car. Doing the nasty, you know?"

"That sounds like your style," I commented.

I hadn't meant to insult him. "You don't know nothing about my style," he told me evenly.

"Okay," I said, "so the guy had a beef with you, and you had to get out of town? Why?"

He leaned forward in his chair. "I ain't worried about some asshole with a beef. But I hear this guy has a contract out on me, and that's serious shit, you know? My uncle, he hit the ceiling when he heard. All my uncle wants is peace and quiet to do his thing. And this was the time there was a lot of shit going on between the families. Very bad blood over Atlantic City, mostly. Then you had the cops and the fucking feds starting to squeeze hard to get Sally Messina. Everybody's freaking, everybody's pissed at each other. It was very tense, you know? My uncle, he didn't want no bloodshed on his turf over a bullshit beef between two guys mad about some blowjob in a car, and not a very good one, either, if you want to know the truth."

"Please spare me. Tell me about Florida instead."

"Okay, so my uncle, he had these businesses down Florida. The guys running them was stealing him blind. He needed somebody he could trust to get things under control, and since I done such a great job running the clubs for him—"

" 'Clubs'?"

"These after-hours clubs—you know, casinos Italian-style that he had out in Queens and the Bronx. I ran them great for a couple of years before Florida. But when the heat went on, he asked me to head down south for a while to get his businesses there whipped into shape."

"What kind of businesses?"

"Supper clubs. Sophisticated joints."

"You ran nightclubs?"

He nodded proudly. "Topless."

"Topless clubs?"

"Bottomless, too. Once I got in charge the girls dropped the g-strings after I reached out to the cops to make sure nobody was going to have objections. But the girls were sophisticated about it, you know what I'm saying. Nothing raunchy."

"Oh sure."

"There was three clubs total, and when I went down there they all had these shitty names: 'Classy and Sassy,' the 'Pink Pussycat,' and the 'My Way Lounge,' which had this sign with a silhouette on it of a cartoon looked like Sinatra in his fucking hat. Old-fart names, you know? So then first thing, I hired a marketing company out of Fort Lauderdale that come up with new names, new signs, new ways of positioning the businesses. Like, you refer to the joints in the ads as gentlemen's clubs, not bars, and for Christ's sake not 'strip joints.' And of course the club names got to have the right image. 'Feelings' was the first one they come up with."

" 'Feelings'?"

" 'Feelings,' that was what they come up with. They done a study on it. You'd be surprised what sells if you put the right name on it. One they tried that I didn't like was 'Foxy Tonight.' Sounded like a fucking TV show. 'Lady Gold' was the other one I told them to forget."

" 'Lady Gold'?" I said, startled that a strip club would use the same name Kevin had used to get under my skin when I was promoted to detective.

"I liked 'Feelings' a lot more," Eugene said.

I said, "So you got the clubs straightened out after you went down there? You ran them like real businesses instead of pross-spots?"

"Right. In a couple of months, they were all running like Mercedes. Bringing in better clienteles, too. You had business guys in suits with the gold credit cards instead of tattooed rednecks with twenty-dollar bills crammed in their pockets. We started to see lots of broads coming in, too. Not lesbos, neither. Office chicks, broads from health clubs, checking out the competition. After a couple of months, every one of them clubs was making money hand over fist. I just kept shipping it back to my uncle after I took my own personal cut, which was fully agreed upon. My uncle took his and sent the rest uptown to Sally. It was working out beautiful. And that's what I was doing till about six months before they busted me."

"What happened then?"

"I retired," he said. "Which is one of the reasons my uncle ain't exactly thrilled to see me back in New York."

The way I saw it, it made sense for a mob outfit to have a guy like Eugene running strip joints in Florida. He'd already proven himself running the illegal New York casinos, which is where I supposed he learned whatever business skills he had, not to mention a few social ones. For years, I knew, the mob had been deeply involved in south Florida, where they had loan-sharking and real-estate operations that branched into savings-and-loan fronts during the 1980s. I knew that Tony Rossi had personally started most of those operations over the years, and that it was still his job to supervise them from New York. They generated a steady stream of cash that moved up the interstate pipeline from Florida to New York.

Eugene said he had set himself up in a furnished condo in a luxury complex on the Intracoastal in Boca. As the manager of the clubs, he oversaw the books, ordered the supplies, and hired the bartenders, dancers, bouncers, cashiers, and valet parking-lot attendants. He awarded contracts for maintenance and janitorial services.

It was a big job for a man without a high-school diploma. He was a quick study. Right then, I knew I could teach him to read.

"So you became a business tycoon?" I said.

"I hired the most beautiful southern babes and the ugliest bouncers," he explained. "Also bartenders who were smart enough to know just how much they could steal before they got their fingers broke."

At first, he explained, the clubs were "half-and-half" operations. That meant fifty percent of the cash flow was legally reported, on the books, and the rest moved under the table. "My uncle Tony is a prick for the percentages—he wanted the legal up to seventy-five, and that was the goal he gave me. The guy wants to be legit someday. I got it up to about sixty before I got tired of working fifteen hours a day and quit."

"You just quit?"

"Sure. Why bust your ass when there's easier ways to make money? My uncle wasn't giving me my just due. His attitude was like, You're lucky I gave you this spot. I had enough dough to live good for as long ahead as I could see. So I quit to show him, and they sent some other hotshot down from New York to replace me. Last thing I heard he was stealing them blind and pawing the girls, which you just do not do in a refined club. All the good ones quit, naturally."

"How did your uncle react to you quitting?"

"Pissed, is how. So I stopped answering the phone. Then he stopped calling. We got out of touch for a while. Basically, I needed to chill in the sun."

. . .

It *didn't take* long for me to piece the whole story together. Eugene's slacker's holiday had come to an abrupt end one morning when he drove to a 7-Eleven for cigarettes. A SWAT team—seventeen agents in camouflage commando gear—tumbled screaming out of jeeps that rumbled into the parking lot like an invasion force. They jumped Eugene and pummeled him to the pavement. When the hollering stopped, his arms were cuffed behind his back. Agents had their knees pressed hard on his legs and chest. Gun barrels pointed at his head like the spokes of a wheel.

Those details came from Rey. What Eugene didn't know, Rey explained, was that the SWAT team had actually grabbed him by mistake, believing Eugene to be another wiseguy named Gino Arguello—a psychopathic killer and cocaine importer from the Lucchese family who was wanted in all fifty states for having shot a DEA agent in the back of the head in Dallas. Aside from a similar first name, it could not have been an easy mistake to make. Eugene was about six feet tall, young, good-looking, with a smooth baby-face. Arguello was five-six, with a half-moon scar from the corner of his mouth to his chin. Arguello had lips that looked like pizza crust and a nose the size of a salami. There was no resemblance whatsoever.

However, Rey explained, Eugene did closely resemble an *actor* who had portrayed Arguello in one of those tabloid television programs that reenact crimes and publicize fugitives from justice. Apparently, a widow who lived in the condo complex had been watching Eugene with suspicion for months, ever since he quit his job and lolled around the pool all day in his little bikini trunks. The widow just kept her eye on him, figuring him for a drug dealer. But one night, she saw the television program with Arguello being portrayed by a young, good-looking Italian actor who resembled Eugene. Bingo, she goes to the phone and drops a dime. They assembled the SWAT team overnight.

"That happens all the time, incidentally," Rey told me.

"What?" I said. "SWAT teams jumping the wrong guy?"

"Well, that too. But I'm talking about these 'most-wanted' television shows. The real actors that play the bad guys on those shows? They're always getting turned in by neighbors looking for a reward."

That afternoon, over coffee in a luncheonette a couple of blocks west of Foley Square, Noah confirmed what I knew and added some detail.

"The FBI had been looking for this Gino Arguello for nearly a year when this went down," he said. He was very amused at the recollection. "Our poor schmuck Eugene was merely in the wrong place at the wrong time. They hit him like a freaking ton of bricks, Gerry. Of course, they didn't want to hear anything out of him—as far as they were concerned, they had nailed a cop killer. By the time they got him into a jail cell, our boy was so scared he had peed his white silk pants.

"Naturally, it didn't take long to figure out they had the wrong guy, which is something that happens a lot with these SWAT teams. They all think the so-called war on drugs means they can act like Rambo storming a compound. They don't worry about legal ramifications, these guys. Anything goes, and they usually get away with it, once they holler 'drugs.' Of course when they checked his prints against the killer and saw they had the wrong guy, they still ran his name through the computer and got a hit. And as they say in law school, *mirabile dictu*! Wonder to tell, they strike oil."

"*Batta-bing, batta-bang, batta-boom*," I interrupted, using the phrase I'd heard from Eugene.

"What?"

"Mirabile dictu. There's a phrase you hear in Brooklyn. You know? '*Batta-bing, batta-bang, batta-boom*.' It means the same thing. Only not in law-school Latin, of course."

Noah frowned at me. Like most insecure people in positions of authority, he was vigilant for any hint of impertinence.

"All right, Noah. What did you mean, 'they struck oil'?"

He cleared his throat. "Well, they find out there's a warrant out on him from the NYPD. They also find out that he's a member of organized crime."

"A warrant for what?" I said, already knowing the answer.

"It was actually bullshit, to tell the truth. But what was important at this point is, the feds in Florida need a way out of this fuckup of sending in the commandos to arrest the wrong guy, who turns out not to be some poor schlemiel in a parking lot, but a made wiseguy from one of the New York families—which means you could have mob lawyers heading down on the next plane, ruining your day.

"So they're relieved that at least they got Eugene on an outstanding warrant from New York. And don't forget, he's still stuck in a cell, scared to death that he's going to prison for some goddamn thing he maybe did once that he thinks we know about. They have him so rattled by this point that he'd believe them if they said they were going to charge him with the Kennedy assassination. So they play it cagey, let him sweat it out while they make some more calls to the NYPD.

"Naturally, the NYPD calls us here at the OCTF: 'Hey, the feds grabbed some wiseguy from the Giavanni mob in Florida, and there's a New York warrant on him. Do we have any use for the guy?' Well, we're thinking, Hello! Why that sounds like opportunity calling. The files indicate that Eugene Rossi isn't just some ordinary mob guy with the gold chains and lizard-skin shoes, although he certainly does have those. No, he's manna from heaven! Right at the time when the feds are really squeezing our nuts on these Mafia cases, who do we have in custody but slick young Eugene Rossi, the favorite nephew of Anthony 'Blackjack' Rossi, senior *capo* in the Giavanni family and number seven or eight on the family chart. So we figure, maybe we stumbled onto the missing link, right when we need a break."

Noah made a temple with his palms and raised his eyes to the ceiling. "Thank you, Jesus."

Still, I thought Eugene was a pretty big reach. After all, he hadn't had much contact with his uncle in two years. Since we'd had him in custody, he hadn't seen the uncle at all. All there had been were a few cordial phone calls. Blood relations aside, Eugene did not strike me as being exactly well-connected.

"Back to the warrant," I said, wanting to see if Noah had a different take on it. "What exactly was he wanted on? It had to be pretty good for you to hold him."

He chuckled. "That's the beautiful thing. It was just some bullshit gambling charge. He got DAT'd a couple of years ago back in Queens and failed to show up for the court date."

DAT was small potatoes, a desk-appearance ticket, the kind of thing that routinely gets blown out on an ACD, an adjournment in contemplation of dismissal. Eugene would have been sentenced to maybe a day of community service. After six months, the record would have been sealed.

"That's it?" I asked.

"Yeah. A three-year-old rap, as I remember it now. He used to run a couple of the illegal casinos in Queens for the uncle, social clubs."

"He told me."

He looked at me quizzically and then said, "Obviously, our Eugene makes a good appearance. He's a sharp dresser. He's a party animal. He's quick-witted enough to run the spot and keep the customers happy. A certain kind of woman goes for him. He runs with a slick crowd. Attracts fast, good-looking women, very hot ladies, in that Queens Boulevard kind of way—just the sort of clientele they need to attract to these joints to keep the customers from taking a bus to Atlantic City."

"He sounds like he's a pretty good businessman. He must have picked it up from his uncle."

Noah shook his head. "Not really, just flashy. All he is, is a wanna-be. As wiseguys go, I know he's not much, but right now he's what we got, Gerry. Frankly, I don't think our boy would know how to shoot a gun if you handed him one. He'd be afraid of getting a callous on his hands. He's really a prime fuckup, a poster boy for the new Mafia, the mob Generation X. No sense of history, no appreciation of myth and ritual. Guys like Eugene, they're the real reason the old Cosa Nostra is in the toilet. Law enforcement efforts actually have had very little to do with the decline of the Mafia."

"So why do we play the game?"

"Because we're lucky enough to have been chosen for the winning team."

"So you got Eugene to basically deed his life over to you on this bullshit warrant? You do know how many people are walking the streets of New York City with warrants out on them, Noah?"

He smiled. "Funny you should ask. Actually, I just saw a figure on that in the *Times*, I think. Something in the neighborhood of seventy-five thousand criminal warrants outstanding in New York. The criminals don't even bother to run away anymore. It's pathetic."

"Noah, I know this guy's no genius, but he's not a complete dope. He got street smarts. He's more perceptive than you think. Given the charge, how did you get him to turn? Where was his lawyer?"

Noah explained, "Luckily, Eugene has these delusions of grandeur from seeing too many movies. Because he's technically a made guy, he actually thinks he's a major player. He figures, what with the SWAT assault and all, he's very big-time to us. He thinks we must have him on something pretty good. After all, who knows what he did that we don't know about?"

"So he didn't lawyer-up when they brought him in?"

"We talked to him about that. After they popped him, he had some time to sit and think before we got down there. He had to be plenty scared about Uncle Tony's reaction. Uncle Tony is pretty strict about his boys getting attention from the law. So when we got down to Florida to talk to him, we told Eugene this was one area we could probably help him out, meaning Uncle Tony didn't have to find out anything."

"And now the guy is giving up his life," I said. "When we're through with him, he leaves with a suitcase and a pat on the back. For Christ's sake, he's just a kid. He can never walk his streets again."

"He was on the wrong street anyway. Look at it this way, we're doing him a favor. He was going to end up in prison at best, more likely dead before he was forty."

"A favor? This is doing him a favor? Does he actually know that you didn't have squat on him?"

"So what are you, his big sister?"

"Do you think he really knows what this means? Believe me, he doesn't. I know. I've read the agreement he signed with you guys."

"So now *you're* his lawyer? I thought you didn't graduate from law school till next year."

I ignored the sarcasm. "Why not be straight with the guy? He couldn't even read the contract."

"Oh," Noah said, "now you're his school teacher?" He softened then and said, "Look, I hear you. But right now, we need him. It's your job to keep him happy and keep him productive. The rest, we'll deal with it somewhere down the line on a need-to-do basis."

"What did you tell him before he signed the agreement?"

The tip of his tongue flicked at foam on his cappuccino. "Well, it wasn't us. I mean, the FBI guys had already laid down the groundwork with him before we got there to talk to him."

"Who's 'we'?"

He reveled in telling the rest of the story. "Me and Frankie DeCarlo, you know the homicide detective that looks like a mob lounge lizard?"

"I know the guy."

"Well, when we hear from Florida that there's been a hit on the warrant that could lead to a big break in the Sally Messina case, we get on a plane to go pick up our boy in Boca. The idea is to shake him enough that he'll turn immediately."

"It couldn't have been that easy."

"But it was. When we get to the cell in Boca, Frankie tells me, You wait outside while I talk to this guy. Okay. So Frankie goes in with his pointy shoes and shiny suit. Immediately, our boy figures Frankie for a mob lawyer, even though he hasn't called one. He figures, I guess, that Uncle Tony somehow heard about him getting jammed up and sent down a mob lawyer, so all's forgiven."

Noah tapped his temple disparagingly with a finger. " 'What took you so long?' Eugene says. Frankie almost fell on the floor when he realized the kid thinks his uncle sent him. So just to break the guy's stones, Frankie plays along and says, 'I jumped on the first bird headed south as soon as I got the call.' Right away, Eugene starts babbling, 'They think I'm a cop killer. I know my uncle's going to be pissed. I still got all his books. What can you do to work things out between me and him?' After about fifteen minutes of this, though, a local cop sticks his head in the room and says to Frankie, 'Detective, you need anything?' All Frankie can do is laugh his ass off."

"So Eugene never got a lawyer?"

"Frankie's good, he's very good. By the time I came in the room, there was no question about any lawyer. Frankie had the guy turned."

"Explain to me how he managed that."

"Well, you understand this part was not my doing. This is police work. Frankie told the kid he was a New York cop and said, 'Oh man, maybe they got your name wrong when they jumped you, but now that they ran you through the computer, they got you on so much other shit, buddy—you're not going to get out of jail till you're an old man with a long white beard. They know how you're connected to the Giavanni mob, Sally Messina's mob, the one everybody in law enforcement wants to bring down. They know who your uncle is that raised you like a son, but now Uncle Tony has other things on his mind in New York. They're RICO-ing everybody's ass; the mighty are falling, buddy-boy. Sally is going down, and it ain't to the seashore, and your uncle goes with him.' So right now, Frankie tells Eugene, 'The only person that gives a shit about you is me.' He says, 'I'm Italian. You're Italian.' "

Imitating Frankie DeCarlo's Brooklyn accent, Noah continued: "He says, 'But you know, peckerhead, your past catches up with you. RICO means just *conspiracy* to do shit—you don't have to actually do it, you just have to *know* some guys that did. In New York, I already know of at least two murders they want to talk to you about in RICO terms. And besides that, *you* know all the shit you did, and all the shit the people who you know did.' "

Noah touched at his lips with a paper napkin. "Frankie is really working him over: 'This is your freaking *life*, buddy-boy. You can make a deal, if you act right here and now. You tell me all you want in life is to open up a restaurant in Boca and catch some rays? Well, you come back to New York with us, you tell us what you know, you spend a little time helping us get us close to your uncle, and we'll take care of you, guaranteed. First of all, no jail time. None. Also, a new identity, and some dough to wipe the slate clean. You leave with a suitcase full of money. So you open up the restaurant in Arizona instead of Boca. They still got sun out there. On the other hand, you can tell me to fuck off, and I will. Then you can call your uncle and get him to send down that lawyer to bail you out. Maybe then you'll know the difference between a mob lawyer and a detective. You think you're in the deep shit now? Wait till your uncle finds out you've been talking to the cops.' " Noah looked at me for approval.

He didn't get any. I said only, "Oh, so you offered to get him into the witness protection program."

He drew himself up straight. "I was not party to any of the original terms of the deal. But just between you and me, there is nothing about the witness protection program in the agreement he signed."

"So I noticed," I said. "Although he certainly thinks that's part of the deal."

"Caveat emptor," said Noah.

"But what specific oral promises *did* you make that I don't see in that agreement?"

"Pardon me, Counselor?"

"Come on, Noah."

"Listen, all I said when Frankie called me in was, I told the guy, 'Eugene, it's up to you.' Remember, I'm not really fully clear on what just transpired between him and Frankie. So Frankie introduces me to Eugene, 'Here is an assistant DA from the prosecutor's office in New York. He's got the authorization to make a deal right now. If you're willing to help us, we'll help you. But the deal don't last till tomorrow, Gino boy. We've got other fish to fry,' Frankie says." Noah loved to talk about tough-guy cop behavior.

"Frankie runs him like a car dealer. 'Don't let them off the lot until they sign.'

"All I told Eugene myself was, 'You cooperate and we take care of you.' And he said, 'What does that mean, "cooperate"?' I said, 'You help us out with information about your uncle Tony's businesses.' Now, these are close to my exact words, Gerry. I told him: 'You come back to New York, you provide what we call substantial assistance. We set you up with a nice place to stay while you're working with us. Under our supervision, you see all your old friends, you see your uncle, you go about your business. Then when you are done with your work for us, we'll take care of you.'"

"That's it?"

"No jail time. I did specifically tell him that."

"But, of course, he wasn't facing time anyway," I said.

"So I told the truth."

"You tell him about money?"

Noah brushed that off. Money was a minor detail. You could always requisition money when it came to high-profile mob cases. "Sure, some cash," he said.

"How much cash?"

"Hell, who knows? There's money available, you know that. It depends on how he performs. If he delivers the uncle, it could be substantial, you know."

He had finished his cappuccino. I hadn't touched my decaf. We were silent for a few minutes.

"You lied, Noah," I said.

"Never."

"You went along with a lie. The charge you had him on was bogus."

"Untrue. We had him on an active warrant. Period."

"But it's unethical."

"Gerry, you haven't told him that?"

"No, of course not. You know me better than that. Besides, I'm the one that has to deal with him."

I wanted to make sure there were no illusions about the value being delivered on this deal, at least as I saw it. My calculations so far showed a lot of expense and wasted time and precious little progress so far. "Well, he hasn't really delivered much of anything worth a damn yet, has he?" I pointed out.

"He will. That's one of the reasons you're working this job."

While we waited for the check, Noah gave me the big-brother pep talk. Since I was a law student, I guess, Noah felt free to lecture me like a professor. "Our boy Gino," he said, "has one of the keys to a warehouseful of information, just at the time when it is at peak value. The law is not always neat. All of the *i*'s are not always dotted. We took the opportunity for the common good. The agreement was legally binding and he signed it as a consenting adult."

I tried to sound reasonable, but the whole idea of tricking Eugene into turning informant turned my stomach. "Listen, I know this isn't a law-abiding citizen here," I said. "On the other hand, what about the moral priorities? I've locked up people who rape and rob. I got some of them to turn. But I did it by the books. *They* made the decision knowing exactly what was going down. It should be done the right way. Not like this, Noah."

"Jesus! What are you, the freaking ACLU? Gerry, he's a piece of crap."

"Yeah, so? The way I see it, you've appointed yourself judge and jury. On a bullshit gambling charge. Even people who murder can come up for parole and go back to the old neighborhood. Eugene can't, not ever, not once they knew he's a rat."

Noah took a deep breath and let it out slowly. "So he finds a new neighborhood. Big deal."

"Fine," I said dejectedly.

"Gerry, don't get involved in any of that part of this. You had nothing to do with it. All you're supposed to do is be his contact person when you're with him. You are the one who is seen with him on the street. You keep him out of trouble, keep him behaved. Rey told me you started teaching Eugene to read, and God bless you, I suppose. But please, Gerry, don't get too personally involved."

He was not smiling.

"Fine," I said again.

"Listen, we did what was necessary here. Don't think for a minute this all wasn't decided at the highest level." His eyes became round. "We're actually doing him a long-term favor."

"Of course he went for it," I said. "A fresh start, the American dream."

Noah nodded sagely. "He absolutely went for it. I never met anybody so thoroughly cocky. The second he decided we were offering him a quick way to get him out of a jam, I think he decided he could manipulate his way around us, no matter what."

"He's a classic manipulator," I acknowledged.

"So finally we agree on something," Noah said.

"You left Boca with the agreement in your hand?"

"Yes. We got his signature, then we packed him up, and Frankie and I flew home with our new CI between us in the middle seat."

"He should have figured out right then that the deal smelled," I said.

"Why?"

"You flew coach."

CHAPTER 8

My *partner had* a lot more undercover experience than I did. That was reassuring, since undercover work is so vaguely defined that you end up making many of the rules yourself, all the while worried that somebody is going to come along and accuse you of breaking one. Undercover work, in fact, was the only job Rey knew as a cop; he'd been doing it almost since the day he was sworn in at the police academy, twenty years earlier. At the academy, they have people who look over the new recruits for the attributes that make for the best deep-undercover cops: an ego resilient enough to coexist with the lie of an alternate identity; a strong presence combined with a vague background; steely nerve and, of course, the ability to keep quiet, which alone would have ruled me out.

Rey was the senior detective already working on the case full-time when I came in, so I tended to defer to him, which he felt was only his due. It didn't take me long to figure out why Rey and Eugene had established a good relationship. It was one of those guy things that become especially intense when you have two dedicated bodybuilding buffs preening for one another, endlessly competing to score physical and social—but never intellectual—points. On the other hand, Rey always made it clear, even if he had to state it explicitly, that he was in charge. One on one with me, they were fine—one quiet and alert; the other boisterous—but together, they made me feel like the short side of a triangle.

Mostly because he had spent his career in deep undercover posing first as a member of an underground Puerto Rican terrorist group for years, and later as a drug dealer, Rey was accustomed to a flashier world than the Jersey suburbs. So was Eugene, of course. Immediately after Noah and Frankie brought Eugene back from Florida—before the OCTF made the arrangements to settle into the rented house in Jersey—Rey and Eugene had been placed for about two weeks in a small, expensive hotel on Gramercy Park.

There, with the NYPD picking up the tab, of course, they charlied it up big-time: room service for dinner and breakfast, chilled Dom Perignon by the buckets—who knows what else was rolling up to the door on a cart. In the afternoons, after they worked out at the gym, they would sunbathe on the grass in Gramercy Park, oiled up in those little bikini trunks that American muscle-heads (and Eastern European men, for some reason) think are irresistible to women.

This well-financed style of living, with plenty of flash money always on hand, gave them certain expectations that they managed to fulfill even after the operation settled into its quiet routine amid the 7-Elevens and highway interchanges and rolling across the river. Police-department spending is like a defense contract—once a base level is set, it only goes up from there. So the health club, which became as non-negotiable a part of the daily schedule as lunch, wasn't a common neighborhood gym, it was more like a resort. When we went out with Eugene's friends, the booze always came off the top shelf, and the prices on the menu never mattered.

Eugene's luxuriating in this excess I could figure. But Rey had me baffled. Once you got beyond the occasional dead-aim wisecrack, he seldom had much to say. My first impression was of an unapproachable man harboring grave secrets, yet haughty with that airtight confidence some guys have when they are accustomed to always getting attention from a certain type of woman. Beyond that, there was something about him—smooth as polished granite on the outside, but under that, wary, watchful and guarded. I didn't like to think about it, but his background in deep undercover had taken him so far off the reservation—he told me he hadn't even owned a police uniform until the year before, and even his paychecks once were automatically deposited into a bank account with a fictitious name—that I wondered what he was capable of under duress. Courage and guts, that went without saying. But what were his rules, after a career in dark worlds where a slip of the tongue, a truth carelessly uttered, could mean a bullet in the head?

It was hard to reconcile the image of the man who must have been—a man capable of living with terrorists and never letting what was real come through—with the man who was now my partner.

Like, who would have guessed he liked to cook? On our way back from the city one night, after I'd complained about being relegated to the role of fraternity housemother, Rey suddenly announced: "I'll cook dinner tonight. So we'll have to stop at the supermarket. I feel like opening a bottle of wine and cooking up a real dinner."

"Oh Christ," muttered Eugene. My own sentiments exactly.

"No, man. I'm a gourmet cook. French."

Eugene stuck his tongue out and made a gagging noise.

"Where'd you learn to cook?" I asked.

"The CIA."

"Get out of here, CIA," Eugene scoffed. "Fucking CIA!"

"Culinary Institute of America. My old man bought me a three-week course there for graduation the summer I got out of high school."

"You actually got to high school?" Eugene said.

"Fuck you, peasant. You want to eat? Show some respect."

"You wear a little apron when you cook?"

"Yeah, and that's all. I cook naked except for my apron."

"You'll burn your johnson that way," Eugene said.

"Not the way the French cook," Rey assured him.

"I'll stop at the supermarket," I said, "but you cook with your pants on."

"As *madame* wishes," Rey said.

My father had a saying: "Don't understand me too quick." As a child, the idea baffled me; I assumed it had something to do with the fact that English wasn't Pop's first language. But as I grew older, and especially as I became a cop, I began to comprehend what he meant. Cops live and die on first impressions, and learn to trust them, but smart cops, the ones who become decent detectives, learn the value of reassessing what at first might seem obvious, to assume the potential for unlikely subtlety, to know that what you hear is often not exactly what the person means to say.

Crossing the bridge, I looked at Rey with curiosity and asked, "Your father knew how to cook?"

"Hey, my father was all man."

"Who said a he-man can't cook?"

"My father was the one that taught me bodybuilding. Every day after work, he'd go down to the basement in the place we had in the Bronx. He had two big paint cans that he'd filled with cement, hooked onto a piece of old brass water pipe. That was his weights. The guy had a build better than you," he said, nudging Eugene.

"But he cooked?" I persisted.

"He was a maintenance man at the Biltmore Hotel. He got to know the chefs. They showed him how to do some stuff, the rest he picked up on his own, out of books. We were the only Puerto Rican family in the Bronx that had French food on the table."

. . .

At the supermarket, neither of them would push the cart, so I had to. The next thing I knew, they were tossing a five-pound sirloin tip roast like a football in the Pampers aisle while I picked out some shallots. The store's Muzak whirred to a halt and a voice came over the tinny loudspeaker. *"Manager to aisle five. Manager to aisle five."* The manager asked them to leave the store, but not before paying the $18.53 for the battered roast, which had left a trail of blood down aisle five.

I had the car keys, so I took my time finishing the shopping, and when I got outside, I found Eugene and Rey in the parking lot like it was detention, with the roast dripping red from its matted shrink-wrap in Eugene's hand.

"You going to take that thing in the car?" I demanded.

"Sure. It's tenderized," Rey said, while Eugene snickered.

The dinner, however, was wonderful, although Danny Flanagan, Lieutenant Campo, and the others begged off when they heard Rey was cooking French. It was just the three of us.

. . .

When he wasn't with Eugene, Rey treated me as a peer, which I liked. I was fascinated by his contradictions, but among other female officers downtown, he was well known for other things. Once, when I ran into Colleen at the OCTF, she asked about the job at the Plant, and then about Rey: "Wouldn't you love to fuck him?"

"The thought never occurred to me," I said coldly.

Now this sounds a little prim, but the question actually shocked me. For me, the police department still was a logical extension of Catholic school, high school, and college as well, where sex occurred without a lot of discussion. Besides, I was offically engaged. I considered this man a friend and a partner. If I sometimes looked for a reason to be around him, well, so be it. I liked being with Eugene, too.

Rooting around in my own conscience, I thought I saw the flash of another motive skittering like a rat out of a dark corner. Rey and Eugene had developed a close male relationship over the months, two experts conning the system for all it was worth. Sometimes they'd be gone all day, supposedly to undercover meetings, but they'd come back with new haircuts and manicures, or carrying shopping bags from Barney's. As a cop I felt affronted, but I also felt left out. Somewhere scratching in that corner, I was afraid I saw jealousy hiding in the dark.

Sometimes I'd simply stay in Jersey till eight or nine o'clock, using the opportunity to catch up on my studying.

The week after Rey made dinner, Eugene decided to match him and announced that he would cook for everyone.

"Let me show you my way of making polenta," he said one afternoon.

From out by the pool, where he was prostrate under the last corner of sunshine on the deck, Rey called out, "Go for it!"

After getting everything ready, Eugene called me to the stove to watch him add water to the cornmeal and stir it as it thickened. A large bubble heaved up in the middle and burst, splattering the stove and our hands.

"Vesuvius!" Eugene shouted. "Watch out. We'll be buried alive! Here comes another one. Stir that sucker down so it don't make a fart noise. I hate it when my polenta farts!"

It popped with a loud Bronx cheer, and we held on to each other laughing.

Rey must have heard us because he came in from the pool and inserted himself between us. "Pretty riveting stuff, right, Detective?"

He was unhappy. "That polenta looks done," he told Eugene. "You should turn it off before it burns."

Eugene stalked into the den. I grabbed the wooden spoon, turned the flame down as low as it would go, and kept stirring the pot.

Rey watched and said, "Getting a little close to the guy, aren't you?"

"That is none of your damn business. You guys charlie it up all the time at the gym and going shopping and chasing girls. So I happen to like to watch the guy cook. He makes me laugh. So give me a break."

"Well, he wouldn't be interested in you anyway," Rey said, stepping back. "How much do you weigh?"

"Excuse me?"

"I said how much do you weigh?"

My jeans suddenly felt tight. "Hey, you don't ask a woman a question like that."

He moved around to look at me critically. "Hey, no offense, Gerry." He edged a little to the side for a different angle.

"What?" I demanded.

"Really," he said, "it wouldn't take you any time at all to get yourself in shape. You could have a terrific body."

I put the spoon down beside a small puddle of polenta that had thickened into a tiny rug on the stove. "I don't think—"

"So stop thinking. Why not come down to the health club with Eugene and me? It's fun, and maybe it'll make you feel more like part of the team."

"Are you crazy?"

"Monday. You come with us Monday."

"No thanks," I said awkwardly. "I have to study."

"Come on, Gerry."

"Really, Rey."

"Listen, you know my girlfriend Monique?"

This would be the one shrieking on the phone about the toilet. Big hair, long nails, spike heels, and one of those behinds that could stop cars on a racetrack. I'd met her once when we were in town. "Yes," I said.

"Monique works out two hours a day. You should see her body." He stood there and closed his eyes tight.

"I saw it when she came to pick you up once," I said. Monique had a lot of time on her hands.

"That's her body, of course," Rey said reassuringly. "Her mind is another thing. But you, *you* could have it both ways. So why not come to the gym for an hour with us—work out an hour, study for an hour. Balance it out."

He was standing close behind me and I felt he was about to put his hands on my shoulder.

"Okay?" he persisted.

The polenta was setting like concrete. I wiped my hands on a dishtowel. "Well, maybe."

"*Okay?*" He had a hand on each shoulder.

"Okay," I relented.

"Good," he said. "You'll work this off in no time." He smacked me hard on the behind and was walking into the den when the wooden spoon I threw bounced off the wall, missing the back of his head by a yard.

CHAPTER 9

By the end of spring, my relationship with Kevin had devolved into an economically convenient agreement between two people over room, board, and laundry. My nights flashed by with my feet barely touching the floors of our apartment. In June, with summer semester starting at law school, I often rushed from class to meet Eugene at some restaurant or bar. Except to sleep, I was seldom at home. My birthday, June 20, passed without apparent notice; even though Kevin certainly had to have seen how I'd propped up on the end table a collection of birthday cards from family and friends. Kevin's inattention, which once would have left me sobbing, hardly affected me at all. In fact, I felt relieved. At least, I didn't have to act grateful to him for a box of chocolates or a bunch of flowers from the Korean grocer's.

On impulse, I went downtown and treated myself to a three-thousand-dollar computer with the works, which consisted of a whole shopping list of odd terms for accessories and options, and a six-inch-thick computer manual that consisted of *entire pages* of words and sentences that were utterly incomprehensible to the point of lunacy.

However, with a phone call here and there to "technical service," a department in the computer store that appeared to be staffed exclusively by passive-aggressive males in their twenties, I learned within about two weeks to make the thing do all I wanted it to, which was type, fetch specified information, and send e-mail.

So now the few hours I was at home were spent fixed silently in front of a computer screen in the bedroom. In the living room, like a mirrored image cracked by time, Kevin took a similar position in front of a television screen. The agitated electrons did not arc between those stations. In the dim cathode-flicker, a relationship dissolved to black.

My consciousness, suddenly freed, and with no prodding from me, arranged itself daily into a flexible split shift. The case was the first thing I worried about in the morning and the last before I fell asleep at night. Law school fit like a mitered corner into the empty spaces. My awareness of Kevin was just punctuation, like the chime of a distant clock.

Occasionally (and I suspect prompted by something manly he had seen on television) Kevin still felt the need to challenge me, even though he scarcely noticed that I reacted like someone approached by a stranger on a subway car. He wasn't jealous of Eugene. He just resented my attitude that Eugene, whatever else he was or imagined himself to be, had dignity.

"That greaser has your number," he said on several occasions, nodding with his brows knit, one higher than the other. "A greaser with a third-grade education outsmarting a college girl." It occurred to me that "college girl" was no less an insult in his mind than "third-grade education."

"He's not fooling me," I said. But my heart really wasn't in it. In fact, the more time I spent with Eugene, the more my frustration grew—not at his company, which I had come to enjoy, but at his lack of progress in moving the ball on the investigation.

One night four months into the job, by which time I had become desperate enough to seek it, I went into the living room to ask Kevin for advice. The operation was like stalled traffic stacked up at the Lincoln Tunnel: lots of horn-honking and frayed nerves, endless heated maneuvering for a few feet of position, so little ground gained. Aside from a few scraps of new information that Eugene had thrown us about his uncle Tony's various lines of business, we were no closer than Miss Manners was to Sally Messina. If there was an intelligent plan to finish the operation, I hadn't been apprised of it. We were drifting in shallow waters close to shore, but spending money like it was a Caribbean cruise. Why was I the only one complaining?

Kevin offered only an impractical plan of action. "If it was me," he declared, "I'd put my foot on his fat fucking guinea throat and press till he pukes eggplant parmigiana."

"I don't think that's helpful," I said dryly.

"Suit yourself," he said. He leveled the remote control clicker at the television as if it were a .38. Larry King's porcine pink face came on, leaning earnestly toward a celebrity transsexual.

"He's just working the system for all it's worth," I insisted.

"Aren't we all," Kevin said, channel-surfing past a sermonizing nun in full regalia, a model selling fake jewelry, a winking Fred Astaire, a wailing Mexican soap-opera mamacita and a quartet of fat red-faced Washington commentators to alight for a few moments on a Beavis and Butt-head imbroglio.

. . .

When I got out to Jersey the next day, I marched in to see Lieutenant Campo, who had ensconced himself in an "office"—a room that the owner's wife had apparently used as a downstairs sewing parlor—to augment the one she had upstairs. There was a Singer sewing machine on a little wood table against the wall. Four gold-framed pastel pictures of ocean surf, sailboats, beach-cottage porches, and sand dunes hung on each of the walls. Campo had his big feet up on the desk, with a *Wall Street Journal* propped on his belly. It was opened to the stock tables.

I cleared my throat to get his attention and said, "Lieutenant, I need to talk to you about something."

He grunted, which I interpreted as an invitation to sit in the metal folding chair in front of his desk, like something you'd see at the Motor Vehicles Office.

"It's Eugene," I explained. "I don't think it's working."

He frowned at his paper, muttering something I didn't catch. Then he looked at me with a trace of curiosity and said, "How many people do you think read this newspaper? I mean actually *read* it instead of buying it as a fashion accessory. *You*, for example." He fixed me with a quizzical look.

"Excuse me?"

"Your financial future I'm talking about, Gerry. You have got to stay abreast of the market. Please don't think I'm prying, but how much money you got in the bank?"

"I'm okay, Lou. I wanted to ask you about—"

"It all goes by so fast, Gerry! You have to start planning a lot sooner than you think. Nobody's going to do it for you. You take me, for example. Thirty years on the job, December the fifteenth. You believe that?"

"Thirty years," I repeated.

"But I'm set, kiddo. I'm sitting pretty because I charted my financial course; I started my planning when I was as young as you are, Gerry, I thought ahead." He put an index finger against his temple to indicate what was required.

"Yeah, Lou. I'll keep that in mind."

"You ought to talk to Brian, too."

"Kevin."

"Kevin. Sorry. You talk to him. You tell him: Planning!"

"I will, sir."

"Well then," he said decisively, as if he had dispensed with my reason for coming in.

I said, "Well, actually, it's Eugene, Lieutenant."

He took his feet off the desk and arranged himself more formally. "What, he getting fresh with you?"

"No sir. He's fine, not as cocky as before, actually. I'm worried that he isn't delivering what he's supposed to."

Nodding vigorously, as if I had put my finger right on the heart of the situation, he said, "Listen, there's something I've been meaning to tell you. I read your DD-5 on this supposed Faffy Fortunato conversation he had with his uncle? Tell me exactly what you remember him saying."

I repeated as much as I could remember. The conversation had occurred more a month before.

"Okay, now let me see your memo book. What date was that?"

Apprehensively, I took my memo book from my purse and thumbed back through the pages, hoping he wouldn't notice how many were nearly blank, and that a couple of them contained grocery lists or doodles. While I was good about turning in my DD-5's, I was casual about my memo book, like many cops. A detective is supposed to keep a detailed daily log, but I'd been a little remiss about mine since there was so little to put down. Theoretically, you were supposed to record every encounter, noting date, time, what was said by whom, and what you observed.

Luckily, I had made notes about the Faffy call. I read from the page, "Phone conversation lasting four minutes. Subject: Faffy Fortunato."

Campo rummaged through a stack of phone records. "Look at this, from the date of the supposed call," he told me. A phone number was circled in red: 1-800-WEATHER.

I was bewildered. "You're kidding me! He was talking to a weather recording? How long have you known?"

"Don't worry about it. Last week, I checked through the phone logs after they started busting my chops about the lack of progress. And goddamn if the phone bill doesn't show he pulled this little stunt on you."

He didn't seem particularly concerned by a slipup that had me mortified. "You're not mad?" I asked.

"Hell no. I've figured for a while that he was just doing a two-step where Uncle Tony's concerned. But now that he's getting to trust you, which takes time, I want you to use this. I want you to confront him with it and tell him the jig is up. Tell him to bring in the uncle or else."

So he was leaning on me to make Eugene deliver, only because a hitch had shown up in the records. I tried to keep my voice even while my mind raced to outline the new approach I was convinced we had to take. "Look, Lou, there has to be a better way to get to the uncle. This little fandango just proves what I've been saying practically since the beginning. It seems like this is a waste of our energy. It's his big million-dollar vacation. When are we going to wise up that he's just pulling our chain?"

"Gerry, Gerry. You always want the quick payoff. I told you this before. On a sensitive undercover job, you must continually revise drastically downward any preconceived notions about the rate of progress. You've been doing a terrific job, letting the information flow naturally over time. Bit by bit it'll all add up, believe me. So don't worry. All's I'm saying, and I'm saying this loud and clear, is it's time to send a message to this joker, that we intend to start holding his tootsies to the fire."

"But Eugene hasn't gotten us anywhere near his uncle, and frankly, I'm not sure he can."

"Don't worry! We're getting there! What about the uncle's annual mob picnic on the Fourth of July? Huh? You just tell Eugene that you and him are going, no *ifs*, *ands*, or *buts* about it. I'm counting on you to make it happen."

Thinking *mob picnic*, I stormed into Eugene's room to confront him. "What is this bullshit about the call to your uncle on the Faffy Fortunato murder? You jerk!"

Eugene remained cool. "What do you mean?"

"You know exactly what I mean, you con. You didn't call the guy! I sat here and watched you make the call to a damn weather recording. You played me for a fool, and the lieutenant just chewed my ass out for it, Mr. Mafia. Let me tell you something, buddy. You better start delivering or we'll just throw your ass in the can. Jail time, *paisan*."

"You can't do that. I got to have a trial."

"Fine! We'll indict your sorry ass and put it in all the papers about how you've been with us all this time, living on the arm while ratting out your uncle."

"Now look. I didn't know you when I made that phony call, not like I do now. I was afraid you might interrupt me or something on the phone if I called Uncle Tony for real."

He was handing me another cheap excuse wrapped with a ribbon of plausibility, which was a concept that passed for reality in Eugene's head. So I told him exactly what I wanted from him now. A personal get-together with Uncle Tony at the picnic he held every July 4 at his sprawling ranch house on Staten Island.

"We're going to that picnic," I told him sternly.

"We'll go, sure," Eugene insisted. "No problem. Just make sure you got something decent to wear so you don't fucking embarrass me."

"Don't worry about me. Just set it up," I said, slamming the door as I left.

. . .

The next morning, Eugene told me he'd made the arrangements for the long-delayed reconciliation with his uncle. He said he had explained to Uncle Tony that he had been back in town for a while, but too ashamed of himself for having quit the Florida job to come see him. Tony understood. Everybody was busy. Everybody had complications. Come, and bring a date, Tony said. July 4.

The date, of course, would be me, wearing a wire. It was well known that Sally Messina himself always stopped by Tony's barbecue for an hour or two, a politician making his rounds. Sally would then head up to his home base in Ozone Park, Queens, where he presided like a prince over his own neighborhood picnic, a big community block party and fireworks extravaganza to which the entire community was invited.

Campo and Rey both thought this was a grand idea, but the plan had little allure for me beyond providing some proof that Eugene was at least going to get me in Tony's physical proximity. But going wired to a mob picnic? What were we going to get from that? These Mafia shindigs were crowded, boisterous social affairs, with wives and girlfriends and kids crawling all over. Press photographers usually stationed themselves outside. So did the feds and the city cops trying to look inconspicuous in their blue city-issue unmarked cars. A scene like that was unlikely to yield much useful information. Besides, Colleen had told me that a couple more retired NYPD detectives were doing private security work for Sally Messina. If that was true and I was recognized, would an ex-cop give me up for a paycheck?

No need to worry. A couple of days later, Eugene told us it was off.

"My uncle passed on a message and says on second thought I should lay low because of that thing," he explained.

"What thing?" I demanded hotly.

"This trouble with the guy that had the beef with me."

"That was ages ago. I thought that was taken care of!"

"It was! But my uncle says a social occasion, I'm going to run into the guy, so let's not rub no salt in no wounds, especially with Sally Messina being under so much stress and all that. My uncle don't want no chance for trouble. So I'm disinvited."

My mind raced. Didn't he realize the time was coming when I would have to expose him as a fraud? That I wouldn't cover for him? "Eugene, don't lie to me."

He looked so unhappy that I eased up and said, "Okay. So the picnic doesn't work. So just tell me now when I'll get to meet Uncle Tony. It has to be soon."

CHAPTER 10

My main law-school course over the summer was Criminal Procedure, which I figured would be a breeze after my ten years with the department. The class actually dovetailed with the ethical issue that kept me awake at night: Eugene.

One of the first classes was about the rights of a suspect and the liberties that the police or prosecutors can take with the truth. It was odd to hear this discussed as theory. In real life, a lot happens outside the textbook.

"What if a perpetrator waives his Miranda and denies involvement in a crime?" the professor asked. "Can the police, use deceit, misrepresentations, and trickery to get a confession?"

Most of my classmates wanted to be prosecutors. A couple were cops. One of them spoke up. "Whatever it takes," he said. Many heads around me nodded.

But I waved a hand until the professor looked in my direction. "Your question is a setup." I said. "You referred to the suspect as the perpetrator, so of course everyone will think deception is okay."

"Miss, ahh, Conte is it? Not only this classroom, but in the United States Circuit Court of Appeals, it has been held that a confession is admissable even when it was obtained by trickery or deceit—provided that the trickery does not shock the conscience or is not apt to induce a false confession."

A couple of the cops turned around and stared at me like I'd cursed at the Pope.

"Professor," I said, "I have a problem with that."

"With what, Miss Conte?"

"With the courts allowing the police to use lies to elicit a confession."

"That's an odd attitude, given your background."

"To me, the courts are just giving the police permission to perpetuate fraud, a license to abuse their authority."

"But surely, Miss Conte, you have seen the police in what we might call blue lies. . . ." He waited for a chuckle from the class and when there was none, he went on, somewhat deflated. "That is, they may hint at leniency, or psychiatric help instead of jail time, or they may suggest the evidence is stronger than it is. If the suspect then confesses, what harm has been done?"

"I simply don't think it should be admissible as evidence. The suspect should confess of his own free will. Those mind games are simply wrong."

"Oh, come on, Gerry," said one of the other cops in the class, a big Irish detective I knew from Torts. "Enough with the goody-goody act. You know as well as I do that by the time we get as far as having somebody in an interrogation room, he's done something, and usually it's what we think he did. Innocent people hardly ever get to that point in the system."

"I'm sorry, but I don't agree that that gives us license to cheat, even if we think we're sure of guilt."

Of course, I was aware of my own hypocrisy, participating in a trick involving Eugene and planning another one to trap his uncle. Still, I'd said what I truly believed: You don't lie just to get what you want out of the law.

. . .

Even if Campo and Rey seemed content with the pace, I figured the prosecutors must be getting impatient. Sounding out Noah seemed like the prudent thing to do before I went any further. This time, I dragged him out of the office to a coffee shop down the street. I was glad I did. After some prodding, Noah conceded what I had feared— that the brass in the DA's office were increasingly unhappy about our end of the investigation, and ready to cut Eugene loose.

"They're afraid that we're going to come up sucking wind again and let the feds get another clean whack at Sally Messina," Noah conceded. "Which is a concern I happen to share."

And it was certainly a valid concern. Messina was still openly mocking law-enforcement efforts to put him in prison. Eighteen months earlier, after a federal prosecutor had blown the first major RICO case against him. Messina waltzed out of court acquitted of charges that could have put him away for life. The cocky bastard even did a victory jig for the television cameras.

"We're the toughest fucking crew in the whole fucking world! Nobody can touch us now!" Messina had crowed, surrounded by fans and reporters like a winning Super Bowl coach.

Messina's lawyer was a surly mouthpiece who looked like an artillery shell cased in sharkskin. The lawyer tugged at his tie and snarled, "You want to get Salvatore Messina? Then you get some goddamn evidence on him that will stand up in a court of law. You goddamn find a credible witness. You do it the right way under the American system of justice. The ends do not justify the means, gentlemen."

The feds were livid, and so was everybody else. Myself, I thought the mob lawyer had a point about doing it legally, because juries were notoriously fussy about police testimony that falls to pieces under assault by a smart defense lawyer. Since then, more than a half dozen federal, state, and county law-enforcement agencies lit bigger fires under their own high-powered investigations, each of them desperate to be the first to bring down this wiseguy who ran his mouth like a movie star. We yapped at his well-shined shoes like a pack of terriers.

The Special Prosecutor's Office supervised the Organized Crime Task Force unit. And Noah was desperate to come out of this with a gold star.

Like Campo, he said he was depending on me. Now the OCTF's problems had become *my* problems. Now that our informant's lack of productivity was finally under official discussion, that became my responsibility. Noah conceded that I was painted into a corner, but his patronizing tone implied that I had done it myself.

He told me, "Okay, you are correct to be as upset as you seem to me."

"I'm not upset! I'm pissed."

"Okay, you're pissed, then. You're absolutely right. The information is *not* being gathered efficiently on your end of the investigation, the investigation that you are involved in, Gerry. Yes, Campo is responsible too, and yes, Detective Vargas is responsible too. All I can say is that a sudden failure at this high level, after all of this time and money, will reflect badly on everybody involved, all of us. I'm talking careerwise. Your career, but more importantly, frankly, mine. The front office, they're leaning very hard on me over this. And just between us, okay, we're about to come down like a truckload of bricks on your boss. This isn't to be repeated. Campo doesn't know it, but they've been auditing the expenses you've all been running up out there at sleep-away camp in Jersey. The vouchers and the overtime have been piling up. Three hundred dollar dinner checks? Clothes for our CI? Fancy health club dues? And what do we have to show for it? Notes! A stack of transcripts two feet high. And do you know what they prove?"

"Nothing," I said firmly.

"Well, very little, I'll grant you that. So as a friend, I'm saying you should be aware of that. And this is totally off the record; you cannot repeat it—"

"Okay—"

"I think you can expect Campo to be relieved of his duties unless we see major results forthcoming by the end of the summer."

This was late June. "The end of the summer?" I said, amazed.

"Right, when everybody gets back from the Hamptons. Now, you probably want to know, do you personally have career problems here, Gerry? Yes, I think you do."

"You said that. Noah, I'm doing everything I can. The end of the summer is a lot longer than I want to wait. I'll ask for a transfer—"

He held up a hand. "I wouldn't do that. They'll say you cut out and ran off the job without accomplishing anything for, what's it been now? Six months?"

"Four." Suddenly, I felt sorry for Campo, as much as I resented his lackadaisical approach. He had always been decent to me and I considered him honorable—two things that go a long way on my sheet. Noah's smugness was appalling. After all, he was the one who had set up the deal.

"Let me run with this one," I said after a minute.

Impatiently, he scratched a fingernail on a flat gold Cartier watch that was too big for his skinny wrist. "Okay, you can move things along, do it." Suddenly, he brightened. "I'm telling you, Gerry, my bosses read the papers and watch the news besides going through all the investigative reports. Maybe now that the air is cleared, we have a golden window of opportunity. Actually, the feds are also getting nowhere, from what I hear, but they're also better than we are at covering up their fuckups and generating positive spin. So it won't be long before they're on the offensive again. The DA wants the New York City taxpayers to know he's on the street looking out for them."

"From his limo?"

He ignored that. "As you say, the trick is to get things moving, obviously. Others in this very office are doing better."

He was referring, I knew, to Unit Two, the other NYPD operation working on a parallel track to ours. They were hitting gushers with informants like Edward "Eddie Mack" McKenny, the turncoat from the Irish Westies. And I'd heard they were already preparing indictments to ram down the throats of the feds, and open a new path to the Messina hierarchy through its disastrous dealings with the Westies, a gang of maniacs who didn't care who they pissed off. The Westies would gag down a sparking hand grenade and jump on an enemy's shoulders if they felt the need to get revenge. The Mafia wiseguys weren't smarter, necessarily, but they were more methodical, better disciplined; they usually factored in at least a small degree of self-preservation.

The Italian wiseguys couldn't *comprehend* the Westies, whose leader, Jimmy Boyle, had once chopped off a guy's head in the back room of his tavern, propped it up on the bar, stuck a lighted cigarette in its lips, and bought drinks for the house all afternoon. When a couple of Giavanni guys came in to do business, Boyle made its mouth move up and down like it was talking to them. Boyle kept the head in his refrigerator for months and pulled the same stunt over and over. Sometimes he just walked around holding it by the hair and swinging the rotting head like a railroad lantern. The Giavanni crew who dealt with him were horrified. Regular wiseguys, they could chop a guy's head off, but they'd put it in the ground. They wouldn't stick it frozen on a bar and use it as a ventriloquist's dummy.

I knew that the Westies end of the investigation wasn't glamorous, and it wasn't clean. Basically, they only had Eddie Mack, who they also called "Wacky Macky," holed up in a hotel room in Staten Island, spilling his guts about the Mafia. He'd killed two dozen people, some just for the hell of it. Eddie Mack, though, was an outsider. As an informant, he lacked sex appeal, not to mention a direct connection to the Italian mob.

The beauty of our unit, at least on paper, was that we had custody of an pedigreed *Italian* gangster; a made member of the Giavanni family, it said on paper, at least, had turned informant as the result of brilliant police work. We had the trophy. But our trophy was just sitting on a shelf. I thought of the row of ceramic clowns on a study in the living room. When I closed my eyes, the clowns morphed in my mind into a ghastly row of tiny severed heads.

. . .

Next, I *sounded* out Rey on my still-in-progress plan to goose things along. "We have got to get close to Uncle Tony, without more delay. It's ridiculous to keep pretending we're going anywhere on this investigation until we turn the uncle. Obviously, Eugene hasn't done anything for us except talk, although he has given us good information about the players and the way they operate."

"Conceded," said Rey.

"So it's time to force the damn issue."

"And?"

I leaned close to him. "Listen to this. Every Monday afternoon, Uncle Tony holds a meeting with his street crew at a place down on Lafayette Street called Nunziata's Pastry Shop."

"Sure. Everybody knows that."

"So we wiretap him there."

He used his spoon to lightly tap his glass of Evian like a bell. "Hold on, detective! You need a court order for electronic surveillance, and that means you have to build a fairly compelling case, at least on paper. How are you going to do that, Sherlock?"

"I'll get it myself first."

"But that's why we have Eugene." Rey looked at his watch. It was almost time to leave for the gym.

"No, wait—what we have so far is nothing times ten. All this guy does is come up with excuses."

"What are you saying, then?"

"Not Eugene. He stays out of this one. He'll never pull it off, but once we got Uncle Tony, then he can come in for the finishing touches. Meanwhile, I take the first big step myself. I want to go down there and get to know Uncle Tony. On my own."

"You're nuts. This guy is too smart. You're not playing in the Little Leagues anymore."

"I'm well aware of that. Listen, I've also done serious undercover before. How about the psychiatrist who ran the prostitution ring? I got over on him, remember?"

"Yeah, but the doctor didn't have a record for smacking people in the head with a tire iron."

"Details," I said.

"Whatever blows your skirt up," Rey said. He thought for a moment.

"So basically, you want to get to know Uncle Tony and start building up the overhears?"

"Right. It'll take time, but it'll work."

"Overhears" are essential in getting the court authorization to wiretap someone. They're reported on the DD-5s, based on undercover conversations and casual surveillance. The first step is to show some indication—even hearsay that wouldn't necessarily rise to the level of admissible evidence—that a crime may have been committed. It's usually pretty easy with known mobsters, if the investigator is close enough to see and hear the subject. Getting the access, of course, is the tricky party. Given time, skill, luck, and, of course, access, I thought I would be able to compile enough overhears to cross the threshold for the next step, which would be filing the detailed affidavit requesting permission to install electronic surveillance at Nunziata's. Once a wiretap was in place, the investigation could then lead to an arrest on some kind of a criminal charge. The next step would be to flip Uncle Tony, like they'd flipped his nephew, by offering him a deal.

Ultimately, flipping Tony Rossi would be Noah's job, assuming we could arrest him on a charge that stuck. That would be the most difficult part, because Tony was a lot smarter than his nephew. Basically, they had merely tricked Eugene, and even then, they did have an actual criminal charge, minor as it was, hanging over him. A man like Tony Rossi, who had managed to avoid arrest for decades, would be unlikely to roll over as easily.

"But think about what happens if you get jammed up," Rey said.

"So I get jammed up. There's always a risk."

"Well, just don't let this guy manipulate you, Gerry."

"I can handle somebody like Tony Rossi. I'm no fool."

"I'm not talking about Tony Rossi, and you know it. Tony Rossi in my opinion won't give you the fucking time of day. I mean Eugene."

"Eugene? All I need to do is light a fire under his butt. Which happens only once I get over on the uncle, which I will do. Then our boy Eugene comes in for the kill, which he will have no choice about doing because his excuses will be gone."

. . .

That *was a* lot of brave talk, and I tried to keep the momentum going before I could decide it was insane to establish an undercover relationship on my own with an organized-crime capo. So the same afternoon, I went in to see Campo for permission. He was trying to get home in time to keep a dinner date with his wife in Long Island. He had to commute to and from Jersey every day across two rivers with the tangle of Manhattan in between, so he liked to hit the road early.

Trying to keep it short, I suggested diplomatically that I'd heard the DA's office was afraid the feds were going to beat us to Messina again.

His frankness surprised me. "Yeah, I heard, believe me. Basically, they want me to wrap things up here and start walking."

"Start walking? You mean put in your retirement papers?"

"Thirty years in December," he said, stuffing papers into a briefcase. "With all the overtime we all put in out here so far, this is the year to retire. Your pension is calculated on your final year's salary—remember that when your time comes, Gerry. Next year, no OT, zilch, they tell me. So I start walking." He made a little strolling motion with his fingers. "Do me a favor, though. Don't let it get around just yet. I still got six months to go. You don't want to be a wounded duck."

"I'm so sorry, Lou, really."

"Not me. Now what did you want to tell me?"

Six months was far more time than I thought I would need. I figured my plan would have to go down under his watch. "Look, I think I can get things moving here. I want to get to the uncle directly—right in that pastry shop on Lafayette Street where he has his business meetings with his crew."

He frowned. "Are you kidding me? How we going to do something like that, for Christ's sake?"

"They wired Sally Messina above the Napoli Social Club on Mulberry Street, didn't they, Lieutenant? A couple of years ago they wired his predecessor's actual *house*, after tricking his wife into letting them in to use the phone, right? That was one of the great bag jobs in wiretap history, remember? Well, we need the affidavits. Eugene isn't getting us anywhere near the point where we can start filing affidavits for wiretaps."

"You got that right," he agreed.

"So why don't I just go down there to where the uncle hangs out, get to know him under some pretext?"

"You mean like set him up for a sting?"

"Well, I haven't thought as far ahead as that. I'm talking surveillance. Overhears."

"With Eugene along?"

"That wouldn't work, I don't think. No, just me. I'll get to know the guy personally."

"How in hell you going to do that?"

"I'll just hang out there, quietly, maybe try to convince him I'm look-ing for work. Like a secretary. These guys are always looking for some-body to do errands."

"You, a secretary?" he said dubiously. "With your lip?"

"Okay, a bookkeeper, then. They all use bookkeepers."

"I guess," he said. "You got balls, I'll say that, Conte. Excuse my French."

"Thank you. Can I give it a shot?"

He had his coat on and was headed out the door. "Go for it."

"Wait, one more thing," I said. "We need Noah on board. You think I should go to him?"

I knew Campo detested him. "No, Gerry," he said. "I'll be delighted to take care of the DA's little peckerhead myself."

. . .

On paper, targeting Tony "Blackjack" Rossi to get to Messina made sense—if you happened to have his nephew on ice as your infor-mant. But I wasn't totally persuaded of that as I listened week after week to Eugene's detailed descriptions of how Tony operated as a business-man. Even though he was still under fifty, Tony belonged to the old guard among the two dozen or so captains, or capos, who were stacked on the Giavanni family organizational charts below the boss and his consigliere Phillip "Fingers" D'Amato and the two senior underbosses. From what I could get out of Eugene, as well as from my own homework, the organizational charts drawn up by law-enforcement mob experts de-picted a cohesive corporate hierarchy that no longer existed, after many years of factionalization within the Giavannis, who had once been the most hierarchical of all.

Messina had murdered his way up to boss, and now he was surrounded by a praetorian guard of diamond-studded cheeseballs, quick-hit oppor-tunists just like himself, fast-lane guys who lived for the moment. Mean-while, the journeymen capos like Tony Rossi managed the vintage street rackets and the routine operations that intersected with legitimate busi-nesses from restaurants and butcher shops to banks and trucking com-panies. Despite their charts, I wondered how close a guy like Tony really was these days to the top.

Of course, so long as things stayed peaceful, the arrangement Uncle Tony had was fine. He lived like a baron, buffered by the loyalty of a crew of thieves and strong-arm men. Tony's greatest vulnerability, from the way Eugene described him, was money. He had an unusual character disorder: On one hand, he was notoriously tight with a buck; on the other, as Eugene told us proudly, he loved to gamble—big-time. Atlantic City, a three-hour drive down the Jersey coast, was his Mecca.

Eugene once said: "My uncle Tony will go down to A.C. at the drop of a hat, and spend money like there was no tomorrow. He's one of them guys who the casinos treat him like a king with comps."

"Comps?" I said.

"Free shit for the high rollers, the select few," Eugene said, his eyes dancing. "My uncle Tony, he has the bucks, too. He's always socking money away in mutuality funds. He's got to be worth millions."

"And he likes to gamble?" I said.

"He has to gamble," Eugene corrected me. "He loses ten thou? Next day, he's back at the table for more. He loves the action more than anything in this world."

So Tony was a man who needed quick gratification. Coupled with the possibility that he had a growing need for quick money. I had an idea that, with luck, might work.

CHAPTER 11

A*nthony "Blackjack" Rossi* was one of the last capos appointed by Jack Ponte before Big Jackie bellied-up on the sidewalk with six bullets in his head. Tony was old-line mob. He was stable and dependable. He showed up for work, kept his crew under control, balanced the books, understood the ground rules, and kept himself out of the newspapers. In today's corporate world, he could have been the competent mid-career vice president at a regional subsidiary, the kind who would get an early-buyout offer when he was fifty. Tony wasn't like most of the capos Big Jackie appointed—tough-guy killer drones who muscled their way to the top of a street crew and then put in their time for promotion. Among the old guard, Tony stood out, not because of his loyalty and ruthlessness, which they all had, but for his business skills.

Big Jackie's murder was Tony Rossi's personal Black Friday, the day his stock lost about half its value. When Messina crowned himself the new boss, Tony kissed the ring, kept up appearances, and started planning his retirement.

In the glitz and flash of the late 1980s, Messina and his new hotshot lieutenants luxuriated like investment bankers on a million-dollar bonus roll. While Big Jackie had bought his suits at Brooks Brothers, these guys went to Barney's. Jackie's crowd rode in Lincoln Town Cars; Messina's boys, who favored Mercedes, laughed and called them "airport limousines." The Big Jackie style was cabin cruisers off Jersey, girlfriends who looked like Vegas showgirls and drank vodka-tonics. Messina was cigarette boats on Long Island Sound, girls who worked out and looked like Victoria's Secret models, Moët by the glass, a stash of blow in the Ferragamo purse. Jackie and the boys ate at restaurants with names like La Bella Napoli. Messina went to Au Bar.

The Messina style required a lot more flash money than Big Jackie's, and it had to come from a volatile mob economy thundering down the grade like an eighteen-wheeler with dicey air brakes. Like the Wall Street boom, the Mafia economy of the Reagan era threw off cash like a sparkler, but drugs and construction shakedowns were speculative money, subject to what the economists would call "volatile market pressures."

Alone among the ranking *goombata*, Tony had actually been through a bear market. So he planned his future accordingly. For example, he got into a long-neglected business that nobody else had much interest in: counterfeiting. With spectacular advances in photocopying and computer technology, counterfeiting suddenly took off. Not counterfeit money, which was a chump's game, but phony *documents*—street paper, SSI cards, work papers, green cards, immigration certificates, fake Medicaid ID's, driver's licenses, credit cards—beautifully done work—all of the engraved invitations to the feast for the steaming hordes of illegal immigrants, bereft of papers, tramping through the gates at Kennedy.

While Jackie tended to the bottom line downtown, the Messina crowd uptown lived off the drug business, where the revenue tended to arrive in gushers. The drug business was labor-intensive, filthy with risk, and merciless with competition. To keep down costs and liabilities, the Messina regime for the first time began going outside the organization to import help—temps. Now the streets swarmed with punks plucked like postmodern day-pool workers from the new urban ghettos of Palermo and Calabria. Instead of a bus, they rode to the job on a plane.

. . .

"Zips," Eugene called them. "They'll do anything you tell them, but you got to watch them every minute."

"Why 'zips'?" Rey asked. We were all sitting around the big shiny conference room table in the Special Prosecutor's Office. The table was polished like a boot-camp shoe. It was a nice contrast to the single dirty window with a bleary view of Foley Square looking like it hadn't been washed since La Guardia was in office.

"Zipperheads. They all got these scars." He drew a jagged line with a finger across his forehead.

"Does your uncle have a lot of these people working for him?" Noah leaned forward with his hands arranged flat on the table, a pose he must have learned at some assertiveness-training seminar.

"Shit no," said Eugene, chin thrust forward, teeth bared in a pose he'd learned on Allen Street.

Noah moved back and scribbled on his pad to cover the retreat. "Why not?"

"He don't trust them, naturally. My uncle has his own people, the old way."

This was Tony Rossi's secret of business success. While the new crew wallowed in fast money, Tony quietly supervised the family's unglamorous but dependable old rust-bucket businesses like loan-sharking, hijacking, price-fixing, small-business shakedowns, and illegal casinos. In a family of high-yield derivatives, Tony was a thirty-year Treasury note.

"So you're telling us that Tony is heavily involved in all of these illegal activities," Noah said, looking up from his clipboard.

"The old shit," Eugene said with a small note of protest.

Noah got pious. "It's illegal activities no matter how long they've been going on. You know that. Now let's get into all of the details you recall. Everything, no matter what."

Eugene caught me rolling my eyes. A small smile flickered on his face as Noah frowned darkly at his notes. We all settled in for a long afternoon.

When we had started these sessions, a regular team of eight prosecutors and detectives always attended, all puffed up like Macy's parade balloons. But now it was a shifting, lethargic crew, sometimes no more than four or five of us. Noah was always there, and so was I. Rey usually drifted out after an hour or so. The rest came and went with their notebooks and identical questions.

Eugene was obviously proud of his uncle. If you put together all the accumulated details Eugene tossed out, you got a pretty good understanding of how Tony's business worked. Essentially, Tony's territory encompassed most of lower Manhattan below Houston Street, including all of the rackets in Little Italy.

Besides counterfeiting, Tony supervised the old Giavanni interests in meatpacking and distribution, which was still a good business, but one becoming more difficult to control as the suburbs expanded outward and overextended the mob's supply lines beyond Manhattan and Brooklyn. Tony also ran downtown gambling and loan-sharking rack ets. These lines were still producing, but there wasn't a lot of growth potential in them, partly because of Atlantic City, which each month sucked out of

New York City many millions in disposable gambling money that otherwise would have gone to the family. The Chinese tongs were another factor. Chinatown was the blob devouring the Lower East Side. No one even had a guess at how many people lived there anymore, as the illegal immigrants poured in and disappeared into cellars and warehouses. There were even a few Chinese businesses now on the northern end of Mulberry Street, the mob's Champs-Élysées. The tongs were coalescing at the borders and pushing hard. Little Italy shrank into itself.

With Messina tied up in court month after month, the street crews were nervous, and even some of the capos were feeling the first creeping chill of panic. Was Messina going down? Few dared even say the words, and fewer still were stupid and impetuous enough to consider making a grab for power. Messina's gorillas monitored attitudes and sniffed for scents of disloyalty.

"What does your uncle think about Sally Messina?" Lieutenant Campo asked.

"I'll tell you the truth, but you didn't hear it from me."

"What?"

"An asshole."

"That's it?"

"That ain't enough? Why don't you try saying it to Messina's face?"

"Eugene, does your uncle think Sally Messina's on his way out?" Campo said.

Eugene seemed to give this some careful appraisal. "He don't say. He's a survivor—my uncle, that is. Messina, he ain't a survivor. That's the difference, if you want to know the truth about it."

"The truth is all we're interested in here, Mr. Rossi.

"Me too."

"Back to your uncle. You say he's on his way out?"

"My uncle? Yeah, he wants to retire."

"Retire?"

"That's what he says. He's putting his dough together, yeah."

"Like a pension?"

"You could say that."

"Early retirement, I take it. Not like a layoff? I mean, he's still in good standing with the boss, right?"

"That's right. Voluntary. When the time is right."

"And when will that be?"

"Soon, I guess."

"Guess better. This year?"

Eugene shrugged. "My guess? This year, right."

There were pig-snorts around the table. But as far as I was concerned, this was the only significant information Eugene had brought to us in all of these interminable interviews. I immediately saw the value in this knowledge. A middle-aged manager quietly planning early retirement, in an atmosphere of uncertainty and fear, not to mention resentment, is a man open to suggestion. He had money, but he would need more cash, maybe five hundred thousand dollars, and a promise of relocation. For the amount we were spending on this Eugene operation to nowhere, we just might be able to buy ourselves an informant who actually knew something. Maybe it was true. Maybe the road to Messina went directly through Tony.

. . .

I *knew Eugene's* time was limited, even if he didn't. In late June, I made my final preparations to pay a visit to Tony's business office, Nunziata's on Elizabeth Street.

With Noah, Campo, and Rey on board, the only dissent to my plan came from Eugene himself. He thought his uncle would see right through it. "No way!" Eugene scoffed, his eyes wide with derision at my audacity. "You think my uncle is stupid?"

"No, I don't think that at all."

"He'll make you for a cop in a second!"

"I got over on your friends, didn't I?" I reminded him. "I think I can get over on your uncle."

He mulled that over sourly and had to get in the last word. "Well, it's your funeral, lady. But take some advice from me. If you get to talk to him, don't pull none of that feminism crapola. He'll backhand you right out the door."

"He'll *what?*"

"Nothing personal, it's just business," Eugene said gruffly.

We were on our way downstairs, where Rey and Danny waited on a couch near the door. I said, "Eugene, would you stop using those lines from the *Godfather* movie?"

Overhearing, Rey jumped in with another *Godfather* line. " 'Leave the gun, take the cannolis.' "

Eugene called back, " 'If history has taught us anything, it's that you can kill anybody.' "

"Please cut it out," I implored them.

Instead, Eugene told me, " 'You give your loyalty to a Jew over your own blood?' "

"Knock it off!"

But Danny piped up. " 'I don't like your kind of people. I don't like to see you come out to this clean country in oily hair and dressed up in those silk suits and try to pass yourselves off as decent Americans.' "

"Danny, this isn't funny," I said, vaguely offended by the way he seemed to be addressing it to both me and Eugene. "Look, Danny—"

Eugene stopped me cold and said, " 'I've lost all the venom, all the juice of youth, all the lust for women. And now my mind is clear.' " He gave me a Brando look. "You ready?"

. . .

Before starting the job, I took home the files on Anthony "Black-jack" Rossi and his crew and spent a couple of hours memorizing faces and matching them to their various criminal exploits. Among the mug shots was an eight-by-ten surveillance photo of Tony on the sidewalk outside the Napoli Social Club, the storefront where Sally Messina liked to hold business meetings when he was making one of his rare state visits downtown.

Tony was in his early fifties, five-ten, barrel-chested, big and wide but not fat, with apparently unretouched jet-black hair and the same dark eyes that were the first feature that had struck me about his nephew. In an assembly of fairly unattractive characters like the members of the Giavanni organized-crime family—I mean, some of these guys would frighten you if you sat next to them in church, and even the supposedly dashing Sally Messina looked to me like the kid in junior high who blew his nose on his shirtsleeve and then smacked someone across the face with it—Tony stood out as ruggedly good-looking, with a face that could have belonged to a man on a horse.

Back in the sixties, he'd done a couple of years upstate for armed robbery, a hijacking; beyond that, his name often turned up on wiretaps in routine family discussions, but basically Tony had managed to keep himself out of major legal trouble as he rose up in the ranks under the tutelege of Jack Ponte. Tony had a bad temper, they said, but he was smart enough to keep it under control. He had a reputation as a ladies' man. Most of the time, he was a notorious cheapskate. But his idea of a big time was Atlantic City, where he was known to drop fifty large in a night, a high roller of such distinction that a half dozen casinos routinely comped him with expensive suites and other favors, some of them in tight dresses. Blackjack was his weakness. When Tony called and said he was headed to a casino, they'd clear a table and put the champagne on ice.

This was about the extent of my knowledge of the man I now intended to personally bust.

. . .

On a warm Monday morning, I made my first visit to look the place over. Nunziata's Pastry Shop was on the western border of Little Italy, a few blocks over from the district along Mulberry Street, from Hester to Prince, that had the biggest congregation of Italian restaurants, outdoor cafes, *gelaterias*, and storefront social clubs with religious statues in dim alcoves. In Nunziata's front window a ruffled cafe curtain hung from a brass pole, covering the view from the street and shielding the pastry counter from the afternoon sun that slanted over the tar roofs on the ancient five-and six-story brick tenements across the street. In front of the pastry counter were four tiny cafe tables with two wrought-iron chairs apiece. A ceiling fan with big wooden paddle blades slapped listlessly at the air, accenting the old-world shabbiness. Toward the rear, where the lighting was dimmer, the shop looked more like one of those neighborhood luncheonettes where the customers linger for hours over racing forms. Four booths stood on either side, defining an unmarked barrier. Occupying them from midmorning until late afternoon was a shifting population of raw characters, mostly men well into middle age who still referred to one another by preposterous nicknames—Tommy "Knuckles," Sal the Jeweler, Mickey "Little Caesar," Joey "Two-Toes," Charlie "Squeals," Frannie "Bang-Bang," Angel "Hot Oil" Mazzola— that would have been childishly amusing if you didn't realize that they tended to reflect felonious behavior, criminal menace, or physical injuries suffered as a consequence of both.

Each Tuesday, at booth number two on the left side, wedged between the table and a slab of dingy maroon Naugahyde, the bulky but still rugged Tony Rossi conducted his business like a monarch, receiving his diffident ministers with a slight bow of the head, dismissing them in turn with a word, a nod, an appreciative chuckle, a pregnant grunt, a hard nudge, a sharp rap on the arm that sent them scurrying back to dim booths, or outside, to do his bidding.

Technically, Nunziata's Pastry Shop was under the ownership of one of those courtiers, a fifty-six-year-old knee-breaker artist named Harry

"Balls" De Luca. He had inherited the shop from his late mother, Nunziata, who herself had inherited it from her third husband, who had been an apparently honest businessman. Balls renamed the shop in his mother's honor and hoped to maintain the business independently, as a monument to his immediate family's brush with legitimacy. Six months after his mother's death, however, a sudden requirement for cash caused by a poor run of luck in Atlantic City induced Balls to mortgage Nunziata's to a finance company owned, through the usual network of interlocking interests, by Tony Rossi and associates.

Balls had acquired his nickname not through a reputation for temerity, but through his preferred method of retribution—to smash victims in the head with a twisted pillowcase filled with five pounds of industrial ball-bearings. He had a great rounded face that protruded roughly in the same shape as his overhanging gut, but the most remarkable thing about him was his hair, painstakingly coaxed into a bouncy bed of tiny and unlikely auburn curls in a permanent he received each Monday morning at a beauty shop in Carroll Gardens, Brooklyn.

Since inheriting the pastry shop when his mother died five years earlier, Balls had begun to regard himself as a restaurateur rather than an enforcer. As time went by, he complained more bitterly about the clientele, sulking that his fellow Giavanni crew members never actually purchased anything at Nunziata's. Instead, the wiseguys chose whatever they wanted from the pastry counter, which was presided over by a dour old man who wore a white apron over a coal-black suit, starched white shirt, and skinny black tie that looked like it had come from an undertaker's spare closet. Every so often, in a spirit of fairness, the crew would dig into their pockets and pile enough money on the table to pay for what they had eaten, but to Balls it was the principle of the thing; the system deeply offended his sense of proprietorship. He never uttered a word of complaint on the afternoons when Tony was on hand.

Because the pastries it sold were excellent, Nunziata's did a robust business with the general public. The neighborhood people knew to buy their goodies and take them *right* home, or at most to sit for a few minutes at a front table and have a cannoli or a quick espresso, to "eat it and beat it," as they said. Occasionally, a tourist or two would wander in off the Mulberry Street path, nose buried in a guidebook, but no recordings of Jimmy Roselli crooning "Al di La" were playing here. Those who peered curiously in the back would get only glares from the hobgoblins in the gloom. Few tourists lingered for a second espresso.

. . .

Lingering was exactly what I had in mind. I thought I had come up with a good cover. Early on a hot and overcast July afternoon, I showed up at Nunziata's. A heavy gray sky pushed down on the city as if to squeeze humidity from the air, but the rain didn't come. I was glad to get inside the shop. It was twelve-thirty. Tony Rossi always arrived at one.

I took a seat at the cafe table closest to the area where the booths were. With only a nod, the old man ambled over and took my order for an espresso and a regular cannoli. My backups—two officers from the detail—were in an unmarked car just up the block, at the corner of Prince. To bring them running to me, all I had to do was tap a button on the beeper in my pocketbook. Also stashed in the pocketbook was my three-inch .38, and under it, my shield. I hoped I wouldn't need either.

A few heads had bobbed up at the booths when I came in and the doorbell jangled the alarm, but I evidently appeared to be dumb or innocent enough, and quiet murmuring resumed. Planning to stick around for an hour or more, I had put some blank accounting-book sheets in my briefcase. This way, I could pretend to do some work while eavesdropping and jotting down notes. I also had the Daily News, which I spread out on the table beside the espresso and cannoli. I was wearing an olive-green dress and a big gold-colored belt that I hadn't put on in years.

Right on time, Tony glided in like a medieval Florentine, accompanied by an entourage of three, two of whom resembled longshoremen dressed for a funeral. These I did not know. The third man I recognized as one of Tony's drivers, a skinny hoodlum named Joey "Two-Toes" Frattiano. He held the door while the heavies filed in behind the boss. With Tony's arrival, conversation stopped. Men rose from the dim booths to greet him. Several of them actually leaned toward him and kissed him on the cheek. He accepted the honors like a society dame receiving air kisses at a charity lunch.

"Sammy Red!" The great Tony's voice boomed at one of these underlings with gruff humor. "Where you been?" He stood with feet spread for the answer. Sammy replied in a nervous rush of words, "Well, Tone, you remember I got no driver since Fatty Falcone went up? You remember I told you that? I got to make the stops myself, you know."

"Didn't I tell you to get somebody? When did I tell you that? What, weeks ago?"

"Well, like you said, I finally got in touch with the guys you told me, and one of them, he tells me he has somebody lined up, but the guy never come to see me. He don't show, this guy. I got another guy coming, though. But I don't know what happened to the guy, Tone."

Tony's eyes swept the assembled faces like a lounge comedian. "What guys? How many guys you got there? Jesus, Sammy! Somebody get me a cup of coffee while I wait for you to count them the fuck up! What are you, some schmuck?" The boss heaved his bulk into a booth amid edgy laughter.

"I'll get it took care of, Tone," Sammy swore.

"After that, maybe I want you start driving for me," Tony suggested. Tony liked having a variety of drivers.

Sammy Red looked a little wary. "Sure, Tone. Anytime you say."

Hunched over my accounting forms, I made some notes, using my left hand as a shield. I felt slightly silly summarizing such trivia, but maybe it all would start adding up in time. I didn't know how to spell *schmuck*. A drop of cold sweat crawled down my arm.

Tony settled down to business with a demitasse that he merely stirred next to a bone-china plate holding a biscotti that he didn't seem to eat. I tried to keep my head down, not wanting to attract any extra attention. On shelves behind the cash register stood rows of bottles, Orzata syrup, red and blue liqueurs. Seeing the big silver-plated cappuccino machine on the side, I regretted ordering the tiny espresso, which was already gone. I nibbled at my cannoli to make it last. A nice Italian girl didn't order seconds.

As far as I knew, no one in back paid any attention to me once they had me figured for a harried office girl taking a long coffee break. I really couldn't make out much of what was being said, but I had studied the files well enough to be able to put names to a few of the men besides Tony and Balls DeLuca.

After about a half hour, the old man shuffled over with the check in his hand, but I wasn't ready to take the hint and beat it. Figuring if I was going to blow it, I might as well fail early, I directed my attention to the old man, but raised my voice so that it would be heard in the booths. My *Daily News* lay open to a regular column on the Mafia that ran every week. The column was written by a reporter who covered the New York Mafia the way a sportswriter covers the New York Yankees. New Yorkers with an interest in the mob turned to that column eagerly—cops, buffs, even the wiseguys who could read—looking for names, gossip, inside dope to handicap their personal conflicts.

"Isn't this unbelievable!" I said, speaking as loudly as I could without sounding like a big-mouthed *gavone*. I rattled the newspaper, and the old man froze in his tracks and began blinking nervously. In the back, the volume of the conversation went down as if someone turned a knob.

Not quite sure where this would lead, but certain of the effect I wanted, I plowed on. "This guy in the paper, that writes about Italians all the time? Every week, like a broken record, it's Sally Messina this, Sally Messina that, like he's some kind of a mass murderer or something—"

With my mention of the sacred name, all talk halted. I had their attention, though I still didn't know what I would do with it.

The old man couldn't escape back to his counter because I kept at him. "You know what I mean?" I said. "And this reporter is an Italian, too. What kind of nerve is that?" Now I looked directly toward the back, where eyes like owls blinked in the smoky dark. I appealed directly to the watchers.

"I'm sorry, these things just get me mad. I mean, there are criminals out on the streets raping and killing innocent people, and all this guy can find to write about is one of his own, who never hurt an innocent person. My own *mother* can't walk down her block for a loaf of bread without worrying about getting hit on the head for her pocketbook! One thing I know, if she lived in Sally Messina's neighborhood, she could walk the streets!"

Stunned silence wafted from the dim cavern like a cold fog. I pressed on. "You don't see the Jews or the blacks talking about their own like that in public. What is it with us Italians?" I waited a few seconds and said, as if suddenly embarrassed by my outburst, "I'm sorry. Excuse me. Sometimes I just get so upset."

With a fast darting move, the old man slapped the check on my table and scuttled away. But as I gathered my things to leave, a huge hand reached around me and snatched the check away.

"No check," said its owner, motioning with his slab of a head toward the back.

There I saw Uncle Tony looking straight at me. He tapped his brow in a small salute and turned back to the discussion in his booth. It made me nervous not to pay, so as I left I unobtrusively slipped a five-dollar bill on the table, $2.30 more than the check had been.

. . .

Coming only on the days when the uncle was there would have looked pretty suspicious, so I made a point to stop by Nunziata's two days later, and again the day after that. Each time, I ordered a cappuccino and went to work for a little while with my accounting sheets, or read my newspaper. About an hour and a half was all I felt comfortable doing, but I knew the routine was establishing me as something of a regular. When I came in, they all looked up, but I avoided eye contact with any of the men in the booths.

The next Tuesday, when Tony arrived at his usual time, he gave me a slight nod and settled with his back to me in the booth that was closest to my table. After a while, I decided to make conversation with him.

"If you want," I called to the back of his neck, "I'm done with the paper. You can have it."

Slowly, Tony shifted his body to look at me. "No thanks, hon. Too much crime in the paper."

The front-page headline was about a bad arson in an after-hours club in the Bronx. Two dozen bodies had been pulled out of the rubble, and the firemen said they expected to find many more. "That fire was terrible, though," I said.

"Ah, it was just a bunch of niggers and spics," called a voice from two booths down.

Tony stiffened and raised a hand as if to swat something away. "Hey! They're someone's children. Show a little respect."

"Sorry, Tone." It was Balls DeLuca, who had been sitting with Joey Two-Toes, handicapping the Met's home stand against the Phillies.

About ten minutes later, Tony again turned around. "So what do you do?"

I was ready with a story. "I'm an accountant. A glorified bookkeeper, actually. Self-employed since I got laid off in June." I gave him a small laugh to let him know I had no pretensions.

He nodded but kept his eyes right on me. "Tough times. So you work around here, keeping books?"

"I've been picking up a little work with small businesses, a few of the new shops over on First Avenue." This was a little chancy because the mob had long relationships in the neighborhood, but so many new businesses had been opening up on that part of town that I wasn't too worried. A lot of the newcomers were Chinese, who the mob wanted no part of, and Koreans, who the mob couldn't figure out enough to bother with yet.

"I've been trying to build up a business doing consulting. Accounting, paperwork—you know, help store owners or small restaurants stay out of trouble with the IRS, handle the city licenses and inspections bureau. Get them in compliance with the new recycling regulations, that sort of thing. There's a lot of red tape for a small businessman to worry about, especially the ones who don't speak English too well. But I'm really just getting started. I'm pretty good with spreadsheets, computers, you know? You don't know of anybody looking for a part-time accountant, do you?"

He let it pass. "Funny you should mention recycling. That's one of the lines that I'm planning to expand in. There's growth in that area, you know."

I moved my chair closer and said, "Interesting."

He was studying my face. "Computers, huh. You got one?"

"A laptop, yes. Not with me."

"Computers is important," he said.

"Is this a job offer?"

"We'll see. Maybe I got something somewheres."

He changed the subject after a minute. "You from around here?"

Even though every morning before I went to work, I jogged from my apartment in the Village down through Little Italy, I wasn't worried about any of them recognizing me. None of these guys were up at that hour.

"Brooklyn," I lied.

"Brooklyn where?"

"Greenpoint."

Tony shot me a look, as if to say I should know better than to live in a slum. Wiseguys study neighborhood real-estate values with true racist diligence.

"Your father lets you live in that neighborhood?" I caught a faint whiff of lime aftershave and cinnamon from him.

"I live with my father and mother there. They've been there since the late forties. They're elderly and they never wanted to leave the old neighborhood, you know, even when everybody else did. I help support them."

"That's a girl. What's your name?"

I figured this was as far as I should venture for now, so I got up to leave, dropping another five-dollar bill on the table. "Gerry Antonucci." Antonucci was my mother's maiden name.

Turning out of the booth toward me, he said, "Well, you be careful, okay, honey?" He lightly touched my upper arm.

I shot him my best "don't screw with me or I'll cry" look, pure Bensonhurst. "I always am."

On the street, I found the five in my jacket pocket.

. . .

Tony *was not* an educated man by any means, but he seemed smart. Like most such men, Tony sought certification more than approval, and lived with the consequences. His crew considered him to be funny when he wasn't angry and went to great lengths to avoid trouble with him. My guess was that, like most of his crew—I had a difficult time thinking of the men in the booths as "Giavanni family soldiers," the way those OCTF charts gravely listed them—Tony had made a stab at high school, and dropped out as soon as he had a better offer. Like everyone in that world, Tony said "don't" when he meant "doesn't," and "them" when it should have been "these." He was surrounded by dopes, but then, who isn't?

To steady myself psychologically as I tried to trespass farther each week onto an edge of their world, I avoided thinking of their criminal records and put from my mind the sudden violence that each one of them had proven himself capable of at one time or another. Instead, I tried to think of them as merely a scofflaw coffee-klatsch. To encourage conversation, I always brought the *Daily News* with me. Within a few weeks, Tony regularly joined me at my table for ten or twenty minutes out of his routine. He'd read the headlines, and we would make comments on the news. I noticed that he always made a point to scan the sports section in the back, which I suspected was only for show, to let me know he was a regular guy, since I never heard him discuss sports with any of the men.

I was amused to learn that Tony loved the opera. One time, after he had become comfortable talking with me, he confided that he always bought annual subscription tickets to the Metropolitan Opera. "Box seats, best in the house, same seats every year, a buck and a half a pop"— that is, a hundred and fifty dollars a ticket. He took his mother, who apparently was the only person he knew who was interested enough in opera to get dressed up and sit through four hours of it. One week when he joined me, he had the Sunday *New York Times*, which surprised me. "The freaking *Daily News* wouldn't write nothing about opera unless the broad actually got stabbed with a real knife on the stage," Tony explained glumly. He stared down at the *Times*, which he had opened to pull out the entertainment section.

"What's the matter, Tony?"

"The only time I read this paper is for an opera review, but that's it. I ain't going to pay them a buck and a half for this crap anymore."

"What'd they do?"

Impatiently, he pointed out a long feature article about the Metropolitan Opera. "This guy, this supposed opera critic, he says the Met has to stop putting on these tired old operas by Puccini and Verdi and find modern works to do, like *experimental* stuff. Can you believe that?"

Uneasily, since in truth I had never been to the opera myself, I skimmed over the article while he watched with a grimace on his face.

"Probably the guy has seen everything a dozen times," I ventured in a breezy tone.

"Yeah? Well, maybe we should repaint the Mona Lisa too, somebody's seen that so many times," he said sharply.

When I didn't reply, he turned in his seat and called back to the booth where his driver was keeping a watchful but discreet eye on us. Joey Two-Toes, I had read in the files, had gotten his nickname by accidentally shooting off the other three toes of one foot while trying to impress a girlfriend with his quick draw. That was five years earlier, during the waning hours of the annual barbecue, beer blast, and fireworks display that Sally Messina always threw for the entire neighborhood in Ozone Park.

"Maybe there's a reason they call it grand opera, ain't that right, Joey?"

"Fuckin' A," Joey said warily.

On my behalf, Tony brought him up, "Hey, watch your mouth."

"Sorry, Tone."

He relaxed. "Do you know 'Che Gelida Manina'? From *La Bohème*?" he asked me.

"No. I'm sorry."

"Sure you do. You're an Italian girl, you heard it a million times. It's a tune that makes you cry. You just don't recognize the words, honey."

Softly, yet in a confident and resonant tenor, he sang,

"Talor dal mio forziere
ruban tutti i gioielli
due ladri: gli occhi belli"

He sat back with a melancholy look I didn't expect. I didn't know what to say; I felt a flush of guilt, not only for being charmed, but for the injury I was preparing to do to this man. In his face, I could see how the boyish features had matured. I tried to think of him as a thug, a thief, a menace to society, a defiler of anything decent, but what I heard just then was music.

"You sing very beautifully, Tony."

"Nah. I'm no singer. That's what we pay fat boys like Pavarotti for." He flipped the paper onto an adjacent table and called back: "Ain't that right, Joey?"

Joey's eyes and nose peered over the back of the booth like one of those "Kilroy Was Here" cartoons. "You better believe it, Tone."

Tony winked at me and declared loudly to anyone within earshot, "Instead of the unspeakable beauty of grand opera, which is an art that you can see over and over and over until you freaking die, because every performance is a one-of-a-kind item, every performance is born new— instead of that eternal beauty, some newspaper schmuck wants every-body to go to the Metropolitan Opera House and pay a hundred dollars to watch a gang of fairies dancing around to drum music with their johnsons wagging in the breeze."

"Marone," said Joey.

"Not me," Tony vowed.

"Me neither," agreed Joey.

It was time to get back. I glanced at my watch, patted my briefcase and stood up. "I have an appointment, Tony. Hey, thanks for the song."

"Where are you going?"

"Back to work. I need to pay the check."

Tony blocked my way. "No check."

The old man watched from the pastry counter, next to the ancient mechanical cash register. I gestured toward him and said, "No, listen, this is how this man makes his living."

This got a big laugh out of Tony, who was gripping my elbow. "Him?" he chortled. "He's no owner! That's Sally's great uncle Thomaso, who came over from Sicily in 1947 and never went back." In a confidential manner, he added, "He still don't know more than twenty-five or thirty words of English, believe it or not. He's a *paisan*." He spat the word out.

"The man was a peasant in Sicily, Gerry, and he's a peasant here. You got to understand that some people are just born peasants, kid. The world is full of them, ready to do errands. Ha-ha! Listen, can you imagine being in this country—what, forty-two, forty-three years? And he don't speak more than"—he mimicked the old man with a high trill—" 'Gooda morning, boss! Okay, Tony!' A peasant, but a good heart, Gerry. There's family obligations here, of course. It's like, you got to feed him, you got to provide him a place to sleep, someplace to hang out all day. Basically, you make sure he don't get run over by a bus. And that's all there is to it." He smiled broadly at the old man, who hadn't moved.

"Ain't that right, Thomaso?"

"Okay, boss," the old man croaked.

This brought another guffaw from Tony. " 'Okay, boss'!" he repeated with delight. He made me put my wallet away. "God bless you, Thomaso," Tony said. He walked behind the counter to put his arm around the old man and pose with him as if I was going to take a picture.

I protested. "Really, I want to pay."

Tony let me know he didn't like saying things twice. There was a definite warning in his voice. "I said, no check, okay?"

"Okay," I replied quietly. "Thanks." As soon as I backed off, the charm came out again. "Thomaso, get the young lady some cannolis to take home to her mother and father in Greenpoint," Tony commanded. "Cannolis, Thomaso."

With a grin that showed broken teeth, Thomaso slid the door of the counter open. Inside was a wonderful array of chilled cannolis, plain and chocolate, anisette and almond, hard waffled cones filled with sweet ricotta, stacked on silver trays like little cords of firewood. Around them was a profusion of fancy Italian pastries: pyramids of biscotti, stockpiles of *zeppole* dusted with confectionery sugar, brightly glazed *frolli di uova*, heaped *mille foglie*. In the center was a plate of *zuccotti*, hollow puff pastries baked to rise like a cathedral dome, glazed and roofed with slivers of almond.

"No, thank you," I said to the old man. To Tony, I added, "No, thank you. Really, I'm fine."

Thomaso waited. Tony became very generous with Balls DeLuca's cakes. "Come on! What kind do your mother and father like?" Tony boomed. "Let's get a couple of dozen!"

There was no way out. "Chocolate?" I said tentatively. The old man carefully placed four chocolate cannolis in the white cardboard box.

"Two custard? The rest regular. No more than a dozen, though, okay? That's plenty. There's just the three of us."

When Thomaso had filled it and tied it up with green cotton string, Tony took the box and presented it like a Christmas gift. "Beautiful," he said.

"Thanks," I mumbled with embarrassment. "My folks will love this."

Out the door I went with the cannolis all done up in this box, feeling worse than a thief. I was in such a hurry to get away that I stumbled into a group of Chinese children in their parochial school uniforms following their teacher up the sidewalk on Lafayette Street. They scattered like tiny figurines tipped from a shelf.

CHAPTER 12

After leaving Nunziata's, my usual routine was to meet my backups and head back down to the OCTF headquarters on Foley Square. Inspector Marcomb and his staff supervised both investigations, ours and the one in Staten Island handling Eddie Mack, the Westies informant. We'd wait there for Eugene and Rey to roll in from the gym or wherever else they had been, usually around four o'clock. Then, most days, we would knock off for the afternoon. One of the guys would take Eugene back to Jersey.

Since our section of the OCTF was only a few blocks over from Nunziata's, I would have preferred to walk, but Inspector Marcomb insisted that I meet the backup car so no one would spot me headed for Foley Square. I couldn't quite fathom how ducking into a unmarked police car parked on Prince Street was supposed to be better, but I didn't want to argue with an inspector.

The first day I came back with the cannolis, Danny Flanagan was waiting behind the wheel of the backup car. Beside him was a sergeant named Phil Geryon, whom I had known when I worked in Midtown South and who had been assigned to the downtown OCTF detail only a couple of weeks earlier, mostly as a driver and backup. Phil was a big lumpy man in his late thirties, a mouth-breather with sagging cheeks and very tiny eyes. Danny and Phil liked to doze in the car, but this time they spotted me as soon as I turned the corner at Mott into the afternoon sun that puddled on the east side of the street. Like a pair of hound dogs, they spotted the bakery box I was carrying and didn't take their eyes off it even after I slid into the backseat. Phil's nostrils twitched; Danny looked anxious.

"What you got in the box?"

"The box?"

Phil reached back and plucked the twine like a guitar string.

I had to cover the box with both arms. "Jeez, Phil, look at you. You've got drool on your chin. It's a bunch of little pastries, for God's sake."

"What kind?" Phil said.

"Just some cannolis the guys in the pastry shop insisted that I take home for my parents. I had to take them or they would have thought something was wrong. But leave them alone! I have to get them up to the office and voucher them."

I might as well have been talking to the Chrysler Building, looming from midtown above the brick warehouses on Houston Street as if it was flipping the bird downtown.

Now that my partners understood that I held edible Mafia contraband, not evidence, they clawed at the box. It was like a backseat grope at a drive-in. I tried to hoist it out of their reach. They pulled the box apart from the sides. Phil came up grunting like a campground bear with a cannoli in one paw. The beautiful *zuccotto* that Thomaso had packed safely in the center tumbled onto the dirty floor mat and left a trail of powdered sugar down my sweater and black wool skirt. It plopped on the floor in a wet heap.

I managed to salvage the rest of the cannolis and get them back to the OCTF office, where my insistence that I voucher the baked goods created a lot of amusement. But the atmosphere soured fast when it became clear there weren't enough cannolis for everybody who tried to grab one.

Now, New York cops at this level make very good money. And I'm certain that you could not have bribed these guys with money. Yet they would have run down their grandmothers in the hall for a free piece of cake.

· · ·

Naturally, they expected me to come back with goodies every week I went to Nunziata's. By the third week, I was tired of having the confectionery sugar spill on my clothes when the free-for-all began, so I asked Thomaso not to give me any powdered ones. Back at the office, you'd have thought somebody robbed my colleagues at gunpoint.

Phil really got under my skin. "It's just like them wops to cheat customers on the fucking sugar."

"*Wop?*" I said, reddening.

"Not you. Them."

"Phil, excusing the fact that you sometimes talk like a cretin, you do understand that they *give* me the cannolis? For free, Phil."

"What, so they charge for the sugar?"

In a while, the guys at the office actually began putting in advance orders from one week to the next, as if I were going out to pick up sandwiches for lunch, written down on little pieces of paper. Week after week, Balls DeLuca's reluctant generosity yielded cannolis, which I dutifully carried back to the office on Foley Square. Each week, Uncle Tony grandly insisted that I take home more pastries than before—presumably not only for my parents but for their friends and neighbors on the block in Greenpoint. By my estimate, we were accelerating at the rate of about a half dozen a week, and I was soon leaving with two boxes. I tried switching to miniatures, but Thomaso still filled the boxes to the brim—which created more of a grab-fest back at the feeding trough.

One afternoon, Richie Connolly, a lieutenant I hardly knew, sidled up with the stub of a half-eaten cannoli wedged between his fat fingers like a stogie. "It's my daughter's birthday tomorrow, Gerry. Do you maybe think you could stop back there on your way home from work and see if they'll give you one of them *cassattas*? You know, the big tall cakes the Italians buy for weddings and christenings? You know, the ones with all the layers held up by little poles, with the cream-cheese icing? All the Italian bakeries have them. Can you do that? It don't matter if they already got something written on the cake, my wife, she can erase it with a knife and put on the 'Happy Birthday Nicole' herself."

The kind of cake he was talking about was an extravaganza that goes for about twenty dollars a layer. I was so stunned by his audacity that I couldn't manage anything better than, "Sorry, no, Lieutenant. I have to go straight out to Jersey tomorrow." He shuffled away, content that at least he had tried.

In my mind, the cannolis began to assume a psychic value far greater than the fifteen dollars a dozen they would have cost if we had paid for them. I fixated on the damn things, seething. One night I dreamed I was trapped in front of the counter at Nunziata's, crying bitterly, Tony's hand on my shoulder, while I hollered out orders for every kind of cannoli known. Thomaso scurried back and forth like the Sorcerer's

Apprentice, unfolding white cardboard bakery boxes, stacking them with the plump cannolis, tying them with green twine, piling them side by side in dizzy rows to the ceiling. And it was never enough! One after the other, police cars with flashing lights lurched to the curb in front of Nunziata's, and we ran to pile in the boxes, but no matter how many we staggered out with, more police cars came, and then officers on foot, a tossing sea of blue that surged around the block. My conscience brooded over the moral debt accumulated from these cannolis. Had I sold out to the mob for a box of pastries?

. . .

Meanwhile, *it was* clear to me I was accomplishing something. Tony obviously looked forward to spending time with me, and to tell the truth, I came to look forward to it myself, whether as a game or just a welcome break in the social routine, I wasn't sure. Tony was a talker, but his crew had heard all of the stories, so he welcomed a fresh listener. At first, I thought that he was spending so much time with me because business was slow, but then I realized that *talk* constitutes most of the business these guys do. The **action** only takes a little time. By the third week, Tony was sitting with me at my table and stayed until I decided to leave. It occurred to me, of course, that he was looking to score, but so far he had acted more like a gentleman than most of the men I knew.

I reminded him regularly that I was freelancing and always looking for accounting work. He didn't mention the computer again, though.

"Stick around," he told me. "Something'll come up."

Did I lead him on? Absolutely, but in an oddly old-fashioned way. I laughed at his jokes, but the fact was, the man was funny and knew it. Yes, I flirted a little. I lied like a thief, batted my eyes, fed his ego, gently led him into discussions about his business, and slithered home at night, feeling like a rat as I sat at my computer typing up notes.

As my fingers tapped at the keyboard, little jokes and snatches of observation that had passed between us in the afternoon became fixed in electric light. Once on paper, ready to be filed as DD-5's, the words looked alien, like ants on the table.

Never did I let myself dwell on the fact, obvious to anybody I worked with, that only a female cop could have gotten close to Tony, and only through a judicious use of sexuality along with whatever other investigative skills and diligence was brought to the table. Dark emotional swamps lay down that path, and I studiously avoided it. Even my assignment to work with Eugene had some of those elements, although in the case of Eugene it was clear, at least, that I had the power.

With Tony, I never knew. At times I wondered whether he wasn't playing the game himself, just to see where it went. Yet Tony behaved consistently in a manner than my parents would have considered appropriate for a man toward a woman. What could he have really thought of me, week after week? I always made it a point to be working on account sheets when he came in at his usual time, but I never acted as if he was intruding. When would he make the next move?

As it turned out, I had to make one first. This happened one Tuesday when two uniformed cops from the Fifth Precinct wandered into Nunziata's and almost blew my cover. One of them took a table near the door, where he straddled the chair haughtily, while the other went to the counter for coffee and pastries. They didn't seem familiar with the place, which was good. Their car was idling at the curb with its radio muttering, so they weren't planning on staying.

I was at my usual table with Tony. He watched the door, but his face showed nothing beyond casual interest. With a quick glance over my shoulder, I recognized the cop straddling the chair, a sergeant named Johnny Moran. We knew each other. He had once worked with Kevin. Kevin and I had even gone to dinner in Chinatown a couple of years ago with Johnny and his wife. I remembered them well because they both agreed that women—present company aside, they assured me— had no business being cops, and Kevin had let it pass.

It took about two seconds for Johnny to spot me, his buddy's girlfriend, with another man in a mob joint. Johnny clomped over for a better look while he did the math in his head.

"Hiya, Gerry," he said. The sentence had a question mark at the end of it.

Tony's face was impassive. Being on speaking terms with a cop was not something he had expected from me.

Flashing a smirk, Johnny launched an intervention on behalf of Kevin. If unfaithfulness was a crime in the state of New York, he'd have been reading me my Miranda. "Gerry! Gerry!" he woofed.

"Johnny," I said, grim.

"What's *up*, hon?"

The leer forced my hand. Quickly I leaned over to nuzzle Tony's shoulder with my cheek while I whispered in his ear, "Let me get rid of this moron." Tony was a block of marble.

Johnny tapped me on the shoulder, almost taunting. "How are you, Gerry? And how's Kevin?"

I decided to try one of the standard brush-offs a woman has to know in New York, one you'd use for a well-dressed creep annoying you on the subway. I hoped he'd be insulted enough to shut the hell up and just go away.

"Kevin is okay, Johnny. The last time I saw him." I barely looked in his direction. "Now, if you don't mind, I'm really busy, Johnny, and I don't have time to talk."

Triumphant, Johnny backed off, to my great relief. "So I see," he said. He was elated at having witnessed sin, which in a street cop's world is usually a lot more rewarding and considerably less troublesome than witnessing crime. He shot a look at Tony, who knew enough from experience with the Fifth Precinct to avoid eye contact with a punk. As if holstering a gun, Johnny turned his eyes to me and said, "Just give my best to *Kevin*."

I didn't reply. In a minute, the two cops grabbed their coffee in a paper bag at the counter, and banged out the door. My heart was still racing. I was trying to project anger instead of what I really felt, terror.

When the squad car pulled away, Tony had a quizzical look. "So who's Kevin?"

"Kevin's my brother."

"Your brother is involved with the cops?"

My mouth went dry. "My kid brother used to be a cop. He isn't one anymore." I pressed my lips tight.

"Come on, *was* a cop?" he said. "What happened there?"

"Tony, I don't want to talk about this." To my astonishment, there were tears in my eyes.

"Tell me," he said, laying a hand on mine. The gesture steadied my nerves.

The tears became soft sobs. "Look, he was a good cop, but he got jammed up. Let me put it this way, the NYPD did my brother wrong. He wouldn't talk about some things going on in his precinct. He protected his buddies and took the heat like a man. Please don't get me started on the police department, Tony. I hate them for destroying my brother's spirit. He's working as a night watchman at Macy's now, and he's not the same man." I couldn't believe how easily the lies could pile up.

"He wouldn't rat, you mean?" Tony asked.

"Yeah." I took out a tissue and blew my nose.

He patted the back of my hand. "That's good. That's good. There's nothing on God's green earth that's lower than a snitch. It's okay, Gerry."

"I despise them, Tony." It was getting late.

"They ain't worth the energy, honey."

"Thanks for understanding," I said.

Someone in the back shouted, "Hey, Tony. Phone!"

He got up. I kissed him lightly on the cheek and left.

. . .

That night, I was miserable as I sat at my computer doing the DD-5. I was a rat with a badge, and so far, not even a very good one. It had now been six weeks, and all I really had were disjointed scraps of information. In time, in the context of a criminal case, the sheer heft of these reports might be enough to tip the scale (along with the other slim handouts Eugene gave Rey), and get a judge to approve the wiretap. But I didn't relish the prospect of ever being cross-examined in court on the kind of stuff I was coming up with.

CASE NUMBER A-112

On the above date the undersigned officer was present at Nunziata's Pastry Shop, 223 Elizabeth Street, Manhattan, and the following information was revealed:

After preliminary discussions about the hot weather and music (opera), subject ANTHONY (aka ''BLACKJACK'') ROSSI, previously identified as a capo in the GIAVANNI organized-crime family, spoke informally but directly of subjects that the undersigned investigating officer believes are related to organized crime activities. On this date, subject ROSSI spoke openly about his contempt for ''new elements'' in the Mafia, whom he said were ''destroying everything for everybody'' with their greed and ''big mouths.'' While subject did not actually mention names, the undersigned, based on her knowledge of the subject, believes he was referring to SALVATORE MESSINA and others associated with the leadership of the GIAVANNI organized-crime family.

On this date, subject also did specifically discuss his admiration for the ''old ways'' employed by the ''Sicilians,'' (which the undersigned believed to be a reference to the Sicilian Mafia). He discussed news reports of the recent assassination of a judge near Palermo, Sicily. These reports had indicated a sophisticated infiltration of the Sicilian Prosecutor's Office by the mob. But subject said there was "nothing high-tech" about the commission of this crime, just "plain old hard work and dedication," which he said no longer can be found in America. Background information states that recent international news accounts of the assassination implied that the perpetrators had acted on information about the judge's activities gleaned from electronic surveillance. This was not the case, subject said, laughing loudly at this.

Subject's words to the undersigned on this topic were, "You know what they did? Six zips sat out in the cold rain for five nights waiting under a bridge for the judge's car to cross. They used binoculars. They had put a bomb the size of a refrigerator under a culvert on this road. They used only their walkie-talkies. The cops kept changing the route every day, but finally the judge's car had to cross over this bridge, and *ka-boom!*—they blew it up." A "zip," subject explained, is a low-ranking Sicilian mafioso.

Subject said that this bomb "killed the judge and caused the destruction of a section of the highway." Subject said, "When all is said and done there is nothing like a hundred pounds of dynamite." Subject then stated, "Court adjourned."

The undersigned did not pursue further details but believes the subject to be speaking from knowledge he obtained through personal contacts in organized crime. The "zips" did things the old way, but they at least "did them right," the subject concluded.

Toward the end of this conversation, two police officers from the Fifth Precinct entered the location, causing the undersigned concern about her identity being exposed, since the undersigned was personally acquainted with one of those officers, Police Officer Johnny Moran. To avoid detection, the undersigned pretended to be a close friend of the subject. P. O. Moran and his partner left without further discussion, and the undersigned has since contacted Officer Moran to advise him of this undercover assignment.

The conversation with the subject ended at approximately 2:30

P.M. on the above date. The next meeting with this subject is scheduled for August 15 at the same location.

Det. Gerry Conte
#423

Many of Tony's stories didn't make it into my reports, but stayed in my mind afterward.

"I was a teenager," he had told me one warm afternoon. "I was a pallbearer for an old lady that died down on Prince Street, a little thing that run a candy store, she was about as big as a broom. But jeez, hoisting that coffin out of the undertaker, it must have weighed three hundred pounds. There was six of us, all big guys, pallbearers, and man, I was afraid we was going to drop it down the steps and dump the old lady onto the steps of Our Lady of Pompeii. I says to my father, 'This is a very heavy coffin with one little old lady inside of it.'

" 'Maybe she ain't the only one inside of it,' he says.

"You can't do that no more. Now you want to get rid of something, you practically need one of them environmental implication statements."

. . .

Every week that I came back to Nunziata's, the group of men made a little more space for me. But except for a polite grunt in greeting, none of them ever spoke to me until two months had gone by, when I came in and exchanged a few words at the counter with one of the younger guys while I waited for my coffee.

Suddenly the guy stopped talking in midsentence and hurried to the back. When I looked around, Tony was glowering in the white glare of the doorway.

"Don't ever do that," he said in a cold and hard voice.

His attitude put me off and I decided to let him know it. "Excuse me?" I said pointedly.

"You come in here, you talk to me, understand. To me."

I decided to back off a little. "Listen, I was just—"

"That's the end of it," he declared, sweeping past me.

I bit my tongue and sulked. Fifteen minutes later, when he joined me, he was smiling.

"I like you," he said. "Get out your notebook."

"What for?"

"You're looking for work, maybe I have something."

"Okay." I took out a spiral-bound notebook.

"You know Italian ice?"

He was referring to the sherbetlike flavored ices that are sold in paper cones in *gelateria* and other shops. "Sure," I told him. "Why?"

"It's one of the businesses I got something to do with." He took my notebook and used a stubby pencil to jot down a name and phone number. "This guy runs the factory in Jersey," he said. "I want you to talk to him, tell him who you're with, get me a full breakdown of the production. How much of the stuff they make, seasonal. What flavors. And how much capacity they got to increase production."

"You mean like a production forecast?"

"Yeah. All we been paying attention to is the revenue, but I want to know about production schedules."

"I think I can do that. You thinking about expanding?"

"Something like that. I got an idea of expanding the business, down in Atlantic City."

"They don't have Italian ice down there already?"

"Yeah, but it's from Philly. They ain't got New York ices down there. Yet."

"Okay," I said, figuring that putting together a report like that would give me access into some of the family's business affairs. "When do you want it?"

"Next Tuesday, okay?"

"Fine."

He grinned. "You didn't ask me how much."

"How much what?"

"How much money I pay you for the job."

"I'm sure you'll be fair, Tony."

"We'll work something out," he said.

. . .

So I *was* in. The production report was easy—I called the man at the factory in Jersey and drove over on Thursday morning to tour the place and get the information, which was given to me in an attitude of profuse cooperation and deep respect. Cherry used to be the top flavor, now it was lemon. They had plenty of excess production and distribution capacity. I left with printouts of all the production schedules and delivery routes. At home, I used my computer to compile all the information neatly into a fifteen-page report, complete with charts. I fastened the report into a folder, like an elaborate term paper, and had it ready for Tony when he came in to Nunziata's the next Tuesday.

He scanned it, nodded, and handed it back to one of the men in the booths. "Beautiful," he said.

There was no mention of pay. To the contrary, from then on, it was apparent that Tony had now claimed me. Wiseguys are notorious for having girlfriends for various occasions—and for keeping each one separate, like a rack of silk shirts. Okay, I was ready to play this one out. That afternoon, he kissed me on the lips when I left.

. . .

Week by week, faithfully I compiled my DD-5's and faithfully took them to Lieutenant Campo, but I wasn't thrilled with the results. The Italian-ice factory seemed legitimate enough—it was one of those niche businesses that made no sense to operate any way but legally. And much of what Tony and I discussed could have come out of a business-management class, or even from one of those talk-radio programs where people drone on about financial affairs.

The man loved to lecture. He had opinions on everything. After a while, it occurred to me that Tony's problem, besides a lack of focus and a serious difficulty with follow-through, was that no one he knew was able to follow much of what he said, once he veered off the subject of criminal intent, which of course he never discussed with me. I gave it my best, but it was becoming more of a chore each week to summarize Tony's chains of thought.

He always signaled that he was prepared to lecture by shaking one of those gnarled black cigars out of a five-pack of flavored Avantis. Coiled in swirls of smoke and burnt anisette, he turned reflective.

"Look, you're smart. You got a good career ahead of you. You don't want to end up trying to make some crumb-bums happy at a corporation where you get two weeks' vacation and twelve bucks an hour, and then they'll throw you out on your behind when they got to . . . size down, they call it?"

"Downsize, right. There's no security left," I lamented.

"Sure there is. I'll tell you where some of the big money is going to be. All the security you need."

"Where?"

He blew a perfect smoke ring that the ceiling fan stirred to a thin gyre. "Something you said you already know a little about. Recycling."

"Really?"

"Just as one example, consider this: Every household and business in America is now being trained, *required* by law, usually—to become garbage sorters, doing *free work*, supposedly for the *environment.* Some places like down Florida, they even got inspectors come around, check your trash, fine you if you don't do it right. Amazing! So okay. New York City, everywhere else, recycling is mandatory. That's good! But what's the environment? Say you're in the hauling business. Say you own a lot of trucks. Your business is trash removal, carting, whatever you want to call it. Big, big business. Okay? The important thing is, you got the trucks, you already got the contacts with the municipals on the one side, you got contacts with the dumps on the other side.

"Now, the law says people got to recycle. There has *always* been a market in recycled material, glass, paper, steel, and aluminum—not so much plastic, but the rest of that stuff you can get money for. The problem was, it used to cost too much to separate it all out. Now all of a sudden, you got the citizens doing it for you! You got to look at this like a business. The citizens are working for free, and the haulers are charging extra to pick the stuff up—and making a profit selling it. Hooray for the freaking environment! You got the trucks, you got the contracts, you do all right, see?"

"I think so."

He blew another smoke ring and watched it fade. "You know how much there was in office-building construction in New York two years ago?"

"How much?"

"Two and a half billion dollars, with a *b*. You know how much there was last year?"

"No."

"Half of that. I read it in the paper."

"The boom's over."

"**That** boom is over."

I looked at him expectantly.

"Asbestos," he said.

"Asbestos?"

"You know how much trouble it is if they find asbestos in a school or a public building?"

"I guess they have to remove it?"

With a wink, he said, "You bet they do. Even though the stuff really ain't that dangerous, unless you basically stick it up your nose over a long time. There's a whole industry built around scaring people about asbestos—the newspapers and TV, they love asbestos scares, like it's goddamn radiation or something—and then removing it. You got guys working in an old building like a city school, maybe some asbestos gets exposed. Right away, it's a goddamn emergency! You know how much money the asbestos-removal industry is worth a year?"

"How much?" I asked.

"Four billion bucks a year."

"Wow."

"A smart company with access to buildings—that's a big racket. Legal, too."

"You in that business, too?"

He shook his head without commitment and kept the discussion away from specifics about himself. Leaning toward me he continued. "I'm going to tell you something else. You know the medical waste that washed up on the beaches five or six summers ago?"

It had been a big story. Week after week, beaches on the coasts of Long Island and New Jersey were shut down because bags of hideous medical debris—dirty needles, grotesque bloody gauze, apparently from municipal trash dumped far out at sea—bobbed in with the tide and washed up on the beaches. And then suddenly, after the headlines, it stopped.

"You don't think that was accidental, do you?" said Tony.

"What do you mean?"

"Well, I ain't talking out of school or nothing, but maybe them dirty needles got pushed overboard off of boats to make a point, you know? Maybe a business that collects trash had a reason to join up with a nature group, some 'Hug the Dolphins' people, to kind of get the public to pay attention to its environment and shit like AIDS."

"You're saying the medical waste as deliberately dumped to make a point?"

He rapped the table with the knuckles of his right hand. "I'm talking business strategies for the modern world, is all. Recycling! Waste! Clean water! Opportunities everywhere! You want a totally different example? The modern-art market. You would be very surprised at how much money moves through them snotty Manhattan art galleries—and it ain't all going to the losers that paint them crappy pictures. Millions and millions of dollars gets shifted around every week in that market. Nobody can tell who's really paying for what and buying what, and where it's going—"

"Drugs?" I prompted.

He acknowledged some familiarity with the subject. "Okay, you take the heroin business, dirty business that it is for sure. But listen to me, the way that business is, is it ain't like you see in the movies." He chuckled. "Screw the movies! The French Connection, the Pizza Connection, the stuff supposed to be coming into the U.S. from Europe? That's from the days of the Wild West! Ancient history! It's amazing what people believe." He leaned closer.

"Now, I know some people who follow this terrible industry as a matter of sad interest. Truth is, Gerry, is that the business goes the *other* way now. That's what's got some of these people tied up in knots. They can't adapt." His tone became insistent. "Nothing moves out of Italy or Marsalays, or whatever the fuck it's called. *Nothing!* It goes the other way. A lot of it comes up from South America, *into* New York, and then *batta-bing*, off to Rome, where the street price is about three times better, or to Paris or Milan. Strictly export." He nodded solemnly, paused and watched to see if I was following.

"Economics, pure and simple, Gerry. You know who runs the domestic heroin business these days, Gerry? *The Chinks!* Chinatown gangs, which are some of the most dangerous and vicious people on God's green earth! Jesus, they'd stick a knife in your eyeball for a nickel deposit on a bottle of Pepsi. They're handling junk from Asia—Burma mostly—that's so pure, ninety percent pure, that the *schvartzes* can snort the stuff! No need for needles. The Chinks have squeezed the Americans out of the market. *Except* for the export business to Italy and places like that. It's a free-for-all."

He snapped his fingers briskly. "Hey, that's business! The global economy! The old ways are no longer useful. You know that, I know that." He looked sadly back toward his crew nodding over their coffee cups and ashtrays and waiting sullenly for him to rejoin them. "These guys, do they know that? What, you think they know anything like that? These guys, they watch movies to get ideas on how to scratch their behinds. That's all they know. Am I right, Joey?"

Back in his booth, Joey Two-Toes halted a desultory conversation. His face turned toward us with a worried look. "I'm sorry, what's that, Tone?"

"Too many movies, ain't that right, Joey?"

Joey considered it for a moment and then nodded. "Fuckin' A, Tone. I mean, right."

"You see what I mean, Gerry?" Tony said with a grimace. "That's why I like to talk to somebody with a brain who understands how the global economy operates. Who knows what's going on and doesn't have pipe dreams about no ancient history. The law of supply and demand! *There is no such thing as a free lunch!* Attila the Hun, there was a guy knew the score. That applies to every industry, every industry in God's free world."

Tony cleared his throat and fell silent, and spent. His eyes were fixed at some invisible spot in the room, perhaps scanning imaginary stock quotes.

Then, like a dope, I blurted out, "What's the main business you're in?"

Suspicion clouded on his well-tanned face. I slowly crossed my legs, letting my skirt ride up enough to put something else on his mind. It worked. He lit another gnarly cigar and tapped a manicured index finger on the table.

"You're good with numbers, right?"

"Sure, pretty good."

"Yeah, I seen that. The kind of work I do, it's complicated, with many facets." He began counting facets off on his fingertips: "You got your consumer credit. You got your restaurant and entertainment industry, supply and personnel, way beyond your Italian ice. You got labor-union organizing. You got investments and collections. And always, always, always, you got employees, all of them constantly yanking on your sleeve wanting something. The truth is, I need professional accounting assistance. I can't keep up myself anymore. Somebody's good with computers, that kind of stuff."

More confidentially, he said, "You see—and this is between you and me, okay—I have a plan for restructuring the business."

"That's what everybody's doing."

He nodded. "Within two years, if God is willing, I want to be up to around eighty percent—higher if possible."

"Eighty percent what?"

He meant *legitimate*, I supposed, but he caught himself. "Put it another way, technicalities aside. Any older business needs restructuring, sizing down. It's got to be lean and efficient, ready to jump on new markets. Maybe we even got to relocate, go somewhere with new opportunities, better positioning."

I started to ask a question but he cut me off with a wave of his hand. "I am aware of the need for change, like they say. You look back there, what do you see? A bunch of men's faces, most of them in their forties, is what! A great crew, but maybe we should be seeing some women's faces back there too, you know? The old days are gone. Mostly, they stank anyway, to tell you the truth."

I pretended to consider what he said carefully. This was the kind of opening I'd been working toward, but it couldn't be rushed. Let him ramble, week after week. Here and there, he would let things drop.

"Well, Tony," I said tentatively, "I'm always looking for work. I'm ambitious and smart. And as I said, things have been very slow for me since I got laid off, but I've been picking up enough freelance work to get by. I wouldn't be interested in anything full-time."

"Well, that's okay. You want to discuss this over dinner?"

Was this the move? I maintained a small smile. "Yeah, I guess. Sure, why not?"

Tony raised his eyes to the ceiling, as if that's where he kept his calendar. "Thursday night?"

"Thursday?" I had law classes on Thursday nights, and finals were coming in three weeks. But I'd manage. "Yeah. Thursday's fine."

"Good!" he said. "There's a terrific place down on Carmine Street where they know how to treat people right. Bella Rosa, it's called."

"I know the place," I said. Mob city. "How about if I meet you there?" I wanted to head off any offer to pick me up at home in his damn limousine. "I'm working late Thursday, so I'll be in the neighborhood at dinnertime."

"Make it eight o'clock," Tony said. "I want to introduce you to a friend of mine."

"Oh yeah? Who?"

"You know Mr. Messina? Salvatore Messina?"

I said I thought I'd heard the name.

. . .

Incredibly, the NYPD told me it had a prior engagement that night. That Thursday happened to be the second payday of the month, when the overtime pay shows up. Cops who cash their checks on the job have a little extra pocket money that their wives don't necessarily know about. So the second Thursday is traditionally social night, a big occasion for what is called working the "four-to-four shift"—start work at four o'clock in the afternoon, go off-duty at midnight, and then commence "bouncing"—hopping from bar to bar—till around four in the morning. For some cops, this is a liturgical feast day on the calendar.

It would have been out of the question for me to meet Tony at the restaurant—not to mention meet the biggest *goomba* of them all—without adequate backup. And it turned out that everybody in the unit who should have been available had something else to do.

I appealed to Inspector Marcomb.

"*This* Thursday?" he asked dubiously. "That's pretty short notice, Conte. I'll see what I can do, but don't get your hopes up."

He could have just ordered two officers to work backup for me, but he didn't. Everybody came up with an excuse. One guy had to take his wife to the doctor. Two of them had a bowling-team championship. Another said his kid was trying out for intermediate midget football in Mineola.

"At night?" I demanded.

"Lights," he explained.

Inspector Marcomb acted like it was my own fault for not giving them more notice. "We don't have anybody in this squad to cover you," he told me. "So just tell this guy Rossi that something unexpected came up, you got to do it another time."

"Inspector, this could be a major break."

"That can't be helped," he said.

Which should have been my cue right there about the brass's real commitment to this particular investigation—and to my place in it. I'd run the numbers in my head. With salary for our unit of officers, with OT and expenses to set up and run the Jersey site, not to mention costs for the care and feeding of our "Confidential Informant" and so on, we had probably already spent an easy million dollars on this investigation. And now I was hearing: Fine, spend the taxpayers' money, risk your neck, use all of your skills as a detective, miss your law classes that you'll have to spend days making up for, but *don't screw with the work schedule.*

Vainly I protested. "Inspector, I'm getting over on this guy. But I can't brush off an underboss! I mean, where are our priorities here?"

Marcomb didn't much like to be challenged. "*I'll* worry about priorities, Conte. And here's one for you: Tomorrow morning, you go down to that joint and leave a message that you can't make it Thursday. It's very simple. Say your mother's deathly sick. You can't expect every situation to be tailored to fit your personal schedule. And let me give you some advice while we're on the subject." He gave me a doleful look over his bifocals. "Don't get so goddamn emotionally involved with these wiseguys, okay?"

What could I say to that? I went home, had a small pizza delivered, and spent about twenty minutes tapping listlessly at the computer. There wasn't any e-mail. Kevin hadn't bothered to leave a note saying when he would be in. Screw it, I thought, and went to bed without touching the pizza.

. . .

The next morning, with a couple of regularly scheduled officers providing backup in the car, I dragged myself into Nunziata's. Thomaso was wiping the counter and there was no one sitting in the booths. I didn't see much point in leaving a message with a man who only knew twenty-five words of English. So I got a coffee and waited. In a half hour, three members of Tony's crew came in, acknowledged me cordially, but marched straight back to their usual booths.

. . .

The flunky I remembered as Sammy Red seemed to have seniority, so I went back to talk to him. They looked aghast that I'd stepped over the invisible wall. "Listen, can you do me a favor? I need to get a message to Tony."

Red had a stricken expression on his face. "Miss, I think you have to see Tony personal," he said. His lips barely moved when he talked, like an amateur ventriloquist. His two companions glanced around as if they'd never seen the wallpaper before.

Hating myself for it, I burbled a new lie. "I'm supposed to meet Tony for dinner tomorrow night, but my mother is extremely sick. She has lung cancer, and we had to put her in the hospital." That could have been a mistake, I realized quickly. Tony was the sort who would send flowers. So I backpedaled.

"She's home now, but she needs a lot of attention. I'm really sorry, but it's an emergency. Can you please get a message to Tony and tell him I can't make dinner?" Uttering this, I felt horribly certain that God was going give my mother cancer to punish me for the cheap way I'd used her name.

Red brimmed with empathy. "Okay, miss," he said. "I'm very sorry as to your mother. I know how that is, a mother. I'll get ahold of Tony. We all know that family comes first. If you don't have family, you don't have nothing."

This made me feel even more despicable. I mumbled thanks and got out of there. When I got to the car, my partners were fuming. Behind the steering wheel, Phil Geryon acted like I'd been shopping. "Where the fuck were you, Gerry? You knew we had a lot of things to do today!"

"I had to wait for the crew to get there. These guys don't keep regular business hours, you know. What was I supposed to do—call you from the pay phone?"

"You just go in there and bullshit with those assholes?" he muttered. "You're getting too close to these ghetto guineas."

"As I recall, that's the idea. . . . This is totally incredible!" I exclaimed. "I must be nuts to keep doing this."

Phil had something else on his mind. "Where's the pastry?" he demanded.

"I threw it in a trash can," I said, to annoy him.

. . .

I *called in* sick on Friday and was planning to call in sick again on Monday and Tuesday. I just didn't have the will. I dreaded having to go see Tony again. I wasn't even sure I could remember the details of the lies I'd told. But that Friday night I was eating Chinese takeout alone at home when the doorbell rang.

It was Rey, who had been away for two days working on something with Eugene. I buzzed him up.

"You alone?" he asked when I let him in.

"As usual. Kevin's disappeared. Working, I guess."

"You okay?"

"Sure. You want some coffee?"

"You got mineral water?"

I shook my head. "Sorry."

"Never mind," he said. "I just wanted to tell you, so we keep our signals straight: We're moving on the uncle." He stood there looking very pleased with himself.

"What do you mean? I've been with the uncle. What's going on, Rey?"

"It's beautiful! Eugene finally came through for us."

"What?" I said uneasily.

"We got it set up. It's magnificent. Eugene finally calls the uncle, tells him he's back in town, ready to get back to work. He has a guy he wants the uncle to meet, a renegade dealer from Cuba with connections, who's looking to unload a shitload of pure cocaine."

Apparently I had succeeded in lighting a fire under both Eugene and Rey. But now things appeared to be moving in a direction I hadn't anticipated. I felt left out once again. "Who's the dealer?" I asked.

He smiled broadly and bowed. "Me."

"Get out of here! You're a Cuban?"

He snapped his fingers and flexed. "I am now, *mida*. What do these guys know?—Puerto Rican, Cuban, Colombian, we all look alike to them. The uncle's being careful, of course. You know how cagey the guy is. He's hard up for cash, but the guy's been around the track a long time. He's no dope. So we start thinking: How do we get the uncle into a controlled situation where we can start working on his ass? We know three important things about the guy, right?"

"Which are?"

"One, he needs dough."

"No doubt about that."

"Two, he's a casino junkie, loves to gamble."

"So I hear."

"And three, he's the cheapest son of a bitch in New York."

"So?"

"So we're taking him to Atlantic City!"

I didn't say anything for a minute. Then I asked, "The two of you?"

"Sure."

"How're you going to manage that?"

"He was invited and he accepted."

"I don't get it."

"Listen to me. You won't believe this, but Eugene just came back from Uncle Tony's house over in Staten Island. He went to see him personally. Wired."

I was astonished. "He went to Tony Rossi's house wearing a wire? You're right, I don't believe it."

"It's true. While you've been softening up the uncle, I've been riding Eugene, hard. He finally worked up the balls to go to the uncle. I'm proud of the son of a bitch."

"What happened?"

"What happened is the uncle went for the initial bait. Eugene gives him this song and dance, it's beautiful. I'll play the tape for you on Monday. He tells him he got this good personal connection that represents a new Cuban operation that wants to start doing business downtown. Eugene says the guy wants to get acquainted, and to do so, the guy's offering a night in A.C., all expenses paid. Just to get acquainted."

"Tony went for that?"

"Yep."

"You're taking him to A.C.?"

"Me and Eugene. A night on the town, courtesy of the NYPD. Maybe we do a little business. If not then, then afterwards."

"You'll be wired?"

"Not me, babe. Eugene."

"Jesus."

He was in a rush. "I'll fill you in next week. Don't say anything about it, okay? You planning to see Tony next week?"

Now I really felt sick. "Tuesday, as usual. I've been working this guy pretty good."

"Yeah. Well, don't say nothing. You be cool, okay? Feeling any better?"

"Fine," I lied.

"I have to meet Eugene at some joint downtown. Now that he's back in the social whirl, it's going to be a long night on the town. So I'll see you when I see you."

"Sure," I said.

I walked him to the elevator, trying to hide my resentment at his attitude that the big boys were taking over. All weekend I stewed over it. By Monday, I had decided to do something about it.

. . .

On *Tuesday I* had to spend the morning downtown filing my DD-5, which was late. The effort seemed useless; I was just going through the motions. Rey, meanwhile, was busy setting himself up in a luxury suite at a luxury hotel on 56th Street to play the part of a Cuban dealer looking to do big business, just in case anybody wanted to check him out. Eugene was staying in Jersey, so I didn't see him, either.

That afternoon, when I met Tony as usual at Nunziata's, I had gotten over feeling sorry for myself. Tony seemed distracted, but I managed to turn the conversation to Atlantic City and his Italian-ice business long enough to get what I wanted.

Afterward I drove all the way out to Jersey to confer briefly with Lieutenant Campo and get his okay on what I had in mind. Then I went upstairs to see Eugene.

There was a note pinned to his bedroom door: "Don't *wake me up. My mussels are growing.*" Seeing any kind of written note, misspelled or not, should have been gratifying, after all the work I had put in trying to bring his writing up to eighth-grade level. Clearly he was getting there, at least from what I knew about contemporary eighth-grade standards. But I wasn't playing teacher now. Annoyed that he would be taking a nap at this hour of the afternoon, I ripped the note off the door and went in without knocking.

Eugene was doing one-handed push-ups on the rug—stark naked.

"Yo!" he said, struggling to his feet. He stood facing me.

Rey had been working on muscle definition with him at the gym, with evident success. Eugene smiled broadly, displaying himself with obvious delight. For a second I let my eyes race over his well-defined body, but quickly caught myself and looked him in the eye.

I turned my head and, in the hall behind me, I caught a glimpse of Phil Geryon and Colleen coming up the steps. They both turned around abruptly and hurried back down.

I was angry and humiliated, but it was my own fault for barging in. "Put something on. Aren't you embarrassed?" I told Eugene.

He took a step in my direction. "Why should I be embarrassed, with a body like this?" he taunted me. "Close the door, I'm getting a draft."

I left it open. He pulled on a pair of tight bikini underwear and walked toward me with those muscles rippling.

"Real men *do not* wear underwear like that!"

"Here we go, you telling me what a real man does and don't do, Miss Crabtree." That was what he had started calling me during our informal reading lessons, after the teacher in the old "Our Gang" comedies.

I grabbed his terrycloth robe from a hook on the door and tossed it at him like I was trying to put out a fire.

"Okay," he said, laughing. "What the fuck do you want, anyway?"

I waited until the robe was on. He looked like a boxer. Then I told him. "I hear you and Uncle Tony are going to Atlantic City with Rey."

"Yeah, so what?"

"So tell me about it."

"Why don't you ask your partner Rey?"

"Listen, dammit, stop screwing around. You really arranged this?"

"Sure."

"By yourself?"

He smiled. "Of course. I told you I was going to deliver. Now we're getting somewheres, right? Ain't you proud of me?"

"Ecstatic," I mumbled. "Frankly, Eugene, I'm surprised. I didn't know you had it in you." I faced the doorway to leave but then turned back. "Oh, incidentally, I forgot to tell you—"

"Tell me what?"

"I'm going to Atlantic City with you guys."

"In your dreams," he snorted.

"Oh yeah? In your uncle's dreams, buddy, because I told him just today how much I love A.C. And do you know what? He's got some business down there he wants me to check out. So he invited me to come along."

CHAPTER 13

Rey *was actually* pleased to hear that I had horned my way in on the Atlantic City sting. For a minute, I thought he was going to pat me on the behind, but he caught himself. "Way to go," he said, knuckling me on the arm instead.

"You don't have a problem with it?" I asked, pleasantly surprised.

"With what?"

"With me coming along."

"Hell no," he said. "I'm glad to have the backup. Plus, with you coming along, the uncle pays a little less attention to me, a Puerto Rican trying to get over as a Cuban. Let me ask you something. How did you do it?"

"How'd I get myself invited?"

"Yeah. I mean, you're not letting this guy think he's going to score with you, are you?"

"What, now you're looking out for my virtue, buddy? Truthfully, I don't believe I'm his type, even if he does have some general ideas. Basically, this is a one-shot accounting job for him, at least so he says. He's been going on for weeks about muscling into some small-time business in A.C."

"What kind of business?"

"Italian ices."

"That thing you looked into for him at some ice-cream factory in Jersey a couple of weeks ago?"

"How'd you know about that?"

"I keep in touch with the big picture on this investigation," he said. "You should too."

If that was a shot, I let it go. "Well, when the uncle mentioned he was going to A.C. on some lark, he mentioned that I could maybe follow up on the Italian ice thing, check out the market there for him."

"The guy's always into something, I'll say that for him. It's amazing how many angles these characters play."

"Think if they put all the effort to good deeds, like us."

"They'd get no money and no respect, like us," he said. "The uncle, he really likes you?"

"Yeah, I think so."

"You like the guy? I mean, aside from the fact that he's a scumbag criminal?"

"Actually, he makes me laugh."

"What's he expecting in return for your attention?"

"I haven't given this guy any ideas about sex, if that's what you mean, and I resent the implication."

"Christ! Why are you so combative? Lighten up!"

"I mean it. As a woman, I—"

"Calm down. As to sex, this guy isn't going to be worried about you, even if he thinks so right now. The guy is a gambling junkie, maybe one of them addicts that you hear about, if there is such a thing. Once he gets to the tables with his stake, the last thing on his mind is getting laid. He'll keep going all night, all right, but not in bed, babe."

"Right."

"Fill me in on the business he wants you to do, so I know what's going on. Eugene and I already got our end worked out."

I had to laugh. "I told you, the *Italian-ice* concessions for the board-walk. The Giavannis already have the restaurant unions, cigarette and condom machines, and a lot of supply businesses, most of which they grabbed from what's left of the Philadelphia mob. Apparently, Tony now wants to expand into flavored ices."

"Sno-Kones?" Rey said in wonder. "Jesus, can you imagine somebody like Sally Messina getting his mob involved in that kind of low-rent shit, selling Sno-Kones on the A.C. boardwalk?"

"Hey, it's not Sno-Kones, it's Italian ices, a much finer culinary product, closer to sherbet. Besides, these hotshots like Messina are driving the mob right into the ground, looking down their noses at these kinds of bread-and-butter businesses."

Sounding a little like Tony, I added, "The potential in Italian ices in

A.C. is forty, fifty thousand a week—for a product that costs twenty cents a gallon to produce and distribute and sells retail at the rate of ten dollars a gallon when you break it down into those little cups. It's a very neglected market since the casinos came in. Of course, Italian ice isn't as glamorous as cocaine—"

"Yeah, you don't want to be sticking no Italian ice up your nose."

"—but it does have the advantage of being a legal product."

"Assuming you don't break somebody's legs to get into the market."

"Correct."

"Fascinating," Rey replied blandly. "And you're supposed to see a guy about this business for Uncle Tony?"

"Yeah, some guy he already has lined up in A.C. that used to work for the Philly mob before they fell on hard times. All I'm supposed to do is check over his books, review the Labor Day revenues. Tony just wants some of the basic numbers about demand, deliveries, that sort of stuff. The guy's supposed to have it ready for me."

"Who's the guy?"

"Some guy working out of a construction trailer behind Convention Hall. It shouldn't take me more than an hour while we're there. Then I'll come back to where you guys are set up."

"There'll be no rush," said Rey. "We're going to try to keep Tony at the tables as long as possible, all night if we can. I want him to stay occupied."

"Why?"

"To make him happy. Let him know I'm there to kiss his ass. It's part of the code for these guys before they'll do business."

"What if he loses?"

"So he drops a bundle. It ain't his money. The department is paying, of course."

Inspector Marcomb came in with a long face. We were talking in a private conference room where Rey had been reviewing a surveillance tape when I arrived. It was the recording that Eugene had made the week before at Tony's house. Marcomb sat down and made himself comfortable. "Let me hear the tape," he said.

"The whole thing?" Rey asked.

"Shit no! Just the part where he goes for the deal. So I can sign off on this stunt."

"You mind if I stay?" I asked.

"Detective Conte is going, too," Rey told him. "For backup."

"Campo okay with that?"

"Yes, sir."

"I'm not approving another goddamn cent of expenses for any extra personnel," Marcomb said peevishly. "This is getting ridiculous, what with what we got to show so far."

"Yes sir," said Rey. He was rewinding the tape to a place he'd cued. When he found it, he said, "Like I told you, this is where our CI went out to his uncle's house in Staten Island. You ready?"

Marcomb nodded, but he wasn't happy. Rey hit the button and Tony's voice grumbled thickly from the cassette recorder on the table.

"You want me to see some goddamn Cuban? Why the fuck would I want to do that, Eugene, unless he wants to give me some cigars? I can see all the Cubans I want down Miami, where they own the fucking place. Ain't I got enough shit on my mind already? Huh? You come back from Florida after your nice long vacation from the business, and then nobody sees your face for months. Suddenly, here you are again, hot to trot. I don't know what the fuck you're doing, where you been, and now all of a sudden you want me to go to A.C. with some goddamn Cuban you met in a whorehouse?"

With a steady self-assurance that I didn't expect, Eugene was explaining, apparently for the second time, how he had become good friends in Boca with a Cuban whose name was "Reynaldo." Eugene described Reynaldo as the American agent for a new and well-financed drug operation that was operating as an independent out of Cuba, deeply clandestine, totally divorced from the powerful Colombian Medellin cartel who had most of the cocaine distribution sewn up. Reynaldo had recently come to New York by way of Mexico City, looked up his good friend Eugene, and asked him if he could introduce him to people who wanted to "do business." Eugene told Uncle Tony he was the first person he thought of.

Eugene went on: "The guy is offering us a night in A.C., all expenses paid, which I know how much you enjoy. All expenses paid, Uncle Tony. All he wants is for you to get to know him, maybe later listen to some business ideas when you're ready to, *if* you're ready to. It's like a courtesy call."

Tony grumbled. "I don't like the sound of going nowhere with no worthless Cuban."

"This guy lives for pussy and money, and he manages to get plenty of both, Uncle Tony. He can do business here. Believe me, I checked this operation out when I was down in Florida. I checked very careful and it's the real deal. Nobody pays no attention at all to Cuba, it's so cut off. These guys really have a new pipeline, and they undercut the fucking Colombians. They want to expand. This would be like getting in on the ground floor. What could it hurt to just meet the guy? You talk later, only if you want. Besides, you been working too hard. A.C. would be good for you. I worry about you, you know."

"But you know I don't like fucking with macaroni! Drugs is nothing but trouble. How many times I warned you about that?"

"This won't be any risk, because everything's all squared away. Nobody we know gets their nose out of joint, because this operation is totally new. Nobody but us knows anything about it. It's serious money, fast and safe, and it don't leave no tracks uptown, you know what I mean."

"You don't talk about uptown. Ever."

"Okay, but none of the usual crapola. They just want to move something in and get the lines open, you know. Sometimes you got to do what you got to do."

Eugene's voice dropped. "Please, Uncle Tony. Please do this with me. I don't have the juice to do it myself. You got the clout. Just meet this guy. What's to lose? Did I ever steer you wrong? Didn't I do good running your clubs down Florida?"

"You done good, till you quit on me."

"Really, this deal—everybody wins, no downside. All Reynaldo wants is to meet you so you can look him in the eye, look him over, you see what you see, and then go from there. It's like, just social. We have a great time in A.C., and he pays."

"You know the guy good?"

"Very good. He saved my life down in Boca."

"I never did get the story of what the fuck happened to you down there. But now that you want to get back to work again, I could use you, to tell you the truth—if you want to get off your ass and work doing something besides lifting them fucking barbells."

"I'll do anything you say, Uncle."

"You always been a good kid, Eugene, but I sometimes wonder if you're not a little flaky, like your father. But okay, let's say I go for it. Just for argument's sake. Tell me what the guy's paying for, this trip to A.C. He's paying for what, exactly?"

"Everything, like I told you. He stakes us at the casino. Free booze, broads if you want. Reynaldo gets a free suite at the Taj, automatic deluxe comps."

"Shit, I get that at any joint in town."

"He'll *stake* us, Uncle Tone."

"Stake us what?"

"Five thousand bucks. Your stake."

"Your guarantee, personal?"

"My personal guarantee."

"Okay. Let me think about it. I could use a break, to tell you the God's truth. This shit going on uptown is wearing me down. Them guys is going to get their dicks on a chopping block if they don't stop shooting their mouths off in the newspapers. So when?"

"Next Thursday afternoon good for you? We'll drive down, hit the casinos, eat, drink, get laid if you want. Reynaldo has a limo and a driver—"

"A limo," Tony said appraisingly. "I got my own Fucking car."

"Right. So are we on?"

"You bring the guy and the money. *Capice?*"

"No problem there. He's serious about doing business with you. He knows he can trust anything you say."

"You tell him I don't need no problems, Eugene. Problems I got plenty of. All right? Call me when you get it set up."

. . .

Rey snapped the tape recorder off. We waited for the inspector to speak.

"This stunt going to work?" he said, facing Rey.

"I think so."

"You better do more than think so if you want me to sign a requisition for that kind of money, Detective."

"Inspector, I firmly believe it will work. Look at my track record. Have I ever dropped the ball?"

"That's certainly in your favor, all the weird shit you've been involved with over the years. You're a freaking legend, nobody can take that away from you, Rey. But yesterdays don't count, not today, not with all the heat on this case. So I want guaranteed results, right? This shit has been going on long enough, not that that's your fault."

"You'll get them, sir."

"And I'm not signing another goddamn voucher like this, sticking my neck out. This is it, got it?"

"Yes sir."

Marcomb got up and left without saying anything to me.

My eyes were still wide. "They're giving you *five thousand dollars?*" I said incredulously. My guess would have been that he could have squeezed a grand, maybe two tops, out of the NYPD, assuming they went for this at all.

"Actually," Rey replied, suppressing a chuckle. "I got a little more than five thousand in flash money. You can run through five thousand in no time with the kind of company we're going to be keeping. I have to be able to look like a player and keep him happy at the same time."

"How much did they give you?"

"Well, I signed for fifteen large. Tony don't come cheap."

"*Fifteen thousand dollars?* They went for that much?" Throwing money around, money like this, made me furious.

Rey said, "You got to be convincing when you try to pull something like this off. The last time the NYPD staked me big, I was running a chop shop and I brought in a profit, not to mention fifteen solid convictions in a stolen-car-ring case. Something like this, the last thing you want to do is look like a brokester. Broke is vulnerable, Gerry. Broke is a weakness. You don't want to be vulnerable, ever."

I didn't argue. He was the one with the experience in a kind of high-wire act without a net. It was another world, far different from my own undercover work. I would defer to his judgment. In a similar position myself, I would have probably gotten jammed up. I would have been afraid to ask for enough money. And this kind of operation, if it were to go wrong, could go very wrong.

Besides, I knew that I had squeezed in on a deal that Rey and Eugene set up themselves. Rey could have been ticked about that, but he was gracious enough to act like he was proud of my initiative. "I'm glad you're in on this," he said.

"You sure?"

"Hell yes. But listen: What are you going to do if Tony gets fresh and makes a move?"

"I don't have a problem taking care of myself. And with you along it's extra insurance. It seems like he trusts me. But then again, you never know. Maybe he's having one of those midlife crises and even a pudgy girl appeals to him."

He looked me over. "You sell yourself short; stop downgrading your-self. I notice you lost some weight."

"I've been running a lot," I said, blushing.

"And if he does make a move on you?"

"I'll tell him to take a hike. I'll tell him I'm a good Catholic school girl."

"He's probably heard that one before."

"So I'll cry. How the hell should I know what I'll do? I'll think on my feet like I always do. I can handle myself."

Suddenly he said, "And what if I make a move on you?"

"You, I'd just shoot."

"How about Eugene? I see how you look at him sometimes. He sees it, too."

"He's an a-hole, and you're his accomplice, which makes you an as-sistant a-hole," I said. Colleen had already warned me that Phil Geryon and a few of the other cops on the job were gossiping about the amount of time I had spent with the "guinea prince," as they always called Eugene behind his back.

Cops don't need much evidence to become suspicious, so I suppose they got theirs months before, when I spent so much time teaching Eugene to read. When Eugene began making up salacious side-plots for the simple childish stories, I knew he was starting to read. Week by week he learned, but it meant that I was closeted with him in his room, and evidently the rumor started that we must be having sex. Colleen advised me to shrug it off. "It doesn't really matter, but just be aware that there's talk," she said.

But, always, it did matter when you were a woman. Who knew what they were really saying, and who was keeping notes on it? I was doing a job, working an informant. That meant establishing a close personal relationship, and I had no apologies for my methods. So I used spare time to teach Eugene. That was one simple way to prepare him for the future, when they were through with him. The effort might help him put some kind of a life together once this was over. So sue me for that.

Besides, whatever personal feelings I had for Eugene were constantly in flux. One day the guy repelled me, and the next day I looked forward to spending time alone with him. Like his uncle, he made me laugh, and I felt an affinity with him I seldom felt in the NYPD. We shared common roots, Eugene and I, even if our immediate forebears branched out in far different directions. But I hadn't yet found the energy or the desire to sort any of that out. My affection for Eugene, if that was in fact what it had become, was my private business, in no way interfering with my official duties, and I intended to keep it that way. The NYPD had deliberately left me to depend on my own wits, in a sensitive situation, and I had no apologies to make. No one else had a right to question it.

But relationships between men and women become confoundingly complicated in intense situations like the one we'd been working through for so many months. It suddenly occurred to me that, just as I was jealous of the amount of time Rey and Eugene spent together, leaving me out, perhaps Rey felt the same way when he was left out. "You're not jealous that I spend time with your good buddy Eugene, are you?" I teased him.

"Nah! But he likes you, is what I think."

"What is this, high school? Besides, Eugene already has a girlfriend. In fact, he even has a substitute girlfriend. That's what he calls her, too. And his dear uncle Tony, who he is terrified of, had already put his claim on me, for whatever reasons he has in his deranged mind. Uncle Tony might think that he and I might be freaking *engaged*, for all I know."

"Tony? My guess is that old fart's probably impudent like his ex-godfather Jackie Ponte. These wiseguys get to middle age and they lose it, if you know what I mean. Like Big Jackie did."

"You mean *impotent*?"

"Whatever. You know about Big Jackie, right?"

"I know a little about him." Jack Ponte, last of the old-style dons to hold undisputed title as *capo di tutti capi*. Brother-in-law and successor to Angelo Giavanni, who died of natural causes in 1976, a manner of death so unusual for a man in his position that the headlines said: AN-GELO GIAVANNI DIES IN BED. Until he bought the farm courtesy of Sally Messina, Big Jackie had lived royally in a mansion in Brooklyn Heights, with a spectacular view of the Manhattan skyline. I thought I had a pretty good handle on Big Jackie, but any sex problems were news to me.

Rey provided the footnote. "Big Jackie had one of those johnson-implant operations a couple of years before he died," he said. "You know, he had an artificial johnson put in that worked mechanically with a little lever? He had the thing put in because he was in love with his cleaning lady, some chick from Costa Rica, a real looker. But on the wiretaps, he's always bitching that the damn thing never worked right. It was like defective."

"You mean he had a penile implant?"

"Jesus, I hate that word. It's crude."

"*That* word you find distasteful? *Penile?*"

"Absolutely. Still. Maybe Uncle Tony had one of them operations, too, is all I'm saying."

"Forget it, pal. He's supposed to be quite the ladies' man, from what I hear."

But then he stopped kidding around. "Listen, I didn't tell you this, but it was nice work the way you got over on this guy. You don't seem like his type, to tell you the truth. How'd you do it?"

"He likes to talk. Maybe the guy has a brain."

"Just be careful if you see him start to get pissed off, okay? I mean it. They say the guy is dangerous when he gets his load on."

"Got it," I said. After a moment, I asked, "The uncle said I'm too opinionated."

He nodded. "The week after Eugene sets up this A.C. deal, after you wormed your way in, the uncle tells Eugene that he's bringing a broad with him. He says the broad talks a lot, and she's a little Goody-Two-Shoes, so don't pay no attention to her. He says, 'She's coming because I owe her a little something for some work she did for me. Besides, she's good with arithmetic.' "

"Nice to know I'm appreciated," I said. Tony's figuring on paying me for the freelance job with an invitation to accompany him to a junket to Atlantic City was typical cheapskate mob mentality. The way they treated women as a matter of course was to throw them an occasional treat, a swell night on the town, maybe give them a microwave oven that came off the back of a truck. Why should I be any different? As to the other comments, why should I have felt insulted? It wasn't me, after all. He was reacting to a character I invented. From my point of view, it should have been the ideal attitude for him to have. But it's hard to separate those things out in your head.

Rey said, "Don't underestimate this mobster, Gerry."

"You think he's dangerous?"

He became all cop. "What, are you kidding me? You know he is. Don't let that 'paisan' crap catch you with your guard down, girl."

"Right," I said.

Tony was fun to be with, as long as it was just a game. The danger was in forgetting how he got where he was.

. . .

They had been badgering me to work out. On Wednesday afternoon, the day before the Atlantic City trip was scheduled, I finally agreed to meet Rey and Eugene at a health club in Chelsea. This was not their regular club, but rather a place where they occasionally worked out to maintain contacts with a couple of the younger members from Eugene's old crew. I waited in a lobby that looked like one of those Euro-modern hotels, all done in high-tech black marble and chrome, with mirrors on every wall that forced you to look at yourself, and flat couches designed more for back stretches than for waiting.

A few minutes after three, the two Adonises bounded out of the elevator. With them were a pair of very bouncy and extremely pretty girls in spandex exercise suits—one royal blue, the other shocking pink. These four perfect bodies in radiant bloom (two of them being maintained, I thought sardonically, courtesy of New York City's taxpayers) made me think, for some reason, of the brown serge bloomers we were required to wear in high-school gym class. Could it have been that long ago? How did a full generation sneak in between then and now? Where had I been?

The girls drifted off, trailing adoring smiles. Eugene and Rey sauntered over. I must have been chuckling. Eugene assumed I was laughing at him.

His hair-trigger indignation went on red alert. "What's so effing funny?" he demanded. Cursing on the premises was forbidden in a long list of rules posted at various spots.

"Nothing's funny!" I insisted. I socked him in the stomach, which was hard as mahogany. It caught him a little off guard because I had never done anything like that before,

Rey and I waited while Eugene stopped at the pay phone to call Uncle Tony and confirm the time for the next day. To avoid driving all the way back to Jersey, where Eugene was supposed to be spending every night while in protective custody, Rey had got permission from Lieutenant Campo for the two of them to stay in Rey's suite, so I assumed they had planned a big night on the town.

While Eugene was on the phone, I suggested to Rey that we ought to get together alone later in the day for a last-minute run-through of the plan. Rey agreed to stash Eugene in the hotel and meet me before dinner.

At the phone, Eugene had one palm pressed hard against the wall, as if holding it up. He spoke deferentially. He seemed nervous—uncertain, apparently from long experience, about how Tony would react at any given time. From what I could surmise, however close Eugene and Uncle Tony might have been when he was growing up, the relationship had become distant. Of course, Eugene had been away from New York—as far as the uncle knew—for much of the past year.

"Yeah, Uncle Tony," he was saying. "Yeah, like I told you, he's paying, everything. . . . He's got the money, I seen it. . . . Reynaldo, yeah. Like I said, Cuban. . . . No, real Cuban, from Cuba, not Miami. . . . No, I know not to discuss business on the phone. . . . Yeah, they want a long-term deal, you just say the word. No rush, like I said. Get to know each other, right. . . . Right. . . . Yeah, it's set—high-roller suite at the hotel. . . . Well, what you said is good. You don't want to stay the night, we stay as long as you want, leave whenever you give the word—you just say the word, Uncle Tone. We're cool. . . . Okay, okay, sure. . . . We'll be there at two-thirty absolutely. . . ."

Eugene then said, "Yeah, we're wearing jogging suits." He hung up. Sweat glistened on his face.

Outside, I couldn't leave well enough alone. "Eugene, did your uncle mention me?"

"No. He told me before, he was bringing a broad. So he's bringing a fucking broad. What else does he got to say? The man has got more important things to think about."

"Did I hear something about jogging suits?"

"Yeah, that's what we're wearing," Eugene said, scowling at my question. Rey had stepped off the curb to hail a taxi and Eugene called to him. "Jogging suits, right, bro?" Rey glanced back with a nod.

I persisted, "Tony's wearing a jogging suit too? I just want to be sure, so I dress appropriately myself."

"Yeah. You ain't thinking about wearing no jogging suit, are you? You got to dress nice."

I'd heard that one before.

"Besides," Eugene continued, evidently for Rey's benefit. "What's it to you what we wear?"

"Well, I just want to make sure I understand this. You *coordinate* what you're wearing? Like ladies?"

He ignored me. "I'm wearing the maroon Sergio Valente," he told Rey.

"That's cool," Rey said nonchalantly. A taxicab skidded across two lanes of traffic to the curb. They got in and headed uptown.

. . .

I **had paperwork** to do downtown, but around five o'clock Rey and I met as we had agreed, in Bryant Park, behind the New York Public Library. It was a very warm night; the late-summer sun was low in the sky, nudging shadows across the lawn from the tall buildings around the park. People passed by with their heads down, walking briskly for the subways and the train stations. A soft breeze brushed through trees heavy with leaves.

We found an unoccupied bench near the fountain. A few feet away, a small boy in shorts and sandals crouched by the pool playing with a toy boat that had a red canvas sail. The boy's mother, a pretty woman who appeared to be in her late twenties, sat on the bench beside us. For a minute, I envied a life that had these quiet joys in its daily routine, but the mood passed quickly. Who could know anything real from a simple picture of a mother and a boy playing with a boat on a string? Once you started imagining things to fill in the blanks between the blank faces, it was always so much more complicated, and the endless potential of sadness and tragedy flowed into the void. I drove from my mind the image of a battered little girl who had spent seven hours dying while her mother watched television and ran the vacuum cleaner. A mother who had played with that girl in the same park.

Rey sensed my mood darkening with the shadows. "You ever sorry you got involved in this racket, Gerry?"

"Sometimes."

For somebody planning a night out and a big job the next day, he seemed tired.

"You always know what you're up against, Rey?" I asked.

"Absolutely."

"You're not worried about danger? Ever?"

"Danger is only nature's way of weeding out the stupid people," he said quietly, as if driving to Atlantic City with a mafioso while impersonating a Cuban drug dealer, accompanied by a nervous rat-informant nephew and an undercover female cop posing as the target's girlfriend, was something people did just to show how smart they are. He ran a comb through his wavy black hair.

Still, I admired his attitude. Here was a cop who had lived his entire career as an impostor, in constant danger every day. You could not discount what that did to a person's sense of identity. Did he know who he was by this point in his life? Did the people in this park realize there were cops like him? I wanted to stop the passersby and holler, Hey, folks! Taxpayers of the city of New York! Stop a second and say hello to this jaded cop who risks his neck for you every day while you're going about your business! Let's give the poor slob a night on the town! Working with Rey, you sensed you could absolutely depend on courage under pressure. I just wished he was a little stronger on the details, though. His way was, Hit the beach hard and work out the fine points when the dust clears.

"You know the uncle goes everywhere with a bodyguard," I said.

"He does?"

He hadn't been aware of that? "You don't think he drives himself, do you?" I felt a little wobbly realizing that he had wrongly assumed that Tony would come alone. "Jeez, man, we really should have some kind of a plan besides just hanging out with the guy all night. What if he finds out you're a phony—"

"He won't find out."

"How can you be so sure?"

"Nobody ever did." he said quietly, as if wondering why. "Listen, don't sweat this. All I have to do is make this asshole believe that I'm a well-connected drug dealer from Cuba. We take it from there. One step at a time. This is just the preliminaries."

"You got a place in Cuba to be from? This guy might ask."

"Cienfuegos," he said, accenting the Spanish. "I looked it up. Not that it matters, though, because the only Spanish word this *chooch* probably knows is *bodega*. Besides, you're going to be there if I get in trouble. Just nail the son of a bitch. We'll dump the body in a ditch and put Eugene on a bus for Alaska."

"Oh, that's a very good plan," I replied with a laugh. "Remind me to bring my bullets, incidentally."

"Just remember I'm Reynaldo, not Rey, okay? I'm a Cuban that you never saw before. And Jesus Christ, remember you never met Eugene. Okay? And don't talk to me unless I talk to you first."

"I think I can remember that," I said dryly.

"What time did Tony say he'd pick you up?"

"Three o'clock."

. . .

I *stayed up* past midnight, too keyed-up to sleep or to study, though I was behind in both my law classes. When I finally went to bed, I felt desperately lonely. I was sleeping fitfully when Kevin rolled in at about two o'clock in the morning. I kept quiet, wanting to get back to sleep without any conversation, but it was odd not to smell booze, considering the hour and his recent behavior.

"Where've you been?" I mumbled as he undressed in the dark.

"I met a couple of the guys after work. I should have called. Sorry. What time you have to get up?"

"Late," I croaked, pulling the pillow around my ears. "So don't wake me up when you go out." I forced my mind to pretend I was arguing a case in court. In a few minutes, I was sound asleep.

At ten o'clock the next morning, when I opened my eyes, Kevin wasn't there. I didn't look for a note on the kitchen table.

Sunlight slanted through slatted blinds. I sat in the easy chair beside the window. *Jogging suits,* I thought. How in the world do you dress to accompany that? Digging through the closet, I pulled out a white silk bodysuit, and came up with a black skirt to go over it. I stepped into a pair of black spiked heels so old they were coming back in style. It was going to be a hot day—down on the street, I could hear the kids yelling in the spray from the fire hydrant they had cranked open, until the cops came to shut it off. At the shore, the breeze off the ocean would be chilly at night, so I slipped on a soft charcoal jacket. Out of my jewelry box came a pair of large faux pearl earrings that Kevin had given me for my thirtieth birthday—perfect for Atlantic City. They looked like something you'd see pop up on a slot machine. Adding what I thought was a classic touch to my ensemble was the five-year-old black Timex on my wrist. To impress the Italian-ice man for Tony, I grabbed the only expensive business accessory I owned, a Gucci briefcase. I had bought it right after I made detective but seldom carried it because the other cops, Kevin included, mocked me for it. The hell with them, I thought. At least the mob recognizes quality Italian leather. Going out, I caught a glimpse of myself in the mirror. I looked like a Mary Kay lady about to go on a vodka bender.

They said they would pick me up at Broadway and Canal Street. Right on time, a cream-colored stretch limo as big as the Staten Island ferry nosed down Broadway and glided up to me at the corner. The glass was tinted very dark, but a window glided down silently to reveal Tony's fresh pink face. He looked me over and gave a perfunctory nod. "Ready?" he said.

"All set," I replied, sounding chipper. Rey and Eugene occupied the jump seats, and remained silent. Tony made room for me on the backseat.

Rey was decked out in a red-and-white jogging suit. I thought he was overdoing it a bit with the diamond-studded pinky ring, not to mention the white Bally's sneakers, obviously brand-new. His expression adequately conveyed the slight curiosity a man would show under the circumstances toward a woman he'd never met. Eugene, his back stiff, had on his maroon jogging suit. His hair looked a little slicker than usual. He pretended not to notice me, keeping his eyes fixed on a spot in the tiny rear window. He seemed anxious for the car to start moving, if only to get him away from where he was. No wonder he was such an inept criminal, I thought. Without the family connection, he would never have been a player. He simply didn't have the required surly air.

"You like my suit?" Tony asked me, fingering the lapels. I was glad to see he hadn't come in a jogging outfit.

"It's really beautiful."

"Armani," Eugene piped up, clearing his throat.

"Mr. Cool here, he don't know anything," Tony said with a scowl. "It's Brioni. Silk blend. Here, feel it."

"Magnificent," I said, lightly touching the sleeve.

"Six grand," Tony said.

"Wow," said Eugene, reaching across.

"You touch it, I break your fingers."

Eugene fell back. "I want one of them."

"In your dreams, kid. They only make about a couple of thousand a year of these. You got to know who to get it from."

Rey decided to pipe in. "Actually, they make about fifty thousand. All by hand."

Tony shot him a look. "Not just any schmuck can get a suit like this. You got to be referred."

Eugene whistled.

Tony was already irritated, a bad sign. Finally, he introduced me to his nephew, hooking a thumb in Eugene's general direction.

"That's my nephew Eugene that I told you about," he said. "He's twenty-five."

"Twenty-eight," Eugene said politely.

Tony ignored the correction and introduced me. "Meet Gerry, one of my new accountants."

Forcing a smile, I said, "Nice to meet you, Eugene," and reached across to shake his hand. His palm was hot and clammy, like half-cooked meat. He mumbled something incomprehensible.

After about thirty seconds, it was clear that Tony wasn't going any farther with the amenities. Rey flashed his white teeth at me and offered his hand. It was sandpaper-dry. "Reynaldo Vargas García," he intoned, rolling the r's lightly. I hoped he wasn't laying it on too thick. "Rey, if you please," he said with elaborate courtesy.

"Gerry," I replied. Tony turned away sourly.

From the driver's seat, which seemed about a basketball-court-length away, a craggy face with nicks in it like an old bathtub turned around and showed itself implacably through the sliding Plexiglas barrier.

Tony acknowledged it. "That's Angel Mazolla, like the corn oil."

"How you doing, Angel?" I said.

"Doing okay."

Tony said, "That's Gerry, like I said."

"Yeah," Angel replied. "Good."

No one spoke while Angel stared into his side-view mirror to gauge oncoming traffic as if through a gunsight. Carefully, he eased the limo into traffic and headed west. Within a few minutes we were in the Holland Tunnel. The sudden change of atmosphere and light allowed everyone to relax.

Settling back for the ride, I said to Tony, "Where's your regular driver—what's his name, Joey?" The air-conditioning was going full-blast.

From his breast pocket, Tony fished out a box of those hard, awful little anisette cigars. They looked like twigs that had survived a fire. He shook one out and lit it up, puffing with a ferociousness that soon had his head wreathed in dirty yellow smoke. Slowly, the smoke wafted downward. Buoyed by the cold wind from the air conditioner, it began accumulating in a thick band inside the car at knee-height. I could feel a headache coming on, but didn't want to risk going into my pocketbook for an aspirin, since I had my gun in there.

Having marked his territory with the fumes, Tony answered my question. "Joey works for me on the routine stuff, neighborhood business. A trip out of town, Angel goes. Joey gets lost finding the john in his own house."

"A city driver and a country driver," I observed.

"Sort of." Tony replied in a way that made it clear he did not want to talk. Eugene looked stricken. His face was pale, and I didn't like the way he kept licking his lips, his tongue darting out snakelike. Rey maintained the blank expression of someone riding beside a stranger on a Greyhound bus.

The limo heaved out of the Holland Tunnel into blazing sunlight on the Jersey side. The highway was lined with a junkyard of gas stations and bust-out motels. I felt a little uncomfortable and looked at Rey, but he wouldn't meet my glance. He sat quietly reading the billboards with his hands resting lightly on his thighs.

Nothing had gone wrong; everything was fine, but I worried. The atmosphere in the car was tense. I watched the highway and reminded myself to stay alert for nuances, to keep my eyes open, make mental notes, to be ready to step in and divert the uncle's attention if Rey needed me. But if things went the way we anticipated, there would be no problem, at least not this soon. This was the get-acquainted meeting. If all went well, we would come home without incident and plan the next step, to bait the hook. Rey's job was to get Tony to drop his guard by showing him a good-enough time that he would be ready to go for the bait later. Mine was to observe and assist when necessary. Later, I would write everything up on a DD-5.

Luckily, I thought as I sat back and relaxed, I knew how to handle myself in a casino. Years before, when I was working in the public-morals division, I spent two weeks at the NYPD gambling school to acquire the skills for undercover investigations of illegal casinos. Afterward, they handed me an embossed diploma certifying that I had completed "a specific course of instruction in Techniques in Gambling."

Gambling school occupied the whole eleventh floor of police headquarters on Foley Square. It was a huge, loftlike space, with an immense rug on the floor, like you used to see in old movie theaters. Gamblers crave atmosphere almost as much as action—it's part of the high.

To simulate the atmosphere, the NYPD went to great trouble and expense to make the place like a real, operating, after-hours illegal casino. It was loaded with elaborate equipment and fixtures. They had everything to make it look real: rattan dice sticks, chuck-a-luck cages, eight-gram monogrammed clay chips with revolving carousels, precision bird's-eye dice, Gemco five-star playing cards, even Las Vegas–style drink holders for the trainees' Diet Cokes and Yoohoos. They were always improving the place with equipment and fixtures confiscated on raids. By the time I got there, it was probably the sharpest casino in New York.

I remembered that by the second day of class, I was hooked. Something kicked in in my brain that allowed hours to fly like minutes. The walls had no windows, so you couldn't tell whether it was day or night. Eight hours a day, for two solid weeks, they taught us how to play blackjack, roulette, craps—using real money.

I'm no big drinker. I don't smoke and I try to keep the cursing to a minimum. If I had a serious vice, it would be gambling, hands down. Every day in that school was a high. Pretty soon I could see they were starting to get worried about me. I was the only woman. The male cops all behaved meekly, the way you did in school. Not me. My eyes would go glassy; I'd fix on the game like a lunatic. I'd bet so heavily—craps, four-the-hard-way, press-it, gimme-the-horn bet, you name it—that I drew spectators. Finally, they flagged me.

"Jesus Christ, Conte! What are you doing?" the inspector in charge hollered at me. I was up a couple thousand. From then on, I wasn't allowed to bet more than twenty on the pass line.

A few weeks after graduation from the school, I went undercover on a real raid in a mob casino on Queens Boulevard. They sent me in with five hundred dollars in twenties, figuring it would take an hour or so. But I stayed in the action for three hours, and by the time the cops banged in to raid the place, I'd made a hundred and sixteen dollars for the taxpayers. They almost had to drag me out of there.

. . .

"**Y**ou want something?" Eugene asked. I opened my eyes. He was pouring drinks from the little bar in the side panel.

"A Coke?"

He passed me a plastic glass with ice that rattled from his shaking hand. Without asking, he poured a Rémy straight for Tony, and the same for himself. Rey had a scotch.

With a drink in hand, Tony addressed Rey for the first time since I'd gotten in the car, "You been in New York long, Rolando?"

As respectfully as he could Rey said, "It's Reynaldo, Mr. Rossi."

"Sure. How long you been in New York?"

"Oh, two weeks and a few days, I guess."

"Business, so my nephew tells me."

"That's right. Perhaps we can converse later." He looked in my direction to indicate that he wasn't sure about me.

"Yeah, maybe later, we'll see," Tony said evenly. "You talk pretty good English for a Cuban."

Rey took that as a compliment, but I thought I detected a trace of sarcasm. "Thank you, Mr. Rossi," said Rey. "My mother was a housekeeper for some rich folks who spoke perfect English, even though they worked for Castro. So I picked it up, gave me a good start."

Tony's eyes narrowed. "You know my nephew pretty good?"

"Yeah. We met in Boca under peculiar circumstances—"

" 'Peculiar'?" Tony said, not much liking that word.

"We were involved in some fucked-up situations," Rey said quickly.

With a silly grin, Eugene jumped in. "Uncle Tony, let's not talk about that now. Let's talk about how we're going to break the bank down there."

Tony turned to me and said, "My nephew, always the dreamer."

Rey was confident enough now to stretch his long legs out luxuriously from the jump seat. "Nothing wrong with being a dreamer. Look at me, I'm living the American dream," he sighed. Tony's jowls tightened like an instant face-lift.

· · ·

In an hour we were on the Garden State Parkway. Traffic lightened up once we crossed the big arch of bridge over the estuary of the Raritan River. The parkway runs down the Jersey coastline a hundred miles to Cape May, but from there the only way to continue south is by ferry- boat across Delaware Bay, so you don't get interstate traffic. After Labor Day, most of the traffic is for Atlantic City. The high-end clientele cruise along in limos or big Lincolns. The low-end people, for the most part, come by bus. All year long, day in and day out, the road is crowded with speeding charter buses subsidized by the casinos, hauling the multitudes of slot machine customers in from all over the Northeast, hauling them back out at night. Watching the Leisure Liners with old faces at the windows nose past us, I thought of those farm-labor buses that used to cruise city neighborhoods soliciting day workers for the Jersey crops.

"You like A.C., Gerry?" Tony asked me after a while. A second round of drinks had come and gone, and his mood had improved. He was picking his teeth, making a sucking noise.

"Yeah," I said, trying not to shiver at the steady blast from the air conditioner, which had by now driven the temperature inside the limo low enough to keep a corpse.

"You went there when you was a kid? Before the casinos started up?"

I almost slipped up and told him that Kevin did. His parents took him to Steel Pier, back in the days when you took kids to Atlantic City, went swimming in the ocean and walked the boardwalk afterward. It is where Kevin developed his appreciation for big-band music. Tommy Dorsey, Harry James, Benny Goodman—he had all those records.

"My parents used to go a lot, before the place turned into a slum— you know, before the casinos came in," I said. Actually, my parents rode the subway to Coney Island before *that* went to the dogs. As far as I knew, they never went to Atlantic City. "They used to like the big bands at Steel Pier. Tommy Dorsey, you know. My mom has all the records. My folks used to love to dance." *Lies!* Like Kevin, my father wouldn't dance if you put a gun to his head.

"Long time ago," said Tony with a chuckle. "Before my time."

"All I remember from the old Atlantic City, back when it was starting to really deteriorate, is I would see a man dressed up in a peanut suit on the boardwalk."

"Mister Peanut!" Tony cried happily. "Outside of the old Planter's Peanut Store on the boardwalk."

"I guess that was it. I vaguely remember it," I said equivocally.

The booze had relaxed Eugene, who said, "A guy in a fucking peanut suit? Must of been some fucking asshole."

"You got to talk like that? A lady in here?" Tony said with a reproving glance.

Unwisely Rey interjected, "Yeah, man. You got some mouth on you, buddy."

Tony turned on him. "This any of your business?"

"I was just—"

"I talk to my nephew," Tony said with undisguised contempt. "Maybe you should mind your business, Rolando."

We rode the rest of the way in silence.

A little before five-thirty, we took the exit off the Parkway onto the road across the marshes. Ahead, the jagged skyline of Atlantic City broke the horizon like a mouthful of bad teeth. One after the other, giant billboards whipped past with beseeching messages:

LUCKY SLOTS! MORE ACTION! KING OF THE CASTLE! HAIL CAESAR'S! WINNERS THIS WAY!

The signs clamored for even more attention as we neared the sea.

Angel pulled up at the VIP entrance under the blazing marquee of the Taj Mahal. Rey bounded out when the door was opened. Keeping his back to us, he conferred with a man in a hotel uniform that looked as though it had come from a comic opera. In a minute, we were swept inside.

CHAPTER 14

Just beyond the VIP reception desk in the lobby was a huge ornate urn overflowing with roses, orchids, and maybe half a dozen other kinds of flowers that looked like they came from the tropics. On the table beside the variegated blooms a laminated sign informed the curious: *These beautiful flowers are actual living specimens changed frequently for your viewing pleasure.*

A businesslike woman in a neat blue suit accompanied the bellhop, who insisted on carrying my briefcase, which was the only piece of luggage among us, to the VIP suite on the Fourteenth floor. Tony sniffed everything over with the prowess of a true freeloader and ran his hand down the fold of the heavy window curtain. From where I stood, just inside the door, I could see a sitting room, and in an alcove ten feet above that, up several steps, a dining room with a huge crystal chandelier. There was a fieldstone fireplace in the wall to my right. Down a thickly carpeted hallway, a big mahogany door led to what I assumed was the bedroom.

Tony lit up another cigar, rocking gently on his feet as he puffed.

The woman who accompanied us up to the suite barely blinked. "I hope your stay will be pleasant, Mr. Rossi."

"Not if you're leaving us," he said, leering.

She laughed shrilly. "Sorry, business over pleasure."

"I always try to combine them both," Tony said as she and the bellhop left, shutting the door quietly behind them.

In the dining room a serving table was piled with plates of roast beef, turkey, jumbo shrimp, salads, breads, and pastries—a ton of food, enough for two dozen people instead of just the four of us. Rey had made all the arrangements, but it was obvious that Tony was the big shot here, the man who got the top-shelf comps, another high roller who could be depended upon, with as much statistical precision as the tides, to drop far more money than he won, year in and year out.

My stomach hurt. All I'd had that day was a piece of dry toast, which had become my regular breakfast after my morning run. Casually, I drifted toward the food, but the men went right for the bar. Not wanting to be the first to get at the food, I detoured downstairs and brooded.

I parted the curtains to find a long picture window that overlooked the herringboned expanse of the boardwalk. Lights were already blazing on tall bulky hotels facing the sea. Just beyond the boardwalk, the beach had been raked clean by tractors that left furrows in the sand, as if a giant comb had been run through it. A few people in street clothes strolled on the wet firm sand where the waves spent themselves and ran back to the sea. The ocean rolled off to the horizon, opaque as a squad-room window. An overcast sky glowed with a dull white fluorescence. A single-engine biplane droned northward along the coast, about five hundred feet above the waves. It towed behind it a long advertising banner that said, ERASE BAD DEBTS!!! FRESH START NOW!!!—and gave a phone number.

Eugene called from the bar, "Hey, Gerry! You want a drink?"

He said it in a way you would talk to someone you knew fairly well, but Tony didn't appear to notice.

I grabbed a handful of beer-nuts from a Waterford bowl. A white-jacketed bartender was positioned still as a statue behind the bar in the corner.

"White wine, please," I said.

"While you're at it, set us up two bottles of D.P.," Rey said. The bartender silently poured my wine, brought out the two bottles of chilled champagne, and worked the cork out of one of them. The sharp *pop!* got Tony's attention. He looked over sharply and said, "Don't speak for me." Tony coddled a glass of cognac, neat. He didn't like Rey giving orders, even to a bartender.

Combined with the booze they'd already had in the limo, the drinking so early in the proceedings had me a little concerned. Rey could hold his liquor, and Eugene considered it a point of honor to keep up, but he always faded fast after a few hours, as though a trap door flipped open and down he went. That was when he inevitably reverted to street form, shooting off his mouth like a semiautomatic.

The trait evidently ran in the family. The only difference was that the uncle also had a habit of physical violence. Meanwhile, I tried to keep count of the drinks. The champagne made it the third round for Rey and Eugene just since they had come to the suite. I'd gulped down a couple of aspirins in the powder room, but they hadn't kicked in yet and my head was pounding.

"Do you think we should eat something?" I ventured. They ignored me. Experience told me not to just march over to the buffet and make myself a plate since Tony had a lot of rules about taking any sort of initiative in his presence. He was already radiating malevolence at Rey, and I didn't want to be included.

Rey handed some champagne to Eugene. Then he stood with his legs apart, bouncing lightly on the balls of his feet, and raised his glass to toast Tony.

"First things first," Rey announced, as if the room was crowded with people and he wanted their attention. "Uncle Tony, I wish you the luck of the angels."

"I prefer the luck of Saint Anthony," Tony said, invoking the name of the most-revered Italian saint. "And I ain't your uncle." Nevertheless, he lifted his glass an inch or two and grumbled, "Salut," before downing the cognac.

"Tony, I wonder if I could talk to you a minute?" Rey said. His fingertips tapped lightly at the zippered breast pocket on his jogging suit. Tony understood and followed Rey to the foot of the stairs. From the corner of my eye I saw Rey fish out a roll of bills—the flash money—and put it in Tony's hand. Tony licked the tip of his thumb and flicked through it for a fast count and then tucked the wad in his pants pocket. He looked a lot happier when he rejoined us at the bar. The bartender refilled his glass.

"Gerry," he said, addressing me for the first time since we got to the hotel. "You ready to do that thing for me? See that guy?"

"I sure am," I said, holding up my briefcase

"Very nice," Tony said, fingering the trademark red and green stripes. "How much you pay for that?" The smell of his after-shave lotion distracted me. What was it? Finally, it occurred to me. Aqua Velva, like my father stubbornly continued using even after my mother scolded him once, "You smell like 1957."

Answering his question, I said, "Three-fifty, something like that. My parents gave it to me when I got my associate's degree."

"I could have got it for half that. Next time, ask."

"I will, Tony."

"You know what your problem is? You haven't been connecting with the right people, Gerry. Now, you know where to find this guy for me?"

The address I had jotted down was what Tony had told me a few days before: "Big construction trailer parked behind Convention Hall. 'Santo' on side. Knock hard."

"Right here," I said.

Tony looked at his gold Movado. "What time you got to see this guy? Don't forget what I said; I need the whole financial breakdown, you tell him I want all the figures. *His* books, not the ones he shows to the tax people."

"Nine o'clock," I said.

"*Nine o'clock?* What kind of a time is that to see somebody on business?"

"He said he was working late on the boardwalk. They have some kind of a parade there tonight," I said.

"Parade? What is it, freaking Thanksgiving?" Tony waited for Rey and Eugene to laugh before adding, "Hah? What is it, Columbus Day?"

"Miss America, they told me," I said.

"Miss freaking who?" Tony roared. He drained more cognac.

"Miss America, I guess. They have some kind of a parade tonight before the preliminary show in Convention Hall."

"Maybe we can get them to parade around up here, hey, Rolando!" Tony croaked. "Huh?"

"I can handle a steady stream of legs if you can," Rey said.

"You don't worry about what I can handle, Rolando," Tony said. Then he turned to me. "Gerry—you be careful down there. Don't get run over by no floats full of broads!"

The men laughed. I faked a smile and asked, "Do you mind if I go down to the casino with you before I go to see this man?"

"Why not? It's a free country," Tony said. He finished his drink and ascended to the buffet table, as if on tour. We followed behind. Tony surveyed the feast. Using his thumb and index finger, he pried up a stack of sliced ham and rolled it into a log. Then he wrapped a slice of American cheese around it and rammed the whole thing into his mouth, devouring the meat log like a hot dog, in two big chomps.

He was ready to go. "Drink up," he announced. "Let the games begin."

While Tony went into the bathroom, Rey and Eugene grabbed some food and them hurried to guzzle another round of champagne. I lingered by the buffet, but only managed to put a piece of ham on my plate before Tony bounded out, rubbing his hands together with anticipation. He ceremoniously tucked the room key into his pocket and winked at me while making a clicking sound with the side of his tongue. My face reddened, and I was furious at myself for not being able to prevent it. With the two younger men around, Tony's gentlemanly behavior toward me disappeared.

In a minute, we were following him single file down the hall toward the elevator where Angel had apparently been waiting all the time. Angel held the door for us, stepped in and punched the button for "casino" three times, as if that would get us there faster.

. . .

When **his snakeskin** loafers touched the two-inch-thick carpet on the casino floor, Tony moved like a hovercraft toward the craps tables at the far end of the room. Dropping back a little, I got in a quick word with Rey.

"How much money did you give him?"

Rey glared at me.

"How much?"

Out of the side of his mouth, he muttered, "Five large. He's farting through silk now. But please shut the fuck up."

Eugene scampered behind his uncle like a puppy as we threaded our way through the ranks of slot machines, our destination a high-stakes craps table at the far side of the room. With at least five thousand in his pocket and the altar in sight, Tony parted the crowd like a bishop. Spectators around one of the tables stepped aside.

"Oh Jesus," Rey said, holding me back.

I saw what he meant. We knew that Tony liked to start off the night at the craps tables, before getting down to serious business at his real game, blackjack. He had gone straight to a craps table full of wiseguys, all of them "wearing it," dressed in a manner that marks them as unmistakably as the colors of a street gang. Expensive sports coats over shirts without ties—the older men favoring pastel Banlon shirts, the younger ones quality silk with pointed collars. Gold-chain embroidery glinted in the blazing lights; jeweled links on cuffs rode up to flash diamond watches over pinky rings glowing neon. The shoes, with tassels like tinsel, were a swamp of gleaming reptile skins of various species and colors. Each man appeared to be accompanied by a woman with big false eyelashes. A full-dress ensemble, right out of *Tony and Tina's Wedding*.

"They must find each other by smell," Rey said.

"Who needs smell? Look at them," I said.

The men at the table acknowledged Tony with the fraternal deference of pickpockets at a Sinatra concert. Neither Rey nor I recognized any of the faces, but Atlantic City drew a lot of the boys from Philly, survivors of the Philadelphia mob that used to control what little there was to control in Atlantic City before the casinos came in during the late seventies and attracted the attention of the New York families, who suddenly developed a taste for the seashore. The result was not pretty. One after the other, the capos of the old Philadelphia mob family went down, just like gangsters in the movies—machine guns blazing, cars blowing up in greasy fireballs, floaters bobbing in rivers or slumped in a bloody heap over a steering wheel. The carnage lasted for years, and when it abated, an entire generation of Philly mob soldiers was in the graveyard. The survivors, some of them probably now gathered around the table in front of me, were crafty young cutthroats from Philly who still called themselves a family. But it was a family that knew to be careful about getting fresh with anybody from New York.

Rey whispered in my ear, "Look how Angel just stands there at attention beside Tony like one of those guards outside a castle."

"Be quiet," I hissed. "He'll see you talking to me."

"Baby, all that guy sees is the boss, and all the boss sees right now is them pretty white dice."

Eugene was coming our way through the knot of people who had reassembled around Tony. Rey edged away to cut him off.

"Where are you going?" I asked.

"Stay with Tony," he told me. "Just hang out and look adoring or whatever you got to do to fit in with the other chicks. I'll be back in a little while. Eugene and me got some dice to roll, but at another table where the clientele is better."

"Don't strand me with this guy."

A cocktail waitress wearing a belly-dancer costume cut up to her behind passed by balancing a tray of free drinks. Rey reached across me and deftly snatched one of the plastic tumblers. He tossed a five onto the tray with a wink that she returned. "You worry too much," he told me.

I started to walk away but he called me back. "Listen, you might need this, but don't look too flashy and for Christ's sake don't blow it too quick. Get it changed into twenties." He pressed three hundred-dollar bills into my palm. "Tell Tony you've been saving up."

Tony already had four stacks of black hundred-dollar chips arranged like a row of marble columns in front of his belly. It was impossible to get his attention, so I just watched. Angel also stood back a few feet, where most of the women stood as watchful as beggars. There were about twelve men at the table along with the four stickmen. I noticed a pretty and very tanned blond girl wearing a tight-fitting silver suit looking me over. She had a perfectly sculpted face, with skin as white and smooth as porcelain, but with a tight mouth that suggested a bad disposition. I tried to ignore her, but I knew she was appraising my clothes disdainfully. Naturally, I immediately felt frumpy and out of place, miserably aware of my hideous earrings. I tugged my sleeve down to hide my cheap watch. My cuffs looked wilted.

When I backed up a few steps I bumped into Eugene, who had come over from the blackjack tables. He eased beside me and put his hand firmly but unobtrusively, so Tony didn't notice, on the small of my back, propping me up without a word. A waitress came by and offered him a drink but not me. It was a little after eight o'clock. With relief, I realized that in another half hour I would be able to get out of there for my business appointment.

Tony loved being the center of attention. The table had gotten hot. Tony kept the dice and ran up a fast seven or eight g's. There were a lot of big bets down; the noise level was intense. When he crapped out, the onlookers moved closer, murmuring with the thrilled sympathy of gawkers. But in a few minutes he was back in business; the table heated up again and stayed that way. People were calling out encouragement in loud voices.

Eugene squeezed my hand and wormed his way back to the table, where I watched him lay down a bet. Of course, Eugene knew the game from managing the mob joints in Queens. Craps is the emotional game, and the high rollers love it for the roller-coaster thrills, the sweat and terror. Eugene was winning with the rest of the table, but he never crossed with more than a hundred, and then suddenly he laid back. I think he was afraid of showing up Tony, who had missed his point and relinquished the dice.

Eugene let me in beside him as the crowd shifted. My own excitement was building and I fingered the bills in my pocket and watched the blonde slide to the other side of the table and lay down five black chips.

Eugene winced. "Never make a no-pass bet while the shooter is trying for the point. That's a very dumb move. You don't bet against the table. It ain't sportsmanlike."

"I know."

Tony crapped out.

"Bitch frosted the dice," Eugene grumbled. From the way the stickman looked up, it was obvious his comment had carried across the table, where the blonde was leaning against a man who watched through slitted eyes that moved slowly from Eugene to Tony and back again. My guess was that he was about thirty-five. Six feet, maybe six-one, with thick black hair that had slick mousse furrows in it. I figured him for an earring, and of course it was there when he turned his head to talk to the blonde—diamond stud, left lobe. He had on a double-breasted charcoal-gray suit, lightweight wool.

Concentrating intensely on the dice, Tony fanned a thousand over the pass line, covering across the board. He didn't make the point. With a deep grunt as the dice passed, he backed up a few inches and finally acknowledged me.

"Where did the *Cuban* get to?" Tony said, taking out a handkerchief to wipe the sweat from his forehead. From what I could tell, Tony was still a few thousand up, but the energy had gone out on the table like air from a punctured tire. Tony was aggravated. He had a drink in his hand.

I spotted Rey absorbed in a hundred-dollar game a few tables away. "Your friend moved to a blackjack table over there," I said.

Tony pushed his fingers into Eugene's arms. "Go over there," he said, "and tell your pal Rolando that I want to see him."

"Right away, Uncle Tony."

Calmly I slipped one of the hundreds out of my pocket and tried to pass it up for some green chips. Tony pushed my hand back. Defiantly, I slapped the bill on the padded armrest. The stickman raised his eyebrows and looked inquisitively at Tony, who shook his head.

"No," Tony told me, keeping his eyes on the dice tumbling up the green felt. "Pick it up."

"I want to play."

"Pick up the fucking money!"

Swallowing hard, I shoved the bill into my pocketbook. Tony's face was flushed. How had I ever regarded this bully as even remotely charming?

Eugene came back, pressed up close again, using the crowd as an excuse to put the back of his hand high on my leg. Another drink or two and he going to be major trouble. Furious, I moved toward the pit, closer to Tony.

The table had gone cold as a tomb. Tony blamed Eugene and said, "I told you to get your friend over here."

"He said he'll be right over."

"Excuse me?" I said.

"Here he comes, Uncle Tony!"

"Excuse me!" I persisted.

"*What?*" Tony exploded.

"Listen, Tony. I have a terrible headache. You're going to be here for a while, aren't you?"

"All night, maybe. That a problem?"

"Of course not, Tony. I just thought I'd get going to see your guy. It's a little ways up the boardwalk and I could use some fresh air. Do you mind if I leave now?"

"It's a free country," Tony replied with no interest.

Drifting away, I managed to catch Rey while he was still out of Tony's sight and took him behind a cashier's cage where we could talk.

"I have to go get some fresh air."

"Do it," he said. "You told him you were going out?"

"Yeah. I have to go see this guy at nine anyway."

"That's good. Because I want to try to slow Tony down. By the looks of him this is going to be a bad night—"

"Good luck, buddy," I said.

"How's Eugene?"

"Still cool, but closer to the warning zone."

"Sober?"

"Barely. Can you keep him under control, Rey?"

"Yes. What about Tony?"

"Getting meaner. But he's still up a couple of thousand, I think."

"That's good."

I asked, "Did you lose a lot of money?"

"Don't worry about it. Go see your guy. But for Christ's sake be careful. I don't like you not having backup."

"It's very routine. The guy sounded squirrelly on the phone when I set the meeting up the other day. You got the Tony watch for a while, buddy. Hose him down."

"When will you be back?"

"I don't know. It shouldn't be much later than ten."

"Take your time. We'll be here for a while."

. . .

The casino was jammed and ferociously noisy as I made my way toward the exit, a football field's length away. Endlessly reverberating, silver dollars, quarters, nickles pelted metal slot-machine trays like cloudbursts of nails, all acoustically calibrated to achieve optimal sensual arousal and basic lust. My head rang with rattling coins, whirring bearings spinning wheels of fortune, pearl-hard roulette balls clattering to nest, with the flutter of cards, the soft tumble of dice, the whoop of jackpot bells.

The noise ceased abruptly when the revolving door panel swept behind me. I was woozy. I tried to remember how many drinks I'd had. Three—could it have been four?—flutes of champagne just at the table. Out on the boardwalk, the sea air was cool and heavy. I gulped deep breaths and walked south, hoping to find something to eat.

Decrepitude clung to the gaps along the five-mile boardwalk between the casino hotel complexes. It was as if the tumbledown fast-food shacks and T-shirt stands were allowed to remain as a deliberate disincentive to chase wandering customers back into the casinos. At one of those old stands that didn't look too dirty, I bought a soda and a slice of warm pizza and went to a bench under a bright streetlamp on the beach side. Behind me, I heard music coming from the darkened front of a boarded-up movie theater and strolled over to investigate.

In the darkness, her features barely discernible from the glow of the street lamp, a middle-aged black woman with matted hair and withered limbs lay on her stomach across an old hospital gurney. Holding her head up with great effort, she was using her tongue to press out, one by one, the notes of "Rain Drops Keep Falling on My Head" on a battery-operated Casio keyboard. Beside it was propped one of the plastic buckets the casinos provide for slot-players to hold their nickels and quarters and silver dollars. On the side of the bucket a single word had been printed in red marking pen: PLEASE.

Feeling more like a thief than a benefactor, I dropped one of my hundred-dollar bills into the bucket and hurried down the boardwalk toward the immense concrete hulk of the Convention Hall looming four blocks in the distance. Suddenly I stiffened as a rumble bore down on me from behind like a train.

I managed to get out of the way as two boardwalk rolling-chairs trundled by, each with three people in the seat chanting taunts at the other chair:

"O-HI-O! O-HI-O" one trio screamed. They rattled pom-poms and shook their pennants.

"ALABAMA!" the other chair's passengers bleated. Side by side the wicker chairs raced, propelled by men in shorts who broke into a full run, racing toward Convention Hall as their occupants squealed in delight. The rolling chairs reminded me of rickshaws from old movies. They'd been a fixture of the boardwalk since Atlantic City's heyday as the first great American middle-class resort, when being pushed in a sedan chair by a coolie appealed to a sad fantasy.

I had never been in Atlantic City for Miss America week, and was surprised to see so many people on the boardwalk who were clearly not in town to go to the casinos. The crowd grew around Convention Hall, men in slacks and women in pants suits, tourists from the Midwest and the South, secure in their sheer numbers on alien ground. The parade must have just ended, because the muffled rumble of drums echoed off the buildings far down the boardwalk where the bands were dispersing. Here the sour desperation of the boardwalk changed to a scene that was more like a Big Ten homecoming weekend. Feeling oddly comfortable, I fell in step with the happy multitude converging on Convention Hall.

I turned right, into an area beside the hall. I tripped on the gnarled tangle of electrical cables that snaked underfoot like jungle vines and made my way to the rickety wooden steps of a rusty construction trailer. A faint light seeped out the heavy butcher-shop paper taped over a small porthole. Uneasily, I knocked lightly on the door and waited. After a minute, I rapped hard. A generator was roaring behind a buttoned-up television trailer off to the side.

The door creaked open about six inches. An old woman with a creased face peered out. Her flabby upper arms drooped out of a yellow print housedress. Her hair, piled haphazardly at the crown of her head, was a startling orange. Behind her I could just make out a table with a small banker's lamp that cast dim light on a room piled with boxes and stacked paper cups.

"Yes," she said, making it sound like a demand. An unfiltered cigarette was stuck to the rim of her bottom lip. It jiggled when she talked.

"I'm supposed to see Mr. Albanese?" I said.

"He's in the bathroom!" the woman said. "What do you want?"

"I was supposed to see him at nine o'clock," I said, squinting at my watch. I was ten minutes early.

"What for? I told you he ain't here."

"I thought you said he was in the bathroom."

"So he's in the shitter!" she screamed. "For Christ's sake!" With a *whump*, the door shut. Then I heard her bellowing from inside, "Hey! Santo! Some lady you got to see? She comes at this time of the night, for Christ's sake!"

A male voice shouted a reply I couldn't make out. Then the door opened again.

"He wants to know who sent you."

"Tony Rossi. I'm supposed—"

The door banged. Inside, more hollering ensued. Something heavy crashed to the floor. Footsteps thumped to the door.

Now she opened it and poked a torn, grease-smudged manila envelope at me until I took it.

"I'm sorry, hon," she said. "I thought you was one of them goddamn girls from that stinking rotten club, no offense."

"What club?"

"The nudie joint down the street! They're always coming around here to bitch about something. The last one that came said the air-conditioning was on too high and made her nipples hurt, like that's my goddamn problem! We're *retired* for Christ's sake. My son runs that business, but the bugger is never around to take the complaints. Spends all his time at the racetrack. Can you believe it? A bunch of goddamn nudie dancers who think they're the goddamn Rockettes. They never leave you alone with their bitching over this and that."

I was worried that she might invite me inside, but apparently she decided our business was concluded. "Santo's too stinking goddamn drunk to see anybody right now," she said. "He got drunk watching the girls at the goddamn parade on the boardwalk. All the nude girls in the world at the club, but my Santo, he gets his rod hard over some goddamn Miss Americas riding on floats. He forgot you was coming to see him, at least that's his excuse."

From the trailer a man's voice called hoarsely, "I got drunk listening to you yap, yap, yap!"

"Shut up!" she told him. "She's here for the papers."

"Up your meathook, Loretta! Give the lady the goddamn papers and close the *god*-damn door."

"I gave her the goddamn papers!"

"Then tell her to have her boss call my lawyer in a couple days!"

The woman ran her hands through her hair trying to pat it down. It was like trying to flatten cornstalks. "You'll have to excuse us," she said. "Everything you need is in the envelope. They got any questions about the sale or the closing date, they should call the lawyer."

"The sale," I said evenly, not wanting to sound ignorant. Tony hadn't indicated that he had already bought the business. In any case, the woman seemed glad to be rid of it.

"You can take these boxes full of stinking Sno-Kone cups with you, if you want. They come along with the business. We ain't taking any junk with us. We're retired." A small smile crossed her face, uncovering disconcertingly nice teeth, very good dental work. As if reading my mind, she went on. "We don't live in this dump, hon. This is just the office, but at the end of the season like this it seems like we'll never get home. We sold our house in Margate and bought a *condo*."

"A condo! That's so nice," I said.

"In Palm Beach. It's in Wellington, a few miles away the Donald Trump mansion. Not in that stinking Miami."

Wellington, where Canarsie migrates to say it's close to Palm Beach. "Good for you!" I told her. "Well, I guess I'd better be going, but just let me have a quick look at this so my boss doesn't get mad." I opened the envelope to find a folder containing ten pages of type—production, distribution, sales, outlets—printed by computer. Tony had said all I needed to do was pick up "the papers," so I tucked the file into my briefcase and thanked her.

"You're Mrs. Albanese?" I asked, in case Tony wanted to know.

"I better be after all these years. Just make sure they get the papers. Don't lose them, hon."

"I won't. Tell Mr. Albanese I'll see that Mr. Rossi gets it."

"Thank you, sweetheart," she said. Before retreating behind the door, she called out, "Have a nice day."

I wanted to make a copy of the file, of course, before giving it to Tony. In any other city, it would have been no problem to find a photocopy machine in a convenience store or even a liquor store. Not in Atlantic City, where most of the businesses on the main downtown streets just behind the boardwalk had shut down, their life sucked out by the casinos. Up and down Atlantic Avenue, the streetlights showed emptiness broken by the occasional spot of blinking neon. Luckily, Atlantic City Hospital was still in business. An ambulance with siren moaning and lights pulsing thumped up the driveway by the emergency ward. I followed the attendants in. When I showed my badge, a nurse in the reception area opened up the accounting office to let me use a copy machine.

. . .

I **had no desire** to go back to the casino right away, so I wandered around to the front of Convention Hall, where a few hundred people milled around outside the bank of doors under a marquee that announced the Miss America preliminary stage events inside. I followed a group of them inside and stood for a few minutes in the back of the hall. The brightly lit stage seemed miles away across a dark chasm of people.

"*Heather Merriwell, Miss ARKANSAS! Preventive Health Care!*" A girlish voice boomed from a toylike figure on stage into the cavern. The crowd applauded, whooped, hollered, barked like dogs. A recording blasted "Body and Soul" into the huge dank concrete cavern. One by one, I watched lithe beauty queens in pastel swimsuits present themselves, step forward several paces, pivot to display a front, side, and rear view, then fade back into the glitter.

"May I see your ticket, miss?" said an usher who used his flashlight like a prod.

"I'm sorry. I didn't know you needed one. I'm leaving anyway."

A block farther south, there were more people gathered in front of a hotel. With nothing better to do, I wandered in and followed the crowd to the mezzanine exhibition hall, where another sign said:

MISS AMERICA TRADE SHOW
Pageants Are Our Business

People were going through the doors freely. I couldn't see anyplace to buy a ticket. But a fussy, pudgy man stopped me at the door and frowned at my lapel.

"Oh, ha-ha. Oh no, *no*. You aren't badged," he said with a little sniff. Evidently, from what I could tell, the show was for trade exhibitors and delegates from the fifty Miss America state committees. Curious to see what it was all about, I lifted my shield from my pocketbook and discreetly showed it. That was fine, he allowed, but I would still need a badge. "I don't have any more Guest," he fretted. "All I have left is Press. Otherwise they won't let you on the floor."

Why not? "Thank you," I said, "I'm just going to be here for a couple of minutes. I'm looking for a place to get away from the casinos."

"This is the place," he said, standing aside.

With my press badge on, I roamed around the huge exhibit areas. In a second, I was accosted by a well-dressed older man whose nametag said, EXECUTIVE COMMITTEE—JACK. Spotting my press badge, he pounced at me with a fat, bulging folder of brochures.

"You know," he insisted, "we spend millions and millions of dollars in this country trying to rehabilitate bad kids. What in the world is wrong with a concerted effort to enhance the life skills of good kids?"

"That's very true," I said. He waited till I added, "There's nothing wrong with that, is there?"

"I'm glad to hear you say that. Look at these kids!" He summoned a dark-haired beauty in a stunning black dress who was standing nearby: "Like this young success story—" Jack introduced her as "Miss Tioga County," who looked like she had had that tight smile pasted on her face for all of her fifteen years.

"It's Lynda. With a y," she said, holding out her hand while staring at my press badge. As Jack hovered, she explained that someday she planned to return as Miss Pennsylvania and compete in the Miss America contest.

"What got you into this?" I said.

"My mom. Moms are the key to Miss America." She smiled, waved, and disappeared into the crowd like a light turned off.

Jack had wandered away. I tore off my badge and dropped it on a table. The place crawled with mothers with desperate looks in their eyes, daughters of all ages in tow. Mothers leading ex–prom queens on forced marches into racks of thousand-dollar sequined evening gowns, standing them at racks of "classic swimwear" with built-in padding. Mothers rampaging past tables and exhibit counters brimmed like carnival booths offering a slithering cornucopia of goods with the same shrieking message. IMAGE IMPROVEMENT INC.—COMMUNICATION CURRENT EVENTS, CRITIQUES. Mothers and daughters waited for consultations at booths like patients; they nodded at sales pitches for seminars on physique, poise, attitude, cosmetic dentistry. At one booth sat a physician in a

white lab coat, whose name tag said only, "Dr. Bob." The signs adver-
tised him as the famous "Cosmetic Surgeon of Pageant Winners." His
medical specialty was liposuction.

I gave Dr. Bob a pretty hard look. "Liposuction for teenagers?" I asked.

Dr. Bob, nonplussed, blinked critically. "I'm sorry, are you a contestant's mom?" he asked pointedly.

I fled to an audience gathered around a little makeshift stage near the
center of the exhibition hall. There a young woman with dry hair so
blonde that it appeared white was introduced as a former Miss America
contestant. She sat with erect fastidiousness on a stool under a sallow
spotlight interviewing a ventriloquist's dummy on her lap about a new
line of cosmetics. In a few minutes, she finished and carried her dummy
off to polite applause. Then a portly young man in a navy-blue blazer
and charcoal-gray trousers two inches too long bounded into the light
carrying a box of shoes, all taupe, which he announced to polite applause
was the "color of the year." Nearby, a beautiful girl, a former Miss America contestant named Sue-Ann, stood proudly at a booth, barricaded by
stacks of pageant-preparation videos and inspirational tapes, one of
which, she declared into a microphone, "shows how as a frightened
teenager I managed to get a short leg to grow two inches through
prayer."

Feeling a little crazed, I ducked into the ladies' room. In the next
stall I could hear someone vomiting.

At the mirror I struggled to brush my tangled hair into some kind of
shape. Beside me was a tall, slim young woman without makeup, her
hair cut short. She was rummaging through her pocketbook. In the mirror, she looked slightly familiar, but I didn't make the connection right
away.

"Do you have a match?" she asked, frowning at her own reflection,
as if trying the expression on for size.

"Sorry. I don't smoke." I saw that she was wearing a press badge and
was glad I had ditched my own. But that was enough for me to recognize
her. She was a reporter for one of the New York tabloids who had
covered a case I was on—that of a lawyer who battered his wife to death.
I remembered her mostly because she was smart enough to figure that
the NYPD probably had a female detective working quietly on the investigation and she was aggressive enough to track me down on her
own. When she knocked on my apartment door one night, I told her I
wouldn't talk on the record, and she didn't seem pushy. So we went out
for coffee and ended up spending three hours, not specifically discussing

the case, but talking generally, mostly about what the wife had been through. I didn't realize how acutely cathartic it would be to talk it through with someone who seemed to care about the facts. Afterward, I regretted being so forthcoming, and opened the papers with dread every morning for a week, expecting to see my off-the-record comments screaming back at me. But she never used a word of what I said. Instead, her stories just showed more insight than the ones written by other people.

The trouble was, I could not remember her name. She spoke to me first.

"Excuse me, but don't we know each other?"

"Yes," I said. "We met last year. The Eli Green case?"

"Right! How are you!"

"Fine, fine," I said. "It's Gerry, remember?"

"Gerry!"

"I'm terribly embarrassed, I forgot your name."

"Eleanor Vanson."

"From the *Daily News*, right?"

"No, *Newsday*."

"Right. Wow. What are you doing here? Writing about this ridiculousness?"

She removed her press badge and tossed it in the trash can. "Oh God, you have to wear these things or they throw you out. Yeah, I'm on assignment, such as it is. I must have pissed somebody off. They sent me down here to cover Miss America, you know, snotty tongue-in-cheek for the sophisticated readers. Like somebody has done every year since the 1970s. I tried telling them this thing defies parody. It just *is*, like the Mormon Church. But they sent me anyway." She tossed her head, and it occurred to me that the last time we'd met, her chestnut hair was shoulder-length. "So here I am, interviewing beauty queens. What are you doing here? You're not working?"

"No," I lied, not wanting to get into a discussion about the job. "I'm just down here with my boyfriend, but I can't pull him away from the blackjack table. So I took a walk and wandered in here to kill time."

We sat down and talked for a few minutes. As I made a move to leave, she put a hand on my arm. "I'm finished here for the night. All I want is a couple of drinks and some food that doesn't come with a casino or a name tag. Want to join me?"

"I can't. Kevin will be waiting for me."

"Too bad. Maybe we can get together in the city for a drink. You still live downtown?"

"Of course. Kevin gets a nose bleed if he goes above Fourteenth Street."

"Me too, I'm still on Morton, just off Hudson," she said.

"Sure," I said. "Let me give you my number."

She jotted it down in her notebook and then flipped back a couple of pages to read something. "Do you know how they keep their bathing suits from riding up on their behinds?"

"Excuse me?"

"Those bathing suits. Do you know how they do it?"

"The question never crossed my mind," I said, baffled.

"No, wait. Listen to this: 'Sure Grip, a spray adhesive that sells for eight dollars per four-ounce can. It glues the bathing suit firmly under the buttocks, preventing unsightly ride up in front of the judges.' "

"They sell that?"

She held up a can from her pocketbook. "You need some? I'm thinking about starting a concession in Southampton."

The door of a stall banged. We both looked up to see a dark-haired young woman come out patting her chin.

"Oh-oh," Eleanor told me in a low voice. "Here she comes, Miss Preternatural Congeniality."

The girl strode past the sinks watching her own image pass from mirror to mirror, as if not sure it would reappear. Her shoulder-length brunette hair looked sculpted, as did her figure in a perfectly fitting coral silk suit. Across her bodice was a white sash with red lettering that said: MISS MONTANA-ELECT.

Miss Montana-elect recognized Eleanor. From the chatty way she talked and the way her eyes drilled straight to the notebook, it was clear that she was picking up the conversation from an earlier interview with Eleanor. "Oh, hello. Nice to see you again! I forgot to say, I'm a hundred and fourteen pounds, but I should be less. Last year, you know, I was fat and I came in third in the state finals." Her lips formed a soft pout. "I had nobody but myself to blame."

"You must work out all the time?" Eleanor said, nudging me conspiratorially.

"At least two hours a day, seven days a week. You have to do that religiously to maintain a pageant-perfect body. Oh, they're waiting for me! Bye-bye now." She did a little pirouette and pranced out the door.

" 'Pageant-perfect'?" I said sourly.

Eleanor laughed. "You ever been to the Ocean City baby parade?"

I had no idea what she was talking about.

"Ocean City is a seashore town fifteen miles down the coast from here. Every June, like for the past fifty years, they have had this baby parade on the boardwalk. Hundreds of kids. Parents who dress their babies up like poodles and dolls. The little girls get done up like beauty queens. It's on television. Quite a big deal, some families spend a fortune on it. There's a whole intensely serious world of pageantry out there that you and I know nothing about. But my point is just that there is one thing the Ocean City baby parade and the Miss America contestants all have in common."

"What's that?"

"They all spend a certain amount of their time throwing up!"

I was anxious to get back. She walked with me outside to the boardwalk. As we parted, she told me one more thing. "For a lot of these girls, this is where it all ends, honey—in this shitty hard-luck town fifteen fucking miles up the coast from the baby parade. You and I probably have a lot of complaints, but at least our parents never did that to us. Take care."

"Call me," I said. I meant it. And in time, I would be glad when she did.

· · ·

I'd been gone for hours, but when I got back to the casino, time seemed to be standing still. Tony still had his gut pressed into the craps table, as if making an imprint. In front of him was a small stack of black chips, very small. But at least he was in the play. I wondered when he would turn his attention to blackjack.

It took me about ten minutes to find Eugene and Rey. They were arguing outside the men's room near the security booths.

"What's the matter?" I said, butting in.

It was about money. Eugene was drunk. He was surly, combative, weaving a little on his feet like a boxer still standing after a sucker punch. At least Rey was in control. From the way he handled Eugene, I could tell that he had tapered off on the booze while I was gone.

Eugene complained, "This shouldn't happen, bro. You got a credit card, man. There's a machine right over there. Get a cash advance! What's the fucking problem?"

"I'm almost at the limit, bro," Rey insisted.

Eugene sniffed and wiped the side of an index finger across his nostrils. It occurred to me that he might have been operating on more than just alcohol by this point. I couldn't tell about Rey. But I had made it absolutely clear that I considered cocaine use anywhere near me totally unacceptable. Drugs were the unforgivable sin in the NYPD.

"Uncle Tony's down, but he'll make it back up when he gets to the cards," Eugene was pleading. "We nickel-and-dime him now and the whole deal can blow."

"I know that," said Rey, who thought of something and grabbed my shoulder. "Gerry! How much can you come up with on your credit cards?"

He had to be kidding. "What happened to your bankroll, darling?" I asked sarcastically.

"Gone, babe. Pissed away," he replied in a matching tone.

"You ran through fifteen thousand dollars?"

He patted his thigh pocket. "And change. Not counting the wad Tony still has at the table, which was about two thousand the last I looked."

"And you need more? How can you need more money?"

Eugene barged in. "Them cheap fucking idiots! They only gave you fifteen? They thought we'd get over on that? Now *my* ass is in a sling! You should have known how much to bring. I told you, twenty-five."

Rey brushed him off and tried to appeal to me. "Listen, you have to come through for me here. Just trust me on this."

"When does this end, Rey?"

"Soon. I just need you to trust me."

It didn't look like I had much choice. The teller at a casino cashier cage effortlessly arranged an extra six thousand in cash advances from my Visa and American Express cards, and casually counted out the money as if I were buying subway tokens. We took the money back to Tony, who thanked us like we had brought him a sandwich. To my great relief, he gathered up his chips from the craps table and, as if this had all been only a warm-up session for the evening's real gambling, marched us over to a blackjack table, where he arranged himself on a seat with the dignity of a cardinal during mass.

Tony had just enough skill playing cards that luck sometimes worked to his advantage. By about one o'clock in the morning, the veins in his neck were relaxed. He was easily five thousand up, and we hadn't even needed the extra cash that Rey had stashed in his wallet. Soon, I fervently hoped, he would be ready to take the money and go home happy.

Across the table, a tall, slim man who appeared to be in his late thirties was staring at me. This was the one who had been with the blonde in the silver suit, but she was no longer around. He had wiseguy written all over him. He caught my eye and glanced at Tony with a theatrical roll of his eyes. Then he made a tiny motion with the finger-tips to summon me over, and opened his palm in a small sweeping gesture that presented the stack of chips in front of him. Instead I moved to the side, closer to Eugene. We watched Tony play in silence.

A few places up the table, Rey was also holding his own, betting sensibly but regularly. So far so good, I thought. Then one of the wait-resses passed by with a tray of drinks. Rey brightened up. "*Mida*, mom-mie," he crooned.

My heart almost stopped. Tony caught the verbal slip immediately. The expression was pure Spanish Harlem. No Cuban talked like that. Tony tilted his head a bit to the right, nostrils flared. He said nothing.

Rey didn't realize that he had tipped his hand. Forgetting about the man staring at me, I drifted casually toward the other side of the table where I would have a better vantage point. Seeing motion, I glanced down. A small stack of green chips slid in front of me.

"My compliments," the tall man said. There was whisky and mint on his breath.

"No, really. I can't."

"Sure you can." He had slipped an arm around my waist.

I wriggled away, but Tony spotted it and began gathering up his chips on the table. I saw him give a curt nod to Eugene, who was next to me in a second.

"Knock it off, Gerry," he said.

"Knock *what* off?"

"Screwing with this asshole," Eugene said, loud enough to be heard by everybody at the table.

"I'm not having anything to do with this guy," I told him quietly. "I just moved over here to watch better."

"My uncle's really pissed." Evidently, his uncle's fury at least had the effect of focusing his attention. Eugene didn't appear to be so drunk now.

"Your uncle's always pissed," I said, tired of jumping through Tony's hoops. "I think your uncle's got some serious problems, Eugene."

"Knock it the fuck off."

The man stepped between me and Eugene. Silently, Tony watched. "You tell Anthony Rossi this for me," the man said, talking to Eugene, but staring at Tony.

"Yeah, what's that, Carmine?" Eugene said.

"You tell him he ain't shit in A.C. You tell him Carmine from Philly says to go fuck himself and the horse he rode in on."

"Okay, I'll do that. Anything else you want me to tell him before we have to help you pull your fucking head out of your ass?"

"Yeah! Take the broad with you and tell him no thanks, I already got laid tonight, and I didn't have to pay for that one."

Things happened very quickly now.

Tony gathered his chips, tossed one at the dealer and crossed over to us. "Excuse me, just a minute," he told me in a calm voice. Angel was already moving toward the door. Tony motioned Eugene and Rey off to the side for a brief conversation that I couldn't hear.

Then he came back and took my hand. "We have to get going," he said, sounding nonchalant.

"I got the papers from that guy," I told him.

"Papers?"

"The ice guy?"

"Oh! yeah, sure. Give them to me when we get back."

I turned to follow his line of sight. Fifty feet away, Rey was propelling a very surprised Carmine ahead of him as if his feet were on wheels. He had the man's arm hooked behind his back, duck-walking him with such expertise and authority to the door that bystanders didn't seem to notice. In an instant, they were out the revolving door. About fifteen feet away, Eugene waited anxiously.

Tony, all business now, firmly pointed me in the direction of the bar, where a three-piece band was playing for six solitary drinkers. "You wait in the lounge. Stay in the lounge, right? Okay? We'll be back in about a half hour." He took out the room key and handed it to me as if there were no question that I would use it. "If we ain't back by then, go on up and wait for me. I won't be late."

With Rey gone, I didn't know what else to do. I took the key, nodded and walked toward the bar. But once Tony was out of sight I doubled back and hid behind a pillar that was big enough to be outside a court-house and tried to eavesdrop.

Tony had his arm pressed so tight on Eugene's shoulder that his nephew tilted. I wasn't able to make out all of what he was saying, but there was no doubt about the fury that had come over him. This part I heard clearly enough:

"Listen to me, shit-for-brains. Listen to me! You get out there with Rolando and you teach this guy a lesson."

"Okay, Uncle Tone," Eugene said firmly, turning to leave.

Tony held him back. "There's some other shit going on that I want to get to the bottom of once this asshole with the smart mouth is took care of. Your friend Rolando."

"Rey?"

"He ain't no Cuban, Eugene. I don't know what he's been telling you, but I been in the joint with Cubans, so don't tell me what I know. The guy is a fucking spic from the Bronx, a fucking Puerto Rican with a bankroll. So that means he told me one lie that we know about. What else is he fucking lying about? That's the question I want answered before this night is over, Eugene. You got that?"

"I got it," said Eugene.

CHAPTER 15

After forty-five minutes, the bartender was elaborately rinsing glasses and giving me the fish-eye. I'd been nursing a Coke, chewing on the ice. The band had packed up and the lounge was nearly empty. I decided I'd had enough waiting. I slapped a five on the bar and didn't wait for change.

I ran into Rey right away. He was coming up the wooden stairs from under the boardwalk, brushing sand from his hands.

"Are you okay?" I asked.

He looked like a man who'd just got bad news on the phone. "I'm fine," he said. I noticed that his sleeve was torn and the knees of his trousers were dirty.

"You don't look fine," I told him.

He chuckled, but it sounded nervous and forced. "You ought to see the other guy."

"What happened?" I said, sensing that something had gone wrong.

"Just a quick tune-up, nothing to get excited about."

"Where are they?"

"Who?"

"Eugene and Tony, for starters."

"Waiting in the car. In fact, I was just coming in to get you. Tony told me you'd be waiting for him up in the suite."

"In his dreams," I said, and then asked, "Where's the other guy?"

" 'Under the boardwalk,' " Rey said, singing the words to the fifties tune in a baritone. " 'Down by the sea.' "

"You didn't hurt him?"

"Me?"

"Dammit, don't play games. You didn't hurt the guy?"

"Nothing he can't get over. I had to make it look good for Tony, Gerry. Nah, he's okay."

"I'm going down there. Show me."

He blocked me. "We are going to the car, so let's not keep our boys waiting."

I wanted some answers. "How bad did you rough him up?"

"Just enough. Some ass got kicked after he made an unwise decision to pull a knife on me."

"Are you hurt?"

"Not a scratch."

"Did Eugene and Tony get involved?"

"No. Tony obviously wanted me to put on a show. They watched."

"What was the beef about? Just because this guy got fresh with me?"

Rey laughed. "That had nothing to do with you or your freaking honor, babe. Christ, I thought I had an ego! This was strictly between Tony and the guy. They go back a ways. Basically, the guy just picked a bad time to piss Tony off. You had nothing to do with it. You were just a catapult."

"A catalyst, you mean?"

"Whatever," he said. *"Vamos."*

I was happy to get out of Atlantic City sooner than expected. I'd had no idea what I was going to do if Tony had returned to the lounge and insisted I go upstairs with him. But first, I warned Rey: "Listen, the uncle knows you're lying about being a Cuban. I heard him tell Eugene."

"No problem, I'll come up with a way to explain it."

"And another thing," I said urgently. "On the way home, keep your head up. Tony doesn't like you."

"I tried."

"Yeah. Also, you probably should ease up on the way you're talking to Eugene. These *goombata* are very sensitive about that."

"Ease up?"

"Seriously. Treat him with more respect."

"That dick?"

"Just be aware," I said.

There wasn't any more time for discussion. Tony's car, Angel like a trained bear behind the wheel, was coming up the darkened street toward us, its headlights pushing twin columns of yellow light through the mist. As we fell in step, I could feel the heat from Rey's body.

"Don't worry about him," he whispered. "I just proved myself pretty good back there, believe me. After this, I think the guy's in for the whole nine yards."

"Okay," I said. "But I mean it. Keep your eyes open."

"Shut your mouth and act like you hate me," he said.

"No problem," I replied, scowling as the car glided up to us.

. . .

Tony moved over and patted the seat beside him. He was blowing billows of smoke from a new cigar, this one as long as a nightstick. He appeared calm and greeted me cordially as Rey scampered over Eugene on the jumpseat.

"I got to apologize to you for the change in plans," Tony said, holding up the cigar to admire it.

"That's okay. I was getting pretty tired anyway. Did you have a decent night?"

"I came out ahead, let's say. We had some unexpected difficulties with that smart-mouth, but nothing we couldn't handle. Some people never learn."

I decided not to pursue that subject until Rey filled me in later.

"That's a different kind of cigar than the little ones you were smoking before," I said.

Pungent tendrils of smoke circled me, but it didn't stink as bad as those little ones he had on the way down. There was a hint of nutmeg in the aroma. "It's a Cuban," Tony said appreciatively. "You can't even buy them legal in this country."

"Oh yeah? Where'd you get it, Tony?"

A wreath of dense blue smoke settled on him. "Rolando over there brought it."

Rey explained modestly, "I figured you'd be a man who'd appreciate a great cigar, Tony. That's the best Havana there is, Hoyo de Monterrey, gauge forty-nine."

"Double corona," Tony explained knowingly. "Big as they get. Feels like silk in your fingers."

"If you like those, I can get plenty more," Rey continued. "My friends in Havana keep me well stocked."

"*Grazie*," Tony said, puffing luxuriously and admiring the even glow on the tip of the cigar. But after a few minutes his mood deteriorated.

"You being from Cuba and all, you'd know your cigars," he told Rey. "Probably had them licked personally by Castro."

Rey snorted. "Castro couldn't lick a donkey's ass unless you put him on a stepladder."

Tony withdrew into his cocoon of smoke while I tried not to cough. I desperately wanted to open the window, but knew better than to ask.

As we started out of town, I didn't need the mirror to know that I looked like death eating a cracker. My stomach was churning. Rey looked just as bad. Eugene's head was slumped against the door like a man trying to get some sleep on a crowded plane. It was as if we all had Do Not Disturb hanging from our necks. Nobody spoke. The car smelled like bad breath and stale booze and tobacco. Angel turned on the air conditioner. I held up my arm to see my watch. It was nearly four.

The immediate problem, at least from my point of view, was to determine whether Rey had as much control of the situation as he thought he did. I didn't mind playing second fiddle here, but I needed the score. There were some questions I wanted Rey to answer soon, such as what condition the man Rey had whisked away was in.

When we were on the highway that crosses the marshes to the mainland, and suddenly my heart was pounding again.

"I sure gave that cocksucker a night to remember," he boasted.

Tony didn't reply, but Eugene stirred. Sounding like he was talking through an army blanket, he said, "When he wakes up he's going to feel like he got hit by a beer truck."

"*If* the guinea wakes up," Rey crowed. I winced at his choice of words. Didn't he know how much Italians loathed that term, "guinea"? I was angry at him for laying it on too thick, but the warning look I shot him was wasted on the dark. "Not that you were any help, Eugene, you pussy," Rey said.

"Hey, bro, you didn't need no help there. I would have been there if you needed me. You know that," Eugene said, falling into a pattern of banter that the two were comfortable with.

Beside me, Tony tensed.

Rey kept at it. I usually deferred to Rey's judgment, but this belligerent verbal horseplay worried me. Did he think he needed to impress Tony with what a bad-ass he could be? If so, he wasn't taking into account the cultural loyalties among Italians—let alone the even more fierce family ones.

"I didn't expect you to be standing there playing with yourself when the guy came back at me," Rey continued.

"You could handle it, bro. I seen that. That was your show, all the way."

"*Maricone*," Rey said.

Tony bolted up straight, shooting a two-inch-long white ash onto my lap. "You ain't talking about my nephew, are you, *Rolando?*" he demanded.

"Hey, of course not, Tony. No offense. I meant the loser we left back there eating a sand sandwich."

"Then you talk about that pussy by his Christian name, which is Carmine Latto, in case you didn't have the benefit of no introductions. Or better yet, how about you just shut the fuck up? Just for your information, I don't appreciate any comments about Italians, and I don't like the way you talk to my nephew. *Capice?*"

"Sure, Tony. I'm sorry—"

Tony hoisted a ham-sized fist. "Don't give me no more sorries. *Sorry* ain't a word anybody can afford to use around me more than once."

. . .

K*evin called me* a control freak. It irritated me when he used annoying phony-psychology terms picked up from some daytime talk show. To me, any leader worth a damn is a control freak, and while I didn't ever say it out loud, I considered myself a leader. Nothing frustrates me more than being in a situation where I don't have at least some control of the information, and this was one of them. Of course, Rey was a master of easygoing duplicity, and I trusted his skills. He seemed not to be worried, so why shouldn't I just relax? I couldn't.

That incident under the boardwalk troubled me deeply, because there had obviously been violence, and experience told me that once that cat got out of the bag, it was difficult to put it back in. Tony knew Rey was lying. What else did he know, or suspect? If he decided to move against Rey, what was our plan? I needed to see Rey alone again, before we got back to the city.

There was a rest stop about two miles north on the Garden State Parkway where I thought I might manage to get Rey aside for a couple of minutes if he was alert enough to take my hint. So I asked Tony sweetly, "Tony, if you don't mind, I need to use the ladies' room. Could you ask Angel to pull into the first rest stop we see on the Parkway?"

To my surprise, he thought this was a good idea. "Tell you the truth, I'm feeling hungry," he said. That was undoubtedly true. This was a man who usually nibbled at food all the time, and he'd probably spent his long shift at the tables without a bite.

In a few minutes the bright lights of a rest stop appeared.

"Angel, pull in up there," Tony instructed his driver. "We'll eat a good breakfast and clear our heads. *Rolando's* buying."

"My pleasure," said Rey.

. . .

Despite the hour, the diner was busy with the homebound flotsam from Atlantic City, but we were seated right away at a half-moon booth in back, with me wedged unhappily in the middle, between Angel and Eugene. Tony and Rey were at either end, across from each other. Nobody was happy, including the waitress, who marched over, sized us up, and waited for our orders.

Food made me anxious in company. What I really wanted was a deluxe cheeseburger, well-done fries, and about a cup of ketchup and mayonnaise. Instead I said meekly, "Can I have a bowl of corn flakes with skim milk, and a raisin muffin? And regular coffee. Not decaf." The waitress's expression seemed to inquire why I wanted to stay awake.

Then Tony ordered as though he just got off a refugee boat with a free meal ticket. "Give me three eggs over-easy, ham and bacon on the side, both, okay? And a side order of hash browns. Rye toast with butter. A glass of prune juice and some coffee. With real milk, hon."

"The same," Angel said. The waitress made a little checkmark on her pad.

Eugene said, "Do you make egg whites, hon?"

Her eyebrow cocked. "Egg whites?"

"Yeah. Tell the cook to break ten eggs, throw away the yokes, and make me an omelette. Add some mushrooms. They can do that, right?"

"I'll ask," she said warily. "That's it?"

"No. And the hot oatmeal with raisins, cooked with water. And a short stack of pancakes, no butter. Plain bagel toasted dark. A large glass orange juice. Fresh-squeezed, like it says."

Dryly, with the pencil point just touching her pad, she asked again, "That's it?"

"Yeah, that'll do it for me."

Rey's bloodshot eyes met hers. "I'll have the same."

"As him?"

"You got it."

When she went away, Tony demanded, "What kind of shit is that for breakfast?"

"We eat clean," Eugene told him.

"That's enough to make me puke," Tony said.

Actually, this was something Rey had introduced Eugene to, a diet designed for weight-lifting and body-toning, which seemed to involve a lot of egg whites. To listen to them, you'd think they adhered to routine diets like monks on retreat. If it had been just the three of us, I probably would have asked them if swilling booze all night in a smoky casino was part of the same health diet, or just the reason they needed one.

After a minute the waitress came back and said the chef had no problem except his egg count, which apparently the boss kept close track of. "I'll have to charge you each for the three-egg combo, times three, which would make twelve egg whites. Or we can do it a total of seven three-egg combos, meaning twenty-one eggs total, split in two."

The arithmetic bewildered Eugene. Back at the house, I had been concentrating on his reading skills more than his mathematical ones.

"Go for the twenty-one, for Christ's sake," barked Tony, the blackjack ace. The waitress drifted off again. In the kitchen, somebody dropped a tray of glasses. At several tables, people cheered, the way they do in a high-school cafeteria.

Hoping Rey would follow me, I excused myself to go to the ladies' room. But he sat there like a sack of laundry. In the ladies' room, I groped in my purse for my .38, experiencing the first feeling of reassurance I'd ever gotten from carrying a gun. I took inventory at the mirror and cupped cold water onto my pallid face. Did Rey have a gun? No, I decided. He wouldn't have taken the chance of its being discovered by Tony. We'd all seen too many Mafia movies with too many bloody outbursts, and reality ran in a parallel loop with the movies. Sometimes, reality behaved like a movie, but without the warning.

The food had arrived when I got back to the table. Rey and Eugene were scooping their hideously white omelets in synchronized motions, elbows crooked. It was not a pleasant thing to watch.

"Jesus Christ," Tony muttered. He averted his eyes, which looked deeply sunk above his cheekbones, and used his toast to swab up his own egg yolks. Angel's motions matched Tony's precisely. Miserably fixed on the wonderful smell of the bacon on Angel's plate, I chewed my corn flakes.

When we were through, Rey paid the check and said he had to use the men's room. I followed the others out, unable to think of a way to slip back inside and get Rey's attention without making Tony suspicious. I considered telling Tony that I had to use the phone, but I decided it would sound pretty odd at five o'clock in the morning.

While we waited for him in the car, I tried to gauge Tony's mood. Why should he be unhappy? I was outraged by the amount of money we'd thrown away, but I couldn't figure where he had a beef. From what I could see, he'd left Atlantic City with at least three or four thousand dollars more than he'd arrived with. The rest of the money, the bottom-line loss for the evening, was coming out of the pockets of the taxpayers of New York City. The taxpayers' largess hadn't bought a lot of goodwill, either. In fact, it looked to me like Tony would have been just as happy to have Angel take Rey out in the sand dunes and whack him.

"Listen, Eugene," Tony said, ignoring me as we waited for Rey. "I don't care for this guy."

"But he done what you told him back there, Uncle Tony."

"Yeah, and that's why he's getting a ride home, but I don't like the way this guy talks to you, Eugene. The guy don't show respect. Plus he's a fucking liar."

"I'll tell him to watch the way he talks, Uncle Tony. He's trying to be funny, but he comes out of a different culture than us."

"Maybe I ought to give him a culture lesson myself."

"Please don't do that, Uncle Tony."

Tony belched resonantly. "And, goddammit, I told you, this guy ain't no Cuban. He's a goddamn Puerto Rican. You understand me on that, Eugene? You can't smell shit if you're standing in it."

Eugene had the sense not to argue. "Yeah, maybe you're right."

"You're goddamn right, I'm right! There ain't no maybes about it, you understand me?"

"Yes, Uncle Tone," Eugene said. "But listen, keep in mind that the guy can do business, even if he's lying about the Cuban thing. Cuban, Dominican, Puerto Rican, Martian, whatever—I seen he's got the ability to deliver. I seen that personally. You can trust my judgment here, Uncle Tony."

I was impressed at how well Eugene lied, but Tony didn't sound persuaded. "Listen, I'm telling you for the last time. I don't like the way you let this asshole talk to you, just for starters. Who the fuck is he, talking to you like that? Ain't you got a bit of sense? Forget about business! I got a good mind to have Angel do a Moe Green on him, right here in this parking lot."

Moe Green? Then it came to me. Moe Green was the character in *The Godfather* who got murdered for showing disrespect to the hapless, well-connected Fredo Corleone. We were parked on the darkest side of the lot, near ten-foot sand dunes that rose out of the marsh like frozen waves. Behind them was the inky black of Absecon Bay, with the first streak of dawn starting to show in the sky over the sea.

It was impossible to know, with Tony or any of them, when they were shooting their mouths off for effect. I forced my concentration away from the movie scene whirring in my head. There had already been violence. How much? My God, what if he really decided to do it? What if he'd made Rey not just for a liar, but for a cop? No doubt Angel was packing a gun. The little .38 in my purse wasn't going to mean a lot if things got out of hand. And which side would Eugene be on?

Tony calmed down. "Eugene, you done a good job in Florida. You're lazy sometimes, but you got good business sense and you always been a good kid, respectful. If you vouch for the guy, I take that into consideration."

"I vouch for this guy."

"Okay, like I said. You just keep this clown in line, okay? You see that he shows some respect, understand?"

"I understand, Uncle Tony. You don't got respect, you can't do business."

"Exactly," Tony said.

Pretending to be dozing, I relaxed a little. At least Tony was planning to take Rey back to New York sitting up straight.

"He can do a deal," Eugene went on. "Listen, maybe he's got an attitude, but he don't know no better. Maybe he drinks too goodamn much—"

"There's the pot calling the kettle black," Tony said.

"But Uncle Tony, he's trying to do business. To show good faith, he dropped a lot of money down here on us tonight. That shows you how much the people he represents—"

Tony chopped at the air with his hand. "This is not the time to talk," he said, cutting him off. He nudged me gently and I opened my eyes and smiled. "I'm sorry, Gerry," he said. "My nephew here, always talking business." He slipped his arm around my shoulder.

"I don't mind," I said, resisting the impulse to move away.

Eugene pressed on with mounting excitement. "The deal he wants to do, I'll set it up myself, keep you at arm's length."

"Later! Where'd you say you picked this guy up, anyway?"

"I met him at a health club in Boca. After that, we took a couple of broads on one of them one-day cruises out of Lauderdale. I got in a jam over some money, a misunderstanding. He was right there for me. Later, we got to know each other better working out at the club every day. You can get a lot of business done there."

"That's what's the matter with you young guys," Tony scoffed, "all you want to do, sniff jockstraps in some gym. That ain't no way to do business, Eugene."

"These days it is," Eugene said.

We watched Rey making his way across the lot toward the car. Tony poked a stubby index finger into Eugene's shoulder. "You get this guy straight before we take another step, you understand me?"

"Just consider it done," Eugene promised.

" 'Consider it done,' " Tony repeated disdainfully, directing himself to me. "He lets some Rican talk to him like he's a bicycle messenger. Lets him call Italians 'guineas.' "

"I guess he's only trying to apologize," I murmured.

"I don't remember asking you for your opinion. Everybody's getting chesty tonight."

Rey opened the car door and slid in. When he was settled, Tony asked, "You comfortable now, Rolando? I mean *Reynaldo*."

"Yeah, fine, Tony. Sorry to keep you waiting."

Angel nosed the limo onto the Parkway, and Tony sat back with a deep sigh. In a few minutes, to my relief, he was snoring lightly, leaning against me. After a while, I looked down and noticed that my pocketbook, which lay on the seat beside us, had come open. My heart nearly stopped when I saw that my .38 was plainly visible. Worse, Tony had opened his eyes and was looking right at it. Barely able to breathe, terrified that if I had been stupid enough to leave the gun exposed when I felt for it in the bathroom, I might have also have exposed my shield in its black leather case. But it remained where I kept it, under a bottom flap in the pocketbook. My mouth went bone dry and stayed that way while I pretended to sleep.

We rode in silence for the rest of the trip. All I remember is the sky bright pink over Perth Amboy, the traffic picking up sharply as we approached New York, the garish tiles of the Holland Tunnel, and at last the sharp smell of the city, the river, the exhaust fumes, the concrete and the comforting din.

. . .

Protocol required that Tony be dropped off first. Angel took him to an address on Kenmare Street in Little Italy where Tony kept a small apartment. He used it whenever he had a reason not to go home to Staten Island, where he had the requisite low-profile wife. There were no children.

Angel stopped the car out front, and Tony turned to look at me. "You come up with me for a minute," he said.

"What do you mean?"

"You come with me. I got to talk to you about something."

"I have to get home, Tony!"

"Not right now, you don't," he said, showing no concern about what Eugene or Rey might think. I could make out a faint trace of apprehension on Rey's face. I knew there was no way he could intervene, even if he had known that Tony had spotted my gun. I let him know with a look that I could handle it.

"Tony, I'm exhausted," I pleaded.

"We'll only be a minute," he said, opening the door.

Trying not to show panic, I glanced at Rey and got out of the car behind Tony.

We rode up silently in a small elevator. I kept my purse pressed right to my side. The apartment was on the fourth floor. It was clean, with polished blond wood floors and shiny kitchen countertops, as if a maid had just left. The furniture was Scandinavian. An abstract print hung on the wall behind the couch.

"Sit down a minute," Tony said, unsmiling, as he went to the kitchen.

"Okay, but I can't stay long."

"You want some coffee? Something to drink?"

"No, thanks."

He came in with a glass of milk and walked over to the stereo, where he flipped through some CDs. Oh my God, I thought, he's actually making a move. A tenor's voice filled the room, and then was joined by the lilting reach of a soprano.

"Do you know this?" he said, standing there with his milk.

"No, but it's beautiful." For a second, I thought of poor Kevin with a beer in his hand, slobbering over the Ink Spots.

" 'La fatal pietro sovra me chiuse,' " Tony said quietly. "From *Aida*."

"It's very sad," I said.

"Very sad," he agreed, and in his face I thought I saw for a fleeting moment the image of a man who might have been different.

"A girl like you, you're full of the warmth and joy of Italy. I know you more than you think. You should learn to speak Italian, Gerry. I could teach you, but you wouldn't want that, I know. You probably think I'm just a dumb slob that got lucky in the world you see me in, and that's true. That was what I was born into, and I made my way through it the best I could. But I always have another world I can visit when I need to. You're going to think I'm lying, but the truth is, I speak Italian better than English. Cultured Italian. None of that Sicilian stuff. Can I ask you a favor?"

"What?"

"Would you believe that about me?"

"Yes," I said, and meant it.

"Thank you," he replied, smiling broadly and raising the glass. When the aria ended, he turned off the CD player and joined me on the couch. Then he asked, "So now tell me about the gun, Gerry."

The quick way these men switched gears always caught me by surprise. I was prepared for the question, though. "My little .38?" I asked, feigning surprise.

His face was set like dried clay. "How many guns you got?"

"Only one. And I always carry it. To tell you the truth, I'd be terrified to use it."

"You got a permit for a concealed weapon?"

"No, actually."

"Let me see it."

I took out the gun, and firmly closed the snap on my pocketbook, hoping that's all the contents he'd see. I tucked the pocketbook beside me, away from him.

My pulse raced while he held the pistol in his palm as if weighing it. "This looks like a cop's gun," he decided, watching my reaction carefully.

"Of course it does, because it is," I said in as steady a voice as I could manage.

"What are you telling me, then?"

Somehow I managed a light laugh that didn't let the fear show. "The gun was my brother's, Tony."

"Your brother? What brother?"

"Tony, you remember. The time in the shop when those two cops came in?"

He rubbed the stubble on his chin. "Oh, yeah. Your brother that you said was the cop that got in trouble."

"When they took his badge, he told them he had lost the gun, but he gave it to me for protection."

The tight lines at the corners of his mouth eased. "What with you taking the train in from Brooklyn and all," he said helpfully.

"Especially at night, because with my work, I never know when I'm going to get home," I prompted him. "Why? Does my carrying a gun bother you?"

"You're carrying a concealed weapon," he told me gravely. "You got no permit. You got to watch out for things like that, Gerry. That's the kind of small shit they love to get you on. Especially when you're with me, okay?"

"I'll be careful," I said with relief. "I won't carry it when I see you."

"Good. I can always get one of the boys to drive you home."

"Thanks," I said. That was an offer I'd never take him up on.

"Of course you don't got anything to hide, right?"

"What do you mean, Tony?"

"What I mean is, suddenly, one day I look up and you're *there*. Week after week, we drink coffee, talk like old friends. You could be anybody, but something deep inside the both of us touches our feet on the same ground. That's why I like it when you come around."

"Thanks, Tony. But I thought you needed my help with accounting."

"I do, don't get me wrong. But who are you? What do you want from this, a nice girl like you?"

"You know who I am," I replied. "What, do you want to see some ID?" That took guts, I thought bravely. "And what I want is work. That's the nature of being a freelancer."

"I even forget your last name," he said, puzzled.

"Antonucci."

"Ah, right. Antonucci. I bet you get tired of having to spell that out all the time for people."

"Constantly."

He reached out with his fingertips and lightly stroked my cheek, which went hot under his touch.

"When's the last time somebody told you how beautiful you are in the morning?" he said.

I was too stunned to say anything, but I knew it was time to leave.

"Now I know you at night, in the afternoon, in the morning, like a day."

Uneasily, I said, "Tony, I have to get going soon. My mother will be worried."

"But there's another time that I don't know you, a time that doesn't show up on the clock, that you keep to yourself."

"A secret?"

"A secret," he agreed. "But deeper. More like a mystery."

"I don't think so."

"I know so," he said, his face now very close to mine. Before I realized it, his lips were on mine. I backed away and stood up, clutching my purse.

"Tony, really, I have to go. My mother's waiting. I have to get her to a doctor's appointment this morning."

"I'm sorry to hear that," he said. "We could have had a nice morning. Nobody ever bothers me here."

" 'Bye, Tony. I gave you the papers, right? You have the papers. Can I send you the bill for my services?"

Without a glance he went over to turn up the stereo and said, "Knock yourself out."

Feeling crummy, I walked home.

CHAPTER 16

I *was in* a deep sleep in my apartment when the phone rang. I fought my way awake. From the schoolyard behind our building came the steady tattoo of a dribbling basketball.

"Hello," I croaked.

"Well, did you have a nice time at the seashore?"

"Noah?" I said with annoyance, as if it were a crank call. The alarm clock said a little before noon. "I'm off today, Noah. I need some sleep. What do you want?"

"We have to talk."

"Isn't this something that can wait, for God's sake?"

"It cannot," he said, sounding so whiny that I felt like reaching into the phone and dragging him out by the hair. "Are you awake now?"

Glumly, I sat up. "Obviously."

"Good! So let me read you something that just came over the news wire. Maybe this will sound familiar:

"ATLANTIC CITY—ASSOCIATED PRESS: A man identified by police as a high-ranking soldier in the embattled Scarfo organized-crime family was found beaten to death under the boardwalk early today. Police identified him as thirty-seven-year-old Carmine Latto, of Turnersville, New Jersey.

"Latto was dead on arrival at Atlantic City Hospital. His body had been discovered by an unidentified homeless man who came across Latto and notified a security guard at the casino, who called the police.

"Police said they have no suspects. But they had found an eye-witness who reported that he saw three burly, dark-haired white males escorting a struggling man, presumably Latto, down a ramp that leads to the beach beneath the boardwalk near the Taj Mahal casino-hotel, sometime around 3 A.M.

"Police were unable to determine immediately whether the homicide might signal a revival of the bloody warfare between factions of the New York Mafia families and remnants of the Philadelphia family. For the past seven years, the Philadelphia faction had been led by Nicodemo "Little Nicky" Scarfo, who was convicted of homicide in April and is serving a life sentence in prison. The last known incident involving the warring mob families occurred more than six months ago, and the authorities have recently suggested that the families had reached a truce, with the New York faction clearly in charge.

"The mob battles over interests in Atlantic City, which have claimed more than two dozen lives, began with the assassination of longtime Philadelphia boss Angelo Bruno in 1981, three years after the first casino opened in Atlantic City. . . ."

Noah stopped reading. "You wouldn't happen to know anything about that, would you?"

"Oh my God," I said, feeling a quick wave of nausea.

"*A revival of mob warfare between the New York and Philadelphia families?*" Noah said with a groan.

"Noah—"

"Do you know how many people I've had to talk to this morning?" he shouted.

What had happened down there? Had he spoken to Rey? I imagined a headline: RENEGADE COPS IGNITE MOB WAR. "Noah," I said weakly, "I just don't know what to tell you."

"Well, it happens that one of the two suspects in that incident is sitting right here in my office."

"Who would that be, Noah?"

There was a muffled sound as he handed the phone over. Eugene came on. "Hey, how you doing?"

"I'm doing real lousy, Eugene. What the hell is going on here?"

He breathed loudly into the phone. I could almost see him inspecting his fingernails. "Looks like there was a little problem. But nothing that can't be took care of. They're working on it now. Don't worry about it, babe."

"Where's Rey?"

"He's on his way down. They woke him up at his girlfriend's house."

I was afraid to ask him where Tony was. Instead, I said, "Put Noah back on."

The assistant district attorney sounded unhinged. "This is incredible! How could you let anything like this happen?! I want to see you in my office!"

"Right now, Noah?"

"Immediately!"

. . .

There was a cab cruising right outside, so I got downtown in fifteen minutes. I found Noah sitting in his red leather chair like a body with rigor mortis, still fuming on the phone. Eugene, on the other hand, looked like he'd just stepped out of the shower and dressed for the gym. He lounged on the couch, with his big feet stretched out across the rug and his fingers locked casually behind his neck. He had on a hideous tight-fitting white T-shirt that said, in letters stretched across the chest against the silhouette of a handgun, NEW YORK FUCKING CITY.

"Okay, well, we're going to owe you big-time on this one," Noah was saying into the phone. For a minute, he listened intently and made notes on a yellow legal pad. I craned my neck to read them, but his scrawl was impossible. When he got off the phone, he looked miserable.

"Noah, are you okay?" I asked.

"What do you think, Gerry? Do I fucking look fucking okay to you, or is that a irrelevant fucking question at this point?"

A little smile crossed Eugene's face, which only made me angrier. Deliberately, I pulled up a chair and rested my elbows on Noah's desk; he drew back instinctively.

"It's being took care of," Eugene piped up from the couch.

"What's being taken care of?" I demanded.

"The *incident*."

I turned to face him while Noah buried his face in his hands. "From what I hear, the incident was a homicide. Or am I mistaken?"

"Self-defense," Noah said.

"Oh," I replied evenly. I still had no idea exactly what had happened. I didn't want to say anthing that would hurt Rey.

"Is that all you can say, Detective?"

"Noah, why don't you tell me what the hell is going on here first?"

His phone rang and he grabbed it like it was on fire. "Yes, Inspector," he said. "I know . . . I know. I'll be right there."

He instructed us to wait there for him, and hustled out of the office with his legal pad. I was too furious to deal with Eugene, so I ducked out to wait for Rey in the lobby. Five minutes later, he arrived looking haggard and hungover, but more cocky than desperate.

I pulled him into a corner near the elevator bank. "What happened when you went down on the beach last night? Damn it, Rey, how could you let yourself be put in that position?"

"What position?"

"Don't be cute. How bad did you hurt that guy?"

He aimed a finger at the elevator call button and glanced around furtively. "I did what I had to do," he said. "I had to slap the guy around, or else Tony could have put a bullet in my head. That, I decided, based on my considerable experience, was at least an outside possibility. So I smacked the guy a few times. It wasn't like he was a cripple. He could fight, and he landed a few good ones, including a kick in the balls, the bruises of which I would be happy to show you."

"No thanks. Then what?"

"The guy would have been okay, except he pulled the knife on me. I'm not talking Swiss Army knife here, I mean a real shiv. All I could see was a severed head. So I grabbed a hunk of driftwood and whacked him. Once." He shrugged. "I connected, okay? This was just a scumbag, trying to kill me. And I had a right to defend myself. All I wanted to do was knock him down and kick his ass so he wouldn't get up till noon or so. Him going out like that, it was just one of those freak things."

His confidence told me that he'd already spent some time speaking to someone in authority. He confirmed it.

"They're taking care of it," he said, shrugging. "Shit happens. I've been in worse than this."

We rode the elevator alone. "You weren't thinking on your feet, Rey!" I hissed. "You should have thought of a better way out of that situation."

"Well, it's history," he said curtly. "The shitstorm is still on, but it'll die down in a day or two. Listen, we do what we have to do. What's done is done." He shook his head and watched the lights blinking the floors as we ascended to Noah's office.

Had he crossed the line? It was just incomprehensible to me that a cop with Rey's experience could have let this happen. Sure, he was on the spot. Rey was tough and fast, but I'd never seen him lose his temper, and I couldn't imagine him deliberately beating someone senseless, even in self-defense. Did he think Tony would have figured him for a cop? I doubted that. Rey had been drinking; he killed a man, obviously inadvertently, arguably in self-defense. For a police officer in that situation, where *was* the line?

. . .

The line was drawn farther than I imagined. By the middle of the afternoon, the situation was already pretty much under control. Phone calls flew back and forth—the DA's office, the feds, the Atlantic City cops. And somehow it was fixed. The incident would go into the files as a random robbery and homicide, a street crime, suspects unknown. Reporters who called to follow up were advised off the record that even a known organized-crime figure can get unlucky enough to get mugged by a stranger in a town like Atlantic City. They were assured that a new mob war was not under way.

By the next day, even Noah had things in perspective, meaning that he had calculated the effect on his career. Okay, something had gone wrong, but there was no question that Rey had acted in self-defense. On paper, which was all that counted, our Atlantic City operation had succeeded reasonably well, that unfortunate hitch aside.

In fact, Tony had gone for the bait. Eugene, it appeared, had done his job and got his uncle on tape, agreeing to a drug deal. Two days later, at four o'clock in the afternoon, Rey, Eugene, and me, joined by a dour Inspector Wallace, gathered in Noah's office to listen to the tape of the conversation between Eugene and his uncle.

"You actually went to him wearing a wire?" I asked, impressed that he had finally delivered on something.

"Absolutely," Eugene said, patting his chest. "I met him at his social club for a long business talk."

"When was this?"

"The afternoon we got back."

Inspector Marcomb interrupted with an order to turn on the tape. The sound quality of the recording was superior. Tony's voice was the first we heard.

"You get *Rolando* home safe and sound?"

"Rey? Yeah, we dropped him off at the hotel. He's okay, Uncle

Tony. Believe me on that. How about you? You get the girl home okay?"

"Sure. She don't know nothing."

I took a shaky breath. Tony's voice rumbled from the tape.

"You get some sleep, Eugene?"

"I don't need no sleep today. Tell you the truth, I leave here, I go right to the gym, sweat it off. I feel great. It clears my head."

"So what do you want from me?"

"All due respect, the reason I asked to see you, I want to get some idea how you feel about this thing."

"What *thing?*"

"You know this thing that Rey wants to do for us?"

"Your Rican friend?"

"Yeah. Hey, you know how much money he dropped on us last night?"

"Why don't you tell me."

"Fifteen *g*'s he dropped, you know that?"

"Must of dropped it down his pants."

"Come on, Uncle Tony. We had some action, right? So we lost, what the hell, it wasn't our dough. We got what he said we would. Tell you the truth, you're right about that Puerto Rican thing."

"No shit I'm right."

"Uncle Tony, after we left you off, taking him up to his hotel, I confronted him on that thing."

"Yeah."

"And okay, he comes clean. Yeah, he's a PR, okay? Now, I don't like that lying to me about being a Cuban any more than you do. I mean, I know the guy over a year; we was in some tight spots down Boca, and he was always there when I needed him. But up to the hotel this morning I go, 'Listen, Rey, my uncle don't believe you're no Cuban.' 'Okay,' he says, 'your uncle's right. That's a guy you can't fool. So I am Puerto Rican, bro.'"

"'Bro.'"

"That's what he calls me."

"I noticed. So why does your fucking *bro* lie to you, then?"

"Very simple. He says, he says it's like nobody in Florida or New York is going to deal with no PR fronting for a bunch of Cubans to get in on business, especially with the Colombians breathing down their necks. *They* don't give a shit he's PR or a Chinaman from the moon. They hooked up with Rey down Boca because he knows his way around New York, okay? He like knows how things get done here, right? But in New York and Florida, there's, like, a lot of prejudice about Puerto Ricans. So to get over, he calls himself Cuban, for simplicity."

"That's wonderful, Eugene. So what the fuck am I supposed to do? He got his meeting with me, like you wanted. What does he want now, Eugene?"

"Well, these guys he works for, they do serious business, like I said. Supposedly, they got an in with Castro himself, because Castro needs the money. Very serious business. They got to be careful, it's very dangerous—"

"Tell me about it."

"They want in quick and clean, get established without the Colombians sucking the eyeballs out of their fucking heads. It's very simple. They need to get to know people here, make important friends. Like what you call networking, you know? *Batta-bing*, a quick deal, in and out, everybody wins. They're in business, we profit, nobody's the wiser. Later, maybe we do more business and so forth and so on."

"Don't give me none of that network shit. Tell me the goddamn bottom line, Eugene. What's the deal? They got the macaroni?"

Hearing that perked everybody up. Glaring at the tape recorder, as if daring it to glare back, Noah began scrawling notes.

"Yeah, sure they got it."

"And?"

"They got the macaroni. And Rey can put this deal together, assuming we're interested. I assure you to that."

"You start watching your ass, you hear me, Eugene?"

"I hear you, Uncle Tony. Please don't worry about me."

"I worry, I always worry. You don't worry, that's one of your problems. What kind of macaroni we talking here?"

"He could get three pounds of zitis."

"Fresh zitis?"

Noah switched off the tape recorder and looked around the table. " 'Zitis'?"

"Cocaine," I explained. Rey nodded in confirmation. In recent years, as the wiseguys finally got paranoid about electronic bugs in the walls and wiretaps on the lines, they had developed code words to avoid making specific criminal references. A really arrogant killer like Sally Messina never managed to break the habit of using incriminating verbs like "whack," and he was paying dearly for it. But for all of them, references to illegal drugs were almost always made in terms that sounded like the import-export food trade. "Macaroni" was narcotics in general; "ziti" referred specifically to cocaine. Everybody knew what it meant, but of course talking about importing pasta wouldn't hold up as evidence of criminal intent in front of a skeptical jury, not with the high-powered defense lawyers the mob had on its payroll.

Noah flipped the machine back on, and I felt a cold sweat trickle down my back. Eugene's voice sounded calm. It still amazed me at how effortlessly he lied.

"Absolutely fresh zitis."

"Where from?"

"The usual, but they got a different way of bringing it in. They got a submarine."

"They got a fucking submarine? Get the fuck out of here, Eugene. What you been sticking up your nose?"

"No shit, Uncle Tony. They got this used submarine from one of them countries down there that the navy sold old boats to."

"Chile."

"What?"

"I said Chile, probably. The submarine."

"Probably you're right."

"They bring a big-ass submarine right into Boca?"

"Nah. They drive it underwater—shortest distance between Cuba and the United States. But they come up a couple of miles offshore at night, shift the stuff onto one of them fishing charter boats."

"Fucking incredible."

"Not for nothing, Uncle Tone, but you know how the other guys is starting to bring the shit in? Not the guys Rey is with, but the regular ones."

"How?"

"Ha-ha! Freaking 747's, them big fucking passenger jets. They land them in Mexico, like they was full of tourists. But then they got to drive the stuff over the border in small trucks and then east from Texas, and the cops down there are all over the highways busting balls anybody doesn't look like Joe Suburbs."

"Them Mexicans are all on the pad, Eugene, but I think some of the border cops are just as bad."

"Totally, from what I hear. But we don't got to worry about them in any case."

"Okay, okay. These zitis your good friend Rolando is talking about bringing in off his fucking submarine. Talk don't mean nothing—"

"Excuse me to interrupt, Uncle Tony. Let me stop you there, all due respect. They already got a part of a shipment up here in New York. Rey has the shit stashed in one of them self-serve storage joints out in Queens."

"Okay then, the zitis, the ones that are in Ronaldo's warehouse and the ones that maybe come in later by some fucking submarine. Just let me ask you out of curiosity—they got a price on these zitis?"

"A dime and a half a pound, introductory offer, exclusive to you."

The tape emitted a sharp whistle. Obviously, the fictitious deal Eugene had laid out was attractive, and Tony was receptive. Mentally, I ran the numbers. A dime meant ten thousand dollars; three kilos, at a total outlay of forty-five thousand, could net about a half million dollars once it was cut and put out on the street. By my calculations, Tony could figure on pocketing about a quarter million, quick and clean, with the expectation of more to come on future deals once the new relationship was in place. To a man looking for money in dangerous times, those numbers would sound extremely attractive. We all knew about Tony's expensive tastes and his gambling. Yes, he lived well, but unlike the capos who sat at the godfather's right hand, the favored few who were practically lighting cigarettes with hundred-dollar bills, Tony was chronically short of cash. In fact, Tony's relative penury was both a career attribute and a life-insurance policy. To Messina's cutthroats, it proved that the old warhorse downtown wasn't stealing excessively from them. As a result, he ran his blue-collar rackets efficiently, without a lot of supervision, and without being under the suspicion that he was any wiseguy's mortal enemy.

Now Eugene started laying it on.

"Later, there's a crate of these zitis available, already in the country. They just got to get a distributor for New York. But they got to move fast, Uncle Tony. This stuff can't stay idle. Time is money, and all that shit. They got other people to talk to if we say no thanks. But they want to do business with us, don't get me wrong here. They know your reputation as an honorable man that can get things done without a lot of *agita*."

"I still don't know about this guy. There's something about him I can't figure."

"That's probably because of him trying to pass off the Cuban thing on you. He's been wised up to that now. I vouch for the man, on my mother's grave."

"So do the deal, then."

"What?"

"Do the deal if you want. It's a free country, ain't it?"

"You mean this?"

"What I mean is *you* set this up. I don't want no parts of details. The price better be what got quoted. You do all the arrangements, whatever the fuck else. Then if the deal sounds right to me, okay. I'm a hard-ass, big-time about that stuff, which you fully know. And you leave me out of the details, understand. I don't get involved."

"You won't, not till the moola comes in, of course. So I can move right away?"

"Don't prove me wrong, Eugene. You done real good down Florida, even if you don't keep in touch. So go ahead. You work it out. You let us know."

"Okay, very good. Very good."

"Who is 'us'?" I said, looking impatiently at the tape recorder.

Noah stopped the tape and shushed me, but from where I sat, the talk was still too vague to be of any use in court. We still had a long way to go before we nailed someone as wily as Tony. Maybe I was becoming too much of a lawyer, and maybe I had my own less honorable reasons now, but I wouldn't want to take what I'd heard so far to a courtroom. Of course, if we could catch Uncle Tony red-handed making the deal, that would be a payoff. I listened anxiously, hoping that Eugene would push his uncle a lot harder for specificity. Instead, like an idiot, he just changed the subject.

"You want to get something to eat, Uncle Tone?"

"No. I still got a bad stomach from last night. Too much booze, too. These days, it takes me two days to shake that shit off. So you work it out, you call me when you got it ready."

"Listen, Uncle Tony. I want to say my honest thanks to you."

"You want to say thanks to me? You get your ass in gear, you hear me? You start coming to work around here regular. I want to see you around a lot more than I been, you understand me?"

"Absolute, Uncle Tony."

"And don't screw this up, Eugene, you hear me? I got enough on my mind without worrying about you fucking up, especially the way things are now. You remember this, you watch what you say, who you say it to, don't trust nobody you don't already trust. Do not talk about this to anyone else."

"I hear you."

"I'm serious here. You can be a real asshole sometimes, much as I like you. You know that—"

"I know—"

"But even you, that's never around, you know things ain't looking so good around here. There's bad shit going down, and I don't want none of it falling on me. You use your head, Eugene. With the luck of God almighty, I'm going to retire one of these days. Soon, too. I'm wore-out, Eugene. I had it with New York."

"You retire? Where?"

"Things work out, down Florida. Where the hell else?"

"So this could be your stake, this deal?"

"You don't worry about my business. You just pay attention to your own."

There was a brief pause. Then Tony spoke again.

"You know, your father and me, we had some times down Florida when we was a lot younger. You don't remember this, but your old man was a real funny guy, a fucking riot to hang out with. Everybody loved the guy, especially the broads."

"When was that, Uncle Tony?"

"The late fifties, before Vegas got big, when Florida was still the place to go for a good time. You could still run over to Havana for the weekend. Both places, man, you could get anything you wanted, didn't matter what."

"You still can down in Florida, as long as you know who to see."

"It's not the same."

"Of course not, Uncle Tony. But they're going to get legal gambling down there pretty soon, people say."

"That's where you hit the nail on the goddamn head, Eugene. Gambling is correct.

"You know how much people in this country spend on legal gambling every year? I seen it in a magazine in the barbershop: three hundred billion bucks! That's just legal! Casinos is coming to Florida, damn right, but it's still years away. That means there's time to get in on the ground floor. But the secret is, you don't want to compete with the big casino outfits like them local schmucks down Atlantic City, that fucking slum, tried to do when gambling passed. Which is a reason I got my eye on a place down Miami. I wouldn't actually *retire*, see. Christ, I only just turned fifty!

"This is just between me and you, understand, but I got an option on this property, down what they call the South Beach. You wouldn't recognize the goddamn place since they chased the old Jews out of them hotels and started fixing up them what you call it, Art Decorator, them pink-and-blue joints. Now it's crawling with your jet set, tourists from Germany and France, disco dancing, flashy cars, big bucks, blondes laying topless on the beach with their tits out."

"What is it you got in mind down there?"

"This restaurant and hotel, a rathole now, but with the right management, it could look like one of them places they used to have down Havana before Castro come in and fucked everybody up. Beautiful! Gambling in a few years; everything else, you name it. Florida today, it's screaming with opportunity to clean up! You listen to me, Eugene—a smart, good-looking kid like you ain't got any future in New York. You better start thinking Florida, Eugene."

"I like being back in New York."

"You won't for long, let me tell you. You watch. Everything's coming down. The only ones with a future here is the Chinks taking over. Me, I got my plans long-term. You look at Florida, Eugene. Take the fucking Everglades—you know how much land-fill you could put in there? You know how much *water* you could take out of them swamps with the right arrangements? And with gambling, even away from the beach, you get yourself into a business arrangement with them Everglades Indians. They already got a bingo hall big as Madison Square Garden right on their reservation, twenty miles out of Miami. You're good with foreigners, Eugene! You could work with them swamp Indians, set up businesses before anybody knows what's happening!"

"I guess—"

"There's no future in New York for a guy like you! Things ain't the same. You listen to me."

"I always pay attention to you, Uncle Tony. Listen, could I ask you something?"

"Ask me what, now?"

Eugene nudged me.

"About the broad—"

"What fucking broad?"

"The one from last night—Gerry? She going to be working for you, you think?"

"What the fuck is wrong with you? That broad don't know nothing more about computers than I do. Who the fuck needs her? She's got a dying mother at home in Brooklyn and she throws hundred-dollar bills around in some gambling joint. What kind of a daughter does that? I don't even want her coming around no more. She has too many opinions, the way I see it. In fact, she won't be coming around the shop anymore."

"I don't know, she ain't so bad."

"You *like* this broad, Eugene?"

"I don't know. Maybe I'm getting a little tired of the bimbos I go with."

"She ain't your type, Eugene."

"Yes, Uncle Tony."

"She ain't your style. And she won't give nothing up easy if that's what you think. I know the type."

"Serious? With all due respect, you want to make a bet on that? Like five hundred bucks I can bag her?"

"Jesus, you ain't got the sense God give a barstool. From what I can see, as far as betting any five hundred dollars, you ain't got a pot to piss in or a window to throw it out of. Be my fucking guest. It's still a free country. Try your fucking luck, with my blessing."

The tape ended. Noah and Inspector Marcomb glared at me, as if I had something to do with what they'd just heard. Finally, I felt the deep shame that had eluded me before, as if I had finally waked up to look at reality. On the other hand, in his own way, Tony had protected my honor.

"I'm sorry about that part," Eugene said, looking at me sheepishly.

I said, "You made a *bet* with him over me? This is the way *confidential informants* are supposed to behave? What gives you that right?"

Eugene grinned nervously. Rey kept his eyes down.

"So you want to help me make five hundred bucks?" Eugene then said.

That did it. "Inspector," I said, "I don't think I should have to put up with juvenile behavior from this idiot."

Marcomb backed me up. "Knock it off, Eugene." He turned to me and said, "Conte, you're the best shot we have at this transcription stuff. Get somebody to transcribe that tape today. I want copies, and I want to see your DD-5 first thing tomorrow morning."

My face was flushed as we filed out of the office. But later, I understood that it was not a bad move for Eugene. Being able to join him socially, closer to the uncle but no longer the object of any attention from the uncle, had its virtues as we moved in for a sting to bring Tony down. Now all we had to do was make it work.

CHAPTER 17

Rey *and Eugene* went to work setting up the arrangements for the drug deal to pop Tony. They promised to fill me in once they had a basic outline.

That meant that for now, my mornings were more relaxed than ever. So I ran. The shadows in the narrow streets grew longer by the middle of October. The cooler air encouraged me to lengthen my morning run to a long loop from my place in the Village to the edge of Chinatown and back.

My weekday run wasn't long, just a couple of miles before work. But on the weekends, my range expanded as I felt stronger in the autumn chill, and I pushed harder and harder until the effort ultimately yielded that great white flash of exhilaration, and my mind felt only pure energy.

One Saturday, I just kept going, oblivious to everything except physical power, and was amazed to find myself, winded with pleasure, collapsing, with no recollection of the last five miles, onto the soft, thick grass near the reservoir at the northern edge of Central Park, ten miles from where I'd begun. I took the subway back downtown and rewarded myself with a cappuccino and a dish of ice cream at a sidewalk restaurant on Mulberry Street, where waiters in clean white aprons prepared for the lunch crowd.

The constricting Italian district on Mulberry with its sidewalk cafes and grottolike restaurants made me think not of Palermo or Naples, to which the denizens laid ancestral claim, but of Rome, with its two thousand years of glory, invasion, reappraisal, compromise, intemperance, and the eternal flow of commerce.

Trotting home, I slowed my pace passing Umberto's Clam House at 129 Mulberry. That was where a hotshot renegade from the Profaci family named Joey Gallo ("Crazy Joe") was gunned down eating clams and scungilli with friends on his forty-third birthday in 1972. Joey and the boys were in Umberto's for a late-night snack after celebrating his birthday at the Copacabana nightclub, where the Broadway columnist Earl Wilson and a couple of well-known entertainers sat at their table for the festivities. Joey was my favorite dead wiseguy. During a stretch in prison in the sixties, Joey learned to read, and soon developed a deep appreciation for Kafka, Camus, and Flaubert. When he got out of the penitentiary, he offered to pay for night-school courses for anyone in his crew who wanted to improve his mind.

Joey had panache. He kept a full-grown lion on a chain in the basement of his Brooklyn headquarters, and had a guy come by once a week to change the kitty litter, which they dumped by the ton down the coal chute. Joey had style, but he had it too soon. The cops who responded to Joey's murder found his sister bent over the bullet-riddled body wailing: "He was a good man, a kind man that had changed his image! That's why they did this to him!"

. . .

A *couple of* blocks north of Umberto's on Mulberry was the infamous Napoli Social Club, housed in a narrow, bricked-up storefront that had an American flag pasted on its window and would have seemed a neighborhood American Legion post except for the clientele, who looked exactly like the Mafia guys you see hanging out in these places in the movies. The Napoli was the downtown clubhouse for the Giavanni family. It was dim and dingy, with a couple of rooms on the ground floor, an apartment upstairs. It had a screen door in front, an MIA-POW sticker stuck beside the flag on the oblong window.

One damp Saturday, as I jogged up the wet pavement, I nearly collided with the boss's only son, Salvatore Messina, Jr., known beyond his earshot merely as Junior. Junior hooked his thumbs in his belt and hoisted himself onto the sidewalk outside the Napoli just as I was passing by. He anchored himself there like a harbor buoy with a child's head on top. He had a low brow and was about Eugene's age, with none of Eugene's physical attractiveness. His physique, the result of what was probably the only intense work he had ever performed, precisely matched that of a lowland gorilla's. I moved wide toward the street as I huffed past, hoping not to attract his attention, but when I got past, I felt his tiny cold eyes follow me up the street. That was probably because I had on high-cut silk jogging shorts that day. I quickened my pace, aware that my passing was also being recorded by the cameras of the federal surveillance team. *Everybody*—especially the wiseguys coming and going from the Napoli day and night—knew the feds were squatting, with binoculars and a telephoto lens, twenty-four hours a day beside the window of a third-floor apartment in a dingy building right across the street. From there, they recorded everyone who came and went on the sidewalks below like a bank surveillance camera. I streaked up the block under scaffolds planked with dripping plywood.

I stopped for a soda at an ancient Italian grocery, now owned by Pakistanis. In wire racks out front was a bewildering profusion of newspapers: the city tabloids, papers with headlines in cuneiform squiggles—*Corriere della Sera*, *Le Monde*, and the *Jerusalem Post* wedged in with the *Times* and the *Village Voice*. The rain stopped. People were venturing back onto the sidewalks now. In Tompkins Square Park, a meandering line of raggedly dressed homeless people, nearly all of them men, waited for a free lunch at a mobile van sponsored by an advocacy group. A city housing official once told me that it is actually much easier and more convenient for all concerned to feed the homeless in a church basement or a soup kitchen, but that civic advocates for the homeless nevertheless insisted on maintaining open-air handouts in parks or near major commuter spots like Grand Central, so that the ragged beggars would be seen in public, like advertising images, as symbols of the dispossessed.

Is there any other city in America demanding such attention to so many agendas? The city was hard, enduring, unshakable, grudgingly accommodating. Its heart was bedrock.

It was just after nine in the morning when my beeper went off. I fished it out of my pocket figuring I'd see Eugene's code. I hated beepers, but the NYPD regarded them as the height of technological sophistication, so we all had them, just like all the fourteen-year-old drug runners on the street. I went to the phone.

"Hello, Eugene," I said.

"Yeah?"

"What do you mean, yeah? You beeped me. What's up?"

"Rey told me to call and remind you about meeting us at the gym at two-thirty."

They'd been on me for months, and finally I'd agreed to go with them.

But I'd totally forgotten about it until now. "What do you mean meet you at the gym? It's Saturday! I'm off."

"Rey says you're supposed to be there."

I sighed. Actually, I had nothing planned anyway. Kevin was nowhere around. But I made a feeble effort to squirm out of it. "Tell him I have a paper to finish for one of my law classes. I forgot. It's due in three days.

"I ain't making your excuses."

"What do you mean?"

"He's out at his girlfriend's, anyway. We're supposed to meet at the gym."

"How are you getting into town if he isn't with you?"

"That bug Colleen is supposed to drive me in, but she's been bitching about it all morning. She'll do it, but I'll have to listen to her all the way across."

"I'm not sure I can—"

"Rey said bring your workout stuff. That's it. Today's the day you start your program."

"Anything else?"

"Did you see the paper this morning?"

"No, why?"

"I just seen where it says the Yankees are thinking about moving over to Jersey, and I wondered if you seen that."

"Eugene, I don't read the sports pages and I don't care where the Yankees go."

"Me neither. But they shouldn't be in Jersey, is all."

"You're probably right, but I could care less. I'll see you at the gym."

When I hung up, I realized he didn't care anything about the Yankees, either. He was merely trying to tell me he was reading a newspaper.

I made a cup of coffee. At least that much had been accomplished. He could read well enough to get by. A man whose reading and writing skills were barely at a sixth-grade level three months ago was reading the sports pages. He'd been doing his lessons, even when I wasn't around. Maybe, I thought for the first time, he might actually have a chance at a reasonable life once they cut him loose, as they would— and, I suspected, sooner than anyone now thought.

Not that Rey didn't deserve some credit, too. Week after week, while I worked on Eugene's reading, writing, and arithmetic lessons, Rey quietly made an effort, usually by edict but more often by example, to help sand down the jagged edges and civilize our jungle boy. Eugene's wiseguy "screw you/get over here when I want you" swagger still stood out, but he made a point to show he could turn if off when he wanted and act like a conventional human being. Week by week, as he learned to read and to write simple sentences, his social skills improved apace. He was even starting to recognize nuances of language protocols between genders and ranks. He seldom hollered "Fuck!" in public now. He began to understand that not all challenges have to end in conflict, that some affronts can be overlooked, that reasonable goals can be set and reached with work and with planning, that subtlety is not a weakness.

True, he had not yet come to understand that the present, which seemed to stretch into infinity, simultaneously becomes the past and the future with a blink of an eye. Again and again, I would implore him, "Eugene, don't you realize that when this operation is over, you have to find a place to live? Your people will know that you turned, and if you think you can go back to the way it was before, you're sadly mistaken." But he remained as oblivious to time as a six-year-old.

. . .

I *went to* the gym because Eugene and Rey had become the bookends of my life. I wanted to fit in. I wanted to lose weight. Running every day wasn't enough.

"Twenty-five pounds," I had told Rey one afternoon when we were headed back out to Jersey. I was driving.

He studied my right thigh. I thought he was going to pinch it, but he just laughed. "You're nuts! Women are absolutely screwy about weight. You should drop fifteen pounds, tops. Then you'll be in ideal shape, but it will take work. You don't just lose weight, you gain a lifestyle."

"Jesus, what are you, in some cult?"

"There she goes with them fucking library words again," Eugene put in from the backseat, his social graces slipping a bit.

Two days later, Rey had presented me with a laminated card, a paid-up six-month membership at a health club called Heavenly Bodies Fitness and Aerobic Center. Despite the name, I figured this was one of those musty gyms with a collection of no-neck muscleheads sweating and grunting under monster barbells. I thanked Rey for the membership. The gesture was touching. It seemed, finally, as if they welcomed my company. But the idea of going to a gym gave me the willies.

Over the months, Rey had been working on Eugene's physical-fitness profile as well as his social one. He was teaching Eugene not to approach bodybuilding the way he approached everything else in life, "like a bull-dozer," but to master technical refinement and build the discipline to reject the fast gratifications of bulk and brute power in favor of tone, definition, endurance, prowess.

"That's what you need to learn," Rey told me.

"I don't think so," I replied with some conviction. "All I have to do is lose some weight."

"You pay attention to me, that won't be a problem."

I regarded him with skepticism.

"I'm telling you. No problem," he insisted. "Results absolutely guar-anteed."

Before I realized what I was saying, I stumbled right in and blurted out, "Okay. I'll go on a diet and work out, but it's hopeless."

"He held up a hand as if to flag me down. "One thing, Gerry. A negative attitude means sure failure. Working out is not a diet, it is a new way of life."

What the hell, I thought. The old one wasn't so hot. The old one was fraying at the edges. "So show me the way," I joked.

"Twelve-thirty tomorrow. That means you're ready and dressed by then, and on the floor."

"Tomorrow's Saturday!"

"You building excuses already?"

"No. It's just—"

"Twelve-thirty."

. . .

S o the time had come. Brooding about spandex and thonged body-suits, I rode the subway up to Macy's and spent two hours finding work-out garb that would call as little attention as possible to my body. I came home with baggy sweatpants and an oversized gray sweatshirt.

On time, miserable, anticipating only humiliation, I arrived at Heav-enly Bodies, which was on Hudson Street not far from where I lived. I figured on putting in about a half hour's appearance and then begging off and going to a movie.

To my amazement, the place looked like a resort hotel. On one side of the lobby was a pro shop with expensive workout clothes and gear, all of it, it seemed, tiny. I realized right away that this is where both

Rey and Eugene bought their own workout clothes, top dollar, of course. On a mezzanine overlooking the lobby was a sparkling glass-walled restaurant called the Greenhouse Cafe.

The workout area itself must have been thirty-thousand square feet spread across two thickly carpeted levels, with a raspberry-and-gray color scheme. There appeared to be acres of gleaming black steel machines with magnificent bodies toiling on them with what seemed to me to be supreme confidence. It was clearly a singles gathering place, with an equal number of men and women diligently working both on their bodies and their social schedules. Everything was shiny.

Carved in the limestone across an broad arch at the vestibule were the words: RESULTS ABSOLUTELY GUARANTEED. With mounting anxiety, I showed my pass and wandered inside. Rey appeared immediately and fell into step beside me.

"Welcome," he said, acting like he owned the place.

"Some gym," I said. "Nothing at all like the police academy."

"You like it?"

"I'm terrified of the place."

"Go get dressed. We'll meet you on the floor in fifteen minutes."

Crossing over to the locker rooms, I felt even more intimidated. Not that I was a physical wreck. After all, I was a regular runner. But to me, this expensive health club was just a high-school gym with better furniture, a torture chamber where only narcissists came out smiling. I really hadn't been in a gym since the academy, where I had almost failed to graduate because I simply couldn't get my behind over the six-foot wall you had to jump. My father, of all people, came to my rescue when he heard about my difficulties. In the alley behind his shop, he actually had a construction man build a six-foot wall out of plywood. On the weekend before the final physical endurance test at the academy, which I was sure I would fail, he spent two full days coaching me. I'll never forget his patience, or his bafflement about my inability to haul myself over that wall.

"You run, spring, boom, you're over," he insisted.

God, I tried, but again and again, I would hit the wall and hang there on quivering fingers.

Finally, late on Sunday afternoon, he said, "Gerry, I'm goddamn tired of this. Get over that wall or I'm going to kick you in the ass."

I ran, sprang, and made it. The next day, I passed the physical test.

. . .

Wishing my father were there, I came out of the ladies' locker room hiding in my baggy sweats. A tour guide, Rey pointed to the busy field of machinery and glistening bodies rising up and down like oil derricks.

"Over there, there's thirty or so pieces of what we call cardio equipment—your basic StairsMasters, treadmills, stationery bicycles. All state-of-the-art."

"What are the little video screens?" I asked, hopping on one foot to show I was ready.

"That's cardiotheater, very expensive equipment. Each piece of equipment has a personal audio-visual command module. We have programmed tapes you can use, or you bring in your own. In a couple of years, this stuff will all be obsolete. It'll be replaced by virtual-reality technology. You'll be able to work out in a three-dimensional multiactive environment simulating anyplace in the world, with whoever you want to be with."

Virtual reality? From what I could gather, this was essentially a View-Master with moving pictures and stereo sound.

"Wow," I ventured.

"And over there, in the rear, is our free-weights area," Rey went on. "See, the familiar barbells, benches, hammer equipment."

"What's that stuff?" I asked, gesturing at some steel-framed machines that looked like highway construction equipment. Most of the people riding these contraptions had on headphones and seemed lost in communion with their inner beings. Yet there was an uncanny uniformity to their cadences, as if they all were getting identical commands through their headphones from an unseen coxswain.

"That's the Cybex machines. They all work on a particular muscle group. Circuit training, it's called. One day for each of six body parts—every day, you do one body part: chest, back, shoulders, arms, legs, abs."

"And you expect me to do that."

"Absolutely."

I nearly bumped into a girl in a tiny workout suit who looked like a model except for the perspiration wetting her chest and armpits. She was mounted obscenely on a machine.

"We call that the butt-blaster," he said, appraising her form. "It gives you a great ass. Better than the one you have, which incidentally is an improvement on the one you used to have. I mean that as a compliment."

"She already appears to have one of those."

"That's true," he acknowledged, and looked me over critically. Even in the baggy sweats, I felt naked.

"Never compare," he said. Just then, Eugene appeared and motioned us over to a lounge at the far side of the room.

Eugene was a vision of self-contentment in a gold cut-off sweatshirt that had written on the front in red letters, ME TARZAN, YOU TRAIN. He looked very warriorlike with his gold sweatpants rolled up above thick fullback's calves. Rey, I noticed, wore a black string tank top which had UNDER CONSTRUCTION across the chest. He was wearing thigh-cut black shorts. Rey was more than ten years older than Eugene, but you'd never know it from the shape he was in. Both of them had shaved their chests.

Rey's father, I knew, had been the inspiration. He claimed his father looked like a Puerto Rican Charles Atlas. Rey grew up even stronger and better toned.

"Man, when I found out the girls liked it, I had no problem doing what my old man said about getting in good shape. Every day before dinner, him and me would go down the cellar and pump like two Hectors on a truck. Not to brag, but when I was sixteen I won my first bodybuilding title, Mr. Teenage New York. I had a good six-pack by the time I got into tenth grade," Rey said.

"A what?"

"Your six abs. They're here whether you know it or not." Boldly, he ran his hand over my belly and slapped me playfully on the side of the thigh. I didn't feel the need to complain.

Eugene stood back admiring Rey. "Man, I can't believe you're not 'roided up on the juice," he said.

"Steroids," Rey explained before I asked. To Eugene, he replied, "You do it the hard way, you'll never regret it, bro."

"Man, I wish I had the guns you do. The guy has twenty-inch guns, Gerry."

"Arms, he means," Rey said.

I looked at Eugene. "Are you sure you two are straight?"

"Fuck you," he said. "You could ask Tina what kind of a sex machine I am."

"Who's Tina?"

"Tina is my girlfriend. The main one. I told you about her. I been seeing her a lot now I'm back in circulation. Rey and me sometimes double-date."

"Usually I bring Monique," Rey explained.

"Tina and Monique are good friends," Eugene emphasized.

Rey clapped his hands to stop the chatter. "Let's go! Workout time. We'll start you with a half hour of cardio work, to burn fat."

"Swell."

"Than a half hour of strength and toning. Circuit training. That'll be the drill, four times a week for a while till you're up to speed."

An hour? Miserably, I followed them.

After we got going on the cardios, I watched how they and the people around them moved. I tried to fall into the same pattern, but I felt fat and lumpy. Eugene paused in his leg squats to frown at me, which made me push harder at the bar and the weights. He nudged Rey, who stopped what he was doing to study my exertions.

"What do you think you're doing?" he said.

"I'm doing what everybody else is," I said in a snotty way. I was panting like a dog on a hot day.

"You are? No, you're not. Look, you have to put your feet closer. Positioning of the feet is very important or you wind up with a big ass."

"Bigger than the one you already got," Eugene said.

I felt like taking a swing at him. A woman made a halfhearted attempt to conceal her smirk when she caught me looking her way.

"Eugene, knock it off," Rey said. "I mean it."

Eugene surprised me, saying, "I'm sorry, Gerry. I'm just trying to be funny."

"Forget it," I told him, furious at the people near us who were watching.

Taking his time, Rey showed me the correct way to do leg presses. I bore down with the kind of determination that had finally got me over that wood wall with my father yelling at me. In about fifteen minutes, I surprised them both. Straining, sweating, and huffing, I was still managing to keep up. They had no idea of the amount of pain I was ready to put up with.

Deep in a squat, Eugene called over to Rey, "What's wrong, buddy? You're not pushing as hard as usual."

"Nothing. I still got that guy from A.C. on my mind."

"Fuck him, he asked for what he got. It was either take him down or go down yourself. He wasn't fucking around down there when he come at you, bro. Besides, you impressed the shit out of my uncle."

"Your uncle's standards for being impressed are pretty fucking high," Rey said, pushing himself up with a mean grunt.

"It's all been took care of, anyway, right?"

"Not in my head. Not yet."

Eugene had barely broken a sweat. His attention was wandering to two girls in high-cut leotards trudging like a alpine chorus side by side on their StairMasters.

"Let's go over and work our magic on them two, to forget your grief," Eugene said, ignoring me. "Look at them. I'm getting a woody just watching."

"You don't take training seriously enough, Eugene—"

I didn't stay for the rest of it. Wobbly, I made my way to the women's locker room, where a hot shower soothed some of the pain in my arms and legs.

Afterward, I was shaky but I could feel the energy burning in a way I never felt running. We'd spent an hour working out, and the time had flown.

I found them, showered and dressed and sitting by themselves in a restaurant off the lobby. After I sat down, a waitress came over and put three liter-size bottles of mineral water on the table.

"Thanks, babe," Rey said.

"Sure thing, boss," she replied sweetly. After a moment's hesitation, she asked him, "Listen, can I ask you a favor?"

"Sure."

"I need to go out of town next weekend. Would it be all right if I took a couple of vacation days?"

"Did you clear it with the office?"

"They said it was okay if you didn't mind. Myra said she'd cover for me."

"It's okay with me, as long as they have the shift covered."

"You're a doll!" she said, and bounced away.

I was baffled. It never occurred to me that he was moonlighting. "You *work* here?"

"Actually, I own a piece of the place," he said.

"You *own* this place?"

"A piece. A percent. It's part of my retirement plan. But don't mention it at the office, okay? I don't like people knowing my business."

"Wouldn't think of it," I said.

Eugene was holding up his mineral water bottle to examine it in the overhead light. The name on the label said, Firenze Water "Minerale Naturale."

"They got the right shit, finally," Eugene said.

Rey inspected his own bottle and nodded. "New product," he explained. "We just started stocking this product as our house mineral water. Everybody asks for it. Water comes in fads, and this is the hot new one. You know where it comes from?"

The label was a square of silvery foil that had in the center a reproduction of Botticelli's *The Birth of Venus*, the one with the naked girl with long flowing hair coming out of a half shell beside a couple of adoring angels. I had to squint to read the tiny type at the bottom: *Bottled by Al Fresco di Taormina, Bayside, N.Y.*

"Oh, Bayside," I said. "They try to make it look like it's imported?"

"Well, yeah," said Rey. "But the name itself isn't phony. You heard of Al Fresco? Alberto Fresco? Better known as Polecat Albie?"

"I know the guy. He's been out of the can for three years," Eugene put in. "He's a good friend of my uncle Tony. They go way back." Eugene paused for a few seconds and said, "One thing, he don't like to be called Polecat. Don't never say Polecat to his face. Just call him Albie, is all."

"Yeah, that polecat," Rey said. "He needed a new start when he got out of the can, so they just bought him out rather than shoot him in the head. He invested in some health clubs, then branched into the mineral water business. Now they got their water distributed in health clubs from Staten Island to Boston. It ain't bad, either. Hey, he's like Eugene's uncle, one of the few smart businessmen they have left in that sorry outfit. Distribution, that's the key. Everything comes out of a truck and goes onto a shelf. In the water business, muscle gets you shelf space." He tapped Eugene on the arm. "Tell her what your cousin that works for Polecat told you, Eugene."

"About what?"

"What did your cousin say that Albie told him. Where did he say the future in the bottling business was?"

Eugene finally remembered "Iced tea!"

"Beautiful!" said Rey.

. . .

Afterward, Rey was the first one down to the lobby. Eugene lagged behind to talk to a girl, leaving me with a welcome opportunity for a couple of private words with Rey.

"You available for a quick working dinner before my law class tonight?" I asked.

"No can do. Monique and me are going to Metro 700."

"You really like those places, don't you?"

"Sure. Besides, I intend to get shitfaced drunk."

"What's the matter?"

"Things."

"The guy in A.C."

"Sure."

"Nothing you can do about it now. Listen, Rey, we need to talk. When Eugene comes down, we'll go back to the office and get somebody to drive him to Jersey. Then you and I can get some coffee. Ten minutes is all."

"I don't drink coffee."

"All right, a *protein shake*, then."

"Ten minutes," he said.

· · ·

We *sent Eugene* downtown in a cab to beg his ride back out to Jersey, which was technically a procedural violation, since one of us was supposed to be with him at all times. We knew he was trustworthy enough to get back without any problems, since he knew that doing otherwise would jam up Rey.

I was anxious to talk to Rey about moving things along. There were a lot of rumors that the OCTF was going to close down the Jersey operation and move us all up to Staten Island, to the apartment building where the other unit was keeping Eddie Mack, the other informant. Staten Island was even more remote—and secure—than Jersey. Personally, I hoped the rumor was true. At this point, I knew we could accomplish a lot more, and most important, maintain better control at a crucial time when we went to pop the uncle, from a new location in the city.

We went down to a health-food cafe on Spring Street where Rey ordered his protein shake. I wanted coffee but had to settle for the closest thing they had, decaffeinated herbal tea.

Right away, Rey snapped at the waitress. "I thought I told you to make this with skim milk."

"No, you didn't specify, so they made it with regular milk."

"I said 'no fat,' goddammit! How hard is that to remember?"

The waitress, a thin-faced woman in her late forties, must have needed the job badly enough to take abuse. Her lip quivered and I was afraid she was going to cry.

"I'll take it back," she said.

"Rey, you didn't say anything about skim milk," I put in, disgusted by his bullying.

He backed down, at least. "If I didn't, I'm sorry. It's fine. I'm sorry I yelled at you, hon."

"It's okay. I'll get a new one," the waitress said.

"No," he replied. "Thanks."

When she was gone, I told him, "You can't take it out on the poor waitress."

"Get off my back." It sounded more like a plea than an order.

"All right. I'm sorry. Try to loosen up a little."

"You're telling me to loosen up? That's a joke. Listen, this is my own problem. I'll deal with it."

"It's different this time, buddy. You're not working alone here. You don't have to carry all the weight yourself."

Rey never shopped for sympathy. "Sure I do. Don't you understand that? You were right about one thing—I can't believe I allowed myself to get in a spot like that. You know, all my years, I never got in a position that I had to do something like that before. Before, the bad jams I found myself in, I always, *always*, talked my way out."

"I'll bet you were never involved in a half-assed operation like this one."

"No, you're right about that. Before, I called all the shots. I was the Lone Ranger."

"Now you got two Tontos and about a half dozen chiefs. Welcome to the end of the frontier, *kemosabe*." I reached over and squeezed his hand and changed the subject. "We have to think ahead about what's going to happen to Eugene."

"What do you mean?"

"The way I figure it, this operation has, at most, two months of steam left in it, whether we pop the uncle or not. At most. Then they cut our boy loose. I mean, we're kind of responsible for him, aren't we?"

His face was impassive. It surprised me to see how indifferent he could be toward Eugene's well-being. I guessed working deep undercover for as long as Rey had did that to a person, but the only term I had for it was "emotional damage."

Rey said, "Hey, I'm not adopting him. Shit happens. He goes into the program with the other five thousand wiseguys that ratted out their own. Did you know, they got five thousand wiseguys in the federal witness protection program! It's like a damn government agency."

"Well, Eugene isn't going to be one of them."

"Why not?"

"They never set it up for him."

"The DA couldn't work out a deal with the feds?"

"The DA never even tried."

"What do you mean, they never tried? That was the deal all along."

It surprised me that he apparently believed there were guarantees for Eugene. "I thought he showed you the agreement they got him to sign," I said.

"It never occurred to me to ask."

"Well, the basic problem they had is, they didn't want the feds to know they had him. All that competition crap."

"Exactly what *is* his deal?"

"He doesn't have one, to get right to the bottom line. You didn't know that? All he got was oral promises that they'll give him some bucks and a plane ticket once he's finished doing whatever they wanted him to do."

"You're kidding me, Gerry. No program?"

"Nope. And he can't seem to get that through his thick skull."

"The way he talks, he's pretty sure that he's going to be set for life once they let him go," Rey said.

"He just doesn't get it. Tony's crew gets ahold of him, he's history."

"He can probably depend on that. He'd have nowhere to run."

"Nowhere to hide," I agreed. "There are no arrangements at all to take care of this guy once the plug is pulled."

"I'd say he's fucked, not to put too fine a point on it," Rey decided. "Because there is no way to keep the wiseguys from finding out, once we grab the uncle. I mean, he's going to have to go to court. His name shows up on the reports."

"Exactly."

"This doesn't occur to him?"

"He won't think about it."

"What a fucking moron. Why didn't he tell me about this?"

"I'm surprised he didn't, frankly. Maybe he was ashamed to let you know how dumb he was, signing what they gave him. Also, my guess is he doesn't believe they'll just ditch him."

"What a dumb shit," Rey said. "This is the deal cooked up by Noah and the cop he went down to Florida with? A Frankie DeCarlo deal? DeCarlo got him to do it?"

"Yes" I said.

"Hankie Frankie, they call him, always with the silk handkerchief in the breast pocket. Buys his suits at 'Guidos "R" Us.' "

"That's Frankie," I said.

"Frankie's always been a dirtbag," Rey said. "He did this for grade, for a crummy promotion. They'll use this kid and throw him out like old pair of sneakers. I'm going to go down to the DA's tomorrow and squeeze a few pairs of balls."

"Calm down." I told him. "It isn't time to hit the panic button, not yet."

C H A P T E R 18

The rumors were true. The other unit was nearly through with Eddie Mack, the Irish hit man, who was ready to testify in great detail about his own associations with the top guys of the Giavanni family, including Sally Messina himself. Meanwhile, from what I was hearing, the feds had regrouped and were coming back strong, thanks mostly to a hot new electronic bug they'd planted right under Sally's big nose. I also heard that the feds suddenly had another high-placed informant on ice, totally top-secret. The traps were about to be sprung. The crew was going down. Tony Rossi's allure was dimming.

Not that I cared what happened to Tony. But Eugene, he was another story.

From what I was hearing, the Jersey operation would be shut down, Eugene would be relocated to Staten Island and most of the cops attached to the unit would be reassigned, except for a small core of detectives who would remain with Eugene until the investigation was officially concluded. For the time being, Rey and I were staying on. Among those who were not, I heard, was Lieutenant Campo, whose retirement papers had already been approved.

With nothing official to go on, we just carried on, playing the hand we'd been dealt.

. . .

Once the groundwork had been laid in Atlantic City, meanwhile, the plan to flip Tony was fairly simple. The drug buy would take place.

Tony would be arrested and presented with his options: Either he co-operated and gave up everything that he knew that would incriminate Sally Messina, or he would go to prison for the rest of his life as a repeat offender under the drug laws. If he cooperated, Tony would get a spot in the witness protection program.

Unfortunately, Tony decided to take a vacation in Florida a few weeks after we got back from Atlantic City.

Even Rey lost patience when he heard about that. "What the fuck is going on?" he demanded, pushing Eugene with the heel of his hand.

Eugene wasn't the least bit defensive. "He has some business to get straightened out there."

"How long?"

"Two more weeks, what I hear," Eugene said.

"As soon as he's back, we go for him."

"If he goes for it," Eugene cautioned him.

"We go for him," Rey repeated, and I concurred.

. . .

While we waited, we did what we could to keep busy. One or two nights each week, when I didn't have a class, I'd go out with Eugene as he got reacquainted with his friends from the Giavanni mob, most of them lower-ranking guys in their twenties whose jobs consisted of showing up when they were told to show up. We always went to young-crowd places uptown where Tony and his flunkies wouldn't be caught dead, and I always wore a wire to collect the never-ending "overhears." It was mob cafe society in which the nights passed on waves of booze, cigarettes, and braggadocio.

One thing that surprised me was the lavish quantities of time and money, not to mention coke, pills, and women, these guys seemed to have. They spent as if there was no tomorrow, and after a few times out with them, it occurred to me that this might be exactly the point: Maybe they knew, with an intuition their elders did not have, that the party was almost over. It was as if they, these well-heeled slackers, were in on the joke. When they did have to show up for work, they were hustlers, con artists, enforcers, chiselers, drivers, gofers, and thieves, but it struck me that there wasn't a hardcore violent criminal in any of the bunch I met. Like the rest of their generation, they didn't have enough faith in history to fight anyone else's old battles.

They also had the snatches of movie dialogue down pat.

" 'I swear on the souls of my grandchildren that I will not be the one to *break the peace that we have made today,'* " someone croaked at the party table one night, quoting *The Godfather* to general hilarity.

" *'Ah, shut up or I'll feed your balls to a wolf!'* " a guy across the table hooted, lifting a line from a different mob movie.

" *'You could do that, but then I'd come back and rip your tongue out and wrap it around your fucking neck like a bow tie.'* "

Another ham stood up. " *'I think you should tell your don what everyone seems to know.'* "

A falsetto shrieked, " *'Michael, this cannot continue! Pulllllease!'* "

Listening to this jeering banter, it dawned on me that the Italian Mafia could survive blood feuds, turf wars, and assaults by law enforcement. But it could not survive ridicule. It could not continue, not with its next generation of leaders playing mob Trivial Pursuit, giddy on forty-dollar bottles of wine.

Perhaps because it was so ridiculous, I began to recognize my kinship with these people. Even more than that, as long as I didn't get too far beneath the surface, assuming there *was* any substance below their surface, I found myself actually liking most of them. Knowing that I was skillfully deceiving them in being accepted as one of their own gave me none of the satisfaction I had felt on other undercover assignments, when the deception itself was part of the emotional high. Here, every time I did it, I felt like a rat.

Since thinking about the cultural roots we shared depressed me, I forced myself to focus intensely on the disagreeable necessity of assuming the submissive pose expected of wiseguy girlfriends. Yet at these social events, Eugene kept his hands to himself, spoke to me (when he spoke to me at all) in an affectionate way, and made it clear that I was someone he cared enough about to treat with a degree of respect. Since he was always the elder statesman of the small dinner groups we joined, his example was clumsily and perhaps unconsciously copied by the other young wiseguys, who began to treat their girlfriends better. The girls, in turn, deferred to me, not only as an older woman but as someone who had, from what they could see, achieved a small measure of dignity, which is all they really wanted for themselves on a night out.

All the while, amid the jokes, I recorded everything with a body wire. Whatever I picked up was strictly insurance evidence to bolster the anticipated case we would soon have against Tony, but it wasn't much, in my estimation; it was hardly worth the cost of hiring a stenographer to transcribe the recordings.

Yet I knew that as the careless words accumulated on paper, peripheral criminal patterns inevitably came into better focus. Given the inexhaustible diligence of the police department's behind-the-scenes bureaucracy, stray comments, jokes, wisecracks, hearsay recollections, and wayward anecdotes could be studied, cross-referenced, collated, and assigned their place, like a row of blocks in a puzzle. Ultimately, snippets of gossip, innuendo, and trivia, synthesized in context, make the bricks to lay one atop another and build a case.

. . .

On one of the party nights, a week or so before Tony was due back from Florida, a low-level meeting we were supposed to attend got cancelled. Suddenly free, Eugene and I had dinner alone. He took me to a popular place on First Avenue called Antoinette's, where we shared a double antipasto and talked idly, not about business, but about summer and beaches. I was just beginning to relax and enjoy myself when the conversation in the room suddenly dropped, as if someone had turned down an audio knob. Following Eugene's wide eyes, I saw the reason. Sally "Seashore" Messina himself was looming over the maître d's podium beside the door, surveying the room like a man looking down a well. His entourage of cheeseballs shifted into place as the maître d', chirping like a bird, marched ahead with the determination of a car salesman. The human wedge rolled in like racked pool balls, thick with menace and cologne. Waiters backed off, bowing their heads.

Eugene fiddled with his napkin and kept his eyes down.

I said, "Aren't you supposed to get up and kiss the ring or something?"

"Gerry, please keep quiet."

At the center of the wedge, a head taller than the others, was Messina, whose tanned skin shone as if it had been sprayed with polyurethane. Eugene, the bulkiest and thus the most obvious presence along their lordly path, barely merited a glance from the bodyguards. But suddenly, I saw a face by Messina's side that startled me. Quickly, I dropped my napkin beside my chair as an excuse to get my head down. The wedge pivoted on point and disappeared into the back of the room, behind a partition.

Eugene frowned and shook his head as I groped for the napkin. Just by raising an eyebrow, he signaled the waiter to bring a new one.

"What was that all about? You look like you seen a ghost," he said.

"I did, actually. One of the guys with Messina. The big dope with the crew cut and the radio earpiece?"

"Oh, that guy. I think that's the new security chief Sally hired. From what I heard, he used to be a cop. You know him?"

"Unfortunately. Billy Bittner is his name. He was a homicide detective. He worked with Kevin, of course."

"Of course," Eugene said. "Did he spot you?"

"I don't think so. But he'd recognize me. Kevin and I went to his retirement party from the job last year. After that, I heard he opened a private-detective agency. He was one of those guys always being quoted in the newspapers on inside cop stuff, then he slid onto radio and television, too. A celebrity, media connections."

"Only the best for Sally," said Eugene.

"Well, it's sure depressing to see a decorated cop working for the other side."

"That doesn't surprise me," Eugene said. "Flip side of the same coin."

"Anyway, we probably ought to get out of here."

"He don't know me."

"He could find out fast enough. He'd sure as hell want to know what I'm doing with a good-looking guy ten years younger than my fiancé."

"You think I'm good-looking?"

I picked up my purse. "Of course you're good-looking, Eugene."

"Really?"

"Please, let's get out of here."

Eugene only moved his fingers to get the waiter's attention. Eugene insisted on paying. He left a big tip.

As we walked out, I said to him, "Eugene, you really do have nice manners—"

"When I want to?"

"No, really. What's the word I want. 'Urbane'? Tell you the truth, buddy, you're really not a bad date."

"I don't have to be back in Jersey till midnight," he said. "Phil's supposed to pick me up in Times Square. You want to go to the movies?"

"Sure," I said brightly. There was an Anthony Quinn festival playing in an old neighborhood theater in the Village. We saw *Revenge*, a story about love and betrayal. Afterwards, we took a walk, just another couple on rain-glistened streets, just another couple. For about a block we even held hands, as if it were expected of us, until I pulled away, afraid that Kevin might see us by chance.

. . .

My *confusion grew.* On the nights I worked, posing as Eugene's girlfriend, partying with wiseguys, wearing a concealed wire, I felt like an actress in a long-running play. But other weeknights, sitting at a desk in law class, taking notes on probate, I felt like an entirely different person, a student, not even a cop. My former personal life, which the whole time I'd been an adult had been built around being Kevin's girlfriend, simply ceased to exist.

Meanwhile at the gym every afternoon, Rey and Eugene put me through fitness boot camp. Rey supervised my workouts at first; Eugene showed me how to use the equipment. In time, Rey left us alone; Eugene became my personal trainer.

Occasionally, he would do something I regarded as physically impossible, and tell me to imitate it.

"Eugene, I'll never be able to do that."

"You can do this," he'd say with patience that I never saw before in him. "You could do anything you put your head to." Then he'd show me. Gradually, I caught on. Slowly, I yielded a little control.

It no longer annoyed me that he knew things like how a woman can do her hair. I realized that in his own clumsy way, he was teaching me about fashion, especially color coordination. When I was with Eugene, for the first time in my life, I felt sexy, though I never allowed myself to consider that his attention made me feel that way. He made me conscious of my body, now in a positive way. I saw possibilities. My attitude changed. Unconsciously, even anxiously, I looked for his approval in the way he had once looked for mine. Day by day, the wall between us lowered.

. . .

Oblivious *as he* seemed to be to the changes taking place in me, Kevin seemed to notice a shift in the ground under his feet.

"What's the matter with you? You're getting skinny," Kevin said, looking at me curiously. It was one of those increasingly rare occasions when we had breakfast together before work.

I was eating a bowl of corn flakes with skim milk. "I've been working out at the gym. I told you that."

"What the hell are you wearing? You never used to dress like that before."

It hadn't occurred to me that I was dressing radically differently. I used to wear simple skirts or jeans, print blouses, flat shoes. The changes had been gradual, but Kevin acted as if he hadn't seen me in years. I had on a short corduroy skirt over black tights and black cowboy boots, a red angora sweater with gold buttons, gold hoop earrings. After my morning shower, I'd begun blowing my hair dry rather than brushing it flat. Physically I felt terrific, and even though I avoided monitoring myself every day on the bathroom scale, I knew I'd lost a good ten pounds, without really giving it a lot of thought.

"What are you doing, dressing like that?" he said.

"What do you mean?" I replied, putting down my spoon.

"I mean you look like a bimbo. You're supposed to be a detective, not some working girl from SoHo on the make."

I tried not to show my hurt feelings. "Kevin, please don't talk to me like that—"

"I just don't get you these days," he said, looking away, waiting for me to engage.

I wasn't in the mood, so I just got up and headed for the door. "Listen," I said as I left. "Fuck you, okay?" My reputation for having a mouth aside, I had never said that to anyone before in my life.

He was nearly apoplectic. Face crimson, he yelled, "Fuck *me*? Fuck *you*! I cannot believe I'm hearing that kind of talk from you, Gerry. *Fuck me?*"

"I'm sorry, Kevin. Really."

"Sorry doesn't cut it anymore, Gerry. My advice to you, babe, is you better start watching your ass. You listen to this good."

"Listen to what?" I said, wanting only to leave.

"There's a lot of talk. A lot of talk. You think I don't hear talk? You think I'm some fucking *moron* that doesn't hear what they say—*about my fiancé*? Which reflects directly on *me*? For the first time, man, I'm glad we never got married. Because I'm embarrassed, from what I hear. My friends are laughing."

"What exactly is it you hear, Kevin?"

"Things, Gerry. Things. So fuck you too." He got up to head for the bathroom.

"What *things*?"

He did an about-face. "What I hear is, you spending all your time making time with the goddamn wops."

"You know I'm on the job, Kevin."

His voice went into a mocking high pitch. " 'Oh, Eugene, let's go meet *your friends. Let's cook an Italian dinner together, Eugene!'* You're hooked on this scumbag! You are *crossing the line and going over to the other side, bit by bit!* You think people can't see that?"

"What people? *Colleen?* Who's jealous of any woman who made detective after she did? *Phil Geryon,* that half-wit? These are the people talking?"

"Everybody's talking," he said. "How about Johnny Moran? He saw you kissy-kissy with that fucking old greaser in some bakery downtown."

"I told you about that! What did you want me to do, blow my cover and get killed? *We discussed that,* Kevin! It's my job, dammit. That's the position they put me in!"

"Well, *fuck me,* but I think you're going over to the other side. That's what I hear, and it's what I think, if you really want to know, Gerry. Which just tells me I was right all along. You should never have got your gold."

"How can you say that after all I've done—"

He waved me off. "You never saw me put myself in a compromising sexual position, did you? *Did you?*"

"You're a man!"

"My point exactly."

Tears welled up but I forced them back. All I wanted was peace. "Kevin, I'm boxed-in here! I'm doing the most professional job I can. Please try to understand that. This thing won't go on much longer. They're ready to pull the plug in a month or two."

"And then what?"

"Then I don't know," I said honestly, looking intently at him.

He glowered. "You blowing this guy?"

It hit me like a wallop in the jaw. "What did you say?"

"You heard me. You blowing this guy?"

There was a plastic sugar bowl on the table. I threw it at him, but it bounced off the bathroom door.

"Go to hell, Gerry!" he said. I stormed out of the apartment and just walked. After a while I found myself sitting beside the fountain in Washington Square Park, stunned with fury.

All right then," I said between clenched teeth. "I'll go to hell."

· · ·

I *tried not* to think about what Kevin had said about the gossip. The powers that be had boxed me in on this job in a way they would never have compromised a male officer. As a confidential informant in protective custody, Eugene was never supposed to be away from the plant without an officer, almost always Rey or me. I even had to take him shopping. At first, I deeply resented the chore because of its sexist overtones. What's more, I hated the idea that the NYPD was buying not only his daily necessities like toothpaste and soap, but his expanding wardrobe. Later, as I lost faith in the mission and the department, the shopping became less onerous. By September, I was actually enjoying it. By October, I was doing it with a vengeance.

One day, he needed new sneakers. Once I would have insisted on taking him, kicking and screaming, to a discount place. Instead, we went to the Paragon sports store on Broadway, and I signed the credit card slip for $135 without a qualm.

Since we had the rest of the day free, and Eugene wasn't due back to Jersey until midnight, I decided to do a few personal errands. We took a cab to my apartment, where I made him wait on the front step while I went up to get a lamp that I had ordered from a store on Sixth Avenue. The lamp had arrived with a broken base, and I had to return it.

Eugene carried the carton. When we got to the store, a small place crammed wall-to-wall with lamps, I asked him to wait outside while I made the return. I didn't expect the hard time I got from the manager, a big, unfriendly man who leaned on the counter like he was trying to push it through the floor when I said the merchandise had arrived in damaged condition.

He yanked the delivery receipt off a thick pile on a spike. "It shows here that you signed for the merchandise," he said, dragging a fat finger across my signature.

"I didn't open the box first. The lamp was broken when I took it out."

"That isn't the way it works, miss. Once you sign for it, you accept delivery. I have no way of knowing how that lamp got damaged."

"I can't believe this. You're telling me you won't take it back?"

"Sorry," he said with no conviction.

"I'm telling you that it arrived broken. What kind of a store doesn't make good on damaged merchandise?"

"Maybe next time you should take your business to Macy's," he said with a smirk.

"You sold me a broken lamp and I want my sixty-five dollars and ninety-nine cents back!"

"Look, lady, you broke it, you bought it. Now I'm busy so—"

He froze in midsentence. Eugene was beside me. He leapt the counter like a cat, grabbed the manager around the neck with one hand, and slid him back against the wall like a coat rack. The man's eyes bulged; he couldn't breathe. I was horrified.

"You sold the lady a broke lamp. So now you just give her the money back, is what I suggest," Eugene suggested calmly.

He let the manager suck in enough air to gasp a reply. "No problem!"

"Eugene, for God's sake!" I shrieked.

Eugene let him go and told me, "He said it would not be a problem. I also think he might want to apologize to you for the inconvenience."

"I'm sorry!" the manager yelped, his terrified eyes fixed desperately on a telephone that rang and rang on the counter.

"Now, you just give her the money back," Eugene said. The shop-keeper lunged at his cash drawer and took out a wad of bills that he would have pushed across the counter to me like somebody being robbed at gunpoint.

I was flabbergasted, unable to talk as Eugene made the man count out the exact amount. Then he made him give me a receipt for the returned lamp, which the man somehow managed to write with a shaking hand.

"There's your fucking lamp back," Eugene said, pointing to the box.

"Yes, sir!"

Without looking back, Eugene took me by the arm and led me out the door.

My heart was still pounding when we got around the corner. I was thoroughly appalled, but Eugene behaved as if nothing unusual had happened.

"You can't act like that!" I said, trying to keep my voice down and practically running to get away from the scene I'd just been part of. "Eugene, you can't do things like that!"

"Sure I can," he said nonchalantly, holding me back as a light turned red at a crosswalk. "I won't let anything ever happen to you. I'll cover you like a blanket."

"You're crazy."

"I'm hungry," he declared, guiding me into a coffee bar.

After I calmed down, I tried to reason with him. "Nobody fights my battles for me, Eugene."

"That's part of your problem," he said.

. . .

Later, we wandered the city, alone in vast crowds, and in a while we found ourselves halfway across the Brooklyn Bridge, on the pedestrian boardwalk. As a cold wind whipped up, we stood in the last pool of sunlight under the western Gothic tower, two hundred eighty feet high, a graceful mass of granite hoisting fat cables from Manhattan's bedrock in a spectacular filigree over the swirling East River. I was suddenly aware of the exquisite balance of force under foot, steel straining against immutable stone above the thrust of the tide.

Silently we watched the city's lights twinkle against an ash-colored sky. Below us, cars rumbled across the bridge, their tires whining against the steel decking. A tugboat tooted its horn, and waves churned in the luminescent wake it made pushing down the river to the sea. For a wonderful moment, everything in my world seemed anchored in rock, fastened with steel, and strung with pretty necklace lights.

Eugene faced me, his back blocking the wind. "If you told me to jump off of this bridge, I would do it. You know why? I trust your judgment. If you say so, there must be a reason."

On the roadway below, a radio car flipped on its siren and darted around traffic. I felt the wind catch the moment and carry it off. "Well, don't jump, Eugene. They frown on it at the Harbor Patrol. I'd have to file a report, and I'm too tired."

Yelping like a boy, Eugene suddenly jumped high, grabbed onto a cable and hung there laughing, demanding a reaction.

A quarter mile upstream, a subway train with toy-railroad lights crawled across the lip of the Manhattan Bridge.

"If you told me to jump off, I know that there would be somebody down there to catch me."

"Get down, you fool! You really think your luck never runs out, don't you?"

He let go of the cable and swung back to land on the balls of his feet, like a dancer. "So far," he said.

"Don't push it, okay?" I said.

. . .

But we both were pushing our luck, I knew. On an impulse, we went out together that night, alone. We took a cab to Foley Square, where Eugene always kept a change of clothes at the OCTF office. Then we went to my apartment, where he waited outside while I dressed, grateful to see no sign that Kevin had been home yet. Then we went to the Rainbow Room on top of the RCA Building for dinner.

By now, I knew that Eugene could adapt to a variety of situations, but I didn't realize until that night that elegance was one of them. I felt uneasy and awkward in a place like the Rainbow Room, where I assumed all of the people at the other tables were aware that I didn't belong. Sensing that, Eugene took control without being asked. When he ordered Caesar salad for us, he told the waiter, "Chill the forks, please."

When the waiter nodded knowingly and replied deferentially, "Of course, sir."

Eugene knew how to have a good time, but he also had the grace, when he chose, to see that those who were with him had a good time as well. That was new to me. Kevin would have been suspicious and peevish in a place like the Rainbow Room. Eugene acted as if he belonged, and consequently we were treated that way. A man with no future snatched all he could hold in the present.

We lingered after dinner, drinking champagne until the show came on: the jazz singer Betty Carter, backed by piano, bass, and drum. Watching the city spilling beyond and below, my thoughts drifted on smoky wisps of melody.

My beeper went off, breaking the spell. Getting up to find a pay phone, I realized it was nearly time to leave anyway. Eugene still had a curfew, and a ride to meet. At the phone booth by the rest rooms, I frowned at the unfamiliar number on the beeper's readout, and dialed it.

"Hello, this is Conte," I said when a man with a husky voice answered.

"Gerry?"

"Yeah, who's this?"

"You don't know me, but I'm a friend of a friend."

"And?" I saw my foot tapping impatiently.

"And what I have to say you're not going to like."

Tugging at my pocketbook with the phone wedged under my chin, I fumbled for a notebook and pen. The voice on the phone sounded muffled, as if its owner was afraid I might recognize it. I couldn't. "Go for it," I said warily.

"Fine. Well, this is about Kevin, your husband."

"Kevin and I are not married," I said pointedly. "Is he all right?"

"He's fine. Husband, boyfriend, whatever. We just wanted you to know that he's been seeing somebody, that's all."

"Seeing who?"

"This lady, Terri. We think you have a right to know. He's with her."

I started taking notes. "With her how?" I said.

"*They're seeing each other*, for Christ's sake! We think it's time for you to face up to this, get with the program."

"Who's 'we'?"

Exasperation gushed from the phone. "That doesn't matter!"

"What is it exactly you're trying to tell me, honey? And what did you say her name was—Tiffany?"

"Terri!"

"Terri," I repeated deliberately. "The traditional spelling, or with an *i?*"

"What?"

"T-e-r-r-*i?*"

"How the fuck else could you spell it? What the fuck difference does that make!"

"It makes a difference to me. I need facts."

"Write this down, okay, Sherlock? Your live-in boyfriend and this chick are fucking. F-u-c-k-i-n-g. With a *g*. You got it? From what I hear, she loves him; he loves her, can't live without her. Anything else you need to know?"

"Yeah. I want to know why some asshole would beep me out of the clear blue to tell me this."

My caller let out a laugh and said, "They're a thousand percent right about you. You are one big ball-buster, for a lady cop that's fucking a guinea rat herself."

There was no point in engaging. I just hung up and slid my notebook into my purse.

My attitude changed once I was off the phone. A rug had been pulled out from under my feet. Apparently, and there was no reason now to believe otherwise, Kevin was having an affair with a woman, a woman named Terri, which meant a younger woman because nobody my age was named Terri. For a minute, I stood by the phone and tried to find my bearings, unsure of what packed the biggest wallop: his sexual infidelity, his effrontery, my stupidity? A sense of abandonment welled up in me, but I forced it out of my consciousness.

I knew Eugene would soon be worried, so I composed myself and returned to the dining room, avoiding my own face in those mirrors, just as I always did when passing shop windows. On the way, I realized that I had been a dope. Small, nearly forgotten clues, tiny fibers of evidence of Kevin's infidelity arranged themselves in my mind. I suddenly recalled the faint whiff of strange perfume on my pillow when I fell into bed exhausted one morning—was it the morning after the night in Atlantic City? I'd simply forgotten about it until now; now I understood that she had been in my bed, and this made me feel even more violated than betrayed. It all started adding up: Kevin's smirks, those taunting references to sex, even the fact that he had begun working out again, toning up.

When I got back to the table, Eugene knew immediately that something was very wrong.

"You okay?" he said, getting up to pull out my chair, which was something Kevin never did.

"Sure."

"No you're not. I can see it in your eyes." I met his look and was touched by the genuine concern he showed.

"No, it's just something with Kevin," I told him, hoping he'd drop the subject.

"Jesus, you know, sometimes I forget you're living with that guy," Eugene said, and waited.

I felt a sudden need to fill the silence. "Listen, this stays between us, okay?"

"Cross my heart," he said, and did.

"It's just that apparently he is having an affair."

"How do you know?"

"Somebody took the trouble to beep me with the information."

"Who?"

"An anonymous caller. Sounded like a cop, if you know what I mean."

"Well, maybe they're just trying to rattle your cage."

"No, I know it's true. All the signs were there. I should have seen it a month ago."

"His loss," Eugene said with a dismissive wave. He put his hand on mine. "Why don't we get another bottle of champagne?"

"No, I really have to get out of here and think. Besides, you have to get back, Cinderella."

"Not if you call in and say we got tied up at a meeting with some of the boys."

"You know I can't do that, Eugene."

He fumbled with his napkin, and motioned for the check. "Look, the guy lied, cheated on you."

"And?"

"And you know I have the most greatest respect for you. But after today, I think maybe there's something between us—"

"That can't happen, Eugene."

"You're sure? I mean, I'm here for you. Always, no matter what."

"Thanks, I mean it. And maybe in another time, in some other world, it would work. But not in this one."

"I apologize, Gerry. I was out of line there."

I squeezed his hand and smiled, feeling much better already. Then I leaned over and kissed him on the lips.

We took separate cabs on Fifth Avenue. I went back to the apartment, figuring if Kevin was there we'd have it out and divide the possessions. But he didn't come home.

CHAPTER 19

All *I wanted* was to love someone very well for as long as I could, and I had done that and really believed that marriage would eventually consecrate the effort. And now it was over and all that remained was to say so and move on. Over the years with Kevin, I had let myself become conditioned to solving problems on my own. We both worked long hours, but I dealt with the tax accountant, the landlord, the plumber, the relatives, the holidays, and the doctors. Craving approval but assured at least of control, I brought solutions to Kevin. For him, it was never a good time to discuss problems. Which, I now realized, was why we almost never discussed marriage.

A week after I got that phone call in the Rainbow Room, a cop who was once a close friend of Kevin's killed himself. The cop's name was Jimmy Dugan, and I think they had gone to high school together. I hadn't seen him in about five years. The last image I had of him was of a puffy man slouching into middle age, his brash good looks gone and his good nature going. Jimmy had never made detective, and he never let you forget about that, and in time the only contact with him was a Christmas card that we glanced at and tossed in a pile, and one year the wife's name was missing on the card and we didn't even bother to ask.

Then Jimmy got himself jammed up, not just with booze, but on the job, where he was shaking down hookers for sex in Brooklyn. One of the girls turned out to be an undercover cop who put the collar on him in the backseat of his radio car with his pants tangled around his knees.

Jimmy didn't wait for the departmental hearing. Late one night, he drove over to Jersey City and parked his Ford Taurus in the waterfront park beside the Hudson. Apparently he was just standing there staring at the Statue of Liberty aglow in the dark when he put the gun in his mouth and pulled the trigger.

For somebody who hadn't seen the man in years and hadn't even bothered to pick up the phone, Kevin took it hard.

"How was the funeral?" I asked when he came in that night. He'd been drinking, which is what cops do after a funeral. Except for an exchange of phone messages about Jimmy's death, this was our first encounter since the anonymous call at the Rainbow Room.

"You should have come," he said, weary and sullen. "The poor sorry bastard. About five cops showed up, along with the ex-wife and two kids. I didn't even know the guy had a second kid."

"I'm sorry," I said, unable to look at him.

"Yeah, well. I guess he ran out of options."

"You look awful," I said.

"Excuse me," he replied, going to the refrigerator for a beer. He took it into the living room and flipped on the television. The eleven o'clock news was on, some anchorwoman in a bright red dress, was giggling with some man about the weather.

"You've been working late these days," I said, testing the waters. I wasn't in the mood for a big scene.

"Yeah." He took a slug of the beer and stared at the television.

"Anything special?"

"Same-o, same-o," he said, forcing back a belch. "We have a sting operation that's probably going to pay off pretty soon. The Dominicans that muscled in on the Chinese smack business started reaching out, big-time."

"To the cops?"

"Yeah, the cops. Jesus, it's amazing some of the scumbags they let on the force now. This just isn't the NYPD I joined, let me tell you. Internal Affairs is crawling all over the precinct and everybody's fucking freaked. Nobody knows who to trust, not to mention the Dominicans don't particularly care who they shoot. You never saw people like this. Some of these shit-for-brains even believe in this mumbo-jumbo voodoo-spell shit, that they have a magic shield around them that bullets can't penetrate, so they're safe from the cops. Unbelievable. It's only a matter of time before a cop goes down out there. At least the fucking guidos go to the same church as we do."

I instinctively put out my hand to caress his shoulder but pulled it back and instead took a seat in the easy chair across from him.

"I know this has been a bad time for you," I said. Kevin feared nothing on the street except a dirty cop, which was something that made him almost physically sick. There was a lot of talk about the mess in his precinct. The clean cops were terrified about who might have said what out of context, or who failed to say what to Internal Affairs. Worse, from my perspective, the NYPD had been nickel-and-diming Kevin and the other detectives in the precinct, to the point where Kevin thought that somebody was going to get killed just because there wasn't enough money in the budget to approve an overtime shift. Everybody knew where all the money was really going, of course. To a more glamorous operation across town, across the river. To fishing trips with Eddie Mack, to Nunziata's and the goddamn Rainbow Room; to months and months of wiretaps listening to Sally Messina discuss his piles.

Rain streaked our window. The rain sealed us in what was left of our private world; for a moment, I was lulled into thinking that things could be fixed, that it wasn't the end, only an intermission. Then I blinked away tears as I realized that it was not an affair that had brought me to this. For some time now, I knew. I had been ready to go.

"Talk to me," I said. In my mind he was receding already into the past along with summer picnics and high-school faces.

"Talk about what?"

"Your behavior, for one. This weird relationship we have, for another."

Lurid colors from the television reflected in his damp eyes. "Gerry, I don't need this right now," he said. He got up for another beer and went to the bathroom. When he came back, I hadn't moved.

"What do you mean, my behavior?" he said uneasily.

"Your carrying-on," I said.

"What, a couple of beers after a cop's funeral, for Christ's sake? Booze is the only drug a cop is allowed to use."

"You know what I mean," I said. "Do you think I'm stupid?"

He didn't quite get my drift. "Gerry," he said, "I don't know what's done you more damage, getting your gold shield or getting involved in that law-school shit. But the bottom line here is your behavior, not mine. You're the one with the priorities screwed up, diddling around with that guinea prince for months. Do you think I'm stupid?"

This sent me into my worst move, the defensive stance. "My behavior is completely proper," I said in a voice that rose higher than I wanted. "I'm doing my job, nothing more."

"Not from what I hear," he said.

"And what is it you hear, Kevin?"

"Talk. Talk that you crossed over the line with this mutt."

"Which mutt is that?"

"Your guinea prince."

"And crossed the line with him how?"

He didn't specify. "Lady Gold," he said, exhaling the words like smoke. "Lady Gold, girl detective. Dickless Tracy, with the wiseguy boyfriend."

Even when he was drunk, Kevin seldom got this surly. "Kevin—" I said.

"Things will never change between us, you know, Gerry."

"What's that supposed to mean?"

"You don't give an inch."

"This isn't the point—"

"You're a freaking dreamer," he persisted, clearly enjoying himself.

"I set reasonable goals."

"Sure, like you had to become a detective, the same as me. Then it was law school, with your nose stuck in a book every time I come home. What's next, Congress?"

"Kevin, I know about her."

He blinked and shifted his position the way a suspect does when you hit a nerve.

"I know about her," I repeated. "Terri."

The smile dissolved. "Who?"

"Game's up, buddy. I got an anonymous call the other night from somebody. Some friends you got, buddy. Then I made a few inquiries of my own, and bingo: Terri Malone, Queens, New York, twenty-six years old—barmaid?"

"Waitress," he said, deflated.

"So that's it," I said.

I was already moving on in my mind. Once I had got over the blow to my dignity, the girlfriend was merely the catalyst for the inevitable. It was my decision, and for the first time ever, it was my life alone. I was already planning where to get moving boxes.

Kevin protested: "It wouldn't have happened if you had been there for me, if—"

"No more," I said, cutting him off. "I'm not buying into that stuff anymore. We should have faced up to this a long time ago."

A minute passed silently. Feeling only weariness, I said, "I hope she's the kind of person you need, Kevin."

"I really didn't want this to happen," he insisted.

"Neither did I. But face it, you and I should never have stayed together this long. Until now, it just wasn't convenient for either of us to admit it."

"We had a pretty good run," he said hopefully.

"Well, our Broadway show closed. I'll get a sublet somewhere until I can find something permanent."

"You don't have to do that. I'll leave."

"No. You stay. This was your place first. The lease is in your name, and it's easier for me to work out other arrangements."

That suited him well enough that he felt compelled to say, "I never wanted to hurt you. I'll always love you."

"Wasted words," I replied coldly.

"Let me ask you this, then. Are you having a thing with this wiseguy?"

"A *thing?*"

"An affair, I guess they call it."

"Are you nuts?"

"You aren't?"

"No!"

"With nobody?"

"Kevin, how well do you know me?"

"Well, an affair doesn't just mean sex," he said.

"On my block it sure does. How do you figure that, Kevin?"

"An affair can be letting somebody else into the circle. That constitutes betrayal."

" 'The circle'?"

"That's right. You talk to somebody, confide in somebody intimately."

"And that's the same as having an affair?"

"I knew you went outside the circle," he said, somehow figuring that now he had evened the score.

Kevin wobbled into the kitchen, but I wasn't willing to indulge him. "I'm going to bed," I said. "Sleep on the couch or in our bed, it doesn't matter to me. Tomorrow I'm not due in till noon, so I'll start making arrangements. All I want is my books and records and the china my mother gave us. The rest of the empire is yours."

"One thing, I don't want any lawyers involved," he said, as if we were negotiating.

"There's no need for that. I'll sort out the property fairly."

"Law school finally pays off," he joked, spilling his beer. I was exasperated until I realized—it was no longer my couch. I went to bed.

For a while, I lay in darkness trying to make a mental list of things that had to be done, but I wasn't able to let go of him totally. It was remarkable how little he had changed over the years. He was fixed in a time that I had nearly forgotten. I had thought that we were moving away from each other over the past few years, but now I understood that I had been the only one in motion. I had him pressed in a scrapbook.

Uninvited, an old image of Jimmy Dugan intruded into my mind. Jimmy, trim and beautiful in his tuxedo, raising his glass at our engagement party to give the toast, which he prefaced by saying he had taken the words from a passage D. H. Lawrence had written in *Lady Chatterly's Lover*. Hearing that, the guests on my side of the room smiled approvingly, without a trace of comprehension; on the Irish side, the mention of a famous dirty book elicited a few anxious chuckles.

Later, I asked Jimmy to write down the passage for me, and I put it in our future wedding album:

So it must be; a voyage apart, in the same direction. Grapple the two vessels together, lash them side by side, and the fight storm will smash them to pieces. This is marriage, in the bad weather of modern civilization. But leave the two vessels apart to make their voyage to the same port, each according to its own skill and power, and an unseen line connects them, a magnetism which cannot be forced. And that is marriage as it will be, when this is broken down.

I heard the refrigerator shut with a dull thud, the gasp of a beer-can tab, Kevin in the kitchen, steadying his stand, sails furled, anchored against the wind.

. . .

Rey had a word for those emotional catastrophes that fly into life like a bat through the window—death, sickness, betrayal, grave loss, grievous fault and irrecoverable blame. Any of them can deliver a blackjack bastinado to the psyche and leave you reeling. "Wartime," he called them. Times when you open your eyes in the morning instantly aware of the trouble, staring at it as you would at a movie screen before which you had briefly dozed off. You move through the day like a guerrilla.

In this state, I managed to move out of our apartment within two days. For the first two nights, I stayed at a hotel on Gramercy Park. It was easier than I thought it would be to find a furnished sublet. It was in Greenwich Village, a studio with high ceilings on the fourth floor of a brownstone. It felt like home.

Meanwhile, my status on the job changed perceptibly. In a closed society like the NYPD, word spreads fast when someone breaks loose from the moorings. The day after I moved, I encountered Colleen at the OCTF office, where we met to drive out to Jersey. She was anxious, as though she believed trouble was contagious.

"I heard about you and Kevin, and I just wanted you to know that I'm here for you," she told me nervously.

"Thank you, but I'm okay," I replied, not interested in getting into a discussion. What could Colleen do for me? Colleen was bitter. She was one of those malicious, chronically depressed people who believe in distributing misery like a papal blessing. I was shaky, but I knew it would pass if I didn't let myself get initiated into the share-the-grief sodality.

"Now you don't have anybody to protect you," Colleen pointed out helpfully.

"What do you mean? I have a lot of friends. I don't need anybody to protect me. A busted relationship, even one as long as ours was, isn't the end of the world, Colleen."

She nodded without any conviction. "Well, I guess it's like there's blood in the water, which is when the sharks move in. You have to watch your back, Gerry. Believe me."

"Are you trying to tell me something?" I asked, utterly baffled.

She touched my arm and said ominously. "A jilted woman is seen as big trouble. She's a threat to everybody."

That made no sense to me, but I said only, "I wasn't ditched, Colleen. I was the one who left."

"Even worse," she said. "Just watch your back."

Colleen was still in her forties, thickening rapidly around the middle, with blue eyes as dull and cracked as an empty swimming pool. Talking to her always made me feel like I was speaking into a door buzzer-intercom. I felt a little sorry for her, but was vigilant about not letting her know that.

She continued, "You say you have friends. Okay, that's true. But let me tell you about some of your friends. Like I know a couple of guys you used to work with in the Tenth Precinct? You know they say you used to give them BJs in the back of the radio car?"

"That's total bullshit, Colleen, and you know it."

"Of course it is. I know that, Gerry. I never wanted to say anything before, but my point is, new stories build on old stories. Now the new story is you're giving the BJs to Eugene."

"Colleen, that is ridiculous," I replied, trying not to let her know that she now had me peeved. "Why are you telling me this?"

"You should know, that's all."

With relief, I spotted Noah coming out of the men's room down the hall and told her I'd see her outside later. When I deliberately followed him into his office and sat down, he gave me the kind of look you see staring at you over the counter at the passport office.

"So I guess you heard," he said.

"Heard what?"

"That we're closing down the Jersey operation and consolidating it in Staten Island."

"No, I hadn't heard officially. That's very covenenient, Staten Island," I said sarcastically. "When's this take effect?"

"By the middle of November. You ought to be talking to your lieu-tenant if you have any problems with this, Gerry," Noah said. A rueful smile crossed his face. "Incidentally, I heard what happened. I'm sorry." He had a quizzical look that I didn't care to indulge.

"Thank you," I said, and waited a second before returning to the original subject. "What does shutting down the Jersey unit mean for me?"

"Not a whole lot, at least until the end of the year, when the budget runs out. Less travel, basically; you won't need to come into Manhattan so often during the day, since we'll have two units consolidated in one place. You and Rey and Danny Flanagan will stay with the CI, at least till the thing with the uncle plays out."

"Which is when?"

"That's something I was hoping you could tell me," he said unhappily. "Rey says a couple of weeks. He says they're working on something to try to bring this to a head."

"What about everybody else in the unit? Where do they go?" I said.

"Just between you and me, everybody else gets reassigned. They'll get the word the end of this week. But I'd appreciate it if you let them hear it officially first."

"No problem," I said. Colleen, who had five years' seniority on me as detective, was going to be furious, back catching four or five cases a day again in a regular detective's precinct job at some grind like Midtown South. Back working the chart, four days on, two days off.

. . .

When Colleen and I got out to Jersey later that morning, there was a phone message for me. It said, *Eleanor ??—call*—and gave a phone number. At first, I couldn't think of anyone with that name, but then it came to me, Eleanor Vanson, the reporter. What did she want? I used the phone in the guest bedroom.

It was answered on the first ring. "Vanson."

"Yeah, Eleanor?"

"Yeah, who's this?"

"It's Gerry Conte, returning your call."

"Gerry! Thanks for calling back. You're a tough one to find. I'm glad my message finally got to you. I've been meaning to call since I ran into you in Atlantic City. How about getting together for dinner or a drink?"

"Eleanor, I'm involved in a heavy job. I really can't talk about anything." The last thing I needed was for someone to link me to a reporter.

Tapping a pencil against something, she said, "Listen, I'm hearing things. We should talk."

"I can't discuss anything about a case," I insisted, not wanting to give her an opening to probe.

"No, actually, that isn't why I called, although I am back on the cops-and-robbers beat. Actually, I have a few things to tell you. I heard about your operation. And that there's not a lot of progress so far, right?"

"Boy, you're persistent. I'm just not at liberty to say."

"Jesus, girl! Listen, you have a confidential informant stashed somewhere in the sticks for six months or so, and he hasn't delivered squat. A young nephew of Anthony Rossi, am I right . . .?"

"Meet me for a drink," she said when I didn't reply. "Not a lot of shop talk, just ugly, vile gossip. Like, I'll fill you in about the famous television anchorman who turned up at St. Luke's emergency ward last week with a lightbulb up his ass after some unwise foreplay at a leather bar. Something you'll never read about in the paper."

"What?"

"Sixty watts, darling."

"Who?"

"Not on the phone." she said. "But there is one small piece of shop talk I've heard that you'll be interested in, if you don't already know."

"What's that?"

"You know they just flipped Sally Messina's consigliere?"

"No," I said, utterly astonished. Could that be true? Messina's consigliere, Vincenzo Amarosa, widely known as "the Hammer"—his most trusted confidante, and heir apparent? The news was flabbergasting, if true.

"The feds?" I asked.

"Who else?"

"You're putting that in the newspaper?"

"I can't. At least, not yet."

"Let's have that drink," I told her quickly.

. . .

W*e agreed to* meet the next night at a place called Cowgirl Hall of Fame on Hudson Street, a boisterous country-western joint with sawdust on the floor, a life-size statue of Dale Evans beside the door, and cowboy hats and lariats hanging from the ceiling. When I arrived, a little after eight, she already had a booth, from which she gave me a quick appraisal.

"Whoa, look at you. What are you doing, working on a pageant-perfect body?"

"I've just been going to the gym every day," I said, sliding into the booth.

"I'm impressed. Make that depressed," she said.

We had a couple of drinks and ordered some potato skins. She started doing most of the talking.

"Doing those little personality features was wearing me out," she said, explaining why she had returned to the police beat. "Like, I interviewed a twenty-million-dollar lottery winner who said he planned to use the money to get his porch fixed, and then I had to interview Jimmy Carter in his little carpenter's outfit. All in one fucking week. So I was pretty amenable when my boss said I either had to return to the cop beat or become the television critic."

"Why not television critic? That sounds like a great job."

"Hah!" she scoffed. "Actually, I did think about it for a week or so, since it's such a cushy setup. But finally I decided that writing about television is like reviewing dwarf-tossing contests. No matter how well you do it, you're promoting a reprehensible spectacle. Meanwhile, my personal life is in shambles, as usual. My boyfriend left me last month. He told me he needed space, as he called it, to reevaluate his life, such as it was."

"Oh," I said.

"Well, actually, he was starting to wear me down. He was an investigator for the Labor Department who worked workmen's-comp fraud cases, which are so fucking dull that he spent the last two years writing a play about a dysfunctional Irish family. I told him Eugene O'Neill got there first, but he insisted that O'Neill didn't have to contend with the homosexual cabal that conspires to keep the straight writers out of the New York theater, the Irish especially. Then all of a sudden, he takes a year's leave of absence and moves up to Lake Placid, where he's rewriting his dreadful play for a summer-stock company upstate. This way, he plans to come in under 'the radar,' as he put it. Can you imagine? Anyway, he's history. So I moped around for a while and then started going out again with a guy I met last year in the U.S. Attorney's office."

"Manhattan?" I asked.

"Brooklyn."

I made a mental note of that. "He's the one who told you about the feds flipping Vincenzo Amarosa."

"Vinnie the Hammer," she said. "Don't you love the name? I wouldn't say where the information is from, of course, but it is amazing what some of these guys will tell you if they think they're going to get laid somewhere down the line."

"You want to tell me about what's going on?" I said. "With Sally Messina, I mean. Are the feds going to nail him?"

"All I know," she said, "is they flipped this guy Amarosa and have him on ice, in protective custody. And he's currently talking up a storm."

So much for the vaunted NYPD organized-crime intelligence. We didn't even know Messina's top man was in custody. After another round of drinks, it became clear to me that Eleanor already knew the essential details of our investigation, so I loosened up a bit and began discussing Eugene, trying not to get too specific about police information, such as it was. Still, it was nice to have someone who listened and, what's more, seemed to understand the uncomfortable position the NYPD had me in.

"So basically the guy is your responsibility," she said.

"Yes, basically."

"And if he hasn't produced anything yet, and the feds manage to grab

Messina first, which is looking like a pretty good bet, you're basically left flapping in the wind."

"It's possible."

"And then your informant goes off into the witness protection program?"

"No." I looked at her.

"No? Why not?"

"That wasn't in his deal."

"You mean they just cut him loose?"

"You got it."

Her eyes narrowed. "You like this guy?"

"Despite my better instincts, yes," I admitted, and explained how Eugene had changed for the better, at least socially, over the months Rey and I had spent with him. She was surprised I had been teaching him to read.

"When did they start remedial English education on the police department?" she wanted to know.

"I do that during downtime. It's amazing how the guy has come along in the past six months."

"How old is this guy?"

"Twenty-nine," I said.

"Cute?"

"Sure. At times. Very muscular. Deep, dark eyes."

"And?"

"And what?"

"Are you involved with him?"

"No."

She snorted and said, "Right, that would be against the rules."

"Absolutely."

"The unwritten rules."

"Right," I said.

We'd been talking for well over an hour. Another round of drinks arrived. I realized I had lost count. On a little stage, an all-girl three-piece country-western band was playing. Their name was spelled out on the drums: She-Buckaroos. The singer had on a fringed western-style dress with red-and-white leather cowboy boots that matched the tablecloths.

"Well," Eleanor said in response to something I said about the body-building regime that Rey and Eugene practiced, "the muscles are impressive, but on the other hand, any guy who spends two or three hours a day in intense physical communication with his body, and a couple more hours thinking or talking about it, you shouldn't be surprised if he turns out to be excessively interested in himself."

"I guess that's true." It was after eleven o'clock. We were both a little drunk.

"So, any chance you're going to sleep with the guy?"

My face reddened. "No," I insisted.

"Excuse my bluntness, but why not fuck him now that Kevin is out of the picture?"

"No, that would cause too many complications. Fantasy is always better than reality."

She was trying to figure me out. "Come on, you're obviously interested in the guy. Hasn't it come up at all? Oops, let me put that another way, hasn't the thought ever occurred to you over all these months together?"

"Not really," I said, dismissing a hint of personal speculation.

"So what's the attraction?"

I gave it a try. "Take Kevin, okay. This was a guy who was never wrong. Even if he didn't have the answer to the question, he acted like he did. Over time I began to realize that showed a sense of deep insecurity that he would never dig his way out of. Eugene, on the other hand, is so hungry for knowledge that he was willing to learn from me; he admired the fact that I was going to be a lawyer. Kevin always called lawyers whores, and it was clear he had no reason to revise that even when I started law school. But Eugene was proud of me; at the same time he saw me as a teacher. Imagine. A guy from his hopeless, sorry background, with all that Italian steerage baggage—"

Eleanor was more interested in sex. "He hasn't made any moves on you?"

"None. In fact, he once told me he thinks of me as Madonna, as corny as that sounds."

"That slut?"

"No, the church one."

"Oh, the well-known virgin," she said. "Actually, I'd feel pretty conflicted in your position."

"Alienated," I said. "Incredibly alienated from everything, including the NYPD. I've never felt that way before as a cop."

"Maybe you're feeling things as a woman, not a cop."

"But I'm always a cop first. That's a right you fight for," I said.

"So being a cop means you have to be a savior around the clock?" she asked. "Can't you climb down off the cross occasionally?"

"Not when they have you nailed up there," I said.

CHAPTER 20

The *official word* about the transfer came a few days later, after a clearly unhappy Inspector Marcomb called me in for an interview. When he got up on his high horse, Marcomb spoke in sentences that started out at a brisk trot and fell off a cliff before he got to the punctuation.

"Christ, Conte, if we can't factually ascertain the capabilities of the other side for shit I'd say no one would give me an argument that we have an unacceptable situation here with entirely too goddamn many excessive unknowns."

"Yes sir," I said, cautiously.

"Beyond that, as you may have heard, we're closing down the Jersey operation and consolidating a small part of your unit with Unit Two in Staten Island. Several officers will be reassigned, but I want you and Detective Vargas to stay with this, ride it out to the end. Detective Flanagan will stay, too. And Lieutenant Campo, of course."

"That's fine, sir."

He sighed and leaned back in his swivel chair with his hands locked behind his neck. The chair looked like it might tilt over, but he held steady. There was a box of reports on his desk, and an open file beside his phone.

"Now, I've been reviewing the case carefully for a week," he said, in a manner that suggested he hadn't given it a lot of thought previously. "Obviously, you're the one who managed to get over on the target,

Anthony Rossi, while the unit was falling flat on its ass. I expect you to spearhead the final assault."

"On the uncle, fine," I said.

"Right. Now tell me, what are your bright ideas?"

"Actually, Inspector, Detective Vargas and I have been working on some ideas."

"So I hear," said Marcomb.

"As you probably know, sir, the uncle has been talking about getting out of the family business in New York, retiring to Florida, where he told me he has some real estate and other ambitions. In fact, the CI tells me his uncle has been in Florida for the past few weeks looking things over."

"Go on."

"Well, the other day, I had the CI contact him by phone in Florida to get a reading."

"He wasn't calling the weather service again, was he?"

So that had gotten around. "No sir. I told him I would be listening on the extension. He talked to the uncle for a while. Supposedly, Tony put together some kind of big property deal down there, buying into a resort or something in South Beach. He sounded vague about the details, but one thing he made clear is he's going to need a big chunk of cash. Soon."

Marcomb brightened. "That's encouraging, a sudden need for cash."

"Which, obviously, gives us our opportunity to set up a sting," I continued.

"What kind of a sting?"

"The way we have it tentatively arranged, as soon as the uncle is back in town, we lure him to the Plaza Hotel. The bait will be the first big delivery on the cocaine that's supposedly being supplied by the upstart Cuban operation that the uncle believes Rey—Detective Vargas—is fronting for."

"Campo tells me the setup is, these Cubans want to move big-time into the New York market. Isn't that a little far-fetched? I mean, the Colombians have a total lock on that market."

"Well, the Colombian lock isn't as tight as it was," I told him, surprised that a man who ran one major police operation wasn't up to speed on the complex and fast-moving international drug business. "The Cali cartel is under a lot of pressure right now, with the top guys in jail. They can't keep a lid on the internal violence. They've been shooting each other down in the streets. Meanwhile, from what Detective Vargas tells me, Castro needs dollars so bad that he has been making his own deals to open up new Colombian supply routes through Cuba, which is something he avoided until recently."

"Right . . ." Marcomb said.

"Because he didn't want to give the American government any excuse to come down there and do a Noriega on him, Vargas says."

"Precisely," Marcomb said hesitantly. "So of course the cover of a Cuban cocaine operation would ring true—"

"It would to a smart guy like Tony Rossi, who keeps his eyes and ears open, especially in south Florida."

"Absolutely," Marcomb agreed.

"So our hope is he'll be smelling the green and ready to pounce when we drop the bait."

Marcomb drummed on his desk. "Good, good."

"One of the reasons it took so long for us to get to this point is the uncle had to believe this wasn't a one-time opportunity to score. He had to believe the Cubans were planning on a long-term relationship with him, just to lead them on. Not just drugs, but money-laundering. Tony, of course, figures if he can do one or two big scores, he's out of here and the Cubans then can deal with whoever takes his place in New York."

"And that's because Rossi sees the Giavanni family crashing down sometime soon?"

"Yes," I said. "That's the key. The uncle wants out before the ship goes down."

"And he'll take the bait? You know, probably better than I do, that this guy's one of the few really cagey capos they got left in that family. It isn't his style to come personally to a hotel. A guy like him usually sends flunkies."

"That's right, sir," I said. "And he was definitely cagey for a long time, no doubt about that. But now, from what Eugene says, there's some urgency on this property deal in Florida. The uncle is going to need a big wad of money, fairly fast. The way Detective Vargas laid it down is, the people he supposedly works for don't know New York City. They're nervous about a setup, so they need to meet the uncle personally on neutral turf, so they can get comfortable. Only the uncle and one of his guys."

"You got all the details worked out? We're not talking anything half-assed here, right?"

"I hope not," I said. "We're just about ready to go, pending your approval and Lieutenant Campo's. The way it's arranged is, we'll have adjoining hotel rooms. In the room to meet with the uncle are Detective Vargas, the CI, and two Hispanic officers we have coming in from Narcotics to pose as the Cuban honchos. I'm in the adjoining room with backup. We'll have a surveillance camera and audio, feeding to a van on the street. Plenty of backup down the hall, in case there's trouble. And three unmarked radio cars on the block in the event there's a chase. You never know."

"That you don't!" Marcomb boomed. "Like in war, nothing ever goes exactly as planned on the battlefield."

How would he know? I liked Marcomb from the few dealings I'd had with him over the years, but most of his police background had been in administration and public relations. Still, it was necessary to get him fully on board.

"But before this goes down, there's one small hitch," I said.

"Jesus—what?"

"The uncle insists that the CI and Detective Vargas come down to Florida for a final meeting. Then they're supposed to fly back to New York with him."

Marcomb looked suspicious. "More expenses?"

"The uncle insists on them coming down."

"Okay," he said reluctantly. "We really have to get this show on the road before the feds make their next move, which by my guess will be sometime right after the Christmas holidays. So let me know." He looked at me expectantly. "Anything else on your mind, Conte?"

Carefully choosing my words, I said, "I was just wondering whether you're hearing anything from the feds. Whether they're making any real headway on their end of things."

"Don't worry about that," Marcomb said with a big dismissive laugh. "They're still working on wiretapping the toilet at Sally Messina's clubhouse. We're miles ahead this time."

"They don't have any top informants?" I said.

"None in the making," he assured me firmly.

It wasn't my place to mention what Eleanor had told me about the feds' grabbing Messina's consigliere Vincenzo Amarosa.

Marcomb's phone rang and while he took the call I let my eyes wander to the top sheet of a requisition file he'd left open on his desk, which I managed to read upside down.

- One Half-Dozen (6) SWD M-10 pistols.
- One Half-Dozen (6) Intretex TEC-DC pistols
- One Half-Dozen (6) Striker-12 semiautomatic shotguns (revolving cylinder)
- Two (2) Steyr Army Universal Rifles.

What in the world did we need with a cache of weapons like that? For the first time in weeks, I thought of Kevin and the officers from his precinct, working a really dangerous street operation that couldn't get funded to save its life.

"That's quite an arsenal there," I said when he put the phone down.

Marcomb closed the file and explained, "Oh, that. Listen, let me give you some advice, okay, because you're exactly the kind of officer, especially being female and all, who will end up running your own unit someday, assuming this operation goes right. So let me give you a little management strategy, strictly off the record. Here we are coming up on the end of the year, which means my budget for next year is being put together right now at headquarters. And despite the expenses your crew has run up with that asshole CI, we're still coming in a little under budget. So the thing is, no matter what, you got to make sure you spend everything in your current budget, even if it's for stuff you're going to put in a closet for a rainy day. Otherwise, the bean counters will cut back your budget for the next year."

"Yes sir," I said politely.

He looked at the clock. "I'd say your plan looks good. Go for it, as soon as you get Lieutenant Campo to sign off on it."

"Thank you, sir."

It was snowing lightly outside. I got up to leave, but Marcomb stopped me.

"How's the CI behaving? He being a good boy?"

"No serious complaints, at least from my perspective. It took awhile, but he's performing pretty good."

"They tell me you've been spending a lot of time working with the guy."

"Only doing my job."

A small smile crossed his face. "I hear you've been tutoring the guy, teaching him arithmetic?"

"Teaching him reading and writing, actually. In fact, I'd say he's reading at about a ninth-grade level now. I figure he's going to need the skills once we turn him loose."

"A washed-up wiseguy? Don't get me wrong, Detective. It's wonderful you're doing the missionary work. They even tell me his manners have improved. Not that it's going to help him where he's headed."

"Excuse me, Inspector?"

He laughed. "Back to the street."

"We can't let that happen."

"You don't worry about that part. You just get this thing on the road, pronto."

. . .

The next morning, when I went out to Jersey, there was a U-Haul van out front. Colleen was crying, but I brushed past her and found Rey at the kitchen table, where he was bent over the *Daily News*.

"This doesn't look good," he said, pushing the newspaper at me.

DEVIL'S NIGHT

Gruesome Rubout on Boardwalk Ride to Hell

ATLANTIC CITY—Mobster Santo Albanese went to hell and back yesterday, but he didn't live to tell the tale. His battered, bullet-ridden body was discovered slumped in a seat on a boardwalk amusement ride called "Dante's Inferno" yesterday when ride operators readied the attraction for the day's business.

On the attraction, an amusement park favorite for over a century, two-seat cars travel on tracks through a darkened cavern illuminated by fright scenes.

"I turned on the switch to check the cars running on the track, and the first car that bumped out of the doors had this body in it," said Kevin Albaugh, 22, an employee of the indoor amusement park whose duties include a daily inspection of the Dante's Inferno ride. "The guy was stone-cold dead, stiff. He had one of those big boxes of chocolates in his lap, a big red satin heart."

After making the grisly discovery, Albaugh called police. The body was identified as that of Albanese, 68 years old. Sources described the victim as a semiretired soldier in the fractious Philadelphia Mafia family who still had interests in a number of small businesses in Atlantic City, including holdings in topless bars and peep shows.

The murder had the familiar markings of a mob hit, but police sources said they had no motive yet. "As far as anybody knew, this guy had been out of the mob picture for years," said one police source. "He and his wife had sold their business and were planning to move to Florida."

The source said that Albanese's son, Anthony, operated the top-less clubs and other businesses owned by the couple. The son was reported to be out of town. Police said they had not been able to question him.

Albanese's wife, Loretta, could not be reached for comment. "They were always fighting, but they loved each other," said one neighbor at the couple's $300,000 ranch house in nearby Margate, who declined to give her name.

Noah called within minutes.

"You seen the paper?"

"I was just looking at it, actually."

He was hollering like I could do something about it. "That's the guy from A.C. that Tony sent you to see!"

"I know that."

"This gets worse," he said.

"Tell me."

"It gets very fucked-up, Gerry. We cleaned up the mess that Rey left. But it turns out there was a hitch. You're not going to believe this. The night Rey hit that guy? Turns out there was a witness after all."

My heart sank. "Jesus, who?"

"The valet-parking guy at the casino. Evidently he's on retainer for the Philly boys, just keeping track of comings and goings in general. This comes from Eddie Mack, who says he got it from an old pal in the Philly mob. It seems that night, you guys didn't know that some of the valets routinely jot down the vehicle I.D. numbers on expensive cars, and pass them on to the Philly guys who run a chop shop and keep the casino parking valets on retainer. The next day, when they found the body, they run the vehicle I.D. numbers and guess what?"

"What?"

"Instead of altering the numbers, the brilliant fucking NYPD leaves its calling card, and it traces back. The Philly mob evidently put two and two together and came up with five."

"Meaning what?"

"Meaning they figured that Anthony Rossi is working for us, for Christ's sake! And evidently they also discovered that one of his supposed people—that would be you, Gerry—had a visit that night with Albanese, a few hours before their guy gets whacked under the board-walk. Naturally, they then figure that Albanese was double-crossing them, ratting them out somehow before he retired."

I felt sick. In Philadelphia's underworld, it was still the 1970s, and the Philly mob thought nothing of gunning down people in the streets. They were the most vicious mob in the country.

"Does Sally Messina know about this?" I asked warily.

"Apparently not, thank God," Noah said. "With all the bad blood between Philly and New York, the lines of communication are cut. The Philly guys are working independently from New York. Every man for himself."

And every woman, I thought, knowing I was in a pickle myself. I was worried about Rey, but especially about Eugene. How long before the dots all got connected?

"The tunnel of love, you got to admit that's a nice touch," I said lamely.

"Fuck that," Noah snapped. "What this tells us is, we got to pop the uncle fast. Before the assholes from Philly catch up with him on their own and screw us up."

If they figured the uncle for one, Eugene would also have been im-plicated as a rat. "What about the CI?" I said.

"That's your responsibility, to keep him alive and well until you peo-ple pull this stunt off. Then all bets are off."

. . .

The new location was in one of those big prewar apartment com-plexes overlooking the harbor from a hill in Staten Island, where you could go up to the roof and watch the nubby ferry boats chugging back and forth past the Statue of Liberty. The apartment complex consisted of four seven-story buildings arranged as a quadrangle around a central court. In the middle was a tiled fountain in which water gushed from the open jaws of four marble turtles. The entrances to the courtyard were through two vaulted arcades with Art Deco mosaic patterns on the ceilings. You felt good about yourself just coming through them and hearing the water splashing from the fountain.

They had had Eddie Mack in one of the second-floor one-bedroom units all the time he was in custody. Next door was a sloppy two-bedroom apartment that the cops used as a headquarters. All of the apartments opened onto landings that were bordered on the courtyard side by four-foot-high concrete balustrades. They put Eugene into the vacant unit, a small studio on the far side.

He wasn't happy about the cramped quarters. The place seemed cozy enough to me. It had high ceilings and a fireplace, though that probably hadn't worked since the Eisenhower administration.

"How long they going to keep me in this shithouse?" he demanded once we got him settled in.

"What did they tell you?" I asked him.

"They said till they shut down the investigation. Then I'm taillights, babe. I'm set. New car, a nice condo, a suitcase full of money. A whole new personality. Maybe you could come with me."

I ignored that invitation and said, "Taillights? You have any idea where you're going when this is over?"

He pulled the curtain aside and peered out the window to a slice of leaden sky that looked like it wanted to snow. "Someplace with sun and buns, maybe Florida."

This was a day before he and Rey were scheduled to go to south Florida at Tony's summons.

"I think you'd better enjoy Florida this time around, because I don't think it's going to be a realistic place for you to settle once you're out of this," I told him gently. "Too many people you know down there, Eugene."

He nodded. "So Arizona, maybe. They got sun there, right?"

"Yeah, they have sun."

"Arizona, then," he said, like he believed he was going to have a choice.

. . .

We were still going through the motions. That night, we were scheduled for dinner with a couple of very low-ranking Giavanni guys who were setting up a phone calling-card scam. They rented an old candy store on the Bowery and had twelve phone lines put in. Illegal immigrants would come in and pay to call back home for a certain period of time. The wiseguys used the stolen card numbers to put the calls through. With what little mob protocol was left, they needed to go up the chain of command and notify Eugene, so nobody could accuse them of working an independent scam and not giving Tony his usual cut. More and more, this was the kind of penny-ante stuff that the younger Giavanni guys were involved in, hustling phone calls to refugees from Senegal. As usual, I'd be wearing a wire and spending the next day searching for a snippet of conversation that might be used to bolster the case against Tony.

It was the middle of the afternoon and I was looking forward to a couple of free hours to study before we had to go out. I told Eugene I'd see him at seven. On a hunch, I stopped down at the rental office to check the lease on the place he was in. Sure enough, it was month-to-month.

I had got to know Eddie Mack just from hanging around. He was a good-looking Irishman with a lot of charm—just the type I fell for once, although of course Kevin hadn't murdered people. The cops all liked Eddie. He was a model informant, well-behaved, full of good cheer, one of those guys who always had a new joke. Eddie was brimming with information that came from the Westies connections with the Giavanni family, and he'd been talking all year. When he took over the family, Messina had unwisely denigrated the Westies as a pack of drunks and morons. He was only half right.

Like ghosts from the nineteenth century, the Westies haunted what was left of the Irish waterfront gang's fiefdom along the Hudson in Hell's Kitchen, on the West Side of Manhattan. A lot of the modern-day Westies were hardcore Vietnam veterans who prided themselves on not being afraid of anything or anybody. Once, on a freezing winter day, one of the Westies stopped a cop and stripped him of his leather coat, just like that. Before the wiseguys made an uneasy truce with the Irishmen, the Westies on at least two occasions dumped the bodies of made members of the Giavanni family into the Hudson River. One of Sally Messina's first mistakes after taking over the Giavanni family was to renege on deals the family had made with the Westies. When Messina went on trial in early 1989, in another case he would beat, Eddie Mack testified against him. Eddie had become that most dangerous of enemies, a professional witness.

At first, I was extremely uncomfortable around Eddie because all I could think of was that this affable character with the quick laugh had murdered twelve people. Then the personality takes over. A part of you is able to overlook even that.

Like Rey, Eddie also liked to cook. One night, he made a terrific dinner for Rey, Eugene, Frankie DeCarlo, and me. He had a cloth on the table and a little vase with a fresh carnation in it.

Frankie always hated Eugene, whom he regarded as a lowlife. He made it a point not to say a word to him all through dinner. Afterward, outside on the landing, Frankie took me aside and told me that there was a lot of talk about my relationship with Eugene.

"You're too nice to the guy, Gerry," he said patronizingly. "People notice things like that. Trust me on this."

"So I should treat him like an animal?"

Frankie himself had been transferred back to the squad effective the following week, and he apparently felt free to speak his mind, such as it was. "Look, I'll tell you straight. You and me, we're Italians. We have a special relationship in an investigation like this. The rest of them, they never forget you got that vowel at the end of your name. Cop and wiseguy, it's like we're all the same underneath—guineas. They scrutinize everything we do differently."

"Being Italian has nothing to do with my job," I told him with a stony glare.

He raised his palms as if checking for rain. "Okay, okay. A word to the wise is sufficient. What I hear, they say maybe you're playing by mob rules. Only you have a badge."

"I don't believe I'm hearing this," I said fiercely. I had no intention of defending myself against something that ridiculous.

"If I was you I'd get off my throne and look around. What is it your father does for a living? Isn't he a supplier to restaurants on Mulberry Street? Am I right? That's what they say."

"Frankie, my father is the most honorable man I have ever known. He has spent his whole life hating everything the mob stands for."

"Yeah, yeah, I know. Believe me, I know. It's all this *Italian* thing. So before I walk, I thought it was my duty as a *paisan* to tell you there's talk." He chucked me lightly on the arm.

This was the man who had used his Italian credentials to trick Eugene into signing his life away? He made me sick. I muttered, "There is nothing I can do about talk."

"Well, and maybe this is none of my business, you can stop being so cozy with that dirtbag Eugene Rossi."

"I'm supposed to be his keeper! That's my job, Frankie."

"Well, maybe you can poke him with a stick through the bars sometimes. Make it look better."

A couple of days later, on a Sunday, all of the cops from the unit went on a fishing trip accompanied by Eddie Mack, who technically was not supposed to be out of the safe location except on official business and under tight guard. In fact, Eddie had set up the trip, an all-day excursion to catch sharks on a charter boat that went out from Montauk Point at the tip of Long Island, twenty or thirty miles out to sea. The point was to haul in as many sharks as possible, kill them, and throw them overboard to attract new ones.

Eddie had been solicitous enough to ask me if I wanted to come along. "The hauls have been the best in years," he said with great enthusiasm. "A boat went out last week, they were up to their keisters in blue sharks—eight-, nine-foot suckers streaking in for a feeding frenzy, with their fins riding high like sails. Mean sons of bitches, they'll eat anything you throw overboard. Garbage, fish guts, an old shoe, they swallow it."

"What do you do when you catch them?"

"You haul them in—very, very carefully. They fight like a Tijuana whore. Once they're on board, while they're still thrashing around and biting the wind, you come up and beat the hell out of them with a baseball bat, then push the mangled carcass back in to make chum and draw some more. I'm telling you, you get things going right and you can be riding in that boat on a whirlpool of churning bloody foam. It's like a bloody water rush. There's beauty in the red water."

. . .

The next day, Rey and Eugene went off to meet Tony in Florida, with girlfriends in tow. Here I was alone in New York during a miserably cold, sunless November day when even the pigeons looked like they wanted to give up and shoot themselves. Kevin was with his Terri with an *i*. And my partner and a Mafia informant were headed to Florida, *at taxpayers' expense.*

Worse, I had to drive Eugene to the airport. "So we need a ride tomorrow out to LaGuardia. Me and Josephine, that is," he said, naming the lucky girl. "Rey and Monique got their own ride."

"You need a *ride* to the airport? You don't expect me to drive you, do you?"

"Come on, Gerry. You're working. What's the difference? You get paid the same."

I tried to keep my voice down. "They have a new invention called taxicabs, you know."

"Not in this fucking burg, they don't. You want I should take the ferryboat with all the luggage?"

"I don't care if you swim," I said.

He smiled. "We got to pick her up at nine o'clock tomorrow morning, her apartment in Queens." He pulled out an airline folder with the tickets that he had wadded into his pants pocket.

I grabbed it, made sure they were coach seats, and then said in a voice laced with sarcasm, "Oh, that won't be out of the way or anything. Let's see, all I have to do is leave my place in the city around, what, seven-thirty? Drive over here to Staten Island for you, then back across the Verrazano Bridge to pick up your girlfriend in Queens. From there, it's an easy swing over to LaGuardia Airport. Anything I can bring you two, incidentally? Suntan oil?"

As if actually considering the offer, he said, "No, thanks a lot. But let me give you the directions to Josephine's so you can pick her up first. It'll give me more time to get ready. The plane leaves at eleven."

I had no intention of going to his girlfriend's place like a radio-car chauffeur. "No way," I said flatly. "I get you first. And make it eight o'clock. You never know about the traffic."

. . .

At least he was ready on time. We drove in silence to the girl-friend's neighborhood in Elmhurst.

The two of them were decked out like a pair of Long Island lawn ornaments. He had on black silk pants and an open shirt with a big gold chain on his chest. There was some sort of pendant on the chain, which had *Eugene* spelled out in tiny diamonds. I thought I'd seen all his jewelry by now, but that was a new one. He wore alligator loafers and had a new gold Bertolucci Pulchra watch.

He carried only a gym bag, but the charming Josephine was packed for a world cruise on the QE2. Counting her makeup satchel, she had three matching Vuitton bags lined up on the front steps of her apart-ment building, where she waited like a vision in a metallic gold suit, the pants of which hugged her tight little butt like a surgical glove. Completing the ensemble were gold spiked-heel sandals, gold hoop ear-rings the size of bread plates, and a thin gold bracelet on her right ankle.

When we pulled up at the sidewalk outside the airport terminal and I opened the trunk, a skycap lunged for the bags. She held up a palm and hoisted the makeup kit out, struggling like it was full of rocks.

"Eugene, honey, carry this for me. It's much too heavy," she said in a little girl's tiny voice. He stood there unwrapping a stick of spearmint gum, which he carefully folded in half.

"Don't call me honey," he told her brusquely, after placing the gum on his tongue like he was giving himself Communion. "How many times I got to tell you, for Christ's sake? You wanted to bring all this shit, you carry it yourself."

Like a Roman movie director, Eugene floated into the terminal with Josephine scampering behind, and a skycap on her heels with the bags. I was ready to pull away when I saw Eugene spin back out to the sidewalk through the revolving door. An airport van blocked me in.

He rapped on the window and stared at me like a pet store puppy. I rolled it down halfway. "Thanks a lot for the ride," he said. "See you in a while. Do everything just like I do it, I mean have some fun." He blew me a kiss. Josephine watched this unhappily from the streaked terminal window.

I drove off in a fury and immediately got boxed up in an hourlong traffic snarl. I was too angry to sort through all of my emotions, but the truth is, now that I look back on it all, at least one of them was jealousy.

· · ·

They were back, amazingly tanned and happy, on Friday. The un-cle took the bait.

"Ready to rock-and-roll?" Rey said.

"As soon as possible." I replied.

"Eugene's making the arrangements today with Tony."

Rey booked the rooms at the Plaza. After work, I stopped by to look over the arrangements, a spacious suite on the eleventh floor, over-looking the park. Afterward, we had dinner at a restaurant on Sixth Avenue. I sensed his mind was somewhere else.

"I'm thinking about retirement," he said.

"Aren't we all," I said.

"No, I'm serious. As soon as this shit's finished."

Most cops tote up their pensions practically daily, like misers with a sack of gold coins, but this was the first I'd heard Rey talk about it. He spoke more openly than usual with me. Clearly, this was the end of the road, and I was, weirdly enough, his closest confidante.

"My first ten years were all spent with the really violent groups during the seventies, heavy-duty shit. Man, what a world for a kid right out of the service. I never really knew who I was, but something exciting was happening every day. Then things settled down. The Vietnam War was over. All the revolutionaries who were shooting their mouths off about how they would burn down the Pentagon, they started having kids and moving out to Long Island and working on their portfolios. Even the motorcycle gangs were mellowing out and getting too old for all the crap. Suddenly everybody had enough money. Terrorism was something that happened overseas.

"But of course that didn't mean they would dismantle the antiterrorism units. Hell, they were *jobs*. There was a *schedule*. The funny thing is, they were spending more money than ever on it. All you had to say was, *'War on drugs!'* and you got all the funding you needed. So what the hell, I wasn't going to bitch. I tended to business, did what they asked me to, filed my reports. Basically, I was infiltrating kid groups. Bullshit sting operations, busting street drug distribution where they'd make a haul, bring in sacks of heroin or coke, piles of confiscated assault weapons—whatever looked good enough to arrange on a table and call a press conference so the brass could pose for their freaking pictures. Man, it was a bureaucracy. For me, the police department became more or less a second job."

"That's what got you into the health-club business?"

He nodded. "I sold the automotive business out near JFK Airport, the one that I told you about. They had me use it as my deep cover all those years."

"The one that you worked the Lufthansa heist on?"

"Right, it was a goddamn gold mine. All the NYPD was interested in was getting back its initial investment. You talk about asinine business accounting. I walked out of that deal with about a quarter million bucks."

"Get out of here!"

"Not bad for police work."

"Not bad."

"So now you've put your papers in?"

"Not yet. I may wait till next year to goose up the pension a little. Monique thinks I should get one more year of overtime before we move. But the pension comes to about fifty thousand a year for life at my grade."

"Move where?"

"Florida."

"Is everybody moving to Florida?" I said.

"Why not? This thing has me exhausted, this fucking baby-sitting. This isn't the kind of police work I signed up for."

"Eugene wearing you down, old-timer?" I asked playfully.

"The guy's young. He always wants to party."

"I thought you liked to party."

"Don't believe it. It's work. This guy is always ready to rock-and-roll all night. We get ready to call it a night, I'm always looking at my watch, he comes over with two beautiful girls."

"Tough work."

"Well, at least we all got a lot of OT in. That counts extra, what you make the year you put your papers in."

"I have nine years to go, myself," I said.

"You ain't going to make it," he told me.

"Why not?"

"You just ain't."

That was debatable, especially in my own mind. I was still operating under the assumption that I'd finish this job, take it where it led, get my law degree and grab a promotion into administration. I thought I'd make a very good boss, someone who could help the department throw open the windows, make it feel like home not only for women, but blacks and Puerto Ricans, Chinese, and whoever else swam our way off that big river of immigrants that flowed through this city like life itself. I really believed that I had that kind of responsibility, not only to the NYPD but to New York. Scratch the surface and you'll find a lot of cops feel the same way. But this was no time for career-gazing. It was still wartime; wander off carelessly down the road and you could get your head shot off.

CHAPTER 21

"*Friday night,*" Rey told me. It was Wednesday already. "Tony says he'll meet us at the room, ten o'clock sharp."

On Friday, Eugene was nervous as a burglar all day, and gulped down two martinis during dinner with Rey and me in the Oak Room. He ordered the porterhouse steak, ignored it when the food came, and called for another drink. I vetoed it, and he sat back without an argument.

By eight o'clock, the unmarked van was in place out front, parked beside the fountain in front of the hotel. For authenticity, Eugene had told his uncle that he was staying overnight with me in one of the suite's two bedrooms, which struck me as unnecessarily complicated even though Rey said he thought it was a good idea. Just in case Tony or one of his boys glanced in the wrong door, I unmade the bed and arranged some lingerie on the bureau, a silk teddy that I hadn't had any impulse to wear for years. Eugene was still edgy, but the teddy got his attention. He got to feeling playful.

"It's only eight-thirty," he mentioned casually.

"So put on the television," I said from an armchair near the window, where I was thumbing through an expensively printed hotel guide to New York City that was nothing but ads for high-priced merchandise.

He looked over my shoulder. "That necklace would shine on your neck," he said.

"For ten thousand bucks, I'll pass," I said. "Listen, why don't you go next door and see if Rey's doing all right? Maybe he needs some help." Rey had to check out the surveillance gear in the room and make sure the backup officers knew where to wait in a linen closet down the hall. Actually, he had asked me to keep Eugene occupied, so I withdrew the suggestion and told him to sit down while I went over to the long bureau to inspect the electronic monitor they had set up in a drawer. Instead, he grabbed me gently by the shoulders and backed me slowly toward the bed. The next thing I knew, I was on it, with Eugene on top of me, trying to kiss me. I was absurdly aware of having my shoes on. His mouth was wet on mine. I kissed him, but kept my hands by my side. Then I turned my face away. "It can't happen, Eugene," I said firmly, feeling his weight lift off my body.

Maybe if he had touched my cheek, if he had just done something tender, or said the right words, maybe it might have been different because I was sad and lonely and angry enough at the situation I had been placed in to say the hell with it and give in.

He tried, but he was hopelessly clumsy. "I have feelings for you," he said with a look as direct as a bullet. Footsteps clumped by outside the door.

"Eugene, don't mess things up."

He smelled sweaty. I moved my arm across my abdomen, casually brushing the front of his pants. He wasn't even hard.

"Mess up what?" he yelped with a sudden laugh. Hoisting his upper body up with his arms, he started doing push-ups, up and down, without coming into contact with my body. I felt ridiculous. "I got to stay in shape!"

"Eugene, get off me. It's getting late."

He braced himself, staring down at me with a funny look that could have even been relief. Then, catlike, he thrust his body up with one arm, flipped off the bed and dropped to the floor. But he continued doing push-ups, alternating from one arm to the other, taking in loud gulps of air, putting on quite a show.

"Eugene, I'm sorry," I said, stifling a laugh.

"Sorry about what?" Now he was doing knee-bends with his arms extended out straight. "What, you really think I would want to ruin what we got?"

"Good," I said. "Whatever it is we have."

"Besides," he went on, "Rey could walk in and get the wrong idea. He's already a little jealous. This is no time for personal trouble."

I had collected myself and was sitting on the edge of the bed. "Jealous? Of what?"

"Of you and me."

"What would give him that impression?"

"You try to fight it, but he knows that you love me in a weird way."

"How's that?"

"It's wrote all over your face. You say it in the things you did for me. The stuff you put up with for me. Why else would you take all the shit?"

Shaking my head, I said, "Eugene, in a very odd way, I've grown to care about you. I regard you as a friend in need, but nothing more. Are you happy now? Will you leave me alone or do I have to call the cops?"

"Listen, Miss Crabtree. I was born at night, but not last night." He clapped his hands together happily and went into the bathroom to towel off. When the phone rang, he was all business. He took the call in the living room.

"Right," he said, silently mouthing to me the information that it was Uncle Tony. "We're ready. Room Eleven-thirteen, okay. You bet. Yeah, it's wrapped good. Okay, see you then. 'Bye."

"Everything okay?" I asked.

"Change of schedule. He'll be here in twenty minutes," he said anxiously.

We knocked on the adjoining door and Rey let us in. Carlos Lopez, the handsome Spanish undercover officer posing as the big shot in the Cuban gang, sat formally in a leather-upholstered chair, dressed to the nines, like a merengue bandleader waiting to go on. He just nodded. He was not supposed to speak English when Tony arrived. Thankfully, the surveillance technology was good stuff, an audio-visual system that had been perfected not by law enforcement but by television news for those hidden-camera stunts they loved. The video transmitter was a little box with a tiny lens that they'd concealed inside the room's smoke alarm in a corner of the ceiling, with one feed direct to the stakeout van, where they had taping equipment, and another one to the room I had, where a normal-looking television set on a stand was wired for live reception.

Leaving Eugene in the reception room with Rey, I went to the adjoining room, making sure the door was locked on only my side, in case something went wrong and I had to rush in. I flipped on the television and watched Rey and Eugene fidget with the two packages they would give to Tony. The packages contained the promised amount of cocaine, genuine stuff borrowed from the police evidence locker, just in case Tony felt a need to verify it. Everything seemed to be in order. In my earpiece, one of the detectives from the van outside confirmed that they were aware of the change in schedule.

Then Noah came on. "We're ready to make the doughnuts," he announced, trying to sound like a cop. Noah had decided to accompany the officers waiting in the van, I knew. I could picture him crouched in the dark, careful not to get his trenchcoat dirty.

In his best command voice, Noah said, "Okay, let's go through this one last time. First, Tony and his flunky come up to the room." He waited for a response.

"That's affirmative," Rey said, rolling his eyes.

"Okay, then what?"

"Then I introduce him to Carlos, say it's to get acquainted, man to man. After the preliminaries, Carlos takes me aside and tells me in Spanish that we're on. I go over the deal with Tony, who then hands over the money. We give him—make that his stooge—the stuff, shake hands, and send him on his way."

"All of which is being recorded out here, and monitered by Conte next door," Noah said crisply.

"Exactly. Then Tony and his man leave, and you guys grab him out front," Rey continued.

"Roger," said Noah. "What could be more simple than that?"

My gun was on the dresser, under the teddy. Two backup officers from down the hall came in quietly and joined me to stare at the black-and-white picture coming through clearly on the television. Then they went back to their posts.

Exactly on time, Tony's Town Car pulled up out front and stopped fifty feet from the marquee. Sammy Red got out from behind the wheel and opened the door. Looking like two businessmen, they walked up the red carpeted steps and pushed through the revolving doors into the lobby, where a string quartet was playing a Strauss waltz in the Palm Court.

In a minute, the elevator doors opened out onto the eleventh floor. Sammy Red came out first. Tony was right behind him, his eyes darting up and down the hall, as if it was a tunnel. Red knocked on the door and they let him in. Eugene greeted his uncle with a kiss on the cheek.

"Where's the other guys?" I heard Tony say. He stared hard at Carlos, who was approaching with Rey. Red stood by the door with his legs slightly apart and his arms folded, watching.

"No need for anybody except my boss here," Rey said. He introduced Carlos and translated the amenities. No one shook hands.

"Well, here's the goodies, as promised," Rey said, pointing to the packages, each wrapped in brown paper and tied with bakery-shop string.

"Introductory offer. If you're happy with this, hopefully we begin a long and fruitful business relationship."

Eugene interrupted, speaking loudly. "How you been, Uncle Tony? You want a drink?"

"No drink. I'm in a hurry. Eugene, you're vouching for this shit."

"Absolutely, Uncle Tony. I checked it out myself. Pure macaroni."

"Okay, let's get this done."

Tony was to pay fifty thousand dollars for enough coke to net him a quarter million. He motioned to Red, who seemed edgy as he took two fat business-sized envelopes from his pocket. He was watching himself in the mirror. Red stretched his neck, looking as if he was trying to pull an extra inch of skin out of his collar, and handed the money over.

Rey took the envelopes and dropped them on the desk beside the packages. Red picked up the goods.

"Money to make money," Rey said.

"It's the American way," said Tony.

"And we hope you'll be a repeat customer."

"I got a money-back guarantee," said Tony. With Red leading the way, they left the room and took the elevator down.

. . .

A *knot of* tourists waited for taxis on the steps in front of the hotel, but it should have been no problem for the five plainclothes cops on the sidewalk to grab Tony and Red as they went to the car. No one except the doorman paid attention to the black Lexus that glided up slowly next to the front of the taxi line as Tony and Red came down the steps. Two Hispanic men got out and waited for Tony and Red to step onto the sidewalk, ten feet from where the tourists stood in a cluster. The doorman was blowing on his whistle to move them away when both men whipped out sawed-off shotguns and let loose with a burst of gunfire.

Tony went down in an instant, clutching his belly. Struggling to get on his feet, he knelt, lurched violently, and fell back into a pool of his own blood. Red didn't even look back as he ran to the car, got in, and made a screeching U-turn before speeding away toward the park. The Lexus sped off before anyone knew what had happened.

People were screaming. Like a crazed referee, the doorman kept blowing on his whistle. Startled by the shots, hundreds of pigeons rose up from the plaza near the fountain and blew into the sky like a plague of locusts. Guns drawn, a dozen cops rushed toward Tony writhing on the sidewalk. He wasn't going anywhere.

Red sure was. The Town Car careened down the street and sideswiped a horse-drawn carriage that was clomping back to the hotel with a family of four. The horse reared in terror, broke its reins, and galloped across the plaza toward Fifth Avenue, where it ran head-on into a downtown bus. Wildly out of control, the carriage spun on a broken wheel and plowed into the line of taxis, where it flipped over, spilling its occupants, a man, a woman, and two teenaged children, across the wreckage. The horse lay on its side, unmoving.

"*Holy shit!*" Noah was screeching in my ear.

Sirens wailed above the screaming of the people on the sidewalk. Three radio cars, light bars flashing, roared off in pursuit of Red at the wheel of the Town Car, but he'd had a good two minutes' head start.

Rey and I ran down the fire stairs and found a surreal scene outside. It looked like a terrorist bombing.

"What the fuck happened?" Rey demanded, grabbing Noah by his trenchcoat lapels. "How the fuck did you allow this to happen?"

Noah could only babble incoherently. All around us, cops were pushing people back, hollering into radios, clearing a path around Tony, who did not move. No one appeared to be in charge.

I flashed my shield and tried to break through to the place where Tony lay, but Rey was right behind me and pulled me back. Two EMS wagons pulled up, sirens wailing.

The family from the horse-carriage looked like war casualties strewn on the sidewalk, but they were moving. Tony was not. They strapped him unconscious on a stretcher and took him away.

Red didn't make it. They picked him up after a chase across town that ended up on the southbound FDR Drive, just below Bellevue Hospital, where the Lexus's front left tire had blown out on a pothole at eighty miles an hour. The car had bounced off a retaining wall and flipped across two lanes into a construction site and come to rest top-down on a bulldozer. It took an hour to cut Red's body out of the wreck. The two packages were not in the car, the officers who got there first claimed.

. . .

Tony clung to life despite two bullets in his gut and two more in his thigh. When he regained consciousness the next day, he was read his rights and placed under arrest at bedside. Two cops were stationed outside the room. The doctors said he'd be paralyzed for life.

The newspapers had a field day, of course. Even though they only had a piece of the story, it was the piece we were missing. The headline the next morning in the *Daily News* was huge:

MOB BIG
GUNNED DOWN
OUTSIDE PLAZA

Innocent Family of 4 Hurt During Gunplay;
Did Philly Mafia Order the Hit?

Other than the description of the pandemonium outside one of the city's top tourist hotels, the morning-newspaper stories were short on detail. The hit men had escaped. Eleanor Vanson and one other well-plugged-in reporter got the information from unnamed sources, quoting a mob informant to the effect that the hit men were in the employ of the Philadelphia mob. But those sources were baffled about what it meant for Sally Messina, since Tony Rossi wasn't considered a player on Sally's starting team. Meanwhile, Tony was in the hospital, and the sources said he would be indicted within days. The family in the horse-drawn carriage, tourists from Minneapolis, were all still hospitalized, but expected to recover from broken bones and contusions. Anxiously, I scoured every paper, but there was no hint in the aggressive coverage that Tony had been lured to the Plaza for a police sting. Nor was there any mention of Red, other than a brief story in the back of the paper reporting a man killed when his car went out of control on the FDR.

. . .

Later in the morning, Rey, Eugene, and I were sitting, stunned, in Noah's conference room, waiting for the brass to arrive. Eugene's beeper went off. He looked at it like it was on fire.

"Who is that?" he wailed. "They know! They know! My uncle knows! I'm fucked!"

"Take it easy," I told him. "Your uncle doesn't have enough wits yet to know what happened to him."

We sat in abject silence. In a few minutes, Marcomb came in looking very grim. We waited anxiously while he arranged his papers.

"Nice police work," he said with ugly sarcasm. We remained silent. It wasn't our fault the Philly mob had accidently spoiled our operation.

"Well, at least we busted the guy," Rey said glumly.

Marcomb glared at Eugene. "Get him the fuck out of here, for Christ's sake." Leaving the room, Eugene kicked over a chair. He had it figured, all right. In no time at all, Tony would, too.

. . .

Later, we brought Eugene in to see Noah, who listened impassively.

"I done what I was supposed to," Eugene said with tears starting to show in his eyes.

"Things didn't go off the way we hoped," Noah replied.

"You can't expect me to do no more than that."

"Nobody does."

With a wet sniff, Eugene stared intently at the polished table, as if looking for a glimpse of his own reflection.

"So now you guys are supposed to give me my suitcase full of money and set me up," he said.

"Whoa," said Noah. "You got to testify."

"Things change! We had a deal! I'm a dead man now. I can't go to no courtroom and show I'm a snitch. My uncle's legs are shot to hell, and I'm the one that got the guy to the place where it happened. Ain't that enough for you guys?"

Inspector Marcomb took a seat by the door, quietly observing.

"What about it?" Eugene demanded.

"Well, we aren't totally finished with you yet," Noah said. "You don't have to worry. You're being protected. Your uncle is in the hospital, in custody. So he isn't going to be doing anything like issuing any orders. Meanwhile, you sit tight."

Eugene jumped up and lunged toward Noah's desk, but Rey rose and pushed him back forcefully.

"What do you mean, 'sit tight'!" Eugene cried. "It ain't your ass in the shitter."

"Sit the fuck down!" Noah ordered. He looked like he was ready to bolt around his desk and dive out the door if Eugene got any closer.

Rey shot Eugene a look that called in a couple of chips. Eugene fell back into his seat, but his muscles were coiled.

After a minute, Noah said quietly, as if going over the fine print on a car lease: "Now. You agreed to assist us, for as long as necessary, in return for certain considerations." Eugene glared. Noah went on, "As you will recall, there were no conditions on how we defined assistance. Nor was there a time limit."

"There's sure as holy fuck one now!" Eugene screamed. He was on his feet. "About two minutes is how much time I got if I show my face on the street—"

"Our agreement," Noah emphasized, "was to provide you protection. You have that protection."

"Listen, asshole, I'm out of this!"

"Now shut the fuck up. You're out of this when I tell you you're out, and not a minute sooner."

Eugene knew he wasn't going any farther. He knew he was trapped.

"Eugene, you don't have to worry. You're in protective custody. No one expects you to go back on the street. As far as your obligations to us, we will exercise them at our discretion. Of course, that means testifying in various cases that are being prepared or anticipated."

" 'Various cases'? What's that mean?"

Angrily, I interrupted, "What he's saying, Eugene, is that they want you to go to court until they tell you they're finished with you."

"Fuck that," Eugene said.

A little chuckle came from Noah's throat. "You always knew that was the deal."

"Testify on what? I told you everything that I know."

"But you have to say it in court—"

"We have an agreement," Eugene stammered.

"And we've respected that agreement, Eugenio," said Noah, all lawyer now, the expert in agreements.

Eugene blinked. "What about the money I got promised?"

"There will be some money, I'm reasonably certain of that."

"How much money?"

Marcomb cleared his throat.

"I can't say," said Noah. "That will depend, of course."

"Depend on what?"

"On your cooperation."

"What about the new personality?" he said petulantly.

Noah allowed himself a tolerant smile. "You mean a new identity?"

"Yeah, what about it?"

"I take it you're talking about the federal witness protection program."

"A new setup, in a new place," Eugene said quickly. "With money to live on. The witness program, whatever it's called."

"Eugenio, nowhere in our agreement is there a word about the federal witness protection program. That is strictly speculation on your part. The witness protection program is operated by the feds, not the state of New York. We have no control over—"

"I don't give a fuck who runs it! Put me in it, like they said!"

"*Who* said?" Noah asked pointedly.

Eugene's eyes went from me to Rey. He couldn't remember exactly what verbal promises they had made when they arrested him in Florida. Noah had been careful to maintain his legal distance even from that. Frankie DeCarlo had done all the talking. Noah had merely been the assistant DA waiting in the hall with a deal and a ballpoint pen.

Frankie DeCarlo was no longer on the scene, either. He had suddenly retired recently to take a job as an assistant security chief at an Indian casino in Connecticut. This left Eugene with his indignation, his faulty memory, and his legal contract that guaranteed nothing except temporary safekeeping.

The fight went out of him. Lamely, he said, "They promised."

Noah said that, as much as he sympathized, his hands were tied. "I'm sorry, Eugene. I am simply not aware of any oral promises. We have to rely on the legal contract. Beyond that, I want you to know that I'll see what I can do to help you with the money. It will be up to you to make a fresh start, but I'm sure Gerry and Rey will give you all the help they can. But remember, we still need you, and I can't make promises." Then he looked from Rey to me and said, as if we were at fault, "This investigation, as you know, has not yet yielded what we expected it to."

Rey's face turned bright red. "Eugene," he said sharply. "Wait for us out in the hall."

When Eugene left, Rey confronted Noah. "What I wanted to tell you for quite some time was"—he flexed his shoulders like a boxer—"you are a big-time scumbag."

"Oh, thank you very much," Noah responded.

"Hey," Marcomb felt the need to interject. "None of that talk."

Ignoring the inspector, I decided to put in my two cents. "Noah, you know the guy is finished as soon as we let him go, and before that, he'll now need to be kept under lock and key. Let's try to get him into the witness program, and bring him back for testimony, the standard way. I know your boss can do that, Noah. Get Eugene stashed away somewhere, bring him back when you need him in court, which is standard procedure in these cases—"

"Don't tell me how to do my job, Detective."

"I'm not telling you how to do your job, Noah. I'm just appealing for playing by the rules."

"I always play by the rules."

I shouted, "*Whose* rules, dammit?"

Marcomb left and took us with him. In the hall, while Rey tried to calm down Eugene, I abruptly turned and banged back into Noah's office alone. At this point, I couldn't imagine how they hoped to build a solid criminal case against Tony Rossi anyway.

Noah listened to me but remained adamant. "Witness protection can't be done," he said with measured patience. "Eugene hasn't given enough for us to ask the feds for that kind of a favor. Besides, they're complaining about overuse of the program. Did you know they have five thousand people in the witness program? It's becoming like a separate government agency."

"Makes you wonder who's running the Mafia."

"The feds wouldn't go for it, Gerry."

There was another reason, I knew. "Noah, you won't even approach the feds because your boss doesn't want to let them know two things. One, that the state's been trying desperately to beat them to Messina. And two, that this investigation has eaten up a lot of time and money— and produced nothing but a wiseguy in a coma who got hit by some guys from Philly operating under a wrong impression."

"That's your interpretation."

"Am I right?"

"The investigation is not yet over."

"Noah, this guy can never go home again."

He didn't blink. "Enough with that. What do you care? So let him join the Marines."

"God damn it, Noah, cut the crap! Play fair. This guy knows two places: the New York streets and the wiseguy hangouts in south Florida. That's it! He's got a fifth-grade education. He has never had a regular job, or a driver's license, or a Social Security card, or even a credit card—"

"In his own name, you mean."

"Yes! So be it! Where the hell is he going to go?"

"He should have thought of that before he decided to become an informant."

"He was given no choice! He's a dead man if we set him loose."

Noah's phone was buzzing like an alarm clock, giving him a welcome excuse to end the conversation. "You're entirely too emotional," he said, brushing me off. "It hasn't reached that point yet. Meanwhile, you're so concerned about his welfare, do what you can to move things along. Let me know how you make out."

He looked at the phone with desperation. "What makes you so sure that we don't have a good case? Tony comes out of it, we have him by the balls."

"I wouldn't bet on that."

"Why?"

"Look, any defense attorney is going to rip through this case like a shredder. How you tricked Eugene. The setup. The evidence is missing. No drugs, Noah. In front of a jury, Tony's already a guy who can turn on the charm. Add to it he's gunned down while surrounded by cops! He's paralyzed, probably for life. Meanwhile, all this coke is apparently on the streets, courtesy of a police screwup. What's a jury going to think of all that? So don't get too comfortable, Noah."

He glared at me. "This conversation is entirely off the record. I'll let you know as soon as we decide to move. Meanwhile, you do your job along with everybody else. I'm personally depending on you to keep a lid on the CI. Keep this guy under control! Now, I don't want to sound rude, but that's the end of this conversation. I have a lot of things to do. Good-bye."

CHAPTER 22

In the commotion, Campo formally announced his long-planned retirement. The party was held at the Union Square Cafe, where about seventy-five cops and their wives and girlfriends jammed into a private room like 1940s college kids cramming a phone booth. I was the only female there without a date. I sat at a table for a while with a half dozen people including Rey and the lovely Monique, planning to duck out before the speeches and the requisite going-away joke gifts.

I'd been intrigued by the hold Monique had on a man who was, otherwise, as independent and self-assured, not to mention socially poised, as Rey. So I perversely welcomed the opportunity to observe her at my leisure. There was no need to revise any initial impressions. Monique was at the peak of her beauty and slenderness, teetering on the inevitable downslide through her late thirties. I worked in an environment where cops cursed all the time, but usually they knew when to behave themselves, and usually the profanity they used at least occurred in context. After a couple of drinks, Monique had a dirty mouth that she brandished like a garden hose. She could put a twist on the f-word like I never heard from a cop or a hooker. "I'm tired as fuck," she whined.

"You can sleep late tomorrow, babe," Rey told her. Now he called her "babe." Ten years from now, if he didn't watch himself, he'd be calling her "mommy."

She glared at me when I talked to Rey, obviously irritated at our social relationship. So I decided to needle her just for the hell of it.

"Rey tells me you sold the beauty shop, Monique," I said, leaning across him to get her attention.

"There was too much business pressure," she said. Though I nodded politely, I knew the truth. Rey had put the down payment on the shop for her a year earlier, but it went out of business because she couldn't get up in time to open it before noon. He lost the $25,000 he put into it, but just shrugged it off.

After a couple of minutes of awkward silence, I excused myself and went up to the head table to shake Campo's hand and wish him luck, then stopped to pick up my things from the chair next to Rey. When I made my good-byes, absently kissing Rey lightly on the cheek, Monique was on me like a subway mugger. While Rey looked on with a dumb expression, Monique followed me from the room, saying there was something she wanted to discuss "outside."

On the sidewalk, it was freezing, but she stood in front of me, long spiked heels tapping a funeral cadence, with bare shoulders and sharp little teeth showing between stretched red lips. Her hair barely moved in the wind that whipped up along the sidewalk. She looked like a crow in high heels strutting beside roadkill.

"What do you want to talk about, Monique?" I said.

"I think you're a cunt."

That certainly put me right in focus. Even cops would never use a term like that directly to a female, not unless they were ready for big trouble. "Excuse me?" I said, deliberately holding back to gauge what was coming. For all I knew, she could have been planning to throw a punch.

"I just want to know what's going on," she said.

"Excuse me, but I don't have any idea what you're talking about. And I don't accept that kind of language."

She was in my face. "I want to know, are you and my Rey doing the nasty?"

I couldn't help laughing. Evidently, as often as Monique used the *f*-word, she didn't like it as a verb. "Are we doing the *what*?"

"The nasty! I know you're doing it!"

"Listen, honey," I said, "I know this may be a burden, but would you mind talking like an adult?"

"You stay away from my boyfriend!"

All I could do was stay calm. "Your boyfriend is my partner, Monique. Furthermore, I think he's a terrific man. You're extremely lucky he's as fond of you as he is. There's no relationship between Rey and me. You can believe that or not, I don't care. Now please get out of my way before I knock you on your bony ass. I have to get a cab. I suggest you go back to your man."

"Now that I seen you up close I ain't worried, especially with that mouth of yours," she said, storming off, trailing perfume and cigarette fumes. I was going to walk over to Broadway to catch a cab when one pulled up to discharge a couple right at the curb. As I got in, I noticed a man loitering under the awning a few doors down from the restaurant. He looked away quickly.

· · ·

A*fter the media* furor over the shooting at the Plaza died down, I called Eleanor and thanked her for not pumping me for information. She obviously had no idea that I had been at the scene.

"You're a friend, not a source," Eleanor said.

"I appreciate that more than you know." I told her. I didn't have the nerve to press her to learn if there was any talk about the botched sting on Tony. If there had been, I figured she would have mentioned it.

"Evidently the Philly guys had a hard-on for this Anthony Rossi guy and hired a couple of freelancers to do the job," she said, sensing my curiosity. What she was hearing happened to jibe with what we were hearing ourselves. She didn't know, and I didn't tell her, that some of us, Rey and me especially, suspected that Sammy Red had ratted Tony out, letting the would-be killers know when Tony would be in a crowded public place, which is the preferred location for a hit. Red's motive was the same as Tony's, we theorized. Anybody with half a brain could see that the Giavanni operation was on its last legs. Like Tony, Red was looking for a stake. With bullets ripping into Tony, Red had the opportunity to take the packages and get away clean as a purse-snatcher. He had no way of knowing the block would be full of undercover cops providing backup for the sting.

Red must have panicked and tossed the drugs out the window as soon as he spotted the cops on his tail. It was anybody's guess where the half million dollars' worth of cocaine had ended up, but Rey said it was certainly possible that a couple of cops in one of the radio cars involved in the multivehicle pursuit might have taken the opportunity to pull over, snatch up the stuff, and provide for their children's college educations.

Of course, Eleanor knew nothing of this aspect of the case. "Everything I hear is that Anthony Rossi is pretty far removed from the big boss," she said. "But at least you have him in custody, which was the goal, right?"

"Right," I said distractedly.

"Meanwhile, I'm hearing that Vincenzo Amarosa is telling all to the *federales*."

I sighed heavily. "You think they're going to indict Messina anytime soon?"

"No idea," she said. "But I wouldn't be surprised."

A while passed before she asked, "So when do you move on to better things?"

"I don't know," I told her honestly.

"You need someone to talk to, have a drink with?"

"Desperately. But I can't. Law school finals next week."

. . .

Along with my finals and my growing concern for Eugene, the pace picked up considerably because everybody wanted to get their work cleared to take time off for the Christmas holidays. The holidays meant nothing to me this year, so I volunteered to work, just to keep myself busy after the stress of my finals and the wreckage of my personal life.

All the while, Eugene was going crazy not being able to get out until the brass figured out how to handle Tony Rossi, who was still hospitalized by mid-December but rapidly recovering. So far, all they had charged him with was conspiracy to purchase a controlled substance. If he could have walked, he would have been free to do so on bail.

At OCTF headquarters, the depositions fell off to weekly sessions, to which Eugene was dragged and badgered with questions about Tony Rossi's personal life. It was clear to me that Eugene didn't have a clue. There was a growing sense of frustration, and I thought they were taking it out on me, too. At one session, a couple of the tough guys working the Eddie Mack case showed up with attitudes.

"All the time and money you spent on this, and your plan gets blown to hell at the last minute by a couple of Hectors in some fluke?" snarled one of them.

I only shook my head. At this point, I wasn't in the mood for arguing, especially with some pudgy detective who had no authority over me.

He kept at it, though. "Maybe you people should get your balls out of the closet and start acting like cops," he said, still looking at me.

"Fuck you," Rey shot back. "Why don't you tell us what you assholes have produced, besides a phone-book-size transcript of bullshit stories from some homicidal maniac mick?"

The detective didn't respond to that. Instead, he said, "Now they got a contract out on your good friend, I mean your CI, for being a rat." His eyes fixed on Eugene, who was sitting quietly at the table with his hands folded.

Eugene's face went white. I gave him a look that said he should keep his mouth shut. He did.

"Who put out the contract?" Rey asked sharply, not ready for any nonsense. "Give me names."

"Some of the boys, is all we hear," the detective said defensively, backing down. "Nothing really definite, just talk."

Eugene stood up unsteadily, but settled back into his chair.

The detective smiled. I wondered how quickly the smile would be wiped off his face if he knew the feds already had Sally Messina's top lieutenant helping them to prepare the indictment for the godfather.

There was one more order of business before the meeting ended. Saying the expense accounts were "out of control," Marcomb announced that all future expenditures over fifteen dollars had to be personally approved by him. He flipped through a stack of expense slips until he found what he had been looking for.

"Here's a perfect example of what I mean," he said, clearing his throat and reading over his glasses. "Ninety-nine dollars for a sweater for Eugene Rossi, from Barney's. I know we have to make sure the CI has clothes, but he's too good for Macy's?"

That made me distinctly uncomfortable. The voucher, one of hundreds submitted by OCTF investigators for a staggering range of expenses, from meals to airline tickets and fishing gear, had my name at the bottom of it. Eugene needed sweaters, and I had found a beautiful maroon cashmere pullover in a half-price sale at Barney's before Thanksgiving.

. . .

While Noah's staff worked on an indictment that would beef up the charges against Tony and give him more of an incentive to flip, we loitered in Staten Island. One night, to break the routine of cards and talk, Rey and I took Eugene to a matinee at a second-run movie theater near a mall. The movie was *Goodfellas*, one of the few mob movies without any heavy romantic nonsense. Afterward, Eugene agreed it was the Mafia movie most like the life he and his associates really led, rather than the one they pretended to lead.

As the walls closed in, an odd serenity occasionally came over Eugene. He knew that time was running out, a door was being shut, and a new one would have to be opened. More often, he stewed in a hash of victimhood.

"You all lied to me. They won't even let me go home for Christmas," he complained, exhibiting an amazing ability to ignore the strong likelihood that any Christmas greeting he was likely to get on the home front would involve a bullet or a knife.

"You people fucked me," he muttered. "Month after month, I told you all everything I know. Everything! I set up the deal with my uncle, like I said I would. I couldn't help it if two morons drive from Philly the same day to do business for somebody else. That was just more of my bad luck."

"Think about Red's luck," Rey told him with a chortle.

Eugene looked from Rey to me and said, with lips quivering, "You two are the only people left I can trust. Please go see your boss about keeping the deal. They got hundreds of people in the witness program—"

"—Thousands," I said.

"Now it's my time," Eugene said imploringly. "They put me in the new life. I come back to testify under guard when they want. I know that's how it works."

It was. It just wasn't going to work that way for Eugene, a confidential informant whose value was plunging like a stock-market crash.

. . .

By the week before Christmas, nothing new had developed. In the hospital, Tony conferred constantly with his lawyers about his legal problems, which actually paled by comparison with his personal ones, since it was now widely believed by the Messina hierarchy that he had already started to cooperate with the police. In his hospital bed, under police guard, Tony began dealing honestly with the reality that he could be paralyzed for life. Once he accepted that, and Tony was a man who didn't argue with the cards in his hand, he spent his idle time charming the nurses, who got together and bought him a three-foot-tall Christmas tree that acquired additional decorations with every shift. As Christmas approached, Tony considered his options and found a measure of hope, if not joy.

A cold drizzle fell on New York all through the afternoon of Christmas Eve. I was off, but on a whim in the late afternoon I took the Staten Island Ferry across the harbor, buoyed by the smell of the river that rose and fell under my feet. Midway across, the rain changed to snow. Snowflakes the size of silver dollars sifted gently onto the skyline of lower Manhattan, which appeared to be enclosed in a glass-domed sky.

From the ferry landing on the Staten Island side, I got on a bus to travel the rest of the way to the apartment complex. The ever-chipper Danny Flanagan had actually bought Christmas decorations from Woolworth's both for the office and for Eugene's apartment. Long ropes of green plastic holly curled over the stone balustrade that overlooked the courtyard. A potbellied plastic Santa Claus with a lightbulb in its middle hung on the office door, and an equally gaudy illuminated wreath was tacked on the door to Eugene's apartment. Inside the office where the cops came and went, a motorized Mrs. Santa rocked back and forth on a pivot, cackling like a fun house fat lady.

Rey was with Eugene. I could tell both of them had already had been drinking most of the afternoon. Christmas music blared from the boom box in the tiny living room. "Feliz Navidad" with a blazing brass section, merengue style.

Tommy went home before dinner, leaving only the duty sergeant on the night desk, along with Phil Geryon, who had pulled the unlucky shift out of a hat. I wasn't hungry, but Rey insisted that we order an enormous quantity of Chinese takeout, which arrived in more than a dozen little white boxes. In keeping with the spirit, the restaurant had fastened small cloth poinsettias to each of the handles, and the cartons spread out before us like a hydroponic garden.

They also had a half dozen bottles of champagne on ice, as if expecting visitors. But only the sergeant knocked on the door; he came in for a minute to grab some food and scamper back to his lonely post in front of a television set. I had some champagne and nibbled on a cold egg roll. In a while, Eugene asked me to dance. "You're a good-time Charlie. Let's Charlie it up tonight."

"I can't stay much longer," I said, patting his hand. "I told you I have to go to midnight mass with my folks tonight."

His face went sullen. Reluctantly, I got up to dance with him in the cramped room.

We had only been dancing for a couple of minutes when Rey cut in. Eugene bowed away, but he wasn't happy about the intrusion. When they had been drinking, their rivalry over me came out, but I also knew that I was just the territory where they found it most convenient to butt horns.

It was almost nine. "I have to get out of here by ten-thirty," I said.

Eugene's shoulders rippled under his black silk shirt. "It's Christmas Eve!"

Shouting to be heard over the loud music, I said, "I told you, I have to go to midnight mass with my parents."

It was more than a family tradition; it was as if Christmas would not arrive without midnight mass. Afterward, we would walk back to my parents' place, where my mother always had a lavish buffet set up for the relatives and neighbors. I think the building could have been on fire and my parents would have insisted that every step of the ritual be complete: mass, the walk home together, the huge seafood buffet in a living room decorated like a Macy's window, the friends and neighbors who dropped in, almost till dawn.

All my life, I had loved that ceremony, its colors and scents and sounds. Until this year, I couldn't imagine spending a Christmas Eve in any other way. Oddly, this year it seemed just another chore before bedtime, made far worse by the fact that this would be my first family appearance since leaving Kevin, a statue missing from my mother's carefully sculpted tableau. The thought filled me with guilt.

By nine-thirty, there was an open, half-full bottle of Dom Perignon wedged into a bucket of shaved ice beside the couch. Tommy's crepe-paper streamers now sagged from the ceiling.

"Time to go," I said. I asked Rey if he would give me a ride back. Monique required him to accompany her to an all-night Christmas party with her fellow manicurists in Queens.

"We have to go soon, bro," he told Eugene.

With a load on, Eugene was planning to party till daybreak. "It's too goddamn early. It's Christmas Eve."

Eugene and Rey wandered into the kitchen while I cleaned up as much of the Chinese-food debris as I could. When they came back Eugene had a bright look in his eyes.

I kissed Eugene on the cheek. "Merry Christmas, Eugenio," I said, reaching for my coat. I went outside while Rey ducked into the office to make a phone call. Eugene was right behind me, unsteady on his feet, looking wounded.

"Eugene, you've had too much to drink. Why don't you call it a night? I'll see you tomorrow morning." I told him gently.

"Fuck it. I'm going to get a cab and find a party."

"You know you can't do that. Listen, good-time Charlie. The only place you're going tonight is to your room."

The sergeant had come out of the office while Rey used the phone and was smoking on the landing fifty feet away. Eugene's loud voice, almost a shout now, caused him to turn in our direction.

Snow was still falling, and I was worried about the roads. Below, in the courtyard, Christmas lights blurred through the mist. Snow swirled in the lights on the high stone garrets of the apartment building.

Eugene sniffed wetly and wiped his nose with the back of his hand. Suddenly he put his arms around me and tried to kiss me, but I turned my face so his lips would catch me on the cheek.

"Merry Christmas, babe," he said.

I pulled away. "We already said good-bye, Eugene. Enough is enough, I think you better get inside."

He stomped away. Now Rey had come out and was headed toward me, jiggling his car keys.

We were startled by a loud crash from inside Eugene's apartment. I ran to the doorway and hollered, "What's going on?"

Eugene, red-faced, breathing heavily, was throwing a tantrum. He had kicked over the wooden chair beside the desk that he sat at when we did his lessons. It was the only furniture we had brought with us from the Jersey site. Now he was standing by the tiny kitchen area with the chair raised above his head, ready to throw it against the wall.

"Get out of here!" Rey bellowed at me. To the sergeant who had come running, he said, "Lock the asshole in for the night!"

But I waved the sergeant back and attempted to control the situation. Approaching him, I said, "Eugene what's wrong with you?"

"Don't come near me, bitch."

Rey moved inside to position himself between the door and me. "Come on, Gerry. Let's get out of here. They'll keep an eye on him to make sure he doesn't break anything else."

"Don't you come near me, Rey!" Eugene shouted over my head. "This is between her and me!"

"What the hell do I have to do with it?" I said.

With a violent swing, Eugene smashed the desk chair into a mirror over the bureau. The glass shattered into long jagged daggers, and I had to duck fast as pieces of the chair ricocheted across the room. One piece narrowly missed my face.

Keeping his eyes on Eugene, Rey took his gun from his shoulder holster and wordlessly handed it to me. Eugene's eyes narrowed. He still had a piece of the broken chair in his hand. Rey moved to him and pushed it away. They stood nose-to-nose.

A marimba version of "I Saw Mommy Kissin' Santa Claus" came on the radio.

"Come on, bro," Rey said. "I want you to put a hand on me. Just put a hand on me, okay?"

Eugene edged backwards but Rey kept at him, poking his chest with the hard tips of his fingers. "Come on, bro! What's the matter? Come on!"

Fear flickering in his eyes, Eugene said, "Bro!"

Bro my ass, I thought, moving warily toward him. But just then Eugene made a great rush past Rey, as if all he wanted to do was run into the night. A kind of air lock swept me right behind him. We both hurtled out the door, but I felt my right foot shoot out from under me on a patch of ice. I went down hard just as he turned to catch me. He missed and stood there breathing hard as I slid shoulder-first into the aluminum trash cans stacked up beside the railing. Luckily I know how to take a fall, but it's not a skill you'd associate with dignity. My dress was soggy and clumped above my waist.

Rey loomed in the yellow light from the doorway with a three-foot weight-lifting trophy hoisted to smash down on Eugene's skull.

"Don't hit him!" I screamed. Eugene dodged and slipped on the ice himself. He went down like a sack of concrete. Snorting furiously, Rey smashed the trophy onto the pavement.

"Buddy. Buddy." Eugene, moaning, scrambled to his hands and knees in the slush to pick up pieces of the trophy. It was one that Rey had given him when he thought Eugene had begun to master the finesse of proper weight-lifting.

Rey yanked Eugene up in a headlock. Eugene's feet skittered crazily, groping for traction on the blackened slush.

"Are you okay?" Rey grunted at me.

"Yeah! Don't hurt him! I slipped on the ice!" I insisted as firmly as I could. It hurt to get up. It felt like a broken rib.

"You want to push somebody around, push me, asshole!" Rey said savagely, tugging hard at Eugene's head wedged in the crook of his arm.

"Stop it!" I cried, seeing that Rey either believed, or chose to believe, that Eugene had body-slammed me in his tantrum. "Rey, he didn't do anything!"

"The fuck he didn't!"

Eugene went limp in Rey's grip and sobbed, "I didn't want to let you down, bro!"

"What the hell are you talking about, asshole? What about *her?*"

Eugene put his hand on my arm. "You okay?"

"Fine," I said, rearranging my dress and scrambling up shakily. "Slippery."

Rey yanked Eugene so hard I was afraid. "Rey, don't hurt him. Let him go immediately!"

With a look of disgust, he released Eugene, who fell to his knees with his head bowed. Rey looked at me.

"I'll jack him up right here, Gerry."

"Calm down," I said, rubbing my side.

He glared at me and said through clenched teeth, "You aren't going to let him get away with this?"

I was astonished. He was acting like a nightstick jockey taking it out on some poor skell in a holding cell. "He didn't do anything. I fell on my own ass, Rey."

Suddenly Phil Geryon was behind him with his gun drawn. Oh Christ, I thought. Now we have an incident. Geryon, fangs bared, waited for a signal from Rey to pounce.

"Shit!" Rey said. "Let's just take the cocksucker downtown and book him for assault. Let him spend Christmas in the lockup, without all these niceties. We don't need the motherfucker anymore anyway. Put him into the fucking system."

"This is ridiculous!" I said, moving between the two of them. A jolt of pain shot through my rib cage.

"Okay, then, I'll have them chain him to his fucking bed for the night, let him wake up and see himself that way on Christmas morning," Rey said, still panting. "That possible, sergeant?"

"This cocksucker assaulted a police officer," Geryon declared, as if addressing a crowd.

"He did not!" I shouted. "You weren't even here!"

Geryon gave me a withering look and snorted. He was taking his signals only from Rey. Twenty yards away down the landing, Eddie Mack watched silently in the dusting snow in front of his apartment door.

"Just let him go back inside," I pleaded. "It's Christmas. Try to understand, he's alone."

"Understand *shit*," the sergeant snorted. "From what I could see, this was an assault on a police officer." He came toward Eugene, but Rey waved him off and made him put the gun away.

"I slipped on the ice," I repeated.

"I can't believe you're going to let him get away with this," said Geryon. "That does damage to all of us. Put the cuffs on the fuckwad right now!"

Finally, to my great relief, Rey shook his head, sighed deeply, and helped Eugene to his feet. "All she ever did was try to help you, bro. I'm fucking finished with you."

Eugene was deeply contrite. "I'm really fucking sorry, bro."

Rey looked at him with disgust, as appalled as I was by the tears. Rey roughly pushed him into the apartment. Eugene yelped with pain but stumbled forward without resisting. He bent down to pick up his jacket as he brushed past me.

When he came out, Rey took me aside. By now, I was bristling a little at his cop-in-charge attitude, treating me like I was a witness at a crime scene. But I realized that this no longer had much to do with me.

"I'm asking you one more time, Gerry. You want him to take a collar on this? It's your call. But I think we should squeeze this son of a bitch right now. I'm sick of his shit."

"No," I said firmly, astonished at the way Rey had turned on Eugene. I thought they had bonded over all this time. They were pals who joked, went to the gym, got drunk, got laid together.

"I mean it, I'll take him in. I'll put the cuffs on him right now, Christmas or no Christmas," Rey said.

"Please, Rey. Settle down."

I was holding my arms tight across my ribs. "Let me see," he said, curtly lifting my shirt without my permission, to look at my lower rib, where the skin was already starting to darken.

"You got to get to the hospital."

"No! It's just a bruise," I insisted. However, I knew that at least one rib was cracked.

He dropped my shirt back down. "When he gets a look at that, Kevin is going to come down here and fucking kill this bastard," he said.

He had forgotten that I had moved out. I thought we were pals, too. And yet a landmark as profound as the end of a long engagement hadn't registered with him. I looked at Rey as if for the first time, and said, "If I still lived with Kevin, which I don't, I'd tell him I fell on the ice." The truth was, in the past few years of our relationship, Kevin wouldn't have noticed anyway. "Let's not push this any farther, okay?"

He thought for a minute. "Fine," he said. "Merry Christmas to you all." He walked away, headed for the office to check out.

I called after him, "Rey?"

He spun around with an angry look. "This is it, Gerry," he said, spitting the words out. "I will never come back to this place again. This guy is a piece of garbage. It took me too long to wise up to the way he was using me. When are you going to wise up? What he just did to you?—if he could do that, after all you did for him? Man, he's capable of turning on anybody. He isn't worth your time anymore. He's a rat bastard, pure and simple, just like they said. Why can't you get your head smart to that?"

"I thought you were on his side."

He laughed and looked at me like I was a fool. "You couldn't see through that? Hell, I must still have the old touch. I thought I was losing it."

"You just walk away? Just like that?"

He replied, "I took this job to fill out the rest of my time the easy way. You think I cared about anything besides padding out that fifty-thousand-dollar-a-year pension I got coming? You think I would risk that for this character?"

"I see the good in this guy," I said, feeling cold and abandoned. He looked at me without saying anything more.

"Anyway, this is a horrible way for the guy to have to spend Christmas," I said weakly.

"Too bad you can't take him to Radio City Music Hall for the midnight Christmas show," he said sarcastically. A gust of snow skittered along the landing like a sagebrush phantom.

All I could do was collect myself and walk through the motions for the rest of the night. We got Eugene secured in his apartment. Rey drove me back to the city, expertly negotiating slippery streets into Manhattan, and let me off at my apartment. We barely spoke in the car and shook hands when he stopped. It would be the last time I saw him as a cop.

A few minutes before midnight, I hurried into the family church, Our Lady of Pompeii, and slipped into the pew beside my mother. They were singing the *Gloria*. Taking short breaths, I prayed for a personal peace, but a deepened sense of loneliness pulsed through me like a toothache. My feet felt the subway rumble of the big pipes in the church organ. I breathed deeply, seeking consolation in the spicy scent of incense, blending like smoke into the almond smell of firm burning candles, the pine boughs bundled like presents at the altar rail, bright in the golden candlelight from the sanctuary. But there was neither consolation nor joy to be found. I mouthed the carols, but my heart was as black as the ice freezing on the church steps outside.

CHAPTER 23

Rey *put in* his retirement papers the day after Christmas and turned in his shield the night before New Year's. Through the cops' pearly gates after twenty, at age 42 hauling in a pension of $4,775 a month for life. A week later, he went to Florida. Monique went along. I called a few times, but never heard back, which made me feel like a fool.

Hoping to cram in a lot of the required reading for my last semester, I used ten days of vacation after New Year's. During that time, Eugene pestered me constantly, calling my beeper, filling my machine with messages that I heard like random snatches of conversation in the park. Always, he ended with, "I'm sorry about that thing."

I made a few calls to Noah, but he didn't get back to me. I didn't need a telegram to get the message that my role in the operation, or whatever remained of it, was diminished. On January 12, I drafted my transfer request, asking for reassignment. At that point, I'd have been happy even to get back to shift work in a precinct. Then I just took it to the post office and mailed it to Marcomb. It wasn't even worth the effort of a personal visit to the office.

Around Thanksgiving, I had promised Eugene I would have him ready to take his high-school GED test in January, but now my heart wasn't in it. He mentioned the promise in one of his phone messages, and then dropped it when I didn't respond.

But it nagged at me. Having heard nothing, I went back to work in mid-January, reporting to the office at the apartment complex in Staten Island. Then I went down to see Eugene.

He was pale, with dark circles under his eyes. After sheepishly letting me in, he pulled out a piece of yellow legal paper from his trousers pocket.

"Here, read this," he said, handing it over the way you would push a movie ticket at an usher. I had to unfold it.

Dear Miss Crabtree—

I write this to you because I feel I have to write. You are the only one that is in my corner. Sometimes I don't understand why God ever brought you into my life. You say why do I tell lies and act up even to you???? I would never let anything hurt you, I would cover you like a blanket. I have been lied to all of my life. I know in my heart that what you do for me you would not do for anybody. Please do not leave me. You are all that I have left, if you walk out on me I don't know what I can do. I would just—you know. . . .
Happy New Years, baby.

"Charlie"

Every word in the note was spelled correctly. I felt a surge of pride in that.

" 'Charlie'?" I said.

"Yeah, like good-time Charlie."

"Why not put down 'Eugene'?"

"You should never sign your name. Never."

"Glad to see you finally learned that lesson," I said, smiling to let him know I was back on his side. So, yes, Rey would have laughed at me for giving in so easily. But that wily old antagonist, my desperate urge to be needed, to be *declared necessary*, pushed me back. When I saw the relief in his face, the ground beneath me got firm once more.

He said, "I'm really very sorry about that thing."

Was that a flicker of triumph in his eyes?

"Yeah," I said, pulling back a little. "Okay, well, everybody screws up. You were drunk and under a lot of pressure. It was a rough year, but just don't take it out on me, okay? I'm the best friend you have right now."

"The only one," he said. Our eyes met, and there was no need to speak of Rey.

Naturally he opted not to leave well enough alone.

"But you were dancing sexy with Rey. You know how that makes me feel?"

"How does it make you feel?" I said wearily.

"Disrespected."

"Disrespected," I repeated with amazement.

"By you. . . ."

"Whatever gave you the impression you have a claim on me?" I demanded. He didn't respond.

"Rey was planning to take a walk anyway, but that incident pushed him out the door. In disgust. You do realize that, don't you?"

"Rey did what he had to do. My only beef is he never came around to say good-bye, after all we've been through."

"Not after what you pulled Christmas Eve."

"I said I was sorry."

"Rey doesn't think the same way I do, Eugene. Listen, I don't want to always sound like Miss Crabtree, which by the way I would appreciate your not calling me anymore, but one of the things you are going to have to learn, and learn soon because you're headed back into the real world, is that actions have consequences. You just can't 'sorry' them away. For one thing, your uncle isn't going to be looking out for you now. What you do builds a history that you have to live with. You can't make the past go away by dropping a quarter in a video arcade machine and pushing the 'New Game' button. Starting here and now, you're going to have to stand on the past and build from it."

Self-pity washed over his face. "That's fine with me. Rey walked out on me. You're next. I start from there."

"Rey was your friend, Eugene. He was always there for you."

"That's not what the other guys told me."

"What other guys?"

"The cops out there. They told me Rey was only spending all that time with me so he could pile up his overtime pay and get a bigger Social Security check."

"Pension."

"Pension, whatever. And it's the same thing with you. You're putting in the time for your check."

I tried to tell him that was ridiculous, but it was like talking to a granite tower.

Minutes later, as if I didn't already have enough aggravation, Colleen showed up in a flurry, saying she had left some files behind and needed to get them for her next assignment. I didn't bother to ask what that was.

With her hand on my elbow, she led me outside. It was a cold day. The sky was the color of a frozen lake. Colleen had a new warning. "You remember when I told you there was a lot of talk about you? Remember, I told you to watch your back?"

"Yes, Colleen," I said with irritation. "So what's the talk about now?"

"Just talk," she said, blowing air through her thin lips as if exhaling smoke. "The talk going around—I hear it, I keep my own mouth shut— is that maybe you went over to the other side. That's what I hear."

" 'The other side'? What are you saying this time, Colleen?"

"Listen, Gerry, I don't believe this for a minute. You had a tough job and there was no way to win. But maybe you weren't careful enough to stay on the right side of the line, that's all."

"They're talking about me and Eugene still?"

She nodded. "Well, I come here and where do I find you? In his room. Now, I know you're a total professional, Gerry. You get the job done. But with some of these other guys, it's like, 'These Italians, they all stick together.' Things like that, a wink and a nod. I'm just telling you because you ought to know. Talk has a way of getting written down in this place, if you know what I mean."

I didn't have a clue, nor did I have much interest in what she said. The way I saw it, I could handle things as long as I did my job, and I'd done my job, thankless as it was. I had met my own personal standards. They had Tony. Though I had been oddly uninformed of it, the word in the office was that Tony had indicated a willingness to consider a deal, once his lawyers signed off on it. So the job was done, except for Eugene. Getting Eugene secure was all that remained. After that, personal mission accomplished.

. . .

Now that I was back at work, Noah magically became available. When I went to see him the next day, he was cool and correct, like a high-school teacher. He said I would get "all due credit" for my help in getting Tony on ice.

"Even though the plan got fucked," he added, as if I shared some responsibility for not foreseeing that Tony's most trusted aide would go over to the Philly mob and double-cross him with a couple of hired hit men in front of the Plaza.

"Thank you," I said curtly. "Now what?"

"Now we get Tony producing fast. And then they make the move on Messina."

" 'They'?"

He blinked. "That phase is not something I'll be involved in."

I didn't pursue that, nor did I feel any need to pass on gossip that the feds would probably get there first. If they did not, the process of indicting Messina by the state would take some time—assuming Tony cooperated, and assuming, as they had from the beginning, that Tony had enough to put Sally away. That was never an assumption I was willing to take better than even odds on.

"He says he's got dates, names, details. Did you know the guy kept a diary?"

"Tony? He doesn't seem like the diary type," I said. "You've seen it?"

"Not yet. That's the next step. incidentally, he says you're in it. In the diary. Among other things, he claims he laid you at his place the morning after you got back from A.C." Noah laughed, but there was a nervous undertone in it.

"He's dreaming," I said with some annoyance. "You have to figure he's going to pull stuff like that."

"Sure he's dreaming, but it's on paper. So far we haven't caught him in any lies. But don't worry about it. He's just a fucking criminal."

"Noah, tell me one thing. How does he know about me? He was out cold on that pavement."

"Well, he had to put two and two together."

"You told him."

He sat up straight. "Not me. The guys did. What the hell, they wanted to bust his chops a little. No big deal, right? It all comes out anyway."

"What did he say?"

"He said he was on to you for months."

"Bullshit. What did he say about Eugene?"

"He said Eugene broke his heart. Then he put his head down on the table and cried like a little kid."

I didn't respond. After a minute, Noah continued in a self-satisfied way. "Now that I've had some time to look back on this whole operation, to postmortem it in my head, the only thing I'm really unhappy about is the length of time it took to get him locked up. I think we could have moved a little more aggressively. You can't pussyfoot around with these shitbirds. You have to come on like John Wayne. Hit him fast and hard."

"The Philly boys did that," I noted.

"That's a good point," he said. "You take immediate advantage of the opportunities that arise."

"And you've charged him with what?" I said, aware that they didn't have enough to keep Tony from walking out on bail as soon as he was able to leave the hospital.

"We got a conspiracy to traffic in drugs that will stick."

"Good luck," I said dubiously.

"Come on, we got him solid there."

I wasn't so sure, not with a good defense lawyer ready to ram it down their throats that there did not appear to be any physical evidence of drugs, not on Tony, not even on poor Red.

"Besides, we hear Messina was told that he was being ratted out. So Tony's not about to walk, no pun intended, even if he does get bail."

"That much I'll grant you," I said. My instincts confirmed for me now that what Eleanor had said was true. Messina was sharp enough to smell a rat, all right, and figure it was Tony. But he was sniffing in the wrong corner.

"So," he said, and waited for me to speak.

"So what about my transfer request."

He nodded. "Ah, yes. Moving along. You'll be hearing in a couple of days."

"Okay, now we need to talk about Eugene."

That made him scowl like a boss being leaned on for a raise he was reluctant to hand out. "They're working on that. I'll get back to you on that, since I know your personal relationship—"

I stopped him cold. "What personal relationship?"

"No offense, Gerry. Really. The question of what we do with Eugene is too complicated right now. Just let me handle this one for the time being."

"Soon, Noah."

"Soon," he promised, and then changed the subject. "Meanwhile, we could use a little more help from you."

"What kind of help?"

"Well, like your official reports and your recollections of your conversations with Tony Rossi. We've reviewed all of them carefully, of course. And to tell you the truth, there are a few little places where you could fill in some of the blanks, to really make a better case."

"What are you telling me, Noah?"

His face craned toward mine like a gooseneck lamp. "Do you have to be so, well, literal?"

"Literal?"

"You're a big girl, Gerry. You know exactly what I mean. Just a few blanks here and there to fill in. To connect the dots, so to speak."

"I connected all the dots I could. You're asking me to go beyond that? To lie?"

He looked stricken. His eyes darted around as if someone might have heard, although his door was closed. "Oh my God, don't say anything like that. All I mean is, you can try to help us out here with some judicious editing of your reports. Here and there."

I hated to sound like some ACLU intern, but I reared back and said, "Noah, I went into this job with one provision. It was going to be done by the books. *By the books*, Noah. That's how I do it. You and I go way back. Give me that much."

He shook his head. "Look, I've walked the mile with you from the beginning of this thing. I know it's been a mess. We should never have invested so much effort, money, and manpower in it. But at this point, we're just dotting the *i*'s and crossing the *t*'s. It's time for all of us to move on, proud of what we did, despite the screwups here and there."

"I didn't screw anything up, Noah."

"Now don't get down in your famous defensive crouch," he said with a smirk that made me want to smack him. "I'd like us to part friends."

Ah, I thought. The sound of a man changing jobs. "Where are you going, Noah? What's your deal?"

His eyes dropped and then he looked up, quite pleased with himself. "Okay. Okay. I've been offered a job in the U.S. Attorney's Office. International Narcotics Task Force, south Florida. Of course, I'll see it through here for another month, till they have Tony producing. But then . . ."

"Then you're taillights," I said. "Very impressive, Noah. Everybody goes to Florida."

"It's where the action is."

"Well, I wish you a lot of luck. You'll do great." I got up and we shook hands.

"Thank you, Gerry," he said. "And listen—"

"Yes?"

"You need anything, you just holler, hear?"

"Sure. Thanks. You keep me posted on the plans for Eugene, since I assume I'm still on the job there."

"Absolutely!" he boomed, a new man. "Don't let the bastards get you down."

"I'll try," I assured him, happy to have the door shut behind me.

. . .

I *went down* the list of people I had been associated with all year. Everybody had made a deal. In one way or another, they were all out the door, Tony included. Everybody except me and Eugene.

There was a pink message slip on my desk, with the name that I recognized as one of those local television reporters who had made a career of associating himself with the Messina case. This guy particularly annoyed me because he bathed in the Messina mystique but was wily enough to strike of a pose of hard-nosed antipathy toward Messina. On television, the godfather and his favorite television reporter would dance their little pas de deux. The encounter between the two of them I remember best was about a year before, when Messina beat the first rap in federal court. Hartley was waiting like a suitor in front of the club on Mulberry Street when Messina and his celebrating thugs arrived. The television star strode right up to him, bowed respectfully, and said, with the cameras rolling: *"Buona sera, signore."*

Sally had paused briefly, considering this sign of respect. A beatific smile lit his shiny face. *"Bene. Bene, grazie."* Messina was so pleased he put his arm around Hartley and they walked past the cameras like brothers.

I called Eleanor. "I have a phone message to call Brent Hartley, the television guy."

"That gaper? What's he want?"

"I thought maybe you could give me a clue."

"Hartley? Well, he's real stupid, for starters, though obviously very good-looking. Basically, we're talking an ambulant house plant with a pretty face and a nice baritone voice. But he can cause a lot of trouble when he gets hold of some half-assed piece of information and runs with it. You never know if he's got it right, or who's been pissing in his ear. Why not call him and see what he wants? Then please let me know."

I said I would, then asked, "What are you hearing these days? Any new rumors?"

"Actually, there are more than rumors. In fact, I was just going to call you. I figured I'd let things cool down a little bit after your pal Tony Rossi went down."

"It was just a coincidence," I told her.

"So I hear. A lucky one, too, since he's still breathing. We ought to get together and talk."

When I hung up, something occurred to me that made me smile. Eleanor was the only one who ever gave me a straight story and the only one who had never betrayed a confidence.

. . .

E*arly the next* morning, I returned Brent Hartley's phone call. "How did you get my name?" I demanded.

"I have my ways."

"What do you want?"

"Ah, a woman who cuts right to the chase. I like that. Okay, what you should know is I'm working on a story about the conflicting investigations into the Messina case. Basically, how the feds and the state have been tripping over each other all year. Almost a comedy piece, if you know what I mean."

"No," I said, giving him nothing. "There's nothing I can do for you, Mr. Hartley. I'm sorry."

The brush-off had no effect. "It's a series," he went on, braying. "There's absolutely no rush, because it won't start airing until the next sweeps. My working title is 'Getting Messina: The Race to Bag the Dandy Don.'"

"I can't help you."

"It's the barn-burner for sweeps week," he insisted. "Let me explain how I work. When I put together a major investigative piece, first I decide who among the cast of characters will have a speaking part."

"A speaking part?"

"Right. Besides Messina and the other usual suspects, there are a handful of good guys who I see as having speaking parts. I mean, you have to understand they will be represented in the story, whether they like it or not. The names will come up, yours included, in the narrative texture. You've had your share of publicity in the past, so you know how this works."

"I never talk outside of channels. But why don't you tell me what you think is going on?"

He chuckled. "As I'm sure you'll see, I haven't pieced it all together yet. There are a lot of loose ends. Listen, I just want to give you the courtesy of knowing that I'm working on this. I hear the investigation that you've been involved with is a major break in the case. Lots of glory coming your way. So if you want to talk to me, you get a speaking part and it comes out your way. It's up to you. Either way, you're in the narrative."

"Suit yourself."

"Listen, I tell *stories*. On *television*. Stories have characters. Characters are actors in stories. Some have speaking parts, some are walk-ons. The script is being written, Detective."

"Good luck. You'll have to call the NYPD's public-relations office. Beyond that, would you do me a favor?"

"Sure."

"Obviously you have my phone number."

"Obviously."

"Lose it." I hung up. The phone rang back four times and my answering machine flipped on. I ignored the creep.

A few minutes later, when it rang again, I was furious. But when I heard Noah's voice I picked up.

"Gerry, Inspector Marcomb is here in my office and he wants to talk to you," he said.

Marcomb got on. "Conte?"

"Yes, Inspector?"

"How you doing?"

I resisted the urge to tell him the truth. "Fine," I said. "I'm just about to walk out the door and head down to Staten Island."

"Fine! You keeping that CI of yours out of trouble?" What trouble could he get into in police custody? He went on without waiting for a reply. "Good," he said. "Incidentally, I've been reviewing your transfer request along with the DA. Everything looks just fine. We should be able to accommodate you nicely after some, uh, small housekeeping matters are cleared up. But that isn't what I want to talk to you about. Right now, I need you to come down here. Downtown."

"Of course," I said, wondering glumly what this was all about.

"We have one little final assignment for you."

How depressing, I thought. "What's that?"

He had his mouth close to the phone. It sounded like whispering through a bullhorn. "Well, our Moustache Pete, Uncle Tony, gets out of the hospital tomorrow. In a wheelchair, naturally. Then he and his lawyers are coming right over to see us and do some talking." He waited.

"That's good. That's what we wanted," I said.

"Yes. Well, he's slick as wet dogshit and still a little high and mighty, even while he's going to cooperate. But I was thinking, for a little added effect, just to kick the cripple a little bit, ha-ha, we'd like you to come down and join the welcoming party."

"Sir, I'd rather not do that."

He was bubbling over. "Wait! The idea is, on your way in, first you stop at a bakery, some Italian joint, and you buy a dozen of those cannolis. See? Then you wait outside the interview room. And we ask him 'Hey, Tony, you hungry? We ordered some food for you.' And then you come in with the goddamn cannolis, Detective!"

The idea appalled me. "I can't do that, sir."

He was deeply disappointed and let me know it. "Fine, it was just an idea for a joke. But I want to see you down here in a half hour anyway. Got it?"

. . .

Marcomb, Noah **and** four of the downtown OCTF detectives were sprawled around the interview table like fraternity boys. Marcomb pointedly ignored me when I sat down. Noah brought me up to date as the other detectives stared.

"Well, today, just to rub it in, we played him excerpts from the tapes Eugene made during his talks with him."

Why torture the guy? I thought. It seemed not only stupid, but cruel and unnecessary.

"What did Tony say when he heard the tapes?" I asked.

Marcomb grumbled and said, "First he got mad. He said he thought the kid was just a dope. But then, actually hearing the words, the *sincerity* in his nephew's voice—hell, would you believe Mr. Tough Guy broke down and cried like a baby?"

Marcomb looked at me soberly and said, "Noah tells me your reports over the months stand as is."

"Anything that was pertinent is in those my reports, Inspector."

"It's your word against his," he pointed out.

"There's nothing I can add."

Marcomb shifted position, cracked his knuckles loudly, and asked the other detectives to leave the room, leaving just the three of us at the table.

"Now, the housekeeping details," Noah said when they were gone.

Marcomb cleared his throat. Suddenly, I felt like I was being grilled.

"Your father owns a bakery business down in Little Italy?" He had opened a file on the table in front of him.

"What's my father got to do with it?"

"Nothing. I just want to make sure we know everything we're dealing with here, so no stink bombs go off. You understand. Questions have to be asked."

"You mean, is my father connected?"

"I never implied that."

"My father is the most decent and honorable man I know," I said fiercely. "He has *never* had anything to do with the wiseguys."

"Okay. Good," he replied, studying my face. "Questions have to be asked. Sometimes feelings get hurt."

My heart was racing.

"Anything else?" I said.

Marcomb shook his head and stuffed his file into a briefcase. "No. Thank you, Detective." With a nod at Noah, he left the room.

"Don't worry about him. He's under a lot of stress," Noah assured me.

"My heart bleeds for him," I said. "Haven't we been over this bullshit before?"

Noah just nodded.

I felt defeated, and didn't even know where the fight had been. "I want some answers," I said.

"Sure."

"First, what does our guy do now?"

He shrugged. "Eugene? They're finished with him. They have bigger fish to fry. So we release him."

"Just like that?"

"Yep."

I drew in a shaky breath. "With just a 'Thanks a lot, don't let the door hit you in the ass on your way out'?"

"Don't be upset, Gerry. This isn't the KGB. He'll get a check and some travel assistance. Where he goes, what he does, that's strictly up to him. He got himself into this situation, after all."

"A check for how much?"

"Reasonable, to give him a start. Generous, considering that he's already had almost a year of free room and board, not to mention all those fancy restaurant bills and even the clothes on his back."

"How much?"

"I don't want you to say anything to him about this yet. But I think we can manage about five thousand. Then he's on his own. He's a survivor, as you know."

Aware that arguing with a man headed for a new job was futile, I asked, "And you'll drop that half-assed warrant you popped him on in the first place?"

"Already done," Noah assured me. "As far as the law goes, the guy's clear right now."

"Big deal, considering he's dead meat the minute they see him on the street," I said, feeling ill. "I told you this was going to happen. Tell me, was it worth it, Noah?"

He rubbed his hands together gleefully. "Without a doubt. Wait till you see how good you'll feel to see Sally Messina perp-walked into his arraignment with the cuffs on. Again, Gerry, it's like war. There are casualties, pointless skirmishes; there is extravagant waste of *matériel*. There are some friendly-fire casualties, unfortunately. But finally you win the big battles and you win the war."

"And the point of the war was all to make sure we got Messina before the feds," I said.

"One of the objectives, sure."

"Well, again—congratulations."

He was quiet for a minute. Then he laughed.

"What's so funny?" I demanded.

"You don't understand history."

"What do you mean by that?"

"They say history gets written by the winners. That's true. But these days it really gets written by the winners' public-relations offices."

. . .

The next night, Eleanor and I got together again. I was glad to see her. It was the first time I had been in her apartment, a spacious one-bedroom with a den just off Washington Square. It was a mild night; the streets were crowded with college kids, and walking up to her place made me feel young. The apartment was done in a minimalist, high-tech style that stated its occupant lived comfortably but without excess encumbrances. It was exactly the kind of place I wanted to have when things worked out, I decided firmly. I'd get her to give me some decorating tips. Meanwhile, there was no way of telling when I would be able to get on with my life. At this point, I couldn't see more than a week ahead.

She opened a bottle of cold white wine and we talked. It was nice to be out. We were just shooting the breeze, cops and media gossip, when I mentioned in passing a former FBI agent from the New York bureau. His name was Michael Marconi. He had been something of an inspiration to me because he went to law school and began a new career after the bureau.

"Sure I knew him!" she exclaimed. "I got to know him when he was in the bureau in New York and I was covering the mob. I ran into him, literally, outside a restaurant in Little Italy, when they were taking some poor schmuck's body away. I mean, I sideswiped his car. He was amazingly good-natured about it. We went out a couple of times. The last I heard, he was happy teaching college somewhere in the Midwest."

"The University of Iowa, from what I heard. He's a law professor there, somebody told me," I said.

"How do you know him?"

"Actually, I don't very well. We just ran into each other occasionally."

As I suspected she knew him somewhat better. "An absolute prize," she said. "Some of these bureau guys are just full of themselves, but they're really just shitkickers from the sticks in good suits, looking to make it big in New York, trying to trade information or access for sex, frankly. You'd be surprised how much of that goes on. Marconi, though, he was different. I was devastated when he quit."

"Why'd he quit?" I had never been quite sure.

She shrugged. "That was back when I was really drinking big-time," she said, raising her wineglass. "You have to keep up with the cops. He wouldn't talk a lot about it. Apparently there was a lot of internal politics over press relations and that sort of thing, the way there always is with the FBI. But from what I could gather from him and from the grapevine, he resigned strictly on principle. Remember when people used to do that?"

"No."

"Well, that's because you're, what, six or seven years younger than I am?"

"What was the principle?"

"He had a theory that the cops, the wiseguys, and the press were all locked together in one single industry, in effect. All feeding off each other. It really, really bugged him the way they were using informants. He had been assigned to South Florida before he came to New York and he said they had hundreds and hundreds of these informants, mostly from the New York mob families, on the payroll, full-time.

"He told me once, 'It kills me that these guys are basically government employees, just like me.' He saw it like one of those revolving-door deals, you know, like lobbyists who leave the government and go to work for defense contractors or whatever. All these wiseguys getting government checks, everybody always thinking up new schemes to keep the game going. Basically, he felt that the government and the Mafia didn't ever belong in the same bed. He said it started back when Kennedy wanted Castro whacked, and it never really ended. Whatever, it made him sick. Evidently he finally had enough of it. I think the New York media kind of put it into sharp focus for him. You never know, of course, but I never heard a single bad word about him, and that's in a pretty cutthroat culture. Why do you want to know this?"

"There's a possibility I might need to ask him a favor," I said.

"Cool," she said, stubbing out her cigarette.

"Cool?"

"Gerry, I'll do whatever I can to help you. On anything. Okay?"

She obviously meant it. "Thank you," I said.

She began giggling.

"Out with it," I told her.

She poured some more wine and leaned toward me conspiratorily. "Okay, just between you and me. The feds have everything they need now. They go to the grand jury next Monday to indict Messina."

"For what?"

"Murder. Conspiracy. RICO. The whole nine yards."

I started laughing. "They won."

"Looks that way."

"And they haven't told the state yet?"

"Hell no! You know how this game is being played. Strictly for credit."

"How'd they get it together so fast?"

"Vincenzo 'the Hammer' Amarosa, of course. I told you they flipped this guy like a pancake. He's been wearing a wire when he meets his boss. You want to hear some of it?"

"Absolutely."

She went into the bedroom and came back flipping through the pages of a steno pad. "Here we have the existentialist dilemma of Sally "Seashore" Messina," she said, and read from her notes:

"MESSINA: Where the fuck are we going here in this outfit? Every fucking time I turn around somebody's going off on his own. Where are we going here? Who the fuck can we trust?

"AMAROSA: Me. You could trust me, Sally.

"MESSINA: I know that."

Delighted, Eleanor flipped through to another place.

"MESSINA: Vinnie. You always done what I asked. But the truth is, even you got sidelines. For Christ's sake, you think I don't know you're into dealing some shit in Harlem? You're running whores out of Queens? You think as a boss I'm not aware of them things?

"AMAROSA: [Laughing.]: Come on, Sally. Small shit, here and there. You never cared about no small shit.

"MESSINA: Yeah, no problem, Vinnie. This I got no problem with. Because you deliver, you ugly cocksucker. Me, I know a guy has to look out for his family. I'm not some selfish boss. Me, all I want is a good steak and a nice pair of shoes on my feet. You always understood that. Which is why you ain't where Ray-Bans Rizzoli is right now.

"AMAROSA: I always done exactly what you told me, Sally.

"MESSINA: That's right. I tell you, Ray-Bans Rizzoli, that thief that would steal a crucifix off his mother's coffin, I don't want to see his fucking fat face no more, and you understand what I need. You do what's got to be done without no problems. You know how important that is to a boss?

"AMAROSA: Sure, Sally. What you told me I done. Shoot him in the fucking head in his fucking kitchen. [Laughing.] We made sure to put a throw-rug down so's his wife don't have to wipe up no messes.

"MESSINA: Sure! You done it with consideration. You couldn't help it if his dog come in and started licking it up, made a mess tracking it all through the fucking house! [Laughing.]

"AMAROSA: I done them all, whenever you asked me. I can't even count how many guys you told me to whack.

"MESSINA: Six. I told you whack six guys, and you whacked six guys. That's why I know I can depend on you."

She shut the notebook and said. "Hammer time! That's some of what the grand jury will hear."

"They got him," I said admiringly.

"By the short hairs. Meanwhile, back at the ranch, Messina's going totally out of control, he's developed a new habit, doing a lot of speed. Not showing any respect to his guys, bitching about how he has to take the heat, stand up to the prosecutors, fighting for the family, and everybody else is scrambling to steal as much money as they can. Not just Amarosa, but everybody else close to the boss, they're all wondering who's going to end up next with a bullet in the head. The rats are jumping off the ship right and left."

"What's Amarosa's deal?" I asked.

"They made him an offer he can't refuse—instead of life in prison for the six murders he admits doing for Messina, he can take a year for a racketeering rap. He'll actually do about six months. Then he walks out a new man, literally, into the witness protection program, executive style, plastic surgery, a monthly paycheck to live on, the works. The guy's only in his forties. So bingo, he cops the plea, he wears the wire, he gets the goods pronto, and the rest, we will soon see, is history."

"Amazing," I said.

"Fucking A."

"So let me ask your opinion. How do I get my guy out safe?"

"Eugene? You already know the answer to that, girl."

"Which is?"

"You do it yourself. And you haul ass."

CHAPTER 24

E_{ugene} *looked scared,* for once, when I told him he was about to be turned out on the street. I didn't have the heart to add any of the details about how his uncle had reacted, nor did he ask. I think he knew. And my own face told him that he shouldn't expect much more than a pat on the back from the NYPD.

"When do I get thrown out?" he said queasily.

"A week, maybe ten days, is my guess."

"Free and clear?"

"Yes," I said, hoping that what Noah had told me was on the level but afraid there was really a catch, that they'd expect him to be available for court testimony whenever they called.

"So what if I just get on a plane and go somewhere?" he said hopefully.

"Go where?"

He thought for a minute. "Brazil?"

"Eugene, you don't speak anything but English. How could you get along in a place like Brazil?"

"I could learn some Spanish."

"They speak Portuguese in Brazil."

"Well fuck them, then," he decided, his eyes brightening. "Maybe I'll go back down to Florida."

"Somebody would spot you there. This is very serious."

"I can't stay in New York, lay low till this blows over in a couple of months?"

"No. You have to look farther down than a few months."

He looked at me imploringly. "Can you do anything for me?"

I told him I would try. My head was spinning when I went home that night. All I could do was crawl into bed and sleep.

Just before I left for work the next morning there was a message from downtown that Inspector Marcomb wanted to see me immediately. What now? I thought gloomily as I waited for the downtown subway. Marcomb barely glanced up from his desk when I came in and said good morning.

"They want to see you at IAB," he announced curtly.

That got my attention fast. "IAB?" I gasped. "What in the world for?" IAB, the internal-affairs bureau, is the agency that investigates complaints of corruption and misconduct against officers. It works in such secrecy, and can operate so far beyond the usual boundaries of procedure, that cops regard it almost as a remnant of the Spanish Inquisition. Most cops would rather take a bullet in the leg than get a blind summons to IAB.

At first I thought they must want to ask me some routine questions in some sort of routine investigation. In that case, there was no problem. One of the unwritten rules of precinct life that I followed without any hesitation was that a cop did not rat on another cop. A cop could arrest another cop, but a cop did not rat. I wondered who they were after, because there was nothing in my recent work that gave me a clue. The only thing I could think of was the jam Rey had got into in A.C, and I had nothing to add to the reports there. Let Noah keep running that muddy ball, I figured.

What else? Certainly not the expense accounts. I was always punctilious about filing my own expenses; I hated to nickel-and-dime them for minor costs, to the point where Kevin would mock me as a fool— the only detective on the force who actually took a loss on expenses.

Marcomb saw my confusion and set me straight. "I don't know the details, Conte. But I should tell you this: *You* are the subject of the investigation."

Suddenly, I felt nauseous. "Me?" I said, keeping the pitch of my voice low. My teeth were clenched like I'd brushed them with Krazy Glue.

Avoiding eye contact, he said, "And you should bring an attorney with you."

My throat tightened. My mouth got dry. If IAB calls you in for questions, that's bad news. But they don't tell you to bring an attorney unless they have something going on you, and that's terrible news. What had I done? I was no saint, God knows, but I had never stolen, never taken a bribe, never lied under oath, never abused anyone on the job. I quickly scanned through the screens of my conscience. Why did I feel guilty? I *always* felt guilty about something.

Lately I was knee-deep in it: Failing to get an indictment on Messina, even though that was not even remotely my fault? Letting Eugene down? Driving Rey away? Tony and his diary? Who would believe something like that? My superiors knew exactly what had gone on in Atlantic City and afterward. I did the job the way I was supposed to. Maybe Colleen was right; alone, abandoned, you're administrative roadkill.

"They want to see you Monday morning, nine o'clock," said Marcomb dryly. Clearly, he wasn't going to give up anything more.

. . .

I *groped my* way through the week in a daze, but I managed to find a lawyer. The detective's endowment association, which is the detective's labor union, supplied me with an attorney who represented cops involved in IAB inquiries. He was a bulky, humorless man in his late twenties with a face like a pumpkin pie and thick black eyebrows that never came unknit. It worried me to notice that he had gnawed his fingernails. His name was Walter Prescott III. I told him I didn't have a clue what they thought they had on me.

Showing no more personal interest than a loan clerk, he asked questions and took notes. Had I compromised the investigation? No. Drugs? Absolutely not. Theft, bribery, adultery? No. He was very businesslike, as if reluctant to get involved in anything that wasn't specifically written on a piece of paper.

He advised me to answer their questions in as few words as necessary, and to address the question and only the question. Add nothing else.

"Fine," I said.

. . .

It *took me* about a minute to break that promise when I got there Monday morning. The IAB had a suite of offices on Barrow Street that looked like a corporate law firm, with thick rugs, mahogany paneling, recessed lighting, leather-backed chairs. In the conference room, at strategic points at the borders of the fifteen-foot-long table, we faced an IAB captain, two sergeants, and a detective. The captain had gray hair in one of those elaborate pompadours that some cops still think is fashionable. Peering down over wire-rimmed half-glasses, he kept his eyes fixed on the papers in front of him.

Somebody cleared his throat. The captain used both hands to square the angles of the report, which appeared to be extensive—a computer printout, all of its pages in an accordian fold about two inches thick.

"Let's begin," the captain said.

"Good morning, Detective Conte." At the far end of the table, a stenographer's fingers jiggled like marionettes on her machine.

"Good morn—" But I stopped, stunned, when I heard him begin:

"You have the right to remain silent. Anything you say can and will be used against you . . ."

How many times had I said those words to a criminal suspect, by rote, the way you would rattle off a Hail Mary. How different it sounded coming at you! Keeping my chin up, I replied that I understood my rights. I was careful not to lick my dry lips, because that was an indication of distress. It was important not to change body position or fidget. In my sudden panic, I was behaving just like a suspect who knew the ropes.

"You understand that you do not have to answer these questions, but if you choose not to, you may be immediately suspended from duty?" the captain said.

"She does," my lawyer interjected.

He winced when I decided to put in my two cents.

"I want to know what generated this inquiry, Captain."

The captain took note of the combative response and said, "I ask the questions. You answer them. Period."

"So ask away. It looks like you got quite a list of them there." My lawyer pressed his forearm against mine, but what did I care if they knew I was being disrespectful?

The first question was the one I expected.

"Did you ever have a sexual relationship with Anthony Rossi?"

"Absolutely not."

Then the captain reared back and threw a curve. "Now then, did you ever use the words 'nigger' or 'spic'?"

That flabbergasted me. "I can't believe you're asking me a question like that!" I said.

"Did you ever use those words? I'm asking a simple question, Detective," the captain persisted.

My lawyer said quietly, "Just answer yes or no."

"No."

"You never used the words?" the captain pressed.

"I never referred to anybody using those terms," I said, firmly and truthfully.

My interrogator sniffed wetly and rubbed his nose with the back of his left hand. The tip of his pen seemed to be snagged on the printed words of question number two. "So, then, you deny being racially biased?" he said.

A sharp nudge from the lawyer. "Yes. I deny it," I said.

Across the table, a few feet from the captain, the detective was watching me through slitted green eyes. With a glance from the Captain as his cue, he piped up, "Well, as regards that, Conte is basically a loner, so it's hard to say, from what I was able to observe."

The captain tugged out some papers and decided this was a judgment call. "Actually, I see from your report here, on several occasions when Detective Conte went to lunch while under observation, she was seen with officers who are Black or Puerto Rican and the like, and these people appeared to be on friendly terms with her."

" 'Blacks'?" I said with astonishment, as the realization that they had been *tailing* me hit me like a baseball bat. "Why would who I go to lunch with be any of your concern?" I demanded, directing my anger toward the detective. I studied his face, that of a nondescript middle-aged man reading the sports pages on the subway. If he had in fact tailed me, he was good. I never knew it. Then he did begin to look vaguely familiar, like someone you occasionally see around the neighborhood, nondescript as a cobblestone.

"You've been followed for several months," the captain explained.

"What in the hell for?"

He didn't elaborate and instead went to the next question. "Have you used, bought, or sold illegal drugs?"

"Why don't you give me a Dole?" That was the standard urine test for drug use, very simple to arrange.

"Just answer the question," my lawyer implored.

"No," I said.

I was breathless with outrage. Witch hunts could be organized over accusations of drugs. Complete innocence, like mine, could be a mere technicality. An allegation of using illegal drugs, not to mention *selling* them, was a grave charge and an easy one to make, even anonymously and with no evidence whatsoever. Once a drug allegation is made, it automatically requires a formal IAB investigation. That had to be part of the reason I was there. Someone, for some reason, had tagged me with drugs.

For the first time, it occurred to me that I should assume they might file a criminal charge. Immediately, I followed the lawyer's instructions like a suspect and kept my answers short and to the point: "No. No. Never. No. . . ." One after the other he worked down the list.

"Now, the weight loss, what accounts for that?"

"The what?" I said.

"You've lost weight. Fifteen, twenty pounds. What accounts for that?"

"I've been working my butt off at the gym every morning for months!"

The lawyer spoke up. "We object to that question, captain, as inappropriate."

"Fine, consider it withdrawn," the captain said, moving efficiently. The questions were all over the field—*"Did you ever steal anything or become involved in a theft as a police officer?"* It was impossible to figure out where they were going.

I felt tense and alone. It was extremely hot in the room. The stenographer bent over her machine like a seamstress.

After about fifteen minutes, sex came back.

"Regarding CI number two-seventeen," the captain said. CI 217 was the case designation for Eugene. "Are you having a sexual relationship with CI two-seventeen?"

All eyes were on me, including my lawyer's and the stenographer's.

"No, I am not."

"Have you ever had sexual intercourse or any sexual contact with CI two-seventeen?"

"No."

"Never?" the captain said, like I might have forgotten one or two times.

"Never. And I resent the question."

After sex came shopping.

"Have you gone to a store to buy something on department time?"

"I'm sorry, Captain. Can you please be a little more specific about how you define shopping?"

He stumbled through an explanation. "There has been an allegation that—"

He had to fan through the printout to find the place where my shopping offenses were evidently documented.

"That on several occasions you returned to your OCTF office during working hours with shopping bags marked—"

He squinted as he read, " 'Hit Or Miss' . . . 'Macy's Cellar.' " My inquisitors watched for signs that I was cracking. And I cracked.

"Yes," I admitted.

"Yes, you have returned to your OCTF office, et cetera, et cetera," the captain prompted, stroking the page with his first and second fingers the way a priest would rub a chalice rim.

"Yes, on occasion I have gone shopping on department time," I said, stunned by the idiocy of this.

He looked deeply grateful. "You have?"

"Yes. But I've also routinely worked twelve-hour shifts without putting in for overtime. My going to a store never took any time away from the NYPD—"

"You *have* gone shopping," the captain said, making a check in his box.

I tried to explain. "If you speak to my supervisor, the inspector will inform you that part of my duties as the main contact officer for CI number two-seventeen—who as you know is in protective custody— among my assigned duties have been to occasionally purchase items of clothing or toiletries for his use. That was part of the investigation. So yes, I've occasionally shopped on department time. . . ."

No one was listening. Well, I thought. They've had a gumshoe following me for weeks, if not months. When did I buy that new bra? They probably had pictures. A triumphant sigh passed around the table like a stale breeze. The stenographer bent to her work with new energy. Now we were getting somewhere.

Before the captain could ask what I knew about the Lindbergh kidnapping, I had a question for the detective who had been trailing me. "How many places did you follow me over those months, Sherlock? Did you ever see me do anything illegal or unethical?"

"Just answer the questions," my lawyer said wearily.

From a manila folder the captain brought out a piece of loose-leaf paper and studied it before declaring, in a tone of reproach, "You were never seen at any drug location. You were never seen with any known drug dealers. That I can tell you. Because if it had ever reached that level, you would not be sitting here free today."

The captain then fished out an opened envelope with a typewritten letter stapled to it. "I'll warn you right now that somebody is very pissed off at you, Conte. We think this came out of your office."

He pushed the letter across the table. My lawyer grabbed it and read silently for a minute before passing it to me.

As I read, my lawyer said, "For the record, this *anonymous letter*, I take it, was sent directly to IAB and triggered this investigation?"

"Yes," said the captain.

"And you don't know who wrote it?" the lawyer said.

"No," said the captain. "According to regulations, an investigation was mandatory upon receipt of charges, even anonymously, as you know, Counselor. After that, one thing leads to another, of course."

The letter was typed on a manual typewriter, which told me pretty certainly that it had come from some cop's desk. Police stations are the last remaining workplaces in America where you will still see a Royal upright on a desk.

TO WHOM IT MAY CONCERN:

This is to tell you about a disgrace to the New York City Police Department, her name is Detective Gerry Conte.

This detective has been sexually involve with an organized crime criminal that she has been working with. She has been involve with him selling drugs, selling cocaine, sleeping with him often.

When she has conversations in the office, she says that she is glad that "her people," meaning Italians, sells drugs to "niggers and spics" because their nothing but "animals." When anyone is arrested that is in the cell and that is black or Puerto Rican, she refers to them as "Nigga and spic."

When she comes in in the morning, she puts her pocketbook with her gun still inside it in her bottom desk drawer, and any time you can open her desk drawer and go in and find her gun unsecured, and there is said to be "coke" in there sometimes.

She has physically lost a lot of weight in recent months, she brags that she has dropped off weight, twenty (20) lbs., which can be an indication of Drug Use. She is often moody in her work and also with her fellow officers.

She goes shopping after lunch and comes back with shopping bags from Hit Or Miss department store. Once the bag was Saks and had in it an expensive mans sweater.

Very Respectfully yours,
CONCERNED COP

Basically that was it. Some shopping on my lunch hour. A scurrilous anonymous letter composed by an illiterate. That was the IAB case.

"Thank you for your cooperation," the captain said. "You'll hear from us when we have made our determination."

My lawyer and I had the elevator to ourselves. I was too stunned to say much. The lawyer let out a deep breath and chuckled. "That was quite a performance they gave to nail you on going to a store at lunch-time. They got you, for what that's worth." He watched the floor numbers blink on the panel and took my hand. Then he gently rapped my knuckles.

"And you did leave your gun in your drawer against regulations."

"So give me the chair," I said. "Absolutely guilty there. The truth is, I seldom gave a lot of thought to the damn gun. I didn't like carrying it. But it's ridiculous."

He said, "You don't understand. A file is *required*. There are separate agencies that then receive copies of that file, and of course that means they also have to assign a new case number. The files live without end. They never die, no matter what the disposition."

"Drugs?" I said.

"Obviously no one gives any credence to that. Nevertheless, bureau-cratically, the accusation slumbers eternally undead in the file cabinets. It gets its own case number in the drug-abuse files. But no one will pay any attention to that unless something else comes up later. So don't worry. The final report will clearly reflect the fact that insufficient evidence was found to prove the only real charges, drugs and racial bias."

"That makes it sound like I got off on a technicality."

He shrugged. "They want the file closed, of course. So next, the captain will make a determination to the effect that no evidence was found. After this, a period of time has to pass. You know the drill: Trouble has been caused, some blame must be assigned, or else the universe is out of whack. There is, naturally, the matter of your culpability on the trivial technicalities, the gun especially. So, technically, some of the charges have been proven."

"But no one would ever have made a case on those two-bit things if it weren't for the other totally false charges that came from nowhere."

"True. But that's the point. The file now clearly reflects that there was at least valid reason for the investigation of you in the first place. Do you understand?"

I did. "So what happens next?"

"My guess, next week sometime you'll receive an official letter from

Command. You'll be sternly instructed to carry your gun. To shop only on your own time. Basically, your pride takes a brutal beating, but that's about it."

"Which means?"

"For your career, it means nothing unless they choose for it to mean something."

"Choose when?"

"Anytime they want, of course. Because there will be a file. And of course, you'll get a tepid administrative reprimand eventually, and that will remain in the file.

"A reprimand saying what?"

"Saying don't cause trouble."

"I didn't do anything."

"Right, and all you have to do is make sure you just don't do it again."

CHAPTER 25

Life improved slightly the next day when a thick envelope with my law-school grades came in the mail. I opened it with trepidation because I was sure I had blown all of my finals. To my astonishment, I'd actually aced them. It was like someone else had taken the finals. I barely recalled being there.

The IAB review rushed through the pipeline like bad food. Marcomb himself called me in to grandly inform me that the IAB case was closed, once my lawyer filed our response. As I had expected, the penalty was only a reprimand for technical violations. "It's no big deal," Marcomb insisted. "Just a command discipline, which is nothing. All you have to do is remember to keep your memo book in good shape, in case they come around to check."

"Fine," I said curtly.

"Now for the good news," he said.

"What's that, Inspector?" I muttered.

"I told you this IAB flap wouldn't matter. So let me now tell you that your next assignment is to the legal bureau, downtown. Effective as soon as we close down this operation. How about that?" He looked like he'd given me a pony.

Actually, being transferred to the legal bureau should have been wonderful news, especially now that I was certain about graduating from law school with the June class—with a reasonable expectation of passing the New York State bar exam in the summer. The legal bureau, where detectives work closely with prosecutors on high-profile cases, was the perfect "next rung up the ladder" for me. I wished I could have reacted with something other than a forced smile that failed to disguise my contempt.

"What about the rest of the IAB case?" I asked.

Marcomb looked puzzled. "Closed," he said. "I told you this was no big deal. Officially, it just gets filed away marked 'Unsubstantiated.' "

That wasn't good enough, though I knew it was final. I faced him squarely and said, "I find that unacceptable, Inspector."

His eyes widened with surprise. "You can't find it unacceptable or anything else, Detective. You file your response and the case is closed."

"Not for me, it isn't," I said. "Excuse me, I have business to do. I'll make sure it's in my memo book." I slammed the door so hard the frosted glass in it rattled like a breadbox. Luckily, it didn't break.

· · ·

There was a lot to do. Eugene would be cut loose well before they shut down, and probably without more than one or two days' notice. So I put in for my last remaining two weeks' vacation. It was approved right away without the usual griping about short notice.

Everything fell into place in my mind. I just had to put a plan into action. Early one morning, I knocked on Eugene's door. He was surprised to see me.

"The conversation we are about to have is totally confidential," I said when he let me in. In his white silk bathrobe with a red sash, he looked like a boxer before a fight.

"Absolutely," he said with a quizzical look.

"First, you haven't been told anything about what they're planning to do with you?"

"Nothing. I'm waiting for the word about where they're sending me."

"You still believe they have a plan, don't you," I said wearily.

"Some kind, at least."

"Eugene, you have to listen to me. They're going to tell you to pack your bags and hit the street. They'll give you a few bucks, but that's it."

"How much moola?" he said intently.

"The money isn't the point! But I'm telling you, it won't be anywhere near what you thought you'd get when you signed that stupid agreement last year. I'm leveling with you here. All of a sudden, your uncle is going to be stale bread sitting on the shelf. Useless. So they're going to jack you up on the money."

"They're supposed to give me enough money for a new start," he protested, uninterested in anything but that.

"Do you know what a new start means for someone in your fix? It isn't just getting together a couple of months' advance rent on an apartment, Eugene. You have to make this new start away from New York. You can't come back here."

"Not for a while," he said thoughtfully.

"Not for years—if that! For once in your life, you have to start thinking ahead, way ahead."

"Bunch of fucking assholes," he scoffed.

"That is no longer a relevant point, Eugene. The point is, unless you let me help you, you are fucked when they turn you loose. Fucked."

"You never said that word in front of me before," he said with wonder.

"I'm saying it now. I've been working on a few ideas, and I think I can help you out. But I need your trust. Blind trust. You can't fight me in any way on this."

"I know I'm fucked. I'll do anything you say," he replied. He understood—finally—that he couldn't just walk out and set himself up.

"You can fix things for me?"

"I can only try my best. You have to be very, very realistic for the first time in your life, Eugene. First of all, forget everything you think you know about arranging a new identity, whatever that means. The best you can hope for is a new name and address, far away from here. You'll be safe, but you'll have to work at it in a strange setting. And you have to understand that there is no way you can come back to New York, not if you want to live."

He was leaping ahead. "L.A.!" he yelped.

"Eugene, Los Angeles would not be a good idea. Why? For one thing, I know you and you'd only get into trouble in L.A. You don't want to get into any trouble, Eugene. But the major reason is, L.A. is very expensive, like New York. You no longer can use your former skills or depend on your old contacts for money. Which means you'll have to go to someplace cheap, and from there start to establish yourself financially. That could take years of hard work."

He looked deeply disappointed. But at least he was paying attention.

"It means you have to have a regular job. A job where you show up every day, and not just for a few months until you get bored. Every day!"

"I could do that if the money was right."

"Eugene, the money has to be only sufficient. You are not being recruited by an executive head-hunter. Your ass is on the line here."

"I know that," he acknowledged meekly.

"Whatever can be arranged, you'll have to behave like a normal citizen. Okay? I can't stress this enough, Eugene. It will mean obeying all the laws. All the time."

He snapped off a comic salute. "Okay! Can I pick a new name?"

"Probably. I guess. Something within reason."

"It probably should be Italian."

"Yes, Eugene. Kelly probably wouldn't work."

He thought for a minute and announced, "Eugene DePalma."

Close enough.

. . .

And so I proceeded to set him up in my own, homemade witness protection program. Over the years as a detective, I'd made a few good friends in various federal agencies. I worked the phones, solicited advice, called in favors.

Besides friendly support, Eleanor's major contribution was to come help work out the arrangements with Michael Marconi.

"A place like Iowa is perfect," she chirped, with the animation of someone planning a summer vacation.

"The man has never seen a cow," I said.

"Exactly! All of the old bad influences will be missing."

"He'll stand out like a Martian, the way he dresses."

"Here!" she said. She tossed me a Land's End catalog. "They deliver in twenty-four hours."

. . .

Meanwhile I hit the jackpot with one of the first contacts I called, an agent with the Drug Enforcement Agency, a very good friend from my Midtown South days who had since been promoted to a high-level DEA job in Washington. I'd bailed him out once on a job in Midtown when he'd blown a collar. After I explained the situation briefly and vouched for Eugene, he was eager to help. In fact, he welcomed the opportunity to show off his clout. He assured me that he could procure a valid driver's license from any state in the country, and produce it within three days, once he had an address.

"Does the guy have a recent photograph of himself?" he asked.

"Undoubtedly."

"Fed-Ex it to me."

At the same time, another friend, an attorney in the Justice Department, came through. After I explained the situation, he said he could easily arrange for a new Social Security number for one Eugene De-Palma, birthplace Rhode Island. It was done all the time, he assured me. The card arrived two days later.

Eugene even reacted positively to Iowa. "Hey, I always wanted to live in the mountains."

"No, you're confusing it with Idaho. Iowa's the one next to Wisconsin. Farms, lakes. *The Music Man.* You know?"

The blank look he gave me said that I might as well have asked him to picture Mesopotamia. But he was still game. "What the fuck," he said. "I'll get a horse."

"Listen to me," I said patiently. "You have to start thinking like a normal person, Eugene. First, you get a place to live. Then you get a car that works. A used car."

"Nobody gets a used car," he declared.

"That's what you think."

. . .

Michael Marconi phoned me at home the same night Eleanor contacted him to let me know he was on board.

"You're taking on a lot of responsibility here," he pointed out.

"Actually, I thought I was relinquishing responsibility," I said with a laugh.

"Well, it appears you've got things under control. I'd say you've thought of everything, from what you say and from what Eleanor has filled me in on."

"Really?"

"Yeah, actually."

"It wasn't really that hard, not so far, anyway."

He chuckled appreciatively. "No, not if you discount the years of work it took you to acquire the right contacts. But all things considered, it's surprisingly easy in a highly technological society to do a Houdini—disappear, reappear. Basically, all you need to do is create two reference points. A driver's license is the best. Then you only need a Social Security number, even just a mailing address, a lease, a telephone number in the new name. Once one computer agrees with another computer that the new name exists, conception has occurred. Data banks have a horrific pro-identity bias. After they agree that the identity has life, it's just a matter of building up the cross-references on mailing lists."

"That makes sense," I said.

"How's he going to get along in a college town?"

"Coed?"

"Right."

"He'll get by."

"There's restaurant job open at a place run by an old friend of mine from the D.E.A., if he thinks he can handle it."

"That's wonderful. What kind of restaurant is it, did you say?"

"French. Imagine an ex-cop running a French restaurant."

"We often used to stop for a quick bite of takeout French when we were on patrol," I joked.

"I know, it sounds like a joke, but it's actually an excellent restaurant. Tom has one of the best chefs in the Midwest, a guy who likes the idea of being a big shot in a college town. The restaurant even got a rave review in a Chicago paper, so it's not just a bunch of yokels strapping on the old feedbag for some fancy pancakes. Here's the point. He's been looking for an apprentice sous-chef who can fill in as maître d' sometimes."

"A sous-chef?"

"A sous-chef is basically the one who helps out in the kitchen, prepares the ingredients for the chef, chops the carrots, bones the chicken, and all that. Your guy ever been in a kitchen, other than collecting on a numbers drop?"

"Actually, yes. In fact, he's a terrific cook, and he even does the dishes afterward."

"From the way you describe him, he sounds like he looks good in a tux and knows how to act like a gentleman."

"When he wants to."

"Then maybe he takes the job, learns how to run a kitchen, and that's his setup. Don't all these wiseguys dream about opening restaurants?"

I didn't want to tell him that that was the old days. Today the young wiseguys only dream about frequenting them. Still, I knew that Eugene had no choice but to go to work.

Michael gave me his friend's phone number and suggested that I have Eugene call him that night. The friend's name was Tom Reynolds.

"One other thing to keep in mind," Michael said. "For about three years now, Tom has been supposedly working on writing some damn screenplay about the mob. He's convinced he'll sell it as a major motion picture. Anyway, I explained the situation to him. Let's just say your boy's background is a major asset."

I thanked him profusely.

"Just out of curiosity, can I ask you a question?"

"Sure."

"No offense, but you seem to be such a goddamn eagle scout. Isn't what you're doing against NYPD rules?"

"Technically," I conceded.

He let that pass. "So let's do it," he said decisively. "From what you say, Eugene has enough manners to get by. Evidently he's smart enough. The way you're setting things up, he won't encounter any legal problems unless he manages to create new ones for himself."

"That's my hope."

"Well, his future is out of your control."

That was the most delightful thing I'd heard in months.

. . .

Eugene liked the idea of Iowa better than ever when I explained that Des Moines was a college town. He also liked the sound of being a chef, conveniently overlooking the "sous," and worried about only one thing.

"I get embarrassed saying any of them French words," he told me. "I can't fake them. Maybe they'll let me use Italian words instead."

"Maybe you'll just make it a point to learn some French," I suggested.

"I never thought of that," he said, mulling it over. "It could be a new lifestyle statement."

I had him call Michael's friend. The conversation quickly became animated. It was hard to follow from just one end, but the two clearly had hit it off right away.

"Yeah, absolutely. I can do that. My pleasure," I heard Eugene saying as the conversation concluded. "Very, very good. . . . No, working holidays is okay. . . . Yes, thanks a million. *Mille grazie.* Let me check on those things and get back to you. . . . Tomorrow. Beautiful. Okay. Yes. Me too, Mr. Reynolds. Okay, Tom. *Ciao,* Tom."

He put the phone down and faced me with a self-satisfied smile.

"Well?" I said.

"So the guy says I can start whenever I get there."

"Seriously?"

He was certainly taking things in stride. "Of course."

The realization that he was actually leaving hit me. Things were moving faster than I'd anticipated. Control was slipping away. "You need a place to live first," I said nervously.

"No problem there," Eugene said. "Tom owns a bunch of rental properties. He says I can start out with a one-bedroom house with a little yard, near a park, included in the job. See how I do."

"Amazing."

"You see the deal, you close it fast," he said.

Within a week, the reborn Eugene DePalma had his papers, his job offer, and his departure date. After that, the rest would be up to him.

. . .

Meanwhile, Noah was bothering me, apparently prompted by Marcomb's reaction to my tepid response to my new job assignment. After three phone calls, I finally agreed to meet him for coffee, even though I was still on vacation.

Noah acted like I was being rushed for a fraternity that I was reluctant to pledge.

"You should be very proud, Gerry. They have to think a lot of you to offer you the legal bureau. The rest of this stuff, let it go. It's over."

"I'm flattered," I said. Actually, I was thinking about getting to the auto-club office in Midtown in time to pick up a map route for Iowa before they closed.

Noah tried to whip up enthusiasm, although as far as he knew, the new assignment was a done deal. I supposed they were looking for gratitude if they couldn't get joy, but all I was prepared to give was a little patience. He bent one finger after the other into his palm, listing the advantages.

"First, obviously, there's the career status. It's a stepping stone right to department headquarters staff. Who knows where that would lead for someone as sharp as you, especially being female?"

"Especially," I repeated.

"Well, it isn't a bad time to be ambitious and female in the NYPD, you know. The commissioner's office, Gerry! Who knows, given that personality of yours?"

Two fingers now bent, he waited for a response. When I didn't make one, he continued, "Next, you'll graduate from law school already ensconced in what is, by all estimations, the finest police department legal staff in the country. Right off the bat, you'll get the opportunity to practice both criminal and civil law at a level that would take most young attorneys many long years to reach on the outside, if ever. Then there's the steady hours: no weekends, no nights, holidays off. Plus your own office, in nice surroundings. And invaluable legal networking and contacts. *Invaluable.* As you probably know, a number of police officers with law degrees left the department to open lucrative practices, just based on contacts made through that bureau."

He had lost count on his fingers, but pressed on gamely with a closed fist. "And most important, within a year, two at the most, you'd be eligible for the joint program between the NYPD and the DA's office in which selected officers with law degrees can take an indefinite leave of absence from the department and become assistant DAs, while still paying into their pension."

Searching my face with the look of a man selling life insurance, he said, "I, for one, would absolutely love to see you come up as a prosecutor, Gerry. I want to see you in court someday."

"Well, that might be sooner than you expect," I said.

"How's that?"

"I'm thinking very seriously about putting in my papers, concentrating full-time on my last semester in law school."

That brought a gasp. He said, "You are shitting me."

"No."

"What about your pension?"

"A pension doesn't enter into things at this point."

"You've really thought this over?"

"Not much."

"No one will be pleased with your attitude," he said, his eyes narrowing.

"Let them put it in my file," I said, suddenly feeling light and free.

"You mean to tell me, Gerry, that you're leaving the police force?"

"I didn't tell you that officially, Noah. So please don't repeat it."

"You're upset about the way this investigation turned out. I know that. Then that IAB mess, obviously. . . ."

"Forget '*upset*,' " I said coldly. "Do you have any idea how much women despise hearing that freaking word come from a man? Besides, if what you're worried about is that I'll make a stink about this case, in-house or in public, don't give it a second thought. It simply isn't worth it to me anymore. I don't see any point in dwelling on history. But I won't rewrite history."

"So," he said uneasily.

"But I do have one favor to ask you, Noah."

Leaning forward he said, "Go for it."

"You're planning to release Eugene next week."

"Tuesday is his last day in custody. He's been informed."

"Make it five days earlier. Make it Friday," I said. "Release him into my custody."

"Why?"

"That's the favor."

He frowned, fished into his briefcase and pulled out a three-inch-thick appointment book. "Let me see," he said. "Today's what . . .?"

"Tuesday."

"Tuesday." He hummed nervously. "Friday? Okay, it'll be a little bit of a pain in the behind to change the order, but I can manage."

"Make it Friday night."

"Fine. Friday night." He made a little note and looked up expectantly. "That's it?"

"And I want to be sure that there are no outstanding warrants on this guy. Right? No screwups there. He'll be absolutely free and clear, yes?"

"That is already taken care of, I told you," he said. "Let's just hope he keeps his nose clean."

"How much money?"

"Five large," he said quietly.

"Five," I said, shaking my head sadly. "How much did we spend on this game all year?"

"You don't want to know."

"And five is what you got for the guy to start a new life."

"I can maybe goose it up to seven," he said hopefully.

"Do that," I said.

"I'll try."

"Come on, Noah. I know there's always some give. This guy has to get out of town and find a place to spend the rest of his life. He has absolutely no idea of how to do that. You can squeeze more out of them."

"Okay, let me try seven-five. But I'll have to have it approved first. And I swear to you, that's tops."

"Do it," I said.

"We'll cut the check tomorrow."

I held up a hand. "Where's the guy going to cash a check, for God's sake? Make it in cash."

He jotted something down. "Okay. But you'll have to pick it up at accounting and voucher it personally."

"Fine. Thank you. Seventy-five hundred dollars cash, then."

"I said I'd try."

"Thank you very much."

"You're quite welcome."

Going down in the elevator, it occurred to me that he hadn't even asked where Eugene thought he might be going on that stake.

. . .

First thing Friday morning, I rushed down to Foley Square and signed for the cash, which the clerk handed over in a regular business envelope, all hundreds, no twenties. Of course, no one had given any thought to how difficult it is to cash a hundred-dollar bill under the kind of circumstances Eugene would soon be facing—such as at a road-side restaurant.

I hurried over to my bank on Hudson Street and shifted uneasily in the long line at the only teller's window that was open. Finally, I withdrew twenty-five hundred dollars from the money-market account I'd set up after Kevin and I broke up and divided our savings. I asked the teller for a thousand in twenties. The withdrawal left my balance at two hundred and thirteen dollars.

So now the stake was ten thousand dollars. I stashed it in my apartment and walked a few blocks to a car rental office where I'd already made a reservation for a mid-sized Chevy, a week's rental, with an extra couple hundred dollars' charge for a one-way return in Des Moines. I paid for it with my Visa. The rental was in my name, so I informed the clerk that there would be an additional driver.

"Name?" she asked.

"Eugene DePalma." The name was on his Iowa driver's license and the other identity papers I'd managed to scrounge up. She didn't ask to see the license.

"Age?"

"Thirty-two." To bust his chops, I had made my born-again Eugene a few years older.

I drove the car to a parking garage and took the subway to Staten Island, where I found Eugene pacing in his room, looking like he was ready to bolt. But both of his bags were neatly packed.

We'd already been over the arrangements for hours on end. "Listen," I told him, "I have a lot to do yet. But I want you ready to rock-and-roll by eight-thirty."

"Absolutely," he said through tight lips.

I'd phoned ahead to make sure Marcomb would see me. Despite that,

the inspector seemed surprised when I strode into his office. I decided
that Noah hadn't said anything.

Marcomb greeted me gruffly. "Hey, this is way to spend a vacation?"

"Well, you know how it is, Inspector."

"What, you don't want your CI now, do you?"

"Not yet. I'll be back for him around eight o'clock, when it's dark.
Daytime, you never know, somebody could spot him."

"I think the threat is exaggerated," Marcomb said, "but there's no
point in taking chances. You're doing the guy a very big favor, Conte.
I respect that."

He didn't show any interest in where Eugene was headed, either. After
spending so much time with the man in his custody, I expected he would
have at least some idle curiosity.

"So, you ready for the new job?" Marcomb said.

I wanted to keep my voice low because I was afraid of getting choked
up. Everything had happened so quickly that I wasn't sure of my grip.
"Well, not really. Actually, that's what I wanted to talk to you about,
Inspector."

Suspicion flickered on his face. Was I was going to ask him for something impossible, like a change of *schedule?*

I didn't want to make a big production out of what I had to do. So
I just took my detective's shield out of my pocketbook. Once I had
cherished that brass plate like a relic of the true cross. Now I gave it up
like a subway token. I placed the shield in the center of his deskpad.
Marcomb stared at it as if it was smoking.

"What's this?" he said.

"I'm taking my bat and ball and going home, Inspector. I don't want
to play on this team anymore."

He didn't get my drift. "What team is that, Detective?" he demanded.

"I'm resigning," I told him. As soon as I said it I felt like I would
skitter away with a gust of wind.

He watched me take my gun and holster from my purse and place it
on his desk beside the shield.

"What are you doing, goddammit?"

"I'm resigning, Inspector. There's the shield. There's my gun. I don't
have any personal weapons. Any other police department property I
have will be in my locker, and I'll give my key to the duty sergeant
before I leave. Of course, I'll still come by tonight to get Eugene."

"What the hell?"

What else could I say? I certainly didn't want to seem rude; I just wanted to get out.

"You can't be serious, Conte! You shouldn't do anything like this when you're upset."

That word again. I let it pass.

Marcomb seemed to be running quick damage-control calculations in his head. As long as I didn't fly off the handle and make noise about the way I'd been required to spend the past year, I knew that my going out the door wouldn't create any real problems. Everything was contained in the file, the file with my reprimand close by, where my departure sheet would note that the resignation had been "for unknown personal reasons."

Marcomb thought it through. There couldn't be any question about whether the resignation was voluntary.

"Gerry, you're letting that reprimand thing affect the rest of your life. That's silly—"

"Actually," I said, getting more involved than I'd wanted, "the reprimand wasn't the reason for my decision."

"Listen, you're on vacation. You come back fresh in a couple of weeks, this is all water under the bridge, this place. Besides that, you're in the next group for promotion. Maybe you're looking at squad commander within a year. As to the reprimand, it's nothing. You should see the awful crap in some of these personnel files. I want to make sure you're thinking this thing all the way through and not just acting out of emotion."

Without bitterness I told him, "No, Inspector. That's it. I'm finished."

After a minute he said, "And you thought this all the way through?"

"Absolutely."

"What about your pension?"

"My pension? I never gave it a thought, Inspector, believe it or not."

"So you're set financially? You can do this financially?"

Why ask? I thought. Clearly, they had snooped into all of my personal business. They'd had someone follow me for months, as if I were a common criminal. My IAB files showed that they had put a pen register on my home phone, so they had all the records. If they'd done all that, they'd certainly had a look at my bank account.

"I'll manage," I assured him, already feeling out of the game.

Marcomb said, "This is your family."

"No, sir. It is not my family."

"A family forgives," he said.

"I didn't do anything that needs being forgiven."

"It's cold out there, Conte."

I got my coat and put it on and said, "I'll be back tonight to pick up Eugene. But since you'll be gone by then, let me say good-bye, sir."

As I left, I had one more thing to tell him.

"You heard about the feds?"

He looked at me with interest. "What about them?"

"They're going to announce the indictment of Sally Messina on Monday."

His mouth was open when I left without another word.

. . .

I *slipped away* after saying quiet good-byes to the other cops on the unit, and stopped at Eugene's apartment again to give him the money and to warn him to be ready on time.

"You have everything?"

"Yeah. What else do I need but a pair of underwear and my freaking good looks?" He flashed his beautiful teeth. Behind him, the television was blaring. When we first started out at the place in Jersey, he never would have put the television on during the day.

"Why not study while you're waiting?" I suggested.

"Not today. I got too much on my mind." A talk show audience hooted and barked from the corner.

"You packed the boots I bought you? It's still winter out there."

"Yeah."

"Eugene, you have got to promise me again that you'll take that high-school equivalency test and pass it the first time." Michael had said he would set it up.

"No problem," Eugene promised.

"And you've studied the maps? You're not used to driving a long way, buddy. And it's a long way to Des Moines." We'd already gone over the tour books and route maps until I was satisfied he understood. It had astonished me that he didn't understand what an interstate highway was. The motel reservations were made.

"Yeah," he said. "So relax."

"Maybe you should take a nap. It's a five-hour drive to the place in Pennsylvania where you're staying tonight."

"No problem," he said. "See you later." He closed the door.

. . .

O*ften I wonder* if there was any good in all the aggravation he caused. Who can say? Perhaps my life was on its axis when he came into it. But he showed me colors where I used to see gray. He made me laugh, more than anyone ever did. During my time with him, I had managed to find security inside myself. Finally I knew that there were really no mysteries outside; there are only interlocking assumptions, quick moves, regrets, and farewells.

I missed Rey. I wanted to tell him what I had just done. I got his new number but when I dialed it, Monique answered in her shrill whine. So I gently hung up. He probably wouldn't have come to the phone anyway.

. . .

E*ugene was ready* on time. He tried to toss his suitcases on the backseat, but I made him stow them properly in the trunk. We didn't say much on the way down over from Staten Island. I drove south and turned on Eleventh Avenue, where there was a ramp for the Lincoln Tunnel just below Forty-first Street.

Just before the entrance, I pulled off to the left side of the avenue and kept the engine running. It was a mild night, prime cruising time for the tunnel crowd. But I didn't see any of the girls on their usual patrol under the streetlamps. A precinct car must have come by to scatter them. I knew they were somewhere under the long shadows reaching into the city.

Even though I never wanted to see it again, I looked at Eugene hard to remember his face. "This is it, buddy. Let me hear from you after you get settled," I said.

"Sure," he said, looking ahead without blinking. "Thanks a lot, babe."

"There's nothing left to say," I told him.

"Say it with your eyes," he said.

In the dark, I leaned across and touched his cheek. I kissed him lightly on the lips. Clumsily I got out and stood on the sidewalk in a puddle of cold white light. I watched him get behind the wheel. It was good to see him adjust the rearview mirror. A fleeting motion from the edge of the sidewalk ten feet away startled me. It was a rat poking out from under a heap of soggy cardboard. He must have been two feet long. The rat sniffed frantically at the air, then shot into the dark like he owned it.

Next to me, the window glided down silently.

"See ya, Miss Crabtree" Eugene said. He tossed a wave.

I said, "See you, Mafia Man."

He grinned. The window slid up. There wasn't much traffic going to the tunnel on Eleventh Avenue. He remembered to use his turn signal pulling out.

Suddenly, the car jerked to a halt. The taillights blazed bright red. He slammed it into reverse and roared back in a wobbly path.

My heart sank. But he only wanted to kiss me good-bye again. He got out of the car and took me in his arms. We kissed long and tenderly. Then I pushed him away and made him get into the car. To my relief, he complied.

"Okay," I said. "Time to hit the road, Charlie."

"Okay. You win. You want to come?"

I laughed and moved back. "Nope. Remember, I have to find a job and get out of law school."

"I got a job," he said, amused at the idea.

"And don't blow it," I said.

"A sauce chef."

"Sous-chef."

"Whatever."

"May God forgive me for what I have created," I said.

"Is that a shot?"

"No, no shot, buddy."

"You save my life, Gerry."

"Well, maybe it was mutual. We're even. Anyway, buckle your seat belt and hit the road, Charlie. Remember there's no toll going out of New York. So don't stop at the end of the tunnel."

And he was gone. I watched until his car disappeared into the tunnel and there was no turning back.